Crushed Yet Conquering

Yet the throbbing of his boyish heart as he crossed the courtyard told him not unpleasantly that he was *"upon adventure bound," like a young knight-errant.*
(Page 225)

The Reformation Trail Series

Crushed Yet Conquering
A Story of Constance and Bohemia
by
Deborah Alcock

Author of *The Spanish Brothers,*
Romance of Protestantism, Dr. Adrian, etc.

INHERITANCE PUBLICATIONS
NEERLANDIA, ALBERTA, CANADA
PELLA, IOWA, U.S.A.

National Library of Canada Cataloguing in Publication Data

Alcock, Deborah, 1835-1913
  Crushed yet conquering

  (The reformation trail series)
  ISBN 1-894666-01-1
  1. Bohemia (Czech Republic)—History—Hussite Wars, 1419-1436—Fiction.
  I. Title. II. Series: Reformation trail series.
PR4004.A105C78 2002   823'.8   C2002-910003-8

Library of Congress Cataloging-in-Publication Data

Alcock, Deborah, 1835-1913.
  Crushed yet conquering : a story of Constance and Bohemia / by Deborah Alcock.
    p. cm. — (Reformation trail series)
  ISBN 1-894666-01-11.
  Hus, Jan, 1369?-1415—Fiction. 2. Church history—Middle Ages, 600-1500—Fiction. 3. Council of Constance (1414-1418)—Fiction. 4.Bohemia (Czech Republic)—Fiction. 5. Reformation—Fiction. 6.Hussites—Fiction.
  I. Title. II. Series.
PR4004.A115 C78 2002
823'.8—dc21

                                                                2001008570

Cover painting: *John Huss before the Council of Constance* by Brozik

Box 154, Neerlandia, Alberta Canada T0G 1R0
Tel. 780-674-3949 Fax 775-890-9118
Web site: http://www.telusplanet.net/public/inhpubl/webip/ip.htm
E-Mail inhpubl@telusplanet.net

Published simultaneously in U.S.A. by Inheritance Publications
Box 366, Pella, Iowa 50219

Available in Australia from Inheritance Publications
Box 1122, Kelmscott, W.A. 6111 Tel. & Fax (089) 390 4940

Printed in Canada

Contents

View of the City of Constance

PREFACE

It is hoped that the following narrative will explain itself and justify its title. All that seems necessary is to answer briefly a question likely to occur to the reader: How much is fiction, and how much fact? Of the central personality, to which the others owe their interest, and the book itself its existence, nothing has been said which is not strictly true. In telling the story of John Huss, the author has not dared to add or to alter but has only laboured to reproduce; and the labour in very deed has been one of love.

The character next, perhaps, in importance has been used with a little, but only a little, less ceremony. The relations of Gerson to Hubert Bohun are, of course, imaginary, but almost every expression of opinion attributed to Gerson has been taken from his writings, and the circumstances of his death are historical.

Strictly historical, too, are the instances of *martyrdom* introduced, or even alluded to. In particular the story of the burgomaster's daughter of Leitmeritz, and that of Pastor Wenzel and his companions, are given just as they occurred.

With the kind help of a Bohemian friend, the author has carefully gathered the incidental notices that remain to us of the good knight, John de Chlum, who made so noble an appearance in Constance. These are very few and very slight; so the attempt has been made to fill them in, and to depict him as fulfilling the dying charge of his friend to "serve God quietly at home."

The unfamiliar Bohemian names may perhaps be considered a difficulty. When an English form is already in use, it has seemed best to retain it. This is the case with the most illustrious name of all, which, properly speaking, should be written *Jan Hus*. For the rest, it may be observed that the *u* is long and open — Chlum, for instance, being pronounced Kloom — and that the *c* in *Panec* is sounded like *tch*. *Pán* signifies lord; *Páni*, lady. *Pánna* is the title of a young or unmarried lady; and *Panec* is young lord or young master.

7

So abundant and so full of romantic interest is the historical material, that the writer's temptation to linger over details, or to wander into by-paths, has been great. Many episodes have been left untouched which are quite as thrilling as those recorded here. The story ends with the founding of the Church of the United Brethren. But after that, how much yet remains to be told in the pathetic, glorious history of Bohemian Protestantism! The battle of the White Mountain alone, with the terrible years that followed it, would furnish materials for more than one grand tragedy, as yet unwritten.

The grandest tragedies, the noblest epics, often do remain unwritten, or recorded only in His Book of Remembrance of whom it has been truly said,

> *God Himself is the best poet,*
> *And the Real is His song.*

PART I

A STORY OF CONSTANCE

John Huss 1369?-1415

I

TWO LITTLE RILLS DIVIDE

The little children come to us
With wonder in their faces.

It was near the going down of the sun on a fair September day in the opening year of the fifteenth century. The broad fields of Northern France ought to have been white with harvest but few and scanty were the patches the harassed inhabitants cared to sow, and of these, fewer still would come to the reaper's sickle. War, long and wasting, and followed by all its attendant miseries, had left its traces everywhere.

In a bare and desolate plain, where no living thing was visible, a strong but gloomy castle, or donjon keep, stood in solitary state, as if frowning upon all around. It was small of its kind, and utterly devoid of ornament, but well fortified — as it had need to be in those times of danger — duly protected by a deep moat, and furnished with a portcullis and drawbridge. Over the arched gateway hung a funeral hatchment.

Toward this castle a goodly train came spurring along over the rough, grass-grown pathway called by courtesy a road. It was composed of knights and men-at-arms, who all paid extreme deference to two great personages, evidently the leaders of the band. One, who was of very stately and noble bearing, wore, over his exquisitely inlaid hauberk, a long mantle of crimson velvet trimmed with ermine, and his cap, also of crimson velvet, had a gold border, shaped like a ducal coronet. He was, in fact, no less a person than Philip the Bold, Duke of Burgundy. His companion wore no mail, but the mitre embroidered on his rich robes, and on the gorgeous trappings of his showy, though not spirited horse, told all men that he was a great bishop, a prince of the Church.

The Duke of Burgundy, and his friend the Bishop of Arras, had ridden from the Burgundian camp, three or four leagues away, on an errand of kindness, almost of charity. The lord of the castle, Armand de Clairville, a good knight and true, had died that morning in the camp, of wounds received the day before in a skirmish with

11

the Armagnacs — the party opposed to the duke in the civil contest at that time rending France in twain, and leaving her an easy prey to the English. Through some accident, De Clairville had been left almost alone to defend a little bridge against the enemy. He had performed what the duke called "prodigies of valour," and, although mortally wounded, had held his post until relieved, and borne back to his tent to die. The bishop himself shrived him, speaking words of praise and consolation, and the great duke asked him, not without emotion, if there was anything he could do for him. The dying knight murmured feebly, "My wife and children" — then added with an effort, "my fortune is spent; my estate ruined; God and the saints have pity on them!" Both duke and bishop bade him be of good cheer, and assured him cordially that they would provide for all. In fulfilment of this pledge they were coming to the castle; and certainly, for those rough times, it was a good and kindly deed.

At the summons of their herald the portcullis was duly raised, the drawbridge lowered, and the great personages humbly invited to enter. A gray-haired seneschal, with tokens of grief in his face and manner, advanced to meet them, and, bowing to the ground, informed them that his dear lady had just departed this life. The tidings of her lord's mortal wound had proved her own death-stroke; a fever from which she had been just recovering returned with fatal violence, and about noon that day she had rejoined him in the other world.

The duke expressed his regret in a frank, soldierly manner, and the bishop added some words of devout consolation. The old seneschal thanked them with all humility; and having conducted them to the reception hall, very respectfully ventured to inquire if his good lords would deign to cast an eye of compassion on the unhappy orphans.

"By all means," said the duke, stroking his beard. "We have come for that purpose, that we may befriend them for their brave father's sake."

The old servant of the house withdrew, and presently returned with a fair-haired boy clinging to each hand. These, my lords, are the poor children," he said, with his lowliest reverence. Then, to his little charges, "Go now, and kneel to your good lord the most noble and puissant Duke of Burgundy, and to your good lord the most reverend Bishop of Arras, and ask them to protect and befriend you, for the sake of God and our Lady."

Neither of the children would do what was expected from him. The younger, a pretty, delicate child of some three summers, clung frightened to the hand of his protector, and began to cry. But the elder, a very handsome, well-grown boy of five or six, walked boldly up to the duke, and gazed into the stern, warlike face, and at the splendid mantle, the armour, the sword — his brave blue eyes full of admiration and delight, undimmed by the slightest shade of fear. Yet those young eyes were red with tears shed that day for the dear mother whose loss he fully understood; but though the sorrow of childhood is far deeper and more lasting than most people dream, it is easily diverted by those momentary impressions which dominate the vivid, present life of the child, who "sees all new."

The duke, well pleased, laid his gloved hand caressingly on the boy's shoulder, and drew him toward him. "What is your name, my little lad?" he asked kindly.

The boy's eyes were on the beautifully inlaid scabbard of the duke's sword, and he answered carelessly, without lifting them, "Hubert Bohun." Then, with eager interest, "If you please, Sir Knight, may I see your sword?"

"There is no doubt," said the bishop, with a good-natured smile, "that Dame Nature has intended this lad for your calling, my lord, and not for mine."

"Not so fast!" said the duke, a look of displeasure stealing over his face, while his hand dropped from the boy's shoulder. "Say your name again, little lad."

"Hubert Bohun," the child repeated distinctly; and he gave the name an English, not a French pronunciation.

The duke, frowning, looked at the seneschal for an explanation. "If it please my good lords," said the old man, "that is my dear master's stepson. My lady, who lies dead in yonder chamber (God rest her soul!) was wedded first to Sir Hubert Bohun, an English knight, who was in her father's house, a captive and wounded. But he lived not long after; and then my dear lord, who had loved her all his life, wooed and won her, as was meet. Yet Sir Hubert's son was ever dear to him as his own. He made no difference, living, between him and the little Armand de Clairville; and he would have no difference made now that he is dead."

The duke stroked his beard again, more thoughtfully than before. "I did not know this story," he said. "Did you, my lord of Arras?"

"No, my Lord Duke. But it is certain that our good friend De Clairville meant this boy as well as the other, when he prayed us, with his dying breath, to protect his children."

"Possibly — but I will have no Englishmen about me," said the duke, with an air of irritation.

Though he had allied himself with the English, perhaps even because he had done so, he gave free license to his personal dislike of them.

Hubert saw quite well that the splendid knight was displeased with him, though he could not guess the reason. His broad, fair brow gathered an indignant frown, and his little hand was clenched. The bishop marked his look and gesture. "That boy will not be easily daunted," he said to himself. "If struck, he will not cry or cower, but strike back, and fight to the last."

"No," said the duke, finally making up his mind "I will have nothing to do with this slip of the English stock. Give me De Clairville's own boy, and he shall want for nothing. I will make a good knight of him, and if he prove himself his father's son, he may hold his head up with the best in Burgundy."

"But, my lord, he is so young," the seneschal ventured.

"What matters that? I shall send for him by a safe hand, and he shall remain with my own little ones, under the care of the duchess and her ladies, until he is old enough to enter 'the Service' as one of my pages."

This was perfectly satisfactory as far as little Armand was concerned; and the seneschal murmured some grateful words.

"But the other boy?" suggested the bishop.

"Take him yourself, and make a churchman of him. Anything you like," said the duke, carelessly.

The bishop pondered. "Clearly he has wit enough," he said. "Moreover, it is the business of Mother Church to take care of the friendless, and of those whom the world abandons." Then, turning to the seneschal, "Well, my good old friend, your love to your lord and lady does you much honour. You may trust this little Hubert Bohun to my care. I will have him sent at once to some monastery, for such training as he must have cannot begin too early. My Lord Duke, I suppose our business here is ended now?"

The duke bowed. "I am satisfied," he said.

"I can scarce say so much," returned the bishop doubtfully. "I greatly fear we are putting the dove into the falcon's nest, and the brave young eyas into the dovecote."

"That is as God wills," said the duke, forgetting, as men so often do, that it was his own will that had settled the matter.

A few more directions were given to the seneschal, who then left the room, but returned presently with spiced wine and manchet bread, which he made little Hubert present on his knees to the duke and the bishop. Armand could by no means be induced to take part in the ceremony. The attendant men-at-arms, who, meanwhile, for the honour of the house had been well supplied with food and wine, were then summoned; and with due state and ceremony the noble visitors mounted their horses and rode away. The seneschal, with the children on either side of him, waited upon them to the gate, and stood bareheaded until they were out of sight. Then he turned sadly away, murmuring as he did so, "The bishop spoke well. It is the dove to the falcon's nest, and the eyas to the dovecote."

II

TWO STREAMS MEET AGAIN

The house for me no doubt were a house in the city square.
Ah, such a life, such a life, as one leads in the window there.
Something to see, by Bacchus, something to hear at least:
There the whole day long one's life is a perfect feast!
— R. Browning

Never surely in a mediaeval town was there such a stir and strain of surging life — never were there such crowds and commotion, such mingling of business and pleasure, such throngs of notable personages from every clime and nation — as the great General Council brought together in Constance. Its sessions nominally began in the autumn of 1414; but throughout the early days of the following year princes and prelates, learned doctors and splendid knights, were still arriving, and bringing with them long trains of attendants, often numbering several hundreds. Among these we also may arrive in spirit, and, unseen ourselves, see what we can of the stirring drama which is being enacted there.

We must needs bring with us the knowledge of a few facts; now only the "dry bones" of history, though once clothed with vigorous, palpitating flesh and blood. At this time the great schism of the Western Church had already lasted for nearly forty years. There had been at first two, latterly three rival popes claiming the obedience of Christendom — John XXIII at Rome, Gregory XII at Avignon, and "that obstinate old man" calling himself Benedict XIII, secure in his fortress on the Rock of Rimini. Of the three, John XXIII had the strongest title. His predecessor, Alexander V, had been solemnly elected during the General Council of Pisa, and John, at his death, had been chosen by the cardinals in his room. He was lawful pope, true head of Christendom and Vicar of Christ, even in the eyes of many who detested his character and despised his person. Detested and despised he was to an extent that makes us wonder how he could have been tolerated so long. His own secretary has drawn his portrait for us with a pen dipped in gall and wormwood. If we are to believe Thierry de Niem, the Head of Christendom was not only stained, but steeped to the lips, in every possible vice and abomination. However, we must make some allowance for the habit of coarse invective universal in those days; when even the greatest and most respectable personages reviled each other, in speech and writing, in a manner which would not now be tolerated.

All devout Roman Catholics desired ardently to make an end of the schism, and to have once more a pope whom they could obey with a clear conscience. According to the theory of the Middle Ages, the Emperor of Germany represented the civil, as the pope did the ecclesiastical, power. The "Head of the Holy Roman Empire," as he was called, had a kind of sacred character; he thought himself, and was thought by others, "a minister ordained of God." It must be owned that the conception was a noble one; and the man who at this epoch had won, though he had not yet received, the imperial crown, rose to the height of its dignity. Sigismund of Hungary was not a good man: he had many glaring faults, and in one memorable instance was basely false to his plighted word. Yet we are forced to admit his genuine zeal and his unwearied exertions on behalf of the unity of Christendom. He it was who forced the unwilling John XXIII to consent to the General Council, who arranged it, summoned it, presided over its deliberations. He dragged the reluctant pontiff to Constance, almost, it might be said, by force, brought him back when he fled, pressed for his deposition, urged that of his rivals. He spared no pains to detach from the anti-popes, even by personal influence, the political supporters who had enabled them to keep their seats. The credit of a large share in the extinction of the schism is therefore due to Sigismund of Hungary.

But there were others of very different character who were labouring earnestly for the same end. It was an age of considerable mental activity; and, except in Italy, the best thought of the age was still ecclesiastical. The universities throughout Europe were full of stir and movement, and eager intellectual strife; though often, it is true, about words and names, and subtleties to us uninteresting, or even unintelligible. It was also an age of great "doctors." Printing was not yet; and manuscripts, though prized and studied by the few with passionate earnestness, were not for the many. In those days the living voice was almost everything; and many noble voices were lifted up in the various centres of learning. All these voices, almost in unison, called for this General Council.

To the best thinkers of the age, the learned, the gifted, the devout, it had become but too evident that the infallible guidance Christ promised to His Church did not reside in the papal chain. The true voice of the Church could not come from the lips of a pseudo-pope, scarcely even from those of a lawful pontiff stained with every crime. Where, then, was it to be found? Where, but in her collective wisdom, in her rulers and teachers, her doctors and priests, gathered lawfully in solemn council, under the personal guidance and superintendence of the Divine Spirit? Hence the Holy Ecumenical Council came to represent a grand and noble idea, intensely believed and passionately cherished. "The supremacy of General Councils over the pope" — which does not perhaps appear to us a very soul-stirring formula — was in those days a doctrine that devout and earnest-minded men not only laboured and struggled to establish, but for which, at need, they would have laid down their lives. This, we have said, was the best thought of the age. Other thoughts, indeed, which were not of the age, but of all time and for all time were vaguely beginning to stir. Here and there a solitary voice arose, like "the earliest pipe of half-awakened bird" long before the sunrise. As the mystic bird of paradise, in the beautiful legend, sang to the monk Felix of the city of God, the New Jerusalem, so these voices, low and tremulous as they were, awakened in the hearts of men the dream and vision of another Church — "not made of popes and cardinals and priests," nor of councils, which might err — but the "general assembly and church of the firstborn, whose names are written in heaven," and whose one infallible Head is the Lord Himself. But even those who awakened the vision did not wholly understand it themselves. Their enemies sometimes understood it better.

Beside the great object of the extinction of the schism, there were two others which the Council proposed to itself; and which, had it really accomplished them, would have been greater yet. These were the reform of the Church and the suppression of heresy. Of the latter, something may be said hereafter. The crying necessity of the former is abundantly witnessed by all the writings of the day. All righteous men, however fiercely they might contend about other things, were at one about this: they sighed and cried for the abominations that were done in the midst of their Zion, the Church. Often, in the anguish of their souls, they turned their eyes heavenward and exclaimed, "Lord, how long!" Then, turning again to the earth, they denounced, in words that scathed and burned — words so fierce and bitter as to be almost unreadable by us — the sins of popes and cardinals, of priests and prelates. If they could have said no more, at least they said no less, than holier lips had uttered before, "Serpents, generation of vipers, how can ye escape the damnation of hell?" Men were asking everywhere what would the Great Council do to cleanse out this Augean stable.

Other matters, too, of less world-wide importance, yet intensely interesting to those engaged in them, and to many of their contemporaries, were to come before it. As it often happens, these frequently obscured the main issues, as well for the spectators as for the actors. They who walked therein "could not see the wood for the trees." It is only from a distance that the whole can be discerned as a whole. The man who fights in a decisive battle does not see the plan: it is well if he even sees his own antagonist clearly. Nor is the mere idler and follower of the camp likely to attain to greater illumination.

*   *   *

On a sunny afternoon in the first month of 1415, such an idler stood upon the steps of the Cathedral of St. Maurice, in Constance. He was very young and fair in face. His long, carefully-curled golden hair was covered by a tall hat, bearing a single plume, and encircled with golden chains fastened in front by an agrafe, upon which there was engraved a carpenter's plane, with the motto, *Je le tiens*. His short crimson mantle had the same device wrought in gold upon it. The rest of his garb followed the prevailing fashion, being made very tight, padded at the shoulders, but elsewhere fitting accurately to the figure, and ending with a pair of crimson shoes, which had long, pointed, metal toes. A slender sword, in a dainty scabbard, hung at his side; but both sword and wearer seemed better adapted for ornament than for work, and more used to the peaceful tourney and the fencing-match than to the stern reality of war.

He was looking on, apparently well pleased, at the colourful and busy scene before him. The Münster Platz was crowded, and with representatives of fully a dozen different nationalities. Some Hungarian nobles belonging to the suite of the Emperor,[1] who was staying at the Leiter House near at hand, rode proudly by, as if the place belonged to them. Just after them came a fancy coach or wagon, covered like a tent with rich silk brocade, supported upon gilded rods; and the livery of the attendant guards marked it as the equipage of Queen Barbe, the consort of Sigismund, who kept her luxurious

---

[1] The Emperor Sigismund had not yet been crowned, and was therefore, properly speaking, only King of the Romans; but he was often called the Emperor.

little court at Petershausen, on the farther side of the river. The foot-passengers were quite as interesting. Among them were stately, handsome Greeks from the shore of Bosphorus, come to see the great Council of the Western Church. German knights and French gentlemen jostled each other in the narrow space; while the dark, fur-trimmed robes of the doctors, and the gray, brown, and black of the monks and friars, toned down the vivid colouring of the rest. Most numerous and obtrusive of all were the gaily-accoutred serving-men, wearing the badges and colours of prelate, prince, or noble — these moved about in the throng, pushing themselves everywhere, and equally ready to take part in a jest, a quarrel, or a show.

The fair-haired youth continued to look on with an air of amusement, until at last something happened which aroused his indignation, made his open brow contract into a frown, and his blue eyes kindle with anger. A young girl of the humbler class, belonging to the town, very neatly dressed and very modest-looking, had emerged from one of the side streets, and was trying to cross the crowded Platz, with a basket of clean linen on her arm. Three or four dark-faced, handsome, insolent Italians beset her and barred her way, one of them snatching the basket from her hand, and another making a feint of restoring it, with some rude unmannerly jest. Greatly frightened, she begged them to let her go; and they replied with insults which were bad enough, and with rough gallantry which was worse. Springing down the steps, the young Frenchman pushed his way to them through the crowd, and, not stopping to measure his strength with theirs, desired them, in his own tongue, to let the maid alone. For answer, they scoffed and jeered at him — if they did not understand his words they guessed his meaning readily. The Frenchman gave back their scorn with interest, calling them the pope's scullions and trencher-scrapers; at which one of them, who evidently understood the taunt, pulled off his embroidered glove and struck him in the face.

The youth drew his sword, and, though only with the flat, returned the blow. Instantly the deadly Italian stiletto flashed in the winter sunlight. It would have gone ill with the fair-haired lad, but for a new combatant who at that moment appeared on the scene — a tall muscular young man, in the dress of a student or scholar, who caught up some sort of weapon from an ironmonger's close by, and with his scholar's gown flying about him, plunged wildly into the midst of the fray. So doughty were the strokes of his strong right arm, and so quick was he in dealing them, that the braggart Italians soon had more than enough. A clever thrust or stab was one thing, a giant laying about him with an iron mace was quite another. The field

19

was speedily cleared; and the two champions had time to bestow a glance upon each other and upon the girl they had rescued, who, pent up meanwhile against a wall, had been unable to make her escape. She was pale and trembling; but the face, partly concealed by the modest white kerchief, was fair, pure, and honest, as the faces of these good German maidens so often are. She tried, though without much success — for of course she spoke German — to thank her champions; and they, with true chivalry, saw her into a quiet street, and lifted their caps in courteous farewell. Then they stood and looked each other in the face.

The young squire was the first to speak. "Bravely done, Scholar," he cried, stretching out his hand. "I warrant me you are a good Frenchman."

"Straight from Paris," was the answer. "A student of the Sorbonne should know how to defend himself."

"And his friends," said the other. "Come with me to *The Golden Lion* yonder, where they keep good French wine, and let us discuss our victory over a cup of it."

"Right willingly," said the scholar, taking off his cap and shaking out his crisp, curling locks. "But stay a moment. I must return this useful piece of iron to the honest merchant I took it from, lest he should make me pay for it. And scholars' purses are not deep."

"I will go with you. But, pray, what is it? A rather uncommon sort of weapon, I think."

"By St. Martin, I believe it is a turnspit!" said the scholar, with a hearty laugh. "I did not wait to pick and choose. Well, it proved good enough to roast those cowardly Italians."

"What ruffians they are! With cold steel out, for any cause or for no cause at all, and before a man could say an 'Ave!' No better than braggarts and bandits! They got their deserts. But I wonder the town-watch or the Elector Palatine's guard did not step in and spoil our play."

"Oh, they cannot be everywhere — the thing happened too quickly. But here is the shop. I shall not be a minute." Nevertheless, the lively scholar may have spent five in trying to tell the owner, in bad German eked out by signs, that his piece of property had come back greatly enhanced in value by the part it had played in a knightly encounter.

This accomplished, the squire led the way to the hostelry of which he had spoken. Like every spot in Constance, it was full to overflowing; but they found seats on the balcony, and were soon supplied with excellent wine from the vineyards of Beauçe.

"Have you been here long?" asked the squire, whose apparently higher rank seemed to give him the initiative.

"Not yet two weeks. I am waiting for my lord, who has sent me and others on before him, being himself delayed by pressing business."

"And who may be the lord of such a doughty champion, able to serve him as well with the sword as, no doubt, with the pen — which I suppose is the proper weapon of your calling?"

"Right there. I have the honour to act as secretary" (he said scribe, or *scripteur*) "to the Chancellor of Paris."

"What? Do you mean the Chancellor of the Church and University of Paris?"

"I mean the great chancellor, and the great doctor, Jean Charlier Gerson, whose renown is in all the world. There is no one else — and there is no one like him," said the scholar, lifting his head proudly.

Instead of raising the wine-cup to his lips to drink to the lord of his new friend, as in all courtesy he should have done, the squire pointed to the agrafe on the hat which lay beside him.

"Do you see the badge I wear, friend?" he said, with a gathering frown.

"Yes, I know that badge and cognisance only too well," said the scholar. "I am sorry you serve the Duke of Burgundy."

"Spare your sorrow, my brave lad of the pen and the iron mace. Jean Sans Peur[2] is a good lord to me."

"I think not much of Jean Sans Peur," returned the scholar boldly. "His right hand is stained with the blood of the Duke of Orleans, the king's brother."

"Well — if it is?" said the squire. "Suppose he did cause the assassination of his rival and enemy, to whom was he accountable for the deed, save his God and his king? Is it becoming, think you, for beggarly churchmen — I beg your pardon, Sir Scholar — for *churchmen* to judge in affairs of state, and to call great nobles to account for their actions? Let them mind their own business, and leave their betters alone."

"Are not right and justice — are not the Ten Commandments — their own business?" asked the scholar indignantly. "Are poor miserable wretches to be hanged every day for stealing or stabbing, or less crimes even — and is a monk of St. Francis, like that accursed Jean Petit, to stand up unreproved in the presence of the king, and to say

---

[2] Jean Sans Peur (John the Fearless) succeeded his father, Philippe le Hardi (Philip the Bold), as Duke of Burgundy in 1409.

that the Duke of Burgundy ought not to be punished at all, since murder, when it is done on a traitor, is no sin before God or man?"

"Do you think, then, that your chancellor played a noble part when he stood up in public to rebuke Jean Petit? That it is well done of him to come here, with the purpose, as all men know, of getting him condemned by the Council? Mind you, Sir Scholar, that the offence of that same Jean Petit was merely to maintain, perhaps too zealously, the cause of that same Duke of Burgundy who had been your chancellor's first patron and friend. *Churchmen* may act in that way, but not knights and gentlemen."

"Then I maintain, Sir Squire, that churchmen act well. I say it *was* a noble part for the chancellor to speak out for the law of God and man, and to rebuke sin, were it to cost him the best friend he ever had. And now, if the Council condemn, as it surely will, the wicked doctrine of Jean Petit . . ."

"Then I say the duke . . ."

"Then I say the chancellor . . ."

But at this point the duke's gentleman, who, to do him justice, was far less excited than the chancellor's scribe, stopped suddenly, and burst out laughing, struck with a sense of the absurdity of the position.

"Do not let us fight with each other, just after having fought so gallantly with those Italian rascals," he said. "Though, if we did," he added good-naturedly. "I have no doubt you would have the best of it, my knight of the iron mace."

"You say well, Sir, that we should not quarrel. But no man speaks a word in my presence against the Chancellor of Paris."

"That is fair enough, since you eat his bread. Likewise, no one says a word in mine against the Duke of Burgundy. I am in his service, and here on his business. But let us talk of ourselves, not of our lords. What is your name, brave scholar?"

"My name is Hubert Bohun. And yours, Sir Squire?"

"I am called Armand de Clairville," returned the other lightly.

"Armand de Clairville?" cried Hubert, staring at him. "Can it be?" Then laying his hand upon his arm, "Your look — your voice moved me strangely from the first. And now, your name — Armand, do you not know? Can you not remember? Did you never hear anyone speak of your brother?"

Armand returned his gaze in a sort of stupefaction. At last he said in a bewildered tone, "My brother? Yes, I had a brother. It is like a dream to me — I had a brother. I do not remember him at all."

"Nevertheless, Armand de Clairville, I am your brother."

"Hubert — you said Hubert, I think? Hubert de Clairville?" hazarded the still bewildered Armand.

"No; Hubert Bohun. My father whom I never knew, was an Englishman. But my mother — whom, child though I was, I remember well" — and his strong voice trembled with emotion — "was your mother too, Armand de Clairville."

The brothers rushed into each other's arms, and embraced each other with all the effusion and abandonment of Frenchmen, and of Frenchman four hundred years ago. Our modern reserve and undemonstrativeness would have found scant favour in the eyes of our ancestors. Both their love and their hatred were proclaimed with a vehemence which with us would betoken an utter lack of self-control; yet they were able to exhibit, upon occasion, the most heroic self-control.

The complete separation of the brothers after their parting in early childhood was the necessary accident of the age. Very few could read or write, and a letter was a serious undertaking — an event in a man's life. To write it or get it written was difficult, to despatch it to its destination more difficult still. There were no regular posts, or means of communication. Especially in a country so disturbed as France, it did not need the added obstacle that the two young brothers had drifted into hostile factions to separate them completely each from the other.

III

SQUIRE AND SCHOLAR

No distance breaks the ties of blood,
Brothers are brothers evermore.

— Keble

In the meantime other guests had come out upon the balcony, and were observing, not without amusement, the frank delight of the reunited brothers. Armand, who was the first to notice this, whispered to his brother, "Let us go to some place where we can talk in quiet."

"With all my heart. But where shall we go?"

A question not very easy to answer. Our ancestors did not understand, as we do, the charms of privacy, especially in domestic arrangements; and if they had done so, the enormous crowds which were then in Constance would have rendered privacy almost unattainable.

There would have been little quiet for the brothers in the lodgings where the Duke of Burgundy's gentlemen lounged and drank wine, and played games of hazard, while they imagined they were watching his interests, or protecting his agents at the Council. It would have been still worse in the house which had been hired for the Chancellor of Paris, in St. Paul's Street, next to the lodging of the Greek archbishop — where Hubert slept in an attic, at the foot of the junior chaplain's bed.

But Armand solved the difficulty by a bribe to the host of *The Golden Lion* large enough to procure them, even there and then, a private room with lights and supper. Established here, the brothers first indulged in a long, earnest gaze at each other. Both were well pleased with the result. Hubert looked into the fair, ingenuous face of a gallant youth, almost a boy in years, and perhaps no more in mind, to whom his own large heart went out at once in brotherly protecting tenderness. Armand saw a more stalwart frame, a taller figure, and a face far more full of power and character. Hubert's brow was broad and high, the crisp locks that curled about it chestnut-brown, the eyes deep blue, but with hidden fire in their depths such as blue eyes seldom have; and very firm were the lines of the finely-moulded mouth, around which, in student fashion, the hair had been allowed to grow. Almost before he was aware of it, Armand spoke out his thoughts, "It is you who should have been the knight and warrior, Hubert, and not I."

"We should both have been what our fathers were," said Hubert. "So, at least, I used to think," he added. "But now that I have come to serve the chancellor, things look a little different. Armand, have you heard that Guillaume le Ferré is dead?"

"I do not even know who Guillaume le Ferré may be."

"Have you no recollection of the dear old seneschal at Clairville, who was so kind to us children?"

"You forget I was but three years old. My earliest remembrances only take me back to the duke's castle, and the toys and sweetmeats given me by the ladies there."

"I have the advantage of you by at least two years. I remember well our father — this is, your father — and our mother, and the day she died. But as for Guillaume — good old man — I had gifts and messages from him several times. I think he must have been nearly ninety when he died. Some time ago he sent me a chest containing a few things which belonged to our mother. They ought to be shared with you, Armand. I have left them in Paris — at the chancellor's house."

"They can wait," said Armand indifferently. In the bright, varied life of the present he had little thought to spare for the past, and little care about it.

"I have one thing with me, however, which you will like to have, and certainly you have the best right to it; it is a Book of Hours, belonging to your father. There were two books — that, and a smaller one, which was *my* father's; that also I have here. It contains certain Psalms in Latin, and bears an inscription in the English tongue, which a scholar from Oxford, whom I knew in Paris, translated for me. It says the book was given to Sir Hubert Bohun, knight, by his good friend, Master John Wycliffe, Vicar of Lutterworth. A fine fright I was in when I heard that! I showed it at once to the chancellor."

"A fright? What about, I ask?" asked Armand, who knew as little of John Wycliffe as he did of Guillaume le Ferré.

"Can you ask? I thought everybody knew that Wycliffe is a great heretic — was, rather, for he is dead. One of the most important affairs before the Council is the condemnation of his doctrines. I could not bear to think that the good knight, my father, had called such a man his friend. Nevertheless, the chancellor says that my little book, being only a part of the Psalter, has no harm in it, and I may keep it."

Armand laughed.

"I will give you the best of my gold chains," he said, "if you will keep the chancellor out of your talk for ten phrases together. I thought I was a good and loyal man to my lord; but you beat me in that, as, no doubt, in other things. Leave the chancellor alone, and tell me how you have been all these years. How have the churchmen used you? And what wind has blown you here?"

"How am I to answer that," returned Hubert, laughing also, "without naming the chancellor, since I have come here on his business? If you do not want to hear of him, you must tell me your story instead."

So it happened that Armand's story was told first. There was not much in it, after all and a few words about it may suffice at present. The Duke of Burgundy's little protégé had been kindly cared for by the ladies of his court, until, at ten years old, he entered "the Service" as a page. He was trained carefully in all manly and knightly exercises; and at fourteen became an esquire. Since then he had taken part with credit in two or three small "affairs" with the Armagnacs; had chosen a young lady of his patron's court (much older than himself) as the object of his chivalrous adoration; and generally had behaved as young gentlemen of his age and station were wont to do. He was very proud of being among the duke's gentlemen who were chosen to accompany his agents to Constance. Of the chief of these agents, the Bishop of Arras — successor to Hubert's first patron — Armand spoke with esteem and liking. But the second, a canon, named Pierre Cauchon, he despised and detested, calling him a true *cochon*, or hog, fit for nothing but the mire, and a very bad companion. "However," he said, "the duke himself intends to come by and by, to look after his own affairs at the Council, and then all will be right."

Hubert's tale was less easily told. Not, indeed, that he cared to linger over his boyhood; he was not yet far enough removed from it to look back without shame upon its numerous sins and delinquencies. "They sent me to school," he said, "to the Franciscan House in Rouen and a pleasant life I led those unfortunate friars! I can afford to pity them now, though I do not remember that anyone pitied me, and I am sure I needed it — a poor fatherless and motherless child, who thought all the people about him were his enemies, and that he was theirs. It was a cruel wrong, thought I, to send me to a monastery, and destine me for the Church, when I should have been a soldier like my father. I wanted — in so far as I wanted anything, save pure fun and mischief — to show that it was no use; that no power on earth should make a scholar of me. I grew up a determined young rebel, and finally I ran away. I meant to go and fight for France against the English; for, in spite of my English blood, I reckoned — and I reckon myself still — a Frenchman. But they caught me and brought me back again. Then the old sub-prior said to me — the first sensible word I remember hearing from any man — 'My son, be reasonable. Submit to discipline, and learn your Humanities. Then, in a year or two we will send you to the great college in Paris; and you will be your own master, and can do what you please.' Overjoyed at even a distant prospect of liberty, I took the hint; and so at last, in a happy day, I found myself at the Sorbonne, entered as student of theology in the College of Navarre. Fervently did I thank my patron, St. Hubert the hunter, for my deliverance."

"Yes; but I suppose that scholars, like squires, are still under discipline?" said Armand.

"Of a sort; but we had plenty of liberty. What I did that first year at the Sorbonne, and what pranks I played, I am not going to tell you now," said Hubert, shaking his head. "It would only corrupt your manners, my good brother the esquire. There were some hundreds of us, all brimming over with life and spirits, and — if say it I must — with a strong touch of ferocity. It was well for us, on the whole, that we had the Cabochiens to fight with, and could give them broken heads and limbs at our pleasure."

"Take care what you say, brother. The Cabochiens are our people, partisans of Burgundy."

"Little cared we whose partisans they were: and little cause you have to be proud of them," returned Hubert. "But it is true that the city rabble, headed by butchers, skinners, and the like, and especially by that gallows-bird Caboche, were all Burgundians, while we of the Sorbonne were good Armagnacs, to a man. So we had plenty of free fights, which, perhaps, kept us out of worse mischief. I know that *my* luck never failed me until, in some passing truce with the Cabochiens, it came into my foolish head to attack the doctors."

At this the squire, used to discipline, made a grimace. "That is as if I were to show insolence to the master of the horse, or even to the duke himself," he said.

"But I think the duke would not have provoked you by small tyrannies, as the doctors did us. We could not stab them with swords, or beat them with clubs, as we did the Cabochiens, so we betook ourselves to arms of another kind. We caricatured and lampooned them all — rectors, deans, doctors, and masters — without mercy. I was foremost in the work, and, coming off scatheless again and again, I grew bolder. At last I posted a notice on the great gate of the Sorbonne: *De part le Roi. A messieurs les Docteurs de la Sorbonne. Il est defendu . . .*[3] Then followed a string of nonsense, turning all their doings into ridicule. Among other things, they were forbidden to let their finger-nails grow, a scandalous story being current of a fight between a scholar and a doctor, in which both had made use of their natural weapons. I thought that piece of insolence would have been laughed at and forgotten, like all the rest. But it was taken seriously, and became the subject of a grave investigation. I was suspected, and no wonder. They put me under arrest, and then — I am not ashamed to tell you, Armand, that for the first time in my life I learned the meaning of that word fear. Punishments are cruel in Paris. Many of the students — for whom such sights had a fascination I could never share — used to haunt the Place de Grève, and tell of the wretches whom they saw there, scourged, branded, tortured. Once a man was burned there — burned alive. It was horrible, oh — *that cry*! But, then, he was a parricide."

"But," said Armand, "they could not surely do any of those dreadful things to you, for a mere jest."

"They could have done worse than — at least than hanging. It was quite possible my ears might have paid for my insolence; while as for the scourge — but *that* degradation I would not have borne — I would have killed myself first. The doctors were all in a terrible rage; it was treason against the king, they said; they would make an example of the delinquent. I determined to confess nothing; no, not if they put me to the Question, as like enough they would. So I was brought before the chancellor. It was enough to freeze a man's blood in his veins. There he sat, in the great hall of council, with all the doctors around him, he looking the gravest and sternest of them all. When asked, I was so much of a coward that I said, 'Not guilty,' laying, indeed, this salve to my conscience, that though I had done the thing, yet there was no guilt in the thing done."

"And where was the harm?" asked Armand, who had been listening intently.

---

[3] "On the part of the King.

"To the Doctors of the Sorbonne. It is forbidden . . ." etc. The usual style of a royal proclamation.

Hubert did not heed the question. He went on, "I do not know how it might have ended, if some too zealous friend of mine had not come forward to defend me by casting the blame upon another. He would have it that the culprit was Bontemps — that same luckless lad who had begun the stir by returning the doctor's blow, and fighting it out with him. Of course, I could not allow an innocent man to suffer."

"Do you mean to say you confessed?" cried Armand, with emotion. "Oh, Hubert! I could not have done that."

"Why, what else could I do?" asked Hubert, staring. "When things had gone so far, there was nothing left for me but to say, 'Gentlemen, it was I. I throw myself on your mercy.' "

"That was brave — splendid of you, Hubert!"

"Brave? Splendid? Is that the way you squires talk? A man is not brave because he misses a villainy by a hair's-breadth. Of course, you would have done just the same. Then my lord the chancellor spoke stern and awful words about law and order, and the sin of violating them. I think my heart stood still the while. But when he came to pronounce the sentence, it was neither scourging, nor branding, nor torture, nor even imprisonment — nothing but a simple fine! My heart beat again, and sent the blood throbbing through my head and ears, and every vein in my body. But in another moment the relief passed away, and the fainting of heart came back. I cried out despairingly, 'But, my good lord, I have not a denier in the world!'

" 'Remove the prisoner,' quoth he, as stern as Minos.

"Removed I was; and you may think what a night I spent in my cell, wondering what they would do with me, since I had nothing to pay. But the next morning early the chancellor sent for me again. This time he was alone. I stood trembling, as far off as I might, but he motioned me to come near him. 'Hubert Bohun,' he said, and his voice was low and gentle, though his face wore still that stern, sad look which, indeed, it always wears, 'Hubert Bohun, you are free.'

"He waited for me to speak; and I, confused and bewildered as I was, at last contrived to stammer out, 'Am I forgiven, my lord?'

" 'No,' he said, 'not forgiven of grace, but released of right, because the fine is paid,' and this time a grave smile softened the sternness of his look.

"From that smile I knew the truth, and my heart went out to him as it had never done yet to living man. I was on my knees before him in a moment. What I said I know not, but this I think it was: 'My lord, you have saved me. No, more, you have bought me. I am your man forever.'

"But he bade me rise. And then he spoke words which even to you, my brother, I can scarcely tell. He said I was worth saving, and he added" — Hubert paused, crossed himself, then went on in a changed and softened voice, "He added, that I must not think of what he had done for me — that was little, but rather think of One who, though He was my judge, had paid for me a debt infinitely greater. 'By His death He has bought you in very deed. My son, serve and thank Him all your life.' "

Armand looked at his brother as if he was speaking to him in a tongue he could not understand. "But at least," he said, "you were grateful to the chancellor. Else were you no brother of mine."

"Grateful? Yes; but I could find no way of showing it then, save by flinging myself head foremost into school Latin and school theology, which last I took to be the meaning of his words about serving our Lord. At first I had far rather have flung myself alone into a mob of Cabochiens; but very soon I came to like it really."

Armand made an incredulous grimace.

"You never know what you can do until you are tried," said Hubert. "And, indeed, the fine fencing, the clever cut and thrust of the schools, have a charm and a pleasure of their own. There is joy in knowing your blade is sharper than any other man's, and in training eye and hand to deal the neatest of strokes with it. I am more proud of my thesis against the Realists, and my refutation therein of the heretical doctrine of the *Universalia à parte rei*, than of any fray I fought out yet with the Cabochiens."

"What doctrine are you talking about?" asked Armand, puzzled.

"That foolish imagination of the Realists, who maintain that Universals have existence apart from the substance of which they are the attributes."

Every particle of intelligence faded out of the face of Armand, leaving it "as blank as his hat."

"But what are Universals?" he asked at last, in a bewildered way.

"Universal ideas, of course. Such as courage, faith, and virtue."

"I am sure I wish they *were* universal," said Armand, with a dawn of returning sense. "How can any man be expected to understand such jargon? Still, I hope your chancellor appreciated your devotion. I am bound to acknowledge he deserved it."

"That and much more," said Herbert. "But, fortunately, I was able afterward to show my gratitude in another way. Last year the Cabochiens got the town almost all into their hands, and fine disorders we had then! They were worse than the wolves in winter, who used to think nothing of coming into the streets after dark, and snapping up a belated burgher. I had a fight with them now and then, by way of keeping myself warm, when snow was deep and wood was expensive. The rascals — I mean the Cabochiens, not the wolves — had the audacity to attack and plunder the chancellor's house. He took refuge in the vaults of Notre Dame, where he lived for some time, reading and writing, and giving himself to devotion, after his wont. Some of us banded together, mounted guard over his house, and saved what we could from pillage. Especially, we saved the books. And so, what with one thing and what with another, I think he trusts me. It is a great honour that he has chosen me to come with him here, and he says I shall write for him in the Council."

"If you write as well as you strike, he will have no cause to complain of you," said Armand.

After that their talk wandered into other channels, and did not come to an end until the host of *The Golden Lion*, appearing at the door with an armful of bed coverings, politely informed them that two Spanish gentlemen had engaged the room as a sleeping apartment.

IV

THE GREAT CHANCELLOR

There are many sides to love — admiration, reverence, gratitude, affection; they are all different shapes of that one great spirit of love — the only feeling which will bind a man to do good, not once in a way, but habitually.

— Kingsley

During the weeks immediately following their meeting the brothers spent nearly all their time together. Armand had really nothing to do; and Hubert very little, pending the arrival of the chancellor, which was now daily expected — but there was plenty to amuse them. Indeed there was amusement, more than enough, just then in Constance, for keen young eyes and fresh young spirits.

Besides the perpetual pageant of the streets, something special was always going on. There were Mysteries, Moralities, and Miracle Plays; there were famous Mummers from distant England; there were *Jongleurs* with their songs and jests, their feats of strength and agility, and their merry antics; there were showmen with dwarves and giants, with learned apes and dancing bears; there were professional fools by the score, in their motley of red, green, and white, or of the other colours pertaining to their princely or noble masters, always to be distinguished by the long donkey's ears, which were their own special badge and cognisance. But the brothers sometimes preferred a quiet talk with each other to these various attractions. Going out by the Schnetz Thor or the Göttlingen Thor, and passing through the gardens and pleasure grounds called the Brühl, the usual scene of sports and pastimes, they would walk along the White Way, as it was styled then, until they reached the lake, where stood the gloomy towers of Göttlieben Castle. Or, taking another direction, they would walk beside the Rhine; or they would cross the bridge and wander in the pleasant fields and woods beyond. Indeed, all the environs of Constance were pleasant and lovely. But even there solitude was difficult; for many of those who had been attracted to the city by the Great Council were unable to find accommodation within its walls, and pitched their tents in the neighbourhood.

Although far from agreeing upon all points, Hubert and Armand grew daily more attached to each other. They had many arguments, usually seasoned with jests and laughter and with an abundance of what we would now style "chaff." Yet sometimes each would grow eager, and for a passing moment they would be on the brink of a quarrel. But the quarrel never came; on the other hand, every meeting cemented their good understanding.

They had two chief subjects of disagreement. One was about Armand's position as squire to the Duke of Burgundy. One of the things in the world which Hubert just then most earnestly desired was the condemnation of Jean Petit by the Council; and through him, of the duke's cowardly assassination of his rival. It is therefore not surprising that, with the usual intolerance of youth, he contended that his brother ought not to remain any longer in the service of a "murderer," as he called him.

"A good way to show my gratitude for all he has done for me," Armand would answer. "And what, I ask, am I to do? If I quit the Service, I have positively no prospect in the world. Would you have me take the beggar's staff and wallet, or enlist as an archer in the guard of the Black Friars, yonder on the island? Besides, I really cannot see how my honour is involved. If the duke were to ask me to help him in a murder, I hope I know my duty, as a true squire and gentleman; but am I to make myself the judge of my lord's conscience and his actions?"

This seemed reasonable; and Armand, so far, had the best of the argument. But he overstated the case when he added, "In my place you would think the same. I warrant me you would not forsake your chancellor, suppose, even, for argument's sake, that he were to do what the duke has done."

But this was asking too much of Hubert; indeed, it sounded in his ears like blasphemy. "Hold your peace, foolish boy!" he cried indignantly. "The chancellor, some day, may perhaps suffer violence from some of the great men whose sins he reproves so boldly — sparing not even the king on his throne. But to *do* it! The notion is outrageous!"

"Softly, Hubert; I did but jest. Though, I think, I *have* heard of churchmen who compassed the death of their enemies."

"Oh, if it was a jest," said Hubert, mollified, "well, if you jest, so can I. Here I promise, with a free heart and a clear conscience, that if ever the chancellor bears part in taking the life of any man, even his worst enemy, I will leave his service forthwith, and tell him why to his face. That promise will not cost me much," he added, laughing.

"My hand on it then," returned Armand. "One never knows what may happen when there are churchmen in the case. But if you love me, cease plaguing me about the duke, for I have no mind to make myself an idle rogue and a masterless man."

The other cause of difference was more serious. Armand had been brought up among courtiers and soldiers, who had little regard for religion. Of course he practiced the outward observances universal in his day; and equally, of course, he had never questioned a single dogma he had been taught — he did not care enough about the matter to do so. But he often used profane oaths, and what to Hubert seemed worse, he never lost an opportunity of sneering at the Church or abusing the priesthood. It must be owned that the corruption of the one and the crying sins of the other gave abundant cause. Much that he said was perfectly true, far more true than he himself knew or guessed; yet none the less was it said in scorn of all religion, and learned from the lips of men who, for the most part, hated the good and not the evil in the religion of their day; disliking, as such men always will dislike, any restraint upon their conduct.

But Hubert, in his passage from a rebellious boyhood into a stormy youth, had been taken in hand, greatly to his benefit, by a very noble representative of the Church, and therefore he revered and loved the Church with all his heart. At least, he thought he did, but what he really revered and loved was the great chancellor. So Armand's mocking tone used to arouse his indignation. All the more did mischievous Armand like to tease him by repeating the scandalous tales that came to his ears day by day — usually beginning with "One of your churchmen" has done such-and-such. To which Hubert would usually answer, "I am not a churchman."

Particularly Armand delighted in retailing the many disgraceful and undignified stories which were current about Pope John. Even Hubert joined him in a hearty laugh at the tale of the carriage overturned in the alpine pass, and the Holy Father (corpulent and unwieldy from a life of self-indulgence) lying helpless on his back in the snow, and greeting those who came to his aid with the characteristic exclamation, "Here I lie, in the devil's name."

"Pope John, I dare say, will be obliged to abdicate," said Hubert, when he recovered his countenance.

"Still, you must acknowledge that at present he is the true pope," said Armand. "Indeed, you say yourself that those in the obedience of Gregory and of Benedict are schismatics."

"Oh, as for that," returned Hubert, "the Council will set everything right."

"Yes, indeed! 'Tis ever with you either the great chancellor, or the great Council, the Holy Council. You are making a Mohammedan idol of the Holy Council. And I, for my part, have no such opinion of it at all."

There was a reason for this. Armand, although a very subordinate person in the service of the Duke of Burgundy, yet knew perfectly well that his lord had sent large sums of money by his agents to Constance, in order to influence the decision of the Council on the affair of Jean Petit. And he knew that the holy fathers were proving themselves by no means insensible to these golden arguments.

But besides these subjects of half-jesting contention, a vague but real feeling of uneasiness grew up gradually in the mind of Hubert about Armand. He himself, in all his conversations with him, was perfectly candid and open, both about the past and the present. It was his character; and besides, he had nothing to conceal. But he could not help suspecting that Armand did not fully reciprocate his confidence. Hubert could see that there were some things about which he did not like to speak, and was uneasy if pressed to do so. The circumstances of his promotion from page to squire appeared to be among these, though for what reason Hubert could not guess. This kind of reserve repelled and vexed the stronger and more openhearted brother, who had already begun to assume somewhat of the position of a protector toward the younger and weaker. Sometimes even a fear would cross his mind that there might be, in the young squire's apparently simple and innocent past, some hidden cause of trouble or embarrassment.

*   *   *

The arrival of the Chancellor of Paris swept the brothers in a measure apart from each other. Hubert had now abundance of work, and could rarely find a free hour, even for a walk with Armand. A part of his duty, and one of which he was very proud, was to attend the sittings of the Council, and to take notes for his lord. Or rather, it would be more correct to say that he attended the sittings of the French "nation." Four "nations," the Italian, the German, the French, and the English (a fifth "nation," the Spanish, was added later), took part in the Council. These held their deliberations — which were called Meetings of the Nations — apart at first. They came to their own conclusions, and voted separately, nation by nation. Then congregations, composed of the most distinguished members of all the nations, met together and compared or revised their decisions, or deliberated on special questions which had been referred to them. Lastly, these decisions were ratified, or otherwise, in solemn general sessions of the whole Council. All these meetings were attended by scribes and notaries, for whom special provision was made.

The French nation held its sittings in the chapter-house of the Dominican monastery on the island, under the presidency of the Cardinal Archbishop of Cambray, the celebrated Pierre d'Ailly, styled "the eagle of France and the hammer of heretics." But the real master-spirit, the "light and soul," not only of the French theologians, but more and more, as time went on, of the entire Council, was Jean Charlier Gerson, Chancellor of Paris.

The chancellor's zealous, quick-witted young secretary, who served him day by day both in the Council and out of it, threw his whole heart into the work. All the enthusiasm of which his nature was capable, and that was well-nigh boundless, was enlisted in the cause of the Holy Council, and in its grand work — the restoration of the unity of Christendom. It would seem a strange object to kindle the devotion of a young soul like Hubert's; but then, with him, the Holy Council meant really the great chancellor. The great chancellor's aims and passions had become his also.

He took an early opportunity of presenting his brother to his distinguished patron. Armand would have excused himself, saying that the chancellor would regard him with scant favour, as the retainer of his enemy, the Duke of Burgundy, but Hubert assured him the chancellor was far too magnanimous to be influenced by such a consideration. He led him accordingly to a small apartment, very simply furnished, where at a table covered with papers sat the great chancellor, in his fur-trimmed doctor's robe fastened at the waist with a plain girdle of leather. Already, at fifty-three, his hair was gray, and his powerful, rugged face was seamed with deep lines, which told of care, of sorrow, of perplexity.

"My lord," said Hubert, "this is my brother Armand de Clairville, whom I had the honour yesterday to name to you."

The stern, sad face softened a little, as the great man looked kindly on the youth, who bowed low before him.

"I am glad," he said, "of any good thing which has come to my Hubert. For his sake and for your own, God bless you, my son."

As they passed out, Armand condescended to say to his brother, "I think the blessing of your chancellor will do me no harm, Hubert."

*   *   *

On a cold and frosty, but very fine day, late in February, Hubert made his appearance at the house where Armand lodged, and found him standing at the door, with two or three other Burgundian gentlemen. They were training a couple of young falcons, allowing them to fly for a little, and luring them back to their wrist with morsels of meat. "Come away with me, Armand," he cried breathlessly. "I have a holiday — the Holy Council is busy enthroning St. Bridget!"

Absurd as it may sound to us, this was the literal truth. The Council, after solemn debate, had decided on the canonisation of the Scandinavian saint, and was now completing its work by exposing, with much ceremony, her silver image for adoration in the cathedral.

Armand untied the embroidered "lure" from his wrist, and asked a friend to see to the birds; which the latter promised to do, muttering, however, that, in this cursed town, there was no room to see to anything beyond the toes of one's own shoes.

"I am with you," said Armand to Hubert. "Are we to go to the cathedral, and see the play of St. Bridget to an end?"

Hubert shook his head. "Anywhere but that," he said. "I want to see the sky above my head again, which I have scarce done for a fortnight."

"Let us go to the Brühl, then," Armand proposed. "A merry company of *jongleurs* are showing their sports there."

But this proposition did not please Hubert better than the other. "I am sick of *jongleurs*," he said. "I have seen enough of them in Paris. Neither their manners nor their jests are to my taste. No, rather come with me to the Rhine bridge. I hear the townsfolk talking of a boat-race they are having on the river. No great affair, I suppose, since it is but a custom of their own. Still, I am rather curious to see it."

"As you please," said the accommodating Armand. They took their way from the Rosgarten Street, where the Burgundian gentlemen lodged, along the market street, to the broad, pleasant path by the lake. Leaving the Kaufhaus behind them, they came to the narrow water which divided the great Dominican or Island Monastery from the mainland. As usual, there were loiterers about, but the function in the cathedral had absorbed a great many, so the spot was fairly quiet, and the brothers were in no hurry.

"How pleasant it is here!" said Hubert. "Look at the swans, Armand."

And indeed the graceful birds, with their proudly arched necks and their snowy pinions were a goodly sight as they sailed up and down the stream, on the banks of which little wooden houses had been erected for their accommodation.

Armand was still enough of a boy to frequent the booths of the clever Italian and German confectioners who were making rapid fortunes in the town, so he was stocked with morsels of *marchpane* and other delicacies, which he threw to the birds, and amused himself watching the eagerness with which they snatched them.

"Eat away, my fine fellows!" he cried, turning out his leathern pouch to throw them the last crumbs. "You will be eaten yourselves one of these days. Roast swan is the best of dishes. For my part, I prefer it even to peacock, which is apt to be tough."

Hubert had little experience of either at the frugal board of the temperate chancellor. But he answered, "The monks appear to be of your opinion." Then, looking across at the stately, spacious monastery — "That is a grand place, Armand. You know I have been there, once and again, for our 'nation' holds its sessions in the chapter-house, which is very handsome, and most fairly adorned. But their refectory — you should see that. What a noble hall it is!"

"Yes, for banquets," Armand threw in. "And noble banquets, I doubt not, are served there, to your good monks and their guests. The Black Friars are known for good eating all over the world! When they tire of roast swan and roast capon, they may fall back on the fish in the lake, which are splendid here — and no doubt the choicest come to my lord abbot's table."

"He has never honoured me with an invitation," said Hubert. "But I have seen their beautiful chapel — yes, and seen it full of bishops and doctors, the greatest in all the world. That was a grand sight. And then the cloisters — some day, Armand, I must bring you in with me, and let you walk in the cloisters, so fine and spacious, so nobly built and adorned with such beautiful paintings. And sometimes one meets there, walking slowly up and down, staff in hand, and in his long cloak, the great and learned Greek doctor, Manuel Chrysolaurus, who is the abbot's guest."

"I have seen doctors enough already to last me a lifetime," said Armand. "The city is black with their gowns."

"Well, you have not so often seen a great house like that, in which, with all its dependants, there is not one who lacks meat or drink, or comfort for soul or body," answered Hubert, still looking proudly at the stately pile of buildings.

"Are you sure of that, Hubert? Is there no dungeon yonder, foul and noisome, without light or air?"

"Dungeon? Of course, I suppose there is; but no one in it." Here, however, he caught himself up suddenly. "At least — that is . . ."

But Armand went on, without heeding him, "Are you quite sure your monks oppress nobody? I think I have heard otherwise, from those who know their husbandmen and vassals."

"Who are always better treated, and more prosperous, than the vassals of the seigneurs and the barons," Hubert interposed, standing up for the Church.

"Then your bishops, and abbots, and so forth, always keep such a train of idle, insolent men-at-arms — archers, *lanzknechts*, cross-bowmen, and what not. Oh, I have known some of them — very truculent ruffians indeed."

"Are they worse than others who ply the same trade, and learn their manners from the knights and squires, their lords and masters?" asked Hubert, in his turn indulging in a gibe. "But — talk of the angels — there is one, coming out of that postern gate."

"An angel?" laughed Armand. "*I* would call him an archer of the abbot's guard."

Armand was not mistaken. As the young man drew nearer, the brothers saw that he bore, on the sleeve of his buff jerkin, a well-known badge and cognisance — an abbot proper, full length, with his pastoral staff in his hand, and in front of him a shield, bearing the special arms of the Island Monastery, quartered with the famous sign of St. Dominic, the dog with the flaming brand in his mouth. The archer came quickly over the little bridge to the road, where Hubert smiled to see him stop, take the hand of a blind beggar, and lead him gently and carefully across the way.

"Not so bad for one of your 'truculent ruffians,' " he said. "But come along; you see the crowds are gathering, and everyone is going toward the river. The boatrace, you know, is to be from the Rhine bridge."

But the brothers were not fortunate that day. The function in the cathedral was over, and the crowds who had assisted at it came pouring down the quaint, narrow streets that led to the shore. To increase the confusion, the proprietor of a dancing bear had chosen that very spot for an exhibition. A motley group of men and boys gathered about the creature, applauding him aloud as he bowed and took off his cap to his master, but running away with shrieks of half-genuine alarm when he showed a disposition to pay his compliments to the spectators. Hubert and Armand were jostled and pushed around, treatment which Armand at least resented all the more because it came chiefly from "Swabians" — "beggarly flat-caps," as he called the citizens.

"What is the good of trying for the Rhine bridge?" he asked angrily. "Like enough, we should see nothing when we got there; and if we did, the game would not be worth the candle. Let us go somewhere else."

Hubert demurred. "When I plan a thing, I do it," he said. "I want to see the boats."

"Perhaps I can help you, my masters," said a voice close at hand, and turning, they saw beside them the archer with the Dominican abbot's badge. The man spoke in German, but by this time Hubert was quite able understand and reply to him.

"We want to see the boatrace," he said. "It is, I believe, an affair of your townsfolk, and on that account the more interesting to us strangers."

The compliment was appreciated, as Hubert intended it to be.

"The Rhine-Thor-Thurm (Rhine gate tower) is the best place to see it from. Just follow me, gentlemen," said the archer, with a brightening face.

ROBERT'S STORY

In a service which Thy love appoints
There are no bonds for me,
For my inmost heart is taught the truth
Which makes Thy children free;
And a life of self-renouncing love
Is a life of liberty.

The archer took the lead, and with right goodwill made way for Hubert and his brother through the crowd. Having reached the tower at the head of the wooden bridge which in those days spanned the Rhine, he contrived, they scarce knew how, to get them up the steps, and to secure for them a standing-place. There they had an excellent view of the broad river, and of the gaily decorated boats which dotted its surface with flashes of light and colour. Taking his stand beside them, the archer pointed out the different boats, explaining the rules and the incidents of the race, and sometimes even naming the rowers.

Hubert, whose English blood stirred unawares within him at every sight of boats or shipping, followed him with keen interest, until at the end, he warmly applauded the winner of the last and decisive race.

"Glad they are done with it!" said Armand in French. "But, for once, Hubert, you were right. If this lad has learned his manners from the Black Monks, certainly he does them credit. I have left my money at home — do you chance to have a florin about you to guerdon his good service?"

"I have, thanks, indeed, to the senior chaplain. He counselled me to leave my purse behind, as you did, for fear of thieves; but Charlier and I are such unfriends that when he bids me do one thing, immediately I do the contrary." Hubert produced the coin from the purse which hung at his girdle, and, with a pleasant word of thanks, offered it to their guide.

But the archer refused it, saying respectfully, "Sir, I owe more than that to you and to your friend, and right glad am I to have the chance of showing you I am grateful."

"How is that?" asked both of them at once; and Armand added in very bad German, "We have never seen you before."

"But I have seen you, Sir Knight, and your good friend, Sir Scholar. Do you remember — no, you must remember — how some weeks ago you gallantly took the part of a poor girl who was insulted by some unmannerly Italians? That girl was my Nänchen, my betrothed. We are to be married at St. Stefan's Church, come Easter, if God wills it so."

"But how is it that you know us?" asked Hubert.

"Nänchen has often seen you together, gentlemen, and she has pointed you out to me. She wished me to thank you for her, and I longed to do it, but could find no way until today."

"Now it is we who have to thank you," said Hubert, well pleased at the meeting. "But, good —" He paused for the name.

"Robert, to serve you, Sir."

"Good Robert, you must take our gift to buy a token for your Nänchen."

"No, Sir, if you please. A gift to Nänchen would be not only a gift to me, but a gift to me twice over, which from you and your friend I cannot take. But I will tell her I have seen you, and so make her very glad."

"Give you good fortune with her," said Hubert, while Armand laughingly complimented him on his choice, and praised the sweet blue eyes of the Swabian maiden, of which he seemed to have a lively recollection.

"Let us know in time," he added, "and my brother and I will go and see the wedding. You will find me at the house of the Burgundians, in the Rosgarten. Ask for the Sieur de Clairville. My brother, Master Hubert Bohun, dwells with the Chancellor of Paris, whose secretary he is. Who, I pray, are these noble-looking knights riding past us on the broad way? Hungarians?"

Hubert looked also, and with evident admiration, at the tall and stately horsemen who rode leisurely by, their steeds, their arms, and all their accoutrements in splendid order, and bearing on them, as sign and cognisance, a lion.

"They are Bohemians, Sir," said Robert. Turning toward them, he doffed his cap to the leader of the band, a gray-haired knight in a crimson mantle, with a strong, thoughtful face.

Hubert said in French to his brother, "I have seen them before. They have come here about the affair of their countryman, Jean Hus, or John Huss!"

"Oh, another 'affair' like that of Jean Petit?" returned Armand.

"Not half so important, or so interesting. The man is a heretic, and, by the way, he is imprisoned in yonder Dominican house."

"'You did not tell me that before. You took good care, when you were vaunting the glories of your monks, to forget the captive in the dungeon."

"I was just going to tell you, when you stopped me."

"Well, tell me now, if you can — you who are so learned — what are his heresies?"

"They are very grave and very dangerous, I fear," said Hubert dogmatically. "Already the chancellor has condemned at the Sorbonne nineteen heretical propositions taken from the works of Jean Hus. But as to what they are, even *I* do not understand them fully, and, of course, to anyone who has not studied theology it would be impossible to explain them. However, as it happens, I remember one, which is so plainly a dreadful thing that it does not need any learning to condemn it. He says that 'heretics ought not to be corporeally punished, or delivered over to the secular arm.' Has any man ever heard the like of that? Besides, he is a pestilent Realist. After the reunion of the Church, and the affair of Jean Petit, I believe the thing about which the chancellor is most anxious is the condemnation of this John Huss."

Robert had been listening to all this as eagerly as though he understood every word, whereas, in fact, he only caught the sound of one familiar name. Now he drew near, and said in a low voice, marked and almost broken by strong feeling, "Sirs, may a plain man speak a plain word to honourable gentlemen, such as you?"

"Surely good Robert, as many as you please," said Hubert, looking surprised.

"Then, Sir, I beg of you, as you prize the grace of God, never to speak lightly that name you said just now, for it is the name of no heretic, but of His holiest servant on earth."

"Bless your honest heart!" cried Hubert in amazement. "What can *you* know of heresies and heretics, and of the affairs that come before the Holy Council?"

"The Holy Council, as you call it, must have infected the air," said Armand, "since the very archers and *lanzknechts* are beginning to talk theology."

"I know nothing of heresies and of theology," said Robert, standing his ground firmly. "But I know Master John Huss, and no man has better right or better reason."

"How?" asked Hubert. "Has he made a convert of you? I thought at least that he could make no converts now, being in prison."

"Sir, it is I who guard the door of that prison. Did I not say well that I ought to know him? You are honest-hearted gentlemen, both of you, you who saved my Nänchen. I may speak out before you without fear?"

"Certainly you may," said Armand willingly, for he scented another scandal about the Church.

"Why should you fear?" added Hubert. "What harm could we do you, even if so minded?"

"Only, Sir, that if the lord abbot chanced to hear how I — and Jacob and Gregory too, for that matter — have learned to love him, it might come into his head to remove us, and to put others in our places. And that would be doing a very ill turn . . ."

"To your prisoner, doubtless?"

"No, Sir, to *ourselves*. As for me — I speak for myself — before I knew him I was no better than one of yonder cattle that are grazing in that meadow over the bridge. I used to think of nothing but meat, drink, and such-like things, which satisfy the beasts that perish. But he has wakened me, Sir, as you would waken a man out of a heavy sleep. He has put a soul in me — I mean, he has taught me there is a soul in me, and a God above who cares for me. He has taught us — me and the others — the Ten Commandments, and the 'Our Father' in German. He has made us understand that we can call God our Father through the Lord Jesus Christ, who died for us. And that if we serve Him, and do His will, we will come at last to live with him forever."

"But that is no heresy. It is good Christian doctrine, such as the chancellor himself would teach," said Hubert, in great astonishment.

Robert went on eagerly, without heeding the interruption, "Moreover, that we may know and remember it all, he has written it down for us, in simple, easy words, such as plain men may understand."

"What? Can you read?" asked Armand.

"I am learning, Sir. It is worth while *now*. He has written a little book, too, for me and for Nänchen, all for ourselves. For I have told him about Nänchen — somehow one tells him everything — and she says a Paternoster every day for his deliverance. He has given us good and holy counsels, that we may so live together on earth as to enjoy God's blessed heaven together hereafter."

"One would think," said Armand, who was listening attentively to every word — "one would think his own peril and the task of defending himself from the charge of heresy would give him enough to do and to think about."

If Robert had ever heard of "a heart at leisure from itself," he would have used the words in answering. But he had only *seen* it, and had no power to describe what he had seen. "I cannot tell you how it is," he said. "But I think he trusts God so entirely, and is so sure he is doing His will, that he rests at peace for himself — and is free to think and care for everyone else."

"But tell me, Robert," Hubert broke in anxiously, "can nothing be done by anyone to turn him from his heresies, and to bring him to a better mind?"

"To a better mind, Sir, than he is in now, no man could bring him; as you would say yourself, if you could only see him, and talk with him — and God knows I wish you could. When you have seen a man suffer, and when you have heard him pray, you know pretty well what he is. Master John lies yonder, in the tower by the lake[4] — you can see it from here — in chains, in darkness, in cold, breathing poisoned air, continually attacked and harassed by his enemies — and yet always brave, fearless, patient. They may kill him; and it is very like they will; indeed, already he is ill. But they will not break his purpose, nor will they kill his words — *Never*!" Robert drew himself up to his full height, and flung the challenge out boldly with an air of strong conviction, almost of fierce defiance. Then, seeming to recollect himself, and perhaps observing the curious looks of some of the passers-by he added in an altered tone, "I have said enough — too much, perhaps — yet I think not — you are gentlemen of honour, who would not betray a poor man's confidence. God be with, you, Sirs, and reward you for your kindness to Nänchen and to me."

He lifted his cap and moved away, the brothers looking after him in silence.

"What a strange man!" said Armand at last.

"Yes, strange indeed; passing strange," Hubert returned. But he meant the prisoner, while Armand meant the archer.

Armand resumed presently, "See how your churchmen love one another!"

Hubert did not even remember to protest, "I am not a churchman." He stood silent, in deep, perplexed thought. Nor did he move until

---

[4] The dungeon is still to be seen in the Insel Hotel, Constance, formerly the Dominican Monastery.

Robert, who, when he left them, crossed the road and disappeared up the Brückenstrasse, came again into sight, and took his way back to the monastery. "Wait for me, Armand," said Hubert, "I will not be a moment," and he darted after Robert. Catching up to him at last, and laying his hand on his shoulder, he whispered breathlessly, "See here, Robert. I come from Paris, where often for light cause they thrust men into loathsome dungeons. But the prisoners, or their friends, give gold, and that presently mends the case. Take this —" The gold which he thrust into his hand was no great sum, but it was all he had.

But Robert rejected it with a sorrowful smile. "No use, Sir," he said sadly. "There are those I know that would not spare their gold, nor their heart's blood either, to help him. But they can do nothing. The wicked priests and prelates, whose evil lives he has exposed, will have their vengeance, now they have got him in their power. It is for *that* they hate him, not because he is a heretic, for he is nothing of the sort. Still, God bless you, Sir, for your generous thought. May He think of you for good, as you have thought of His servant!"

Hubert quickly returned to his brother, who asked him what he had been doing. "Nothing," was the short reply, and he relapsed into silence. Then he burst out suddenly, "I don't understand this matter. I always thought that man was an obstinate, arrogant heretic, who turned Prague upside down, and stirred up revolts and tumults. I thought he preached all the errors of Wycliffe, with more, and worse, of his own added on to them. But this is evidently . . ."

Here he stopped, perplexed, but Armand completed the sentence for him. "Evidently a very ill-used man, whatever he may have preached or believed. Oh, those churchmen! No wonder people are afraid of offending them. However, the affair does not concern us. Come with me over the bridge to Petershausen; I want to speak to a gentleman of the queen's household whom I know about those falcons you saw me trying this morning."

"No," returned Hubert, "I must go home. I have writing to do for the chancellor."

"A plague on that writing! I wish you were a squire like me. 'Tis hard for you to leave the sunshine and the free air to stoop over pen and paper."

But to Hubert the joy had gone out of the sunshine and free air for that day. "Perhaps there may be some harder lot than mine," he said musingly. "And yet," he added, as he stood gazing at the tower by the lake which Robert had pointed out to him, "I will own that the longing for a free fight is sometimes almost too strong for me!

Would there were a hundred stout Cabochiens, with white hoods and strong staves, between me — and anywhere I wanted to go — say yonder tower! How I would enjoy fighting my way through them! But then, after that, *what* should I do? It is not the doing which is hard, but the knowing what to do."

Hubert announced this as a fresh discovery, which certainly it was to him. The first faint shadow of a perplexity, the first vague beginning of a doubt, stole into his heart that day. Could the Holy Council possibly be mistaken? And could it, of course under a mistake, but still under any conceivable circumstances, be unjust? Robert's story affected him much more than he cared to confess, because he could never hear of any noble doing or enduring without that "quiver of deep emotion," half joy, half pain, which those to whom it is given know so well, while others know it not at all. Such things drew his soul as the magnet draws the steel.

Still, of toleration for heresy he had absolutely none. It was to him quite inconceivable that a heretic could be a good man, worthy of sympathy. But it was very conceivable that a good man might be falsely accused of heresy through personal malice and hatred. This was what Robert said, and certainly it looked very probable. Could a wicked man bear suffering patiently, care unselfishly for others, pray devoutly, teach holy words to the ignorant? Such holy words were associated in Hubert's mind with one, and one alone. It was only from the lips of Jean Gerson that he had ever heard the like. This may seem surprising, since he had been brought up in a convent, and used to all sorts of ecclesiastical observances, even to the length of being wearied and disgusted by them. Yet something these had never brought to him, had never seemed to mean (indeed, for him they had meant nothing at all), reached and touched him the day the chancellor bade him serve the Lord Christ, who had paid the great debt for him. It was strange that the words of the reputed heretic should sound to him so like the words of the great chancellor.

But then came a thought which made him sternly silence the voices that had begun to plead within him for Robert's friend. The great chancellor had condemned him. To Hubert's loyal heart this was decisive. There was simply nothing more to be said on the question. Not a word must be breathed, not a whisper even must stir in the depths of his soul.[5]

---

[5] Robert's story is entirely true. The little treatises, or tracts, which Huss wrote for his prison warders, Robert, Jacob, and Gregory, still exist. Robert had two at least: one on the Lord's Prayer, and one on Marriage, the latter written at his own request.

VI

THE SILENCE OF ARMAND

He saw the tourney's victor crowned
Amidst the knightly ring.

"Are you going to the great tourney tomorrow?" This was the question which a hundred thousand people in Constance and its environs were asking each other on the evening of March 19, 1415. "Would not miss it for the world," was the usual answer, with the addition of words like these: "It will be the grandest show we shall see in a lifetime. Everyone knows what a magnificent prince our Lord Frederick, Duke of Austria is, and he will spare neither pains, nor gold, nor good contrivance to make this the proudest day of his life. He is a gallant knight, too. It is like his brave spirit to challenge Queen Barbe's own brother, the young Count of Cilly, to single combat. Probably he wishes it was her husband, the Emperor, and that the jousting was right earnest sword-play." For the enmity between the duke and the Emperor was well known to everyone. The duke was the ally and maintainer of Pope John XXIII, whom he would fain have delivered, if he could, out of the hand of both the Emperor and the Council.

Armand asked all his acquaintances, who by this time were many, the question of the day. He did not omit to ask it of his brother; but Hubert, though for him the clash of arms and the waving of banners had ever a strong attraction, gave him an undecided answer — he would go if he could. Armand called for him, accordingly, the next day. Hubert, in his ordinary dress, and with a pen behind his ear, opened the door for him softly.

"Hush," he said, "don't let the chancellor hear your voice. His people, chaplains and all, are gone to see the tourney. He thinks I am off with the rest. But if he thought I was going to leave him alone he was mistaken — for once," laughed Hubert. "Not for all the jousts in Christendom. Bring me back a full report of the doings, Armand."

"A plague on your devotion to the chancellor!" said Armand, as he turned away.

Armand was disappointed, certainly; yet the enjoyment of the day was by no means spoiled for him. Remembering something he wished to do, he turned aside from his way into a narrow street, where his favourite Nuremburg confectioner had set up a booth. Here he made pretty extensive purchases, which he stowed away in his pouch and in a wallet which he carried. Then, observing with concern that the town already looked deserted, he quickened his steps, that he might not be late for the show.

Presently there passed by him, in the now empty street, a corpulent, ill-dressed groom or postillion, in a gray cloak, mounted on a sorry horse, with a cross-bow fastened on the pommel of his saddle. Next to hawks, Armand loved horses better than anything else in the world; so he felt irritated at the clumsy way in which the fellow was managing his steed, and was tempted to give him a sharp lesson. But on second thoughts he refrained, thinking neither horse nor rider worth the trouble.

"Besides," he said to himself, "that varlet has been in a fray, since his head is bound with a kerchief. No doubt he has consoled himself for his bruises with a cup or two of their strong, heady German beer. There is not much of his face to be seen; but what there is — that coarse, sensual mouth and heavy jaw — brings to my mind no one else, no one less (and I presume there is no one greater here) than our most holy, or unholy, lord the pope. I always thought Pope John was no gentleman, but rather a fitting companion for grooms and kitchen-varlets, in manners as well as in mind — and this sorry rascal's likeness to him goes to prove it."

Then, dismissing the circumstance from his mind, he overtook the excited crowd streaming out of the city to the Brühl, where, with great pomp and splendour, the lists had been prepared and arranged. Here he met his Burgundian friends, and with them looked idly about him for some time. By and by, however, he left their company, and gradually made his way through the crowd to the decorated platform, where Queen Barbe and her attendant ladies sat in state, to animate the combatants by their presence, and in due time to award the prizes.

The young squire had already made friends among these ladies, and among the German and Hungarian nobles who formed their escort. His French skill in the training of falcons had enabled him to render them some slight services, which were graciously acknowledged, and his winning exterior and pleasant manners did the rest. On the present occasion the crafty youth produced the choice confections with which he had provided himself, and in the somewhat tedious pauses of the tourney ventured to offer them, "with his most devoted homage," to the ladies near him. This procured for him admission to the platform. Once there he watched his opportunity, and drew quietly near a young lady wearing the colours of Queen Barbe, but seated modestly in one of the lowest places, among the least distinguished of her suite. She was a slender, dark-eyed girl, very pale — too pale, some thought, for beauty — but her features were exquisitely formed, and her face was full of expression. She flushed slightly at the approach of Armand, who was evidently no new acquaintance, and he addressed her in rapid French.

She answered in the same language, and in a low, very sweet voice. As the trumpets and hautboys were sounding at the time, they were able to maintain a conversation under cover of the noise, unheard by those around them.

"Both of us French, both of us Burgundians, surely we were meant to be friends," urged Armand.

His first boyish fancy, half real, half affected, for a lady much older than himself, had now given way to a far more genuine adoration of this bright, particular star, the Demoiselle Jocelyne de Sabrecourt.

"Ah, Sir Squire, if you knew all about me you would not say that," she answered.

Armand quite lost himself in high-flown compliments and romantic protestations, which, however, the young lady brushed quietly aside with as little ceremony as if they had been cobwebs. Then he spoke seriously, and the best that was in him came out. The martial music had ceased, but his immediate neighbours were talking loudly enough, and besides were not likely to understand him, as he spoke in French.

"Fair Demoiselle," he said, "you are not happy here; I know it."

"I have no cause of unhappiness," returned the young lady. "The queen is kind to me; and though the Hungarian and German ladies of her suite may not care much for the solitary Burgundian girl, yet they are not unkind."

"How did you come here?" asked Armand. "Since we knew one another as children at the Burgundian court — yes, and were partners in the dance, as you have graced me forever by deigning to remember — I had not heard your name until you rose on me like a star that happy day when I went to Petershausen about the falcons. I shall bless those birds all my life long. No! Let St. Maurice hear my vow. I shall have a falcon in effigy made of the purest wax, and present it to him in the great church here, which is dedicated to his name."

"It is always well to hold the saints in honour," said the lady, "but as for the falcons, I doubt that you, or I either, have special cause for gratitude to them."

Armand protested eagerly, but Jocelyne continued without heeding him: "I can, however, answer your question about my coming here. And in so doing I shall prove my point, that our meeting is not specially fortunate, at least for you. Do you remember my brother — my brave, brilliant young brother — the most promising squire at the court of Burgundy and the most favoured of his lord?"

"I have only the honour to know the Demoiselle Jocelyne by that sweetest and most musical of names," returned the courtly Armand.

"It is true that the name of De Sabrecourt is but seldom heard now."

Armand started and turned pale. "Was Godefroi de Sabrecourt your brother?" he asked quickly.

"You knew him, then? Yes, he was my dear and only brother, and my mother and father are both dead. Tell me, Sir squire, what have you heard about Godefroi de Sabrecourt?"

With a quick, half-involuntary gesture, Armand turned away from her, and was silent.

"Do not be afraid to speak," pursued the lady. "I can bear anything but want of truth. What have you heard about him?"

"That he was killed in a *duello* — in single combat," Armand answered at last, in a low voice and without turning toward her.

"You heard more than that," said Jocelyne.

Armand was silent. Had his face been visible she would have seen it was very pale.

At last Jocelyne resumed, with a sort of cold composure: "Since you will not speak, I am forced to do so, though I do not like the task. After that fateful day when Fancroix gave him his death-wound (Fancroix was not to blame, you understand that; I bear no malice against him), a packet of important papers belonging to the duke was missing, and it was soon found that it had fallen into the hands of the Armagnacs. Surely you remember it, though you will not speak, doubtless lest you should grieve me. It was much talked about at the time, just four years ago, and, as I remember, you got your promotion from page to squire just then. The packet had been sent to Godefroi by a safe hand, and he was to ride to Paris, and deliver it secretly to Caboche. Nothing was done about the affair, my brother being dead, but everyone believed him guilty of culpable carelessness, if not of treason. The duke spoke no word of blame; yet it did not please him to see me about the duchess after that. And it was best that our name should be mentioned no more in his hearing. So I was very thankful when the Countess de Cilly (as the queen then was), being a guest at our court, compassionately offered me an asylum."

Armand did not dare to lift up his face to hers. He knew that it was white with shame and fear, and he felt as if the solid ground was reeling beneath him. No one had suspected the young page, to whom the fatal packet had been entrusted to bring to Godefroi, of being the real delinquent. Godefroi's own lips were sealed in death, and on that very account all inquiry had been silenced; Armand, up to this hour, had honestly believed that no living person was the worse for his cowardly silence. Was it so cowardly after all? It would probably have cost him — and at the time he was but a boy — all that makes life desirable to break it.

The next moment a general stir and movement about him showed that something unusual had happened, and he felt like a criminal reprieved from the scaffold. A lady who was sitting near Jocelyne begged him to go to the lists and find out what was the matter. He was about to obey, as in duty bound, when one of the queen's Hungarian gentlemen came toward them.

"Do not disturb yourselves, ladies. What has occurred is of no consequence. Some impudent fellow, who had business with the duke, must needs force his way to the lists, and beckon him to speak with him, as if, forsooth, his business could not wait until the tourney was over. They spoke together for a moments space, then the duke returned to his place, and quite in good-humour too. He and the Count de Cilly are continuing their tilting-match — as you see, ladies. However, you cannot see very well where you are. Let me find you seats higher up," he said.

But Jocelyne did not care to move; and Armand was only too glad to keep his white face hidden from view. Meanwhile the disclosure which burdened the heart of one greatly relieved the other. Jocelyne had now discharged what, according to her code of honour, was a paramount duty. She had informed a young gentleman, who was plainly showing himself her admirer, of the cloud that rested on her name and her fortunes. Moreover, she had intimated to the same young gentleman that, as a squire of the Duke of Burgundy, who hoped everything from the favour of his patron, she was the very last person he ought to allow his fancy to dwell on. Now, for every reason, the best thing she could do was to talk lightly on indifferent subjects.

"I would the Emperor himself had condescended to enter the lists today in place of his young brother-in-law," she said. "Is not the Emperor splendid, Sieur de Clairville? Handsome as Apollo, with his long, golden hair, his fair face, his stately figure."

Armand agreed carelessly, not thinking much at the moment about either king or Emperor.

Jocelyne continued, "He is brave too, and quick of wit, and has a noble heart, I believe. But just now he is in a difficulty. I wonder what he will do. Do you think the Council will prevail with him to be false to his plighted word, and to give up that poor priest to his enemies?"

"Do you mean the Bohemian heretic?"

"Heretic or not — that is a matter of opinion. There is a certain Jew, physician to the pope, of whose skill the queen has a high opinion. She often sends for him to Petershausen, and I have heard him tell very strange things of this man, whom he visited by the pope's command when lying ill of fever and ague in his prison."

"I have heard," said Armand, rousing himself with an effort, "that churchmen are far less in favour with the queen than with her lord the Emperor."

"That is true. Indeed, Queen Barbe — but this is only for your own ear, Sir Squire — believes little enough of all churchmen tell us.[6] Sometimes it makes me shudder to hear her talk. She says — oh, I dare not tell you what she says! But this I know, if the Holy Council were to meddle with *her* on the ground of heresy, it would have enough to do. Still, whatever we may think of her, I say this of the Emperor — if he breaks his word to that Bohemian and gives him up to his enemies, he will of course be lawful Emperor, but he will be true knight and gentleman no more — he will be a dishonoured liar. Of all things on earth or in heaven, I hate a liar."

"Is silence always a lie?" said Armand in a low voice, and as it seemed irrelevantly.

---

[6] It is said she believed "neither in a God, nor in a future life." However, it ought to be mentioned that a different and much more favourable estimate of her character is given by Mrs. Napier Higgins in her very interesting book, *Women of the Middle Ages*. She thinks that Queen Barbe was slandered by the priests because she inclined to the opinions of Huss, and at least we may give her the benefit of the doubt.

"It will be the worst of lies if the Emperor stands by in silence and lets other men break his word for him," returned Jocelyne, rather surprised at his remark. "But listen! I think the tourney is over."

"What, already!" cried Armand. Indeed there was ground for astonishment in a termination so speedy and so abrupt. A great shout of applause rent the air. The Count of Cilly had unhorsed the Duke of Austria. But, in truth, it was an easy triumph. Since that mysterious whisper from the unknown messenger, the Duke had been only anxious to bring the proceedings to a close and to get away. He gracefully yielded the victory to his young antagonist, and, as soon as he decently could, left the place.

Armand slipped away also, very heavy in heart. His one boyish fault, which he thought unknown to all the world, and which he himself had well-nigh forgotten, was coming back now, like a ghost from the tomb, to overshadow his life, and to wound him in the tenderest part. Purposely avoiding his acquaintances, he walked slowly home. As he did so, he lived over again the events of the day when, although still a page, he had been trusted by the duke himself to bear an important packet with speed and secrecy to the neighbouring town. There Godefroi de Sabrecourt was to meet him, to take it from his hand, and to bring it on to Paris. But Godefroi was not to be found when Armand came to the trysting-place — unluckily for him, a tavern, in front of which a tennis-match was going on. The young page saw the match out, drank to the health of the winners, enjoyed himself thoroughly, and finally went to bed with the fatal packet in the pouch at his girdle, instead of where it should have been, under his pillow. In the morning it was gone. Then Godefroi came — too late — and found the boy in utter distress and perplexity. Being a kind-hearted youth, and feeling also that he himself was partly to blame for the misfortune, he proposed that, before saying anything to the duke, they should make every effort to recover the packet. If they were unsuccessful, then, of course, the duke must know. But he said that before doing anything else he must fight out the quarrel which had been the cause of his delay. He did so in the course of the day, and met his death at the hand of his antagonist. Everyone regretted the promising young squire, and in the first excitement the packet supposed to have been given into his charge was scarcely remembered. But a little while afterward it was very unpleasantly recalled, for it became evident that the Armagnacs were aware of its contents, and were using them to the injury of the duke. Then inquiries were made about it. Armand was questioned in his turn. The terrible Jean Sans Peur had never spoken an angry word to his bright young page, yet Armand trembled like an aspen-leaf before him. The very sound of his voice, the very glance of his eye, seemed to paralyze the boy, and to force him, in spite of himself, to deny his fault. He faltered out that he had given the letter up safely to the Sieur de Sabrecourt, and he was readily believed. The duke did not suspect "that child" either of failure in a simple, easy duty, or of deceit in hiding it. Suspicion therefore fell, and rested, on the dead. Remaining suspicion, and no more, it still did its evil work. How evil that work had been Armand did not know until this day. And now that he knew it, he was overwhelmed.

Armand had been taught to ride, to fence, to tilt. He had been instructed in the noble art of falconry and the mysteries of the chase. He had been even taught, after fashion, to read and to write — but he had never been taught to *think*. This lack of mental training and discipline helped to throw him, in this his first real trouble, into utter and hopeless confusion. He had cruelly injured the one whom of all others he most passionately desired to serve and please. Was he not sinning against her more and more every day he persisted in his cowardly silence? Yet, if he would decide to break that silence, would he not ruin his cause with her forever? Would she not despise him and execrate his name? Moreover — and Armand could spare a thought for this too — the duke, when he heard it, would forever withdraw his favour from him, and would dismiss him from his service with ignominy. It seemed that he must still keep silence, let it cost him what it might.

Yet he could not rest satisfied with this conclusion. After tossing on his hard pallet for more sleepless hours than he had ever known in his life, he said to himself at last, "I will tell all to Hubert. Hubert is brave and strong; and above all, he is true. He is kind too, and fond of me. He will know what I ought to do." And so he fell asleep.

VII

ST. MICHAEL AND THE DRAGON

Like the snake 'neath Michael's foot,
Who stands calm just because he feels it writhe.
— R. Browning

Armand was awakened the next morning by the noise of a great tumult in the street below. The two gentlemen who shared his room had gone out already, so he dressed hastily and followed their example. He found the town in utter confusion. Many of the shops had not been opened at all; others, especially those of the goldsmiths and money-changers, were being shut up again, and carefully barred and bolted. Excited groups stood at the street corners and in the market-place, conversing together with ominous looks and shakings of the head. Someone, whom Armand knew, called out to him as he passed, "Have you heard the news! The pope is gone!" Presently the same cry was repeated from another quarter. Everywhere he turned he heard it. The words echoed and re-echoed in every direction; they seemed to fill the air — "The pope is gone! The pope has fled!"

He hurried to the chancellor's house, expecting a full explanation from Hubert. But even that household, usually remarkable for order and decorum, seemed to share the general panic and excitement. The chancellor's people were running to and fro, and those whom Armand accosted and asked about his brother could only tell him he was busy.

At last, however, Hubert himself came hurrying downstairs with a letter in his hand. Seeing Armand, he cried, "Have you heard the news? The pope is gone!"

"I have heard nothing else since I opened my eyes this morning," said Armand. "But I want to speak to you. Where are you going?"

"To the lodging of the Cardinal of Cambray with this letter. Come with me; I may not delay."

Armand could scarcely keep pace with his brother's rapid footsteps as he hurried along, talking eagerly the while.

"The pope is gone — slipped out of town yesterday while everyone was away at the tourney. In fact, we suspect now that the tourney itself was only a blind, got up by his friend the Duke of Austria, to favour his escape. He went off, it is said, in the disguise of a groom, leading a sorry horse, and with a kerchief around his head to hide his face!"

Armand came to a dead stop in the midst of the crowded street, and, after an instant's silence, broke into a volley of knightly oaths.

"Have you lost your wits?" cried Hubert in amazement. "But, whether you have or not, I can't stay for you. Come on!"

"No — not my wits; but the best chance I am ever like to have of making my fortune," said Armand, obeying him mechanically. "For I saw him yesterday, on my way to the tourney."

"Saw *him*? Saw whom?"

"Our most holy father the pope. Just as you say, dressed as a groom, on a wretched horse, which he managed very ill. What I saw of his face — not much indeed — made me think of the High Mass in the cathedral, when . . ."

"Why did you not give the alarm?" broke in Hubert indignantly.

"Give the alarm! Where is your sense, Hubert! How was I to think for one instant that the head of the Church, the Vicar of Christ, could be found in such a guise? Of course I thought it was only a chance resemblance that struck me."

"You knew, everyone did, how he dreads the Council and hates the Emperor, and how glad he would be to see more than the length of his pastoral staff between himself and both. If only you had come back to the chancellor's and told me!"

"If only I had been a wizard, like Virgil,[7] or a father of magicians, like Prester John!"

But Hubert, not heeding him, went on in strong excitement, "And now, I suppose, we shall have all men thinking this will dissolve the Council — break it up in confusion. Not so, by the help of God! Rather will it prove how strong, how great, how irresistible it is! The Holy Council can do without the pope, for the Holy Council is above the pope. It is the voice of the Church — no, it is the Church herself. It is his superior, his ruler, it may one day be his judge. Oh, he has done very well, this renegade pope! Not for himself, but for us — that is, for the Council. By this flight he has put himself in the

---

[7] Virgil in the Middle Ages was believed to have been a great wizard.

wrong, and has shown to all the world where the right is. For once, might and right are together, and might and right both are, not with the pope, but with the Holy Council."

"Curse the Holy Council!" said Armand to himself. "At this rate a man will never get a reasonable word from him about anything else." But, after the first sense of annoyance, there came to him a feeling of relief. If from sheer lack of opportunity he could not make his confession to Hubert, that was no fault of his. No man could do the impossible. After all, it would be a very hard task to tell that story, especially to one so brave and truthful as Hubert, who would never himself have acted with such weakness. All this had flashed through the mind of Armand before they reached the cardinal's lodging.

"Here we are," said Hubert. "I will have to wait for an answer."

"No use in my standing in the street while his eminence spoils a sheet of good paper," returned Armand, now thoroughly convinced of the insignificance of his private affairs in Hubert's eyes, compared with those of the Council and the pope. "But — wait one instant. All the Burgundians will be asking how can the Council possibly go on without its head. No, how can it live for a single day, thus decapitated — not being like St. Denis. What shall I say to them?"

"Say to them that the Council will go on and prosper, since its true head is no renegade pope, but One whom for reverence I name not now," said Hubert, looking back over his shoulder as he disappeared within the open door.

The tide of public events was now sweeping onward, with so strong and full a current that many an eddy of private feeling and interest was caught up and carried away with it. Young Hubert Bohun was not so much carried away as borne triumphantly on the crest of the advancing wave — like a flake of foam, in itself a thing of small importance and swiftly vanishing, yet for its little moment flashing in the sunlight, the brightest, gladdest spot in all the scene. Probably no one else so thoroughly enjoyed the grand triumph of the Council over the pope. Certainly no other eye saw the vision that gleamed in the ardent fancy of this young enthusiast, of the Holy Council, in the guise of the Archangel Michael, standing sword in hand over a prostrate dragon wearing a tiara.

Yet in this enthusiasm there was just a hint, a suspicion — no more — of something overstrained and unnatural. There was a touch of exaggeration, quite unconscious, of course, but still betraying the truth that, after all, the passion was only a reflected one. A youth of Hubert's character could not fail to believe what the chancellor believed, to worship what the chancellor loved. But the chancellor believed and loved like a toil-worn, world-weary man, with more than fifty years of sad experience behind him; still clinging in faith to high ideals, yet knowing how far the actual always falls short of the ideal. His young satellite, on the other hand, believed and loved like a dreamer. So entirely had he given the reins to his imagination, that up to this time he actually thought the council was composed, for the most part, of men like Jean Gerson. Armand, with not half his brains, yet saw the men and things around him much more truly. Armand's position as a Burgundian had early given him a personal knowledge of the shameless venality of the Council. If he was not himself behind the scenes, he knew those who were; and he had learned from them how bare, how coarse, how unsightly were the wires that moved most of those stately figures, so grand in the eyes of his single-hearted brother.

The morning after the flight of Pope John, the Emperor rode in state through the city, and proclaimed that the council was not dissolved, that its sessions would continue, and that he would protect it. The Chancellor of Paris was requested to prepare a discourse setting forth its rights and its duties. Gerson responded with a trumpet-blast. Never before had the place of the General Council, as the true representative and mouthpiece of the General Church, been so ably, so eloquently, so irresistibly set forth. Never before had the usurped supremacy of the so-called "Vicar of Christ" received such a tremendous blow. Never before had it been proved so clearly that it was the Council, not the pope, which was infallible!

What the "soul of the Council" devised and dictated, the hands of the Council were strong and very courageous to carry out. The fugitive pope was cited to appear before the Council, was brought back to Constance a disgraced and humiliated captive, and was suspended and imprisoned. Not even then was the degradation of the successor of St. Peter, and the triumph of the Council, complete. A tremendous list of accusations was drawn up against him, from which, if but one-tenth part of them were true, it appeared that Balthazar Cossa was not only unworthy to reign over the Church of God, but unworthy to live on the earth which God had made.

Among the voices raised against him there was one which said aloud, in the Council itself, that he deserved the crowning torture and ignominy of all — the death of fire. This was the voice of Robert Hallam, Bishop of Salisbury, an Englishman of whose part in the Council Englishmen have no need to be ashamed, and who in this instance uttered his righteous indignation in the rough accents of his time.

Our young scribe had abundant occupation in those days for his ever-ready pen. There was one business, however, in which the chancellor would not allow him to meddle. His hand must not copy, his eye must not even rest on, the articles of accusation against the pope; so hideous were the enormities, so unutterably foul and abominable were the sins enumerated there. This work was for older hands, for eyes that had already looked shudderingly — or, perhaps, alas, *not* shudderingly — down into the blackest "depths of Satan."

Was it wonderful that the great chancellor himself, in this hour of his glory, showed no exultation? All was going well with the causes he had at heart — with the greatest of them all, the cause of the Council as against the pope and above the pope — with "the affair of Jean Petit" — and with the condemnation of Wycliffe's teachings and his works. Yet the lines of sorrow and perplexity deepened every day on that sad, anxious face. No one knew the secrets of his breast, for he spoke of them to none. But it was easy for loving eyes, like those of Hubert, to see that this heart, so strong, so brave, so true even, was not a heart at rest.

VIII

MORE OF ROBERT'S STORY

In darkness, in hunger, in pain,
Which the haughtiest spirit will break,
He was linked to the wall with the riveted chain —
And he looked for the torturing stake.
Song of the Hussites
— By the Hon. and Rev. Baptist Noel

The brilliant Easter festivities drew on apace. Queen Barbe had taken a fancy to the young "squire of the falcons," as she called Armand, and he was invited to share the pleasures of her little court at Petershausen. Nothing loath, he entered into all with the careless enjoyment of his age and his character. But his great attraction was in the presence of Jocelyne. In spite of the secret which lay between them, and the pain its recollection never ceased to give him, he could not keep away from her. Every day found him more thoroughly fascinated, more ardent, not to say extravagant in his devotion. At last he gave himself up without restraint or afterthought to the sweet and potent charm. Everyone about the court came to know him as the loyal knight and humble adorer (according to all the rules of chivalry) of the pale-faced, dark-eyed French demoiselle who waited on the queen.

Thus it happened that in some degree he drifted apart from his brother. The desire to confide to Hubert the story of his past grew fainter and fainter, partly for lack of opportunity, but still more because it had now become his wish to bury that past altogether.

Nor did he even care to talk much with him about Jocelyne. On such subjects Hubert was decidedly unsympathetic. His own time for the softer feelings had not come yet, and nothing in his training had taught him to reverence them in another. Singularly pure-hearted and high-toned, he had already trodden under foot, or passed by on the other side, those gross temptations which in a horribly vicious age could not fail to assail him. But, like most very young moralists, he was apt to be a little hard and intolerant; and he was also endeavouring, though that was decidedly against the grain, to regard all things from the churchman's point of view. Such love as Armand's for Jocelyne belonged to the "lower," the "worldly" life, and, as Armand at least imagined, Hubert would look down scornfully on it from the cold and lofty heights of his superior learning and sanctity. Nevertheless, there was no lack of cordiality between the brothers, nor did Hubert intentionally neglect Armand or forsake his company. There was, in fact, but one subject from which at this time he resolutely and determinedly turned away. One "affair" which was before the Council, he banished as much as possible from his mind, or rather he drove it down, and buried it in a deep grave beneath the region of conscious thought. This was not because it gave him pain, but because it stirred within him doubt and perplexity. From pain, whether of mind or body, he did not greatly shrink. But doubt he abhorred with all the abhorrence of a strong, determined nature — a nature which must express itself in action, and which instinctively recognizes in doubt the paralyzing foe of action. What would become of him if he were forced to doubt the infallibility of the Council? Hubert spoke a great deal, even to himself, of the infallibility of the Council, but what in truth he believed in, though he could not have put it so, was the infallibility of the Chancellor of Paris. Whenever it became his duty — as it did on more than one occasion — to write, or copy, anything about what he called "the affair of Jean Hus," he was haunted by a sort of double feeling, which he did not like. The Council, influenced by the great chancellor, was surely doing all that was right, even toward a reputed heretic. Yet Hubert could not quite forget Robert's story, and its impression was deepened by one of the papers which it fell to his lot to copy: a simple, manly, pathetic letter, from a Bohemian knight named Chlum, complaining of the cruelty and injustice with which his friend was treated.

One evening, about the middle of May, Robert himself made his appearance. Hubert, when he heard that an archer from the Dominican Abbey wished to see him, knew it could be no one else. He went to the door, greeted him kindly, and asked him to come in.

"No, Sir," said Robert, looking with no friendly eye at the dwelling of the chancellor. "Rather, if you will be so good, speak with me a moment out here."

Hubert stepped out into the street.

"No doubt you have come to redeem your promise, and tell me of the wedding-day," he said. "But I thought it was to have been at Easter."

"Your memory is good, Sir; and for the affairs of a poor man, which does you honour. So I said, and so truly it should have been. But when Easter came we were in sore trouble. One most dear to us was very ill. The trouble has not passed — but that is not what I came to tell you, Sir. Nänchen and I go to the altar together next Sunday after matins, in St. Stefan's Church. If it will please you, and the noble esquire your brother, to honour us with your presence there, you will do us much grace and favour."

"I will tell my brother, who will be sure to go, as I shall also," said Hubert. "And I wish you joy, and all good fortune with your bride, friend Robert."

Robert thanked him, but lingered still, looking wistfully at Hubert, with something in his honest eyes that seemed to say, "Have you nothing to ask me? I at least, have something to tell you."

Hubert, however, did not speak, and Robert at last drew near and whispered, "About him, Sir, for whom you offered me that gold . . ."

"I would have done the same for anyone who suffered," said Hubert, rather shortly. Perhaps he was ashamed of his impulse of compassion for the heretic. Certainly he did not want to be troubled about him now. "But you no longer have anything to do with him. I hear he has been taken elsewhere," he added.

"I have something to do with him, Sir, and he with me, as long as my life lasts, and beyond it — forever and ever. But it is nearly two months now since I have seen his face. God knows if I shall ever see it again. And, perhaps, I should not wish it. They took him from us, Sir, not too soon for him, for the foul air of that horrible dungeon was killing him — but it was a dark day for us. He was very ill with fever and ague first in our own house, afterward in that of the Franciscans, where the pope himself was. There the pope's own physician attended him, and the pope's own guard had charge of him. Those outlandish men, who knew no Christian tongue, proved nevertheless that they had Christian hearts. God Himself — or else His grace shown in His servant — touched and won them. But when the pope fled from the city his guard had to follow. That was on Palm Sunday. They did the best thing, as they thought, for their prisoner. They brought the prison key straight to the Emperor himself." Here he paused, as if struggling with some strong feeling.

"Well?" asked Hubert.

"Sir, the Emperor and his people *forgot him*. After three days, the Bohemian lords, his friends, not being able to hear anything of him, grew disquieted, and, coming to the Emperor, begged leave to see him. They were led to his dungeon, which for those three days

About him, Sir, for whom you offered me that gold . . .

and nights had been unopened. All that time, sick and weak as he was, just recovering from fever, he had been wholly without food. When they came he looked like a dying man. Few words were spoken, as I have been told, for he could scarce speak for weakness, nor they for weeping. He raised himself with pain and difficulty, trying to embrace them, but sank back again, fainting, in his chains. But for all that," Robert went on, and his voice, which had been low and sad, grew strong again, "his faith and patience have never failed. All he can be got to say of his sufferings is just this: 'They are only so many proofs of God's love to me.' "

Hubert bit his lip, and was silent. He felt the wrong and the cruelty, but he would not allow himself to own it.

Robert presently continued, "And now the Emperor, who ought to have done him justice, has yielded to the Council, broken his solemn safe-conduct . . ."

"You should not say that," Hubert interrupted, glad of something he *could* contradict. "No safe-conduct can prevent a heretic being judged after his deserts. If the Emperor had not yielded, the Council would have broken up."

"Well, Sir, be it so. There is One who will judge both Emperor and Council. When He does, He will not forget that, instead of opening the prison door and letting the oppressed go free, the Emperor gave the key into the cruel hands of the Archbishop of Riga. God forgive him — I try to pray God forgive him — else how could I say the 'Our Father,' which Master John taught me himself? But it goes hard with me."

"The Archbishop of Riga is keeper of the seals of the Council, therefore it is his business to take charge of offenders against the Council," said Hubert.

"The Archbishop of Riga is —" A bitter German word, too bitter for rendering here, completed the sentence. "He has brought him to Göttlieben Castle, and God only knows what he is suffering there. No, we do know something about it."

Hubert knew something, too, from that letter of De Chlum's, which had in it certain terrible details. The words came back to him now. "Grievously tormented with heavy fetters, and with hunger and thirst."

He said uneasily, "I am sorry, since he is your friend."

"My friend, Sir? It is not fitting you should call him that, I being but a poor, simple man. There at Göttlieben none of us who love him can come near him, but his enemies come when they will. It is said they examine him in secret, to try and get something for which they may condemn him. That they will not, for he is no heretic, but a good Christian and a good Catholic, the best I ever knew. Already while with us he was denied an advocate; denied leave to call a witness in his favour, or to object to the witnesses who were brought against him. And now, do they mean to condemn him unheard? Will they not let him speak at all before the Council?" Robert's voice had risen, and he looked eagerly, almost fiercely, at Hubert, expecting an answer.

But Hubert had none to give. "I know," he said, "that the Bohemian lords have been beseeching the Holy Council to grant him a public hearing. I do not know the result."

"The *Holy* Council, Sir? Well, no use for hard words. They only hurt the tongue that speaks them."

"True," said Hubert. "And in this case they might do serious hurt. Your Master John's disciple, he whom they call Jeronymus or Jerome, lies in fetters yonder in the tower of St. Paul for coming here to take his master's part, and for railing against the Council."

"Yes, Sir. Master John wrote from his prison to entreat him not to come. Yet he came, as it may be, you, Sir, would have done in his place. But I did not think of the hurting of one's feet with irons, I thought of the hurting of one's soul with sin."

"Robert, what did you mean when you said just now that perhaps you should not wish to see his face again?"

Robert gave him a look full of significance, and also full of sadness. Presently he said, "Prison bars cannot shut God out — nor God's angel, Death, who has been near him more than once."

"I cannot think of this man as you do," said Hubert, "for I know him to be a heretic, and I think him a dangerous one. Yet I do not wish him so ill as that."

"So *ill*, Sir? Heretic he is not — that I say and swear; and if they killed me for it, I would say it still with my dying breath. Yet if the Council condemn him, what then? You, a scholar — you, learned, I suppose, in the Canon Law — you know it. But you ought not to make me speak the word."

He turned away, and something like a shudder shook his strong frame.

For the first time the thought occurred to Hubert that this "affair of Jean Hus" might have a termination very different from "the affair of Jean Petit." Jean Petit was dead and safe, even if he had been a heretic, which he was not. But here was a living man, whose process might end in a horror, such as had once made Hubert run from the Place de Grève, veiling his face that he might not see, and stopping his ears that he might not hear, careless of the jests and laughter his softness of heart brought on him from his comrades. But he dismissed the idea in a moment. How could one think of such things in bright, joyous, festive Constance, where all was going forward so prosperously, so triumphantly?

"Oh, you need not fear anything of the kind in this case," he said lightly, "the matter will be arranged; even if all he is accused of can be proved of him (and I fear much of it can, and will), there will be penance imposed, and satisfaction made. Learned doctors, such as the chancellor, will argue with him, and get him to retract, and to promise not to hold or teach his heresies any more. So everything will come well to an end, with an *Absolvo te* and a *Pax vobiscum*. And every man will go to his own home."

"Yes," said Robert slowly and sadly, "every man will go to his own home — and he to his. Goodnight, Sir, and thank you for your promise about Sunday."

Robert moved away, thinking sorrowfully that the scholar's warm young heart had grown cool since he spoke with him on the Rhine-Thor-Thurm. Hubert, who was just then in some danger of becoming a fanatic, thought the archer of the abbot's guard was expressing opinions on subjects on which he, and such as he, ought not to have any opinions at all. So each was rather out of humour with the other.

Nevertheless, the brothers went to St. Stefan's Church the next Sunday morning. They both, but particularly Armand, duly admired the pretty, modest-looking bride, who indeed appeared to great advantage in her crimson bodice and petticoat of English cloth. Her head was adorned with a wreath of roses, which had been carefully preserved since the previous summer by a process in use among the Germans of that day. Hubert and Armand even graced the marriage festivities by drinking a cup of wine to the health of the bride; and Hubert made the acquaintance of the priest who had performed the ceremony, Master Ulrich Schorand, a learned man, especially versed in the Canon Law, and full of eager interest in the doings of the Council.

It is somewhat difficult for us to say whether Hubert, who considered John Huss a dangerous heretic, or Robert, who thought him no heretic at all, was in the right, accepting, of course, the word "heretic" in the mediaeval or Roman Catholic sense. His creed did not differ *apparently* from that of the Church of his day, from that of the Council itself. Confident of his innocence (though by no means assured of his safety — a very different matter), he had come of his own free will to the Council, and referred his cause, already prejudged by the wicked pope, to its decision. He came armed, not only with a good conscience, but with the strongest testimonies to his orthodoxy and piety that his own archbishop and other recognized authorities of the Church could give. Like other good men within her fold, he had attacked, not the doctrines of Rome, but their abuse. He accepted transubstantiation, but rebuked the blasphemous arrogance of the priests, who boasted that they could "make God." He believed in purgatory, but indignantly denounced indulgences. He was ready to honour a good pope as the successor of St. Peter, but maintained that Christ, not St. Peter, is the rock on which His Church is founded. "A man must believe in God alone," said he, "not in the Virgin, not in the saints, not in the Church, not in the pope, for none of these are God." He vindicated, moreover, in the strongest terms, and with the most unswerving consistency, the authority of the Holy Scriptures as the supreme rule of faith.

It may be said that this creed contains in it the living germ of so-called "heresy," but neither Huss himself, nor his persecutors, knew it. Perhaps his greatest crime in their eyes was the dauntless courage with which he attacked and exposed the vices of the corrupt hierarchy of his day. But, it will be asked, did not others do the same, and yet live in peace and safety, and die in honour? Truly the words of John Gerson were almost as bitter as those of John Huss — both of them cried aloud and spared not: "Woe be to the shepherds of Israel that do feed themselves! Should not the shepherds feed the flock? Ye eat the fat, ye clothe yourselves with the wool, ye kill them that are fed, but ye feed not the flock." How came it then that the one sat among the judges, while the other stood fettered at the bar?

The reasons were more and deeper than we can tell of here. One, the chief, may suffice. Gerson, and other good men of his type, expected the Church to reform herself; he looked for the remedy of the evils he felt so painfully to the action of the hierarchy, the heads and teachers of Christendom. He might as well have expected the Ethiopian to change his skin, and the leopard his spots. Our great English Reformer, Wycliffe, was the first to recognize this fact. Instead of plucking off the leaves and twigs, he laid his axe boldly to the root of the evil tree. He proposed to deprive corrupt and unworthy priests and monks of the wealth and power they had usurped. "Tithes," said he, "are only alms, and may be withheld from those who misuse them." Huss did not follow Wycliffe in everything, but he followed him in this, in the eyes of a covetous hierarchy, the unpardonable sin. It is on this account that he has been called, and truly, "the martyr of Wycliffe." He was, in a very real sense, "baptized for the dead," with the baptism of fire. The hierarchy wreaked on him the passionate hate and rage which the teaching of Wycliffe had aroused, but which Wycliffe himself escaped by that quiet death at Lutterworth.

One of the greatest of modern poets has drawn for us, in lines of undying force and fire, the picture of a great prelate of this, or a somewhat later age, on his deathbed. Let every reader of these pages study and ponder well how "the bishop orders his tomb at St. Praxed's Church."[8] Then let him imagine such a bishop, summoned from his "brave Frascati villa and its bath," his "white grape vineyard," his "jasper, green as a pistachio nut," his other and more guilty delights of the flesh and of the mind, to sit in judgment on a simple priest, a poor man's son, who dared to challenge his right to all these things, and to bid him go and follow in the footsteps of that Master who had not where to lay His head, and of His apostles — else was he no true successor of theirs. Many such bishops, only without the learning and the taste of the Renaissance, sat in the Council of Constance.

This may explain, at least in a measure, the conduct of the Council. But with their victim it would have fared ill indeed had he been labouring merely to cast down and to destroy — even that which was evil and fit for destruction. What for him represented "the everlasting Yes," what was the eternal truth for which he was struggling, the solid rock upon which he was resting, will be seen hereafter.

---

[8] See *The Poetical works of Robert Browning*, vol. V, *Men and Women*.

IX

BEFORE THE COUNCIL

Cover my defenceless head
With the shadow of Thy wing.

On the morning of the 5th of June the heart of Hubert Bohun was lifted up within him. He was to take notes for the chancellor, not, as he had often done before, in a meeting of the French nation, but in a solemn congregation of the whole Council, assembled to transact important business. The chancellor, it must be owned, showed especial favour to his young *protégé* and brought him forward whenever he could. He destined him, as a matter of course, for the Church, but he never intended to make a saint of him, nor did he direct his training to that end. He did not think him the material out of which saints are made. But the mediaeval Church had room, not for saints only, but for scholars and statesmen, for men of letters and men of action. Gerson hoped that Hubert, in whom he thought he discerned unusual abilities, might have a brilliant career before him as a man of action, and possibly as a great statesman. He recognized the active life as good and useful in its own degree, though certainly lower than the life of contemplation.

That day the Council was to meet in the splendid refectory of the Franciscans. Vast as was that lordly hall, it was sure to be densely packed, for the Council was now to redeem the promise made to the Bohemians, and allow their countryman to appear and to speak in his own defence.

Hubert was more eager to see and hear him than even to perform his duty to his lord. Owing to some mismanagement, he was not permitted on this occasion to go in with the chancellor, and take his seat at his feet, as he used to do in the meetings of the nation — an obviously convenient arrangement. He had to fight for an entrance, at the door of the hall, with a crowd of priests, notaries, scribes, and spectators.

A portly abbot blocked the way, disputing with the janitor about his right to some special place. Hubert could not slip by him, and dared not push him rudely aside. But a tall young Bachelor of Arts, who was next him, seemed to be troubled by no such scruples. He jostled the abbot without mercy, and rushing past Hubert in hot haste, tore the sleeve of his gown. Hubert, freeing his right arm with difficulty, dealt him a blow in payment.

"Strike, but let me on!" said the other, unconsciously parodying the great Athenian. Then, seeing what he had done, "Pardon me, 'twas an accident."

Hubert, looking at him for the first time, observed that he was as tall as himself, though more bony and angular. Pleased at once with his height and his good-humour, he said, "Let us stay together." Of course they spoke in Latin, in which language also the proceedings of the council were conducted.

Pushing together, shoulder to shoulder, they soon made their way into the hall. They had brought with them small portable seats, which were bought or hired in the Platz outside.

"I want to sit where I can see that man," said Hubert. "I have never seen him yet. Have you?"

The other did not answer, but busied himself in securing their places. At last they were settled; not too soon, for the day's work was beginning. First, a very impressive prayer for the guidance of the Holy Spirit was recited, all present kneeling or standing. Then a few verses taken from the fiftieth Psalm were read aloud, intended, as someone remarked to Hubert, for a description of the dangerous heretic with whom they had to deal. "But unto the wicked God says, 'What do you have to declare My statutes, or that you should take My covenant in your mouth, seeing you hate instruction, and cast My words behind you? When you see a thief, you consent with him, and have been partaker with adulterers.' "

"Put on that cap of infamy yourselves, for it fits you, not him!" said the scribe at Hubert's side, in a fierce whisper.

Hubert turned to him. "But the man is not here. Why don't they produce him?"

The scribe made no reply; probably he did not hear. When the Psalm was finished, the clerk of the Council began to read a long list of articles taken, as the act of accusation set forth, from the writings of John Huss.

Presently the scribe started up. "Will you keep my place for me?" he whispered hurriedly.

"Yes, if I can; but it will be hard. What's the matter?"

"I am summoned. Look yonder!" Following the direction of his eye, Hubert distinctly saw a person standing up on a seat behind the clerk of the Council, and making signals to his companion. "There's foul play afoot," said the latter, as he hastened out.

It was not without its difficulty to guard his place for him in his absence. The reading of the articles of accusation went on, but Hubert knew he need not take notes of them, as it would be easy to procure them afterward. He was growing tired of the whole proceeding, when a picturesque incident diverted his thoughts. Two personages, splendidly dressed, and evidently of the highest rank, entered the hall, one of them carrying a couple of large books. They had a conference of some length with he cardinals who sat at the upper end, but those at a distance could not hear what was said. Then they retired, leaving the books on the table. Whispers ran from mouth to mouth down the hall, and reached at last the ears of Hubert.

"The Emperor has been told by someone that the Council was about to condemn the heretic unheard, and in his absence. So his Highness has sent these princes to forbid them, on pain of his high displeasure. Moreover, he has sent copies of the books of Master John Huss, lest unfair and garbled extracts should be given of them!"

At the same moment Hubert glimpsed the friendly scribe pushing through the crowd, trying to regain his place. He had turned to give him a helping hand, when someone cried out, "Here comes the heretic at last!"

There was a trampling of armed men, and another lower sound, as if iron clanked on iron. Hubert turned again, and looked up eagerly — far too eagerly to note that his companion, now back in his place, gave but one quick glance, then buried his face in both his hands, and looked no more.

Hubert's eager eyes rested on a tall, slender figure, and a face so worn and wasted, so pale and hollow-eyed, that at first he could read nothing in it but pain. Yet, as he continued looking, the impression of character, which was permanent, came out more and more, effacing that of suffering, which was temporary. Unawares he said to himself, "If this man were not a great heretic, I would take him for a great saint." For there was in his face an austere and lofty purity, as of one who dwelt much in the presence of God; yet a gentleness also, as of one who came forth from that presence to do much loving service to man. The brow was noble, if not commanding, though perhaps the lines of the sensitive mouth expressed sweetness more than strength. The hair and beard had grown long in prison, and their black was touched with silver — not from age.[9]

[9] He was forty-five.

Thus Hubert looked for the first time on the man whom bishops and cardinals hated so bitterly, while simple, honest hearts like Robert's opened to him everywhere, and the men who really knew him loved him as Jonathan loved David — loved him with that love greater than which no man has. Many would have died for him — *one* did so die, vindicating with his latest breath his "dear master's" name and honour rather than his own.

"Do you acknowledge these books to be yours?" asked the clerk of the Council, pointing to the volumes that lay upon the table.

The accused took the books, and Hubert heard again the clank of the iron, as he raised them up in his fettered hands and examined them carefully. He turned to the assembly and said in a calm, firm voice: "I acknowledge them to be mine. If any man among you can point out an erroneous proposition therein, I will amend it with hearty goodwill."

"A fair beginning," thought Hubert; "this heretic will not be obstinate, or hard to deal with. All will end well, as I said to Robert."

After this, certain articles were read, said to have been taken from the books which were thus acknowledged.

Then the accused began his answer. But no sooner had he uttered a word than cries of rage and scorn broke out from every part of the hall, entirely drowning his voice. Hubert's amazement was beyond words. He could hardly credit his senses. He thought he must be the victim of an evil dream. Was this the "Holy Council?" Was it not rather some lawless gathering of students in the Sorbonne?

During a momentary lull the prisoner raised his voice again. "Allow me to explain my meaning . . ."

"Drop your sophistry," someone cried; and then from many voices the shout arose, "Say Yes or No; say Yes or No!"

"Yes," he answered; "for it is written in the Holy Scriptures . . ."

"That is nothing to the purpose." The cry came from the bishops' seats, and echoed and re-echoed through the hall. Again and again he tried to speak — always with the same result. Mocking laughter, cries of rage, jeers and insults, drowned his voice. An eye-witness has thus described the scene for us, "It was more like a herd of wild beasts than a grave assembly of fathers of the Church."

At last he stood silent, looking from one to another in sad surprise, and not without a mute appeal for justice. But even silence availed him nothing. "He is dumb!" they shouted. "He is dumb! He has nothing to say. This is a sign he confesses his errors."

Then once more he lifted up his voice, and its penetrating tones were heard above the clamour.

"I expected a different reception. I thought you would have heard me. I cannot make myself audible in so great a noise, and I am silent because I am forced to it. I would gladly speak, if you would listen."

That was all. He made no further attempt to speak, but stood perfectly silent, perfectly motionless, and let the storm sweep over him. Sweep over him it did; from every part of the hall, and without order or method taunts, accusations, and reproaches were flung at him. "Some did outrage against him, and others did spitefully mock him." Mockery, abuse, and insult — insult, abuse, and mockery; so raged the tempest, until its own fury made it impotent. At length the fathers of the Church could not even hear each other's voices.

Long before this Hubert's amazement had changed to indignation. One man alone against a hundred, and not allowed to speak a single word in his own defence! Heretic or no heretic, he ought to have justice and fair play. To shout him down after this fashion was mean, cowardly, horrible. Forgetting for the moment that this was the Holy Council, until now the object of his own admiring worship, he longed, with a wild, passionate longing, to stand up and cry out his protest before them all. But why should *he* do it? Was not the great chancellor there? Would not Gerson interpose in the cause of right and justice? Hubert could not see him from the place where he sat, but he looked toward his seat, listened anxiously for his voice. In vain; no word was heard from the honoured lips of Gerson. He did not swell the tide of mockery and insult, but neither did he stem it — perhaps he could not.

From the time that he despaired of help from Gerson, Hubert's eyes never left again the face of the accused. He stood before them all, undaunted and unflinching. Yet in his look there was neither scorn nor defiance, nor the fierce courage of despair — only patient endurance. More and more a strange calm seemed to come to him. If still there was sadness, Hubert could not help thinking it was rather for the degradation of the Council than for the shame and scorning heaped on himself.

Finally a priest who had been sitting on the bench appropriated to the witnesses, stood up and began, "Since the days of Christ there has not been such a pestilent heretic, except Wycliffe."

The prisoner turned and looked reproachfully at the speaker, while a visible quiver of pain passed over his patient face. This solitary voice — it must have been the voice, and not the words — seemed to have more power to wound than all the others raised against him. Hubert could endure it no longer; that look shattered the last remains of his self-control. He was on his feet in a moment,

74

hurling at the head of the offending priest the wrath accumulated against the whole assembly.

"*You coward*!" he cried.

But the strong arms of the scribe beside him forced him back to his seat.

"Be quiet," said he in an angry whisper. "Would you have us turned out and no witness left to tell of *this*? Go on with your writing."

"There is nothing to write," said Hubert, showing his tablets, which were nearly blank. "There is nothing — and if there were, for very shame I would leave it unwritten."

"Then look where you looked before, at the one calm face amidst all this uproar."

Hubert looked; the momentary pain had passed now, and there was peace. In the midst of his indignation he could not help wondering: he turned to his neighbour. "Are you a friend of his?"

"His disciple. A Bohemian. But hush! It seems the fathers are returning to their senses, and are going to dismiss the assembly."

It was true. The more moderate and reasonable members of the Council (among whom we may surely reckon the chancellor of Paris), feeling the uselessness as well as the disgrace of the scene, and perhaps also afraid of the Emperor, proposed the adjournment of the congregation. Hubert soon found himself again in the free air, amidst the glorious June sunshine. But in his heart there was no sunshine, only fierce anger, bitterness, and shame. Never again would he think the Council an assembly of men for the most part like Jean Gerson.

As he walked slowly along, someone overtook him and laid a hand on his shoulder. It was the Bohemian scribe. "Can I speak to you, Master Scholar?" he asked, in a low, eager voice.

"Surely; but who is it that would speak to me?"

"Petr Mladenowic, Bachelor of Arts in the University of Prague. And you?"

"Hubert Bohun, scholar of the Sorbonne, secretary to the Chancellor of Paris."

"I thought you belonged to the chancellor — whom God forgive. All the better for my purpose if you will aid me. Your witness to what was done this day in the Council will be of great service."

"To whom?"

"Master Bohun, though you are the chancellor's man, I have marked your looks and words, and I will swear you have a true heart. You will not refuse a service — which you may render in all honour — to the man whom you saw so cruelly outraged today."

Hubert threw back his head, looked up to heaven, and repeated as if to himself words he had found in the chancellor's Latin Bible, and learned by heart because they pleased him so well: " 'To crush under his feet all the prisoners of the earth, to turn aside the right of a man before the face of the Most High; to subvert a man in his cause, the Lord approves not.' I am with you, Master Scribe," he said briefly.

"First then, let us go to the Bohemian lords. I doubt not they will bring us to the Emperor, to tell him how well the Council obeyed his command to give Master John a fair hearing."

"These lords, then, were not present themselves?" said Hubert.

"They came, but could not get in. I fared better, thanks to you. No doubt they have gone home."

"Who is that fellow?" asked Hubert as two priests passed by them talking eagerly, one of them being the man whose attack John Huss appeared to feel so keenly.

Instead of answering, Petr shook his clenched hand at him with a fierce look of rage and scorn. "*Judas!*" he cried. Then to Hubert: "He was Master John's disciple and his familiar friend. Well, when He who tarries long comes at last to avenge His own elect, He will not forget Stephen Palec."

"And the other?"

"Michel Causás. Along with Palec his chief accuser and bitterest enemy — a villainous priest, who is selling his soul for gold. Everyone knows what he is, and how much his word is worth. But at least he is only a villain, not a traitor, like his comrade."

Hubert and Mladenowic learned afterward that the Bohemian lords, though unable to obtain an entrance to the crowded hall, had *not* gone home. They waited patiently outside until the assembly was dismissed. The prisoner was led forth so near to where they stood that they were able to exchange a word with him. He stretched out his hand to them with a smile.

"Don't be afraid of me," he said.

"We are not afraid of you."

"I know it well — I know it well," he answered, with a bright, calm look. Then, "blessing the people with his hand" (they seem to have shown some sign of sympathy), "he passed up the steps" that led to his prison, "going away joyfully after all the mockery he had endured."[10]

---

[10] From the narrative of Petr Mladenowic.

THE BOHEMIAN LORDS

For the wrong that needs resistance,
For the cause that lacks assistance,
For the future in the distance,
And the good that I can do.

Hubert Bohun and Petr Mladenowic walked quickly from the Stefan's Platz, where the Franciscan Monastery was, to the Ober Markt, which they crossed, and turned into what was then called the street of St. Paul, but now bears the name of the Husenstrasse. They stopped near the Schnetz Thor, before a modest but substantial house, now called the Husenhaus, although the man whose name it bears lodged beneath its roof for only twenty days. In the town that witnessed his long and bitter agony, his, after all these centuries, is the name best remembered and most highly honoured. As one said on the spot, "That man's spirit pervades the place." This is something more than the slow revenge of Time; it is surely His hand who says, "The righteous shall be had in everlasting remembrance."

Petr knocked, and the door was instantly opened by a handsome, dark-eyed boy of eleven or twelve, in the bright dress of a page of chivalry. He asked an eager question in a tongue unknown to Hubert, and Petr answered by a torrent of words in the same. Then, turning to Hubert, and resuming the Latin in which they had been conversing, "The lords have not yet returned, which is strange. We must wait for them." He led the way into a room where the presence of various articles of knightly use showed the quality of the occupants. But though arms and armour hung on the walls, paper, pens, and an inkhorn lay on the table.

The boy disappeared immediately, for he knew what became his father's son when a stranger crossed their threshold. Almost before Petr had time to say that he was the young lord (or Panec) Václav, the only son of the knight of Chlum, "whom I serve in the same capacity that you serve the Chancellor of Paris —" he returned, bearing a cup of wine, which, with modest grace, he presented to Hubert. A gray-haired woman, whose dress showed her to be the widow of a citizen of the better class, and who was, in fact, the owner of the house, followed him, and with a look full of anxiety asked Petr in German what was done in the Council.

"Nothing was done there, Mother Fidelia," said he in the same tongue. "However, God's Providence so ordered it that our friend Ulric chanced to stand in the outer ring, behind the clerk of the Council, so that he could read over his shoulder the papers he held in his hand. What think you he saw among them? Master John's condemnation, forsooth, ready drafted and prepared, before he had been tried or heard at all!"[11]

Hubert cried out in amazement, but Petr went on unheeding: "Then Ulric beckoned me and told me what he had seen, and I ran here with the tidings to my lords, as doubtless you know already. They went in all haste to the Emperor, and he sent the princes to stay the hands of the Council, and to prevent such gross miscarriage of justice. Small use in that! But at least the Emperor shall know how they used him today."

"I can't believe it," said Hubert. "About the draft of the condemnation — there is some mistake."

"Can you not, Master Hubert? I think what your own eyes have seen might have prepared you for that, or any other injustice."

Fidelia shook her head sorrowfully. "They will never let him out of their hands alive," she said. "I knew it the day they took him from us, and I believe he knew it too. Standing on yonder stair, he said farewell, and blessed me and my house in the name of God."

"Yes, and how you wept that day," said Václav. "But here they are!" he cried, springing to the door. He admitted three tall, noble-looking men in sword and cloak. Two were quite young, and the third was not old, though his hair and beard were gray. He had an oval face and a high forehead, with a thoughtful, steadfast air. This was Jan z Chlum, or John of Chlum, "that loyal knight," "the best and dearest friend" of John Huss. To him chiefly Petr addressed himself, using the Czech, or Bohemian tongue, in which he had spoken to Václav.

It was easy to read in their looks and gestures the anger of the knights when they heard his tale. The voices of the young men were loud and passionate, and one of them put his hand on his sword.

---

[11] All this is strictly a narrative of fact.

Chlum, outwardly the calmest of the three, laid his on the arm of his companion, as if to check his violence.

Then turning to Hubert, he said in German, "Good Master Secretary, please hold us excused. It is not the custom of Bohemian knights to leave a stranger in their house ungreeted and unwelcomed, especially when he has come on an errand of kindness. But the tidings brought by our friend here of what passed in the Council — where we could not obtain admittance — have made us forget all else. He says you can confirm them. Is it so?"

Here the young knight broke in, "They promised him a fair hearing, and this is the way they keep their word! Liars — hypocrites!"

"Be quiet, Henri," said Chlum, looking toward him for moment. Then to Hubert, "*Was* it a fair hearing that they gave him, Master Scholar?"

"Sir Knight, it was no hearing at all!" cried Hubert passionately. "He was not allowed to utter a single word. Each time he began, they shouted him down, or stopped him with jeers and insults."

"Good! What you have said now in the presence of these our friends, Baron Václav of Duba and Baron Henri of Latzembok, will you say, and stand to without fear, in the presence of our lord the Emperor?"

"That I will, for it is the truth," said Hubert boldly.

"Right and bravely spoken! Come with us, then, to the Leiter House."

Although the distance was short, the knights called out their servants and their horses, that they might present themselves with due ceremony before the Emperor. Hubert and Petr accompanied the party on foot.

There was ready admission at the Leiter House for the Bohemian lords. Sigismund, indeed, was afraid of offending them. Wenzel, the present King of Bohemia, was his brother, and was childless, and he expected at his death to succeed to his throne. It is easy to understand, therefore, what tremendous pressure must have been brought to bear on him by the Council in order to induce him to violate the safe-conduct which one of these very lords, Duba, had himself obtained from him, and given to John Huss at Nuremburg.

The bold, free-hearted barons of Bohemia came into the presence of their Emperor with due respect, but without servility. It was, as we know, for the second time that day. They found him seated at the upper end of the great hall, surrounded by knights and nobles, and engaged in inspecting certain handsome falcons, which some foreign merchants were exhibiting. The beautiful birds were resting, carefully hooded, on the wrists of their keepers. One, however, was in the hands of a slight, graceful youth in crimson velvet, who, on giving it back very cautiously and cleverly to the keeper, turned for a moment — and Hubert was surprised to recognize his brother Armand. As the Bohemians advanced to the dais where the Emperor sat, the nobles and merchants made way for them. Armand, with others, came down the hall, and soon approached the spot where Hubert and Petr stood, modestly awaiting a summons to draw near and give their testimony.

"What wind has blown you here?" asked Armand of his brother, in great surprise.

"I have come with the Bohemian lords," said Hubert briefly, not at all choosing to tell his errand. He was far too anxious to hear what was passing on the dais to question Armand in his turn, but Armand was quite willing to take questions for granted.

"Doubtless you want to know what brings *me* here," he said. "My slight skill in falconry, being talked of in the queen's court, and generally among the Hungarians (where they think much of our Burgundian training in these matters), and these new Flemish falcons being brought to the Emperor, I was invited with the rest to come and judge them. Do you see yonder bird with the blue hood, and the white feathers in his tail? No, not that one — the other, which the little gray-headed man in curried leather has on his wrist. That is the best I have seen yet. Just like one my lord of Burgundy had last year. But you are not listening, Hubert. No use to talk of falconry or other knightly sports to churchmen like you. And why — why in Heaven's name — when you were coming into the presence of the Emperor, did you not at least take the trouble to put on your holiday gown? Look, your sleeve is half torn off! One would take you for a poor scholar, going about to sing *placebos* for a penny and a piece of bread."

"They are beckoning me forward — I must go," Hubert interrupted hastily.

"Go, and I am sure I wish you well out of the business that has brought you here, whatever it may be," said Armand, very doubtfully.

Summoned by Chlum, Hubert and Petr advanced. Touching every step with their knees, they ascended the dais, and stood humbly before the splendid, terrible Emperor. Armand came as near as he could, and tried to see and hear what passed. With a thrill of pride he observed his brother's modest, manly bearing, and the ease and grace with which he moved and spoke, for the first time in his life, in the presence of royalty. In this he showed to more advantage than his companion, and proved how well the Bohemian lords had done to bring him with them. His part, however, was soon over; Sigismund gave the lords an answer which seemed to content them, and they, with thanks to their "most gracious Emperor," respectfully but proudly took their leave, Hubert and Petr following them out.

Before he mounted his horse, Chlum stretched out his hand to Hubert. "Brave scholar," he said, "take our thanks for your true and honest words. Not ours alone," he added, lowering his voice, "but His who regards what is done unto His servant as done unto Him. And if you ever need a friend, come to my lodging in St. Paul's Street. Farewell!"

He rode away with the other knights, and Armand came up. "What have you done?" he asked anxiously.

"This," said Hubert, joyfully. "The Emperor has given his word that when Master John Huss is brought again before the Council, he will himself preside, and see him used with fairness and courtesy."

"Indeed!" said Armand. "I was under the impression that — speaking with all due reverence — the Holy Ghost Himself presided over the meetings of the Council."

Hubert was silent, but there was in his face such bitter pain and shame that even his thoughtless young brother forbore to press him. Yet he said with some anxiety in his voice, "But what thanks do you think your chancellor is liable to give you for the work you have been doing today?"

Strange as it may seem, Hubert had not thought of this before. He knit his brow; he even grew a little pale. But at length he answered confidently, "The chancellor will say I did well. He is so just, so generous, above all, so true, that when I speak the truth most entirely, then I know that I please him best."

"Possibly! Yet I advise you not to speak more than you can help about this affair. Do not think me over-bold. I am younger than you, and far less learned; but then I am a man of the world, and you are only a scholar, and a half-fledged churchman, so to speak. Still, I wish you would tell me in one word how they used that Bohemian today in the Council, for I could not hear half what was said on the dais, though I saw those knights were in a mighty chafe. And there is a lady at the queen's court" — Armand looked conscious, and even flushed a little — "a lady whom I hold in high esteem, and who takes an interest in his fate."

"In very truth," said Hubert, his brow darkening, "they used him shamefully. Don't let me talk of it or, churchman as you call me, I will make your ears ring again. Any man would swear who saw what I saw today."

"What? In the *Holy* Council? However, Hubert, I may congratulate you. So boldly and so well did you speak to the Emperor that I was proud of my brother."

"I deserve no praise," said Hubert shortly. "I did not heed the Emperor. Indeed, I scarcely saw him."

He said no more. He could not tell Armand that what he saw all the time was not the royal pomp and state of the Emperor, not even the "terrible eyes" that so often made the stoutest tremble — but one noble, patient face.

That face was stamped forever on his memory. Wherever he went he would carry its remembrance with him, together with the bitter sense that the "Holy Council" had degraded itself; that it could be cruel and unjust, and — what was perhaps worse in his estimation — undignified and contemptible.

XI

THE DARKENED SUN

God is light, and in Him is no darkness at all.

Hubert was burning to tell the chancellor everything, and to hear from his lips some explanation of the extraordinary and disgraceful scene in the Council. But he had to crush down his angry, impatient heart, and to give the whole of the next day to hard, monotonous toil. The Council did not sit, but a formidable mass of papers about the affair of Jean Petit had to be arranged and prepared. Hubert was now reaping the usual reward of doing his work well, in having more and more work given to him to do. He dared not ask a question beyond what was absolutely necessary of his careworn and pre-occupied lord; still less could he trouble him with a personal confession. His own prolonged absence the day before seemed to have passed unnoticed, except by subordinate members of the household, to whom he felt justified in refusing an explanation.

On the following morning, that of the 7th of June, he rose very early. He knew that the Council was to meet again that day, that the emperor was to preside, and that, in his presence, John Huss was to be heard in his own defence. He knew also that he was to be there himself, as the chancellor's secretary. He wanted first to be quiet and alone; so he went out by the Göttlingen gate toward the Brühl. But avoiding the pleasure-gardens, he wandered into a solitary meadow, which, as it happened, had an ill repute with the townsfolk as a place of execution for malefactors and of burial for horses and mules. Hubert, however, knew nothing of this; in the dawn of the bright summer day all looked fair, pure, and peaceful. It was a lovely morning; the blue sky without a cloud, the grass fresh and dewy, a soft breeze slightly stirring the leaves of the linden trees, and the birds "that sing among the branches" chanting their early hymn of praise.

Hubert was perplexed and troubled in spirit, and he remembered that he had heard the chancellor exhort men who were in trouble to meditation and to prayer, and to the study of profitable books. So he had taken with him the only book he possessed, the part of the Psalter which had been given to his father by John Wycliffe. He intended to read several Psalms, and then to pray a great deal; which with him meant chiefly to recite a great many Paternosters. He ought perhaps to have known better, since he lived with a man who understood the nature of spiritual prayer so well as to leave us counsels on the subject which may still be read with profit. But his soul was not yet awake; he had never really felt the presence of God — never cried to Him "out of the depths." Moreover, the chancellor, not thinking his young favourite "had the Divine vocation," had never singled him out for special religious instruction, though he loved him with a natural, human, fatherly love very honourable to them both.

This love was a sheet-anchor to Hubert, even when so much else to which he clung seemed giving way. Michael the Archangel, to whom in his youthful enthusiasm he had likened the all-conquering Council, seemed to have dropped his beautiful blazing sword, and veiled his face in shame. *What* was he crushing beneath his feet? The wicked pope, the dragon of heresy, or — was it perhaps an innocent man falsely accused? It was not well to recall that scene in the Council Hall; there was danger, there might even be sin, in the passion that made his cheek burn and his heart throb as he thought of it. He tried to lay the blame on the Italians, and indeed they had been the worst offenders; but he could not conceal from himself that Germans, Frenchmen, Englishmen even, had taken part in the uproar. What could have stirred them to such a tempest of rage and hate toward a man against whom, after all, they seemed to bring no such very heinous accusations?

Of course a heretic ought to be convicted, and, if obstinate, duly punished. But it should be done soberly and decently; in a pious, orderly manner, like what it most surely was, a good work, well pleasing unto God. In the tumult and confusion of Wednesday, it had been impossible to ascertain if the accused was really guilty. *Was he*?

Before Hubert's mental eye rose again that calm patient face; and the few quiet, dignified words which, amidst the confusion, he had been able to utter, sounded in his ears. Certainly his demeanour was that of an innocent man, and, as Hubert thought, with a quick flash of sympathy, of a brave man too. At least it was no sin to hope him innocent; no sin, but a good and charitable work, to pray for him that if innocent he might this day be cleared; if guilty, that he might be led to abandon his errors.

Choosing a sheltered spot beneath a linden tree, Hubert knelt down. He repeated a great many Paternosters and other Latin prayers which he had learned. Then he rose, opened his book, and began to read.

This is what he read: "The LORD is my light and my salvation; whom shall I fear? The LORD is the strength of my life; of whom shall I be afraid?" What was very unusual, he stopped there and began to think. What did it all mean? That light was to come from God, God Himself and no other? Not the pope, not the Council even, but God Himself was the light. Whose light? "*Mine.*" But then only great saints, such as the chancellor, could say this. Yet, if so, why was everybody directed to read and to repeat these Psalms? Not priests alone, but acolytes, choristers, laymen of all sorts might and should recite the Psalms. From where, then, was the light to come for himself? He was beginning to feel very sorely that he needed light. But that God could be *his* light, *his* salvation, was beyond his comprehension — beyond his dream even.

While he was thinking thus, a little bird dropped down at his feet with a wild, frightened cry. Perhaps a hawk was pursuing it — he looked up, but saw nothing. Then similar cries were heard from the trees around him, and in a strange, unaccountable way the day began to darken. He looked up again — could a sudden storm be coming? No, the sky was without a cloud; not a breath swayed the boughs above him, or moved the tall grasses underneath. Yet the darkness grew and deepened; grew and deepened still. He sprang to his feet; he gazed around; he listened intently. "No rain; no wind; no thunder;" no sound of any kind, for even the birds had fallen now into the silence of utter terror. The sparrow which had dropped at his feet lay there as if dead, and, stranger still, a wild cat which had begun to creep stealthily toward it stood motionless, transfixed with terror, her fierce eyes blazing in the darkness.

Deeper — deeper yet, that darkness grew. A dread more awful than he had ever felt before seized Hubert; he stood trembling like an aspen-leaf. But at last, rousing himself with a desperate effort, he looked up again. Where was the sun? Had it vanished wholly from the sky? No, but what seemed worse — more terrible, more unnatural — the eye of day itself was darkened, and a black veil drawn over it. Faint, strange reddish flames played around its edge, and in the surrounding heavens he could see the stars glimmering through the darkness. Quite sure now that the end of the world had come, he threw himself down on his face and muttered faintly:

Dies iræ; dires illæ.

After what seemed to him an age of horror, but what was really only a few minutes, he thought the gloom a little less profound. Yes — there was hope. Gradually the shadow lightened, passed away, and the sun resumed its usual splendour. Still trembling and awe-stricken, Hubert rose and looked about him. Once more all things were smiling peacefully in the joy and glory of the fair June morning, while everywhere the little birds were pouring out their rapturous songs of thanksgiving and praise. Should Hubert's voice alone be wanting? Most unfeignedly thankful that his own day of grace, and that of the wicked world, was not to end so quickly, he chanted, by way of a *Laus Deo*, the first words that occurred to him: "The LORD is my light and my salvation; whom shall I fear? The LORD is the strength of my life; of whom shall I be afraid?" Yes, he could say that, now the sun was shining once more, but — had he been able to say it in the darkness?

Presently, and with rapid footsteps, he returned to the town. There he found everything in confusion, and read dismay and consternation in every face. What evil had this terrible eclipse been sent to foreshadow? Did it threaten the Council, the Emperor, the city, or, more likely, all of them at once? But the chancellor called his household together, and calmed their minds by a few wise and quiet words, telling them that if they were in the grace of God they had nothing to fear. Yet, certainly, this was a solemn warning to all men that they should repent of their sins and amend their lives.

XII

BEFORE THE COUNCIL AGAIN

He is brought before the Council;
There are chains about his hands.

* * *

And strange it was to witness
How the false king turned aside,
For he dared not meet his captive's eye.
Thus ever the spirit's royalty
Is greater than pomp or pride.

Notwithstanding the terror and excitement caused by the eclipse, the Council met that day, although not until after noon, which then meant after dinner. This time Hubert sat in his proper place, at the feet of the chancellor. In this convenient, though far from comfortable position, he could hear everything, but he could see nothing except the broad back of the Bishop of Litomissel, who happened to sit in front of his lord. For Gerson, although one of the ablest and most distinguished men in the Council, still took rank only as a doctor, and had his seat behind those of the cardinals and the bishops.

Hubert's longing to see the face of the prisoner therefore had to remain ungratified. He only knew when he was led in by hearing the footsteps of his guards, whom he judged to be more numerous than on the preceding occasion. After the formal opening of the session, certain articles were read, taken, it was alleged, from the writings of the accused. To these Hubert listened with scant interest; they did not seem to him of much importance. If there was heresy in them, at least he did not think it could be very heinous. He failed to see any special significance even in such a proposition as this: "There is but one Holy Universal or Catholic Church, which is the Universal company of all the Elect."

Much to his relief, the proceedings were soon interrupted by the entrance of the Emperor and his nobles. "He will see fair play, as he promised," thought Hubert.

Rising from his seat for a moment, like the rest, to do him reverence, he caught a glimpse of the stately imperial head, and its halo of golden hair, as Sigismund advanced to the throne prepared for him at the upper end of the hall. He saw also the faces of some of his suite, and recognized among them with pleasure, Duba and Chlum. He could not see, however, what others did not fail to note, the look of trouble and perplexity on the commanding brow of Sigismund. For once, those terrible eyes were disposed to quail; they rested anywhere, or on anything, rather than on the poor priest who stood fettered before him.

Just then an "article" was being read, purporting that the accused had asserted the material bread remained on the altar after the consecration of the Host; in fact, that he denied the doctrine of Transubstantiation.

Hubert listened eagerly for his answer. This would be a heresy indeed!

"I have not done so," said he; and he added an explicit declaration of his belief, which was that of all, or nearly all, his contemporaries. "But," he said, "it is true that I have called the Host, even after consecration, by the name of bread, for Christ calls Himself the living bread that came down from heaven."

Then the great Cardinal of Cambray, Pierre d'Ailly — "the Hammer of heretics" — stepped into the arena to measure swords with the Bohemian "Realist."

"Do you not believe in the *Universalia à parte rei*?" asked he. "Then it is impossible for you to hold aright the doctrine of Transubstantiation."

Hubert was all attention now; these scholastic disputes were familiar ground to him and highly interesting. To the accused apparently they were equally familiar; for he took up the challenge with promptness and dexterity.

"Transubstantiation," he said, "is a perpetual miracle, and therefore exempt from logical forms."

A rejoinder was made, and the argument went on. John Huss soon proved that he could wield as deftly as any man the well-tempered blade of scholastic logic. That acute and subtle intellect, for which even his enemies gave him credit, enabled him to hold his own, not against the cardinal alone, but against the whole assembly, for everyone threw in, as it pleased him, a syllogism, a question, a remark. He met them all, and parried or answered them, as the case might be, with unfailing quickness and presence of mind. To one who spoke foolishly, he even said with touch of scorn, "A boy in the schools could answer that."

Not until a long time had been spent in this way an honest Englishman closed the discussion by saying, with English common sense and fairness, "What is the use of all this irrelevant matter? He thinks aright concerning the Sacrament of the Altar."

This was, so far, a victory for the accused. But what, on such a stage, could victory avail him? In a sense it was even worse for him than defeat — it exasperated his enemies.

An attempt was made, very skilfully, as even Hubert could discern, to entrap him into an acknowledgment of error. The Cardinal of Florence, in a tone of studied moderation, reminded him that in the mouth of two or three witnesses every word must be established, and added, pointing to the witnesses, "almost twenty men," who were arrayed against him, "How you can defend your cause against so many, and such reliable men, I cannot see."

Hubert listened breathlessly for the answer. Would the accused, by owning himself even partially in the wrong, consult his safety and propitiate his judges?

There was nothing further from his thoughts. "I call God to witness," said he, "that I have never taught, or even thought of teaching, as these men have dared to testify in regard to what they never heard. And though there were many more arrayed against me, I make more account of the witness of the Lord my God, and of my own conscience, than I do of the judgments of all my adversaries, which I regard as nothing."

Other accusations followed, and other replies. Hours went by, and still the tide of talk rolled on. At last Hubert's attention flagged. In that crowded hall the heat was stifling; and more than once he was half asleep when his lord's command to him to write down something roused him up again.

Still, one thing did not fail to strike him — the continual appeal of the accused to "the Holy Scriptures." This came back again and again, like the keynote of a melody. He might play with the keenly-tempered weapons of the schools; but it was with this sword — the sword of the Spirit — that he fought the battle of life and death.

"This," he said, "is the highest authority in the faith; not so the statements of holy doctors or the pope's bulls, to which it is proper to give credence only so far as they state something out of Holy Scripture, or that is founded on Scripture."[12]

But at last something was said which woke Hubert up completely. It was laid to the charge of the prisoner that he had expressed a doubt of the damnation of the great English heretic, John Wycliffe.

"Heretic he was, and that a great one," thought Hubert with a sigh. "Yet still, he was my brave father's friend, and if there is any man on earth bold enough to say a word for him, I would like to hear it."

The voice of the accused rang through the crowded hall: "I did not say whether John Wycliffe was saved or lost. This I said, that *I would willingly have my soul with his.*"

A shout of insulting laughter, which even the presence of the Emperor could not restrain, greeted the dauntless words. Perhaps it was not mockery alone, but fierce exultation. Wycliffe was beyond their reach; let this man, who would have his soul with his, take the doom that he had earned!

Before Hubert had recovered from his angry amazement, they were accusing him of another crime. From the sentence of the pope (and that pope John XXIII) he had dared to appeal — to Jesus Christ Himself. He owned the fact.

"No appeal," said he, "can be more just and more holy. It is right and lawful to appeal from the inferior judge to the higher. But who is higher than Christ the Lord? Who is more just than He, in whom neither error nor falsehood can be found? Is there anywhere a surer Refuge for the unhappy and the oppressed?"

Again arose the mocking laughter, the cry of rage and insult. In spite of the presence of the Emperor the assembly vas getting beyond control, and the disgraceful scene of Wednesday seemed on the point of renewal. The prisoner himself dared to remonstrate.

"I thought," he said, "that in this Council there would have been more reverence, piety, and good order."

Then some effort was made to restore quietness, and more accusations and answers followed. Thus, one said, for instance, that Huss had called on the people to take up arms in defence of his doctrine.

---

[12] It ought, perhaps, to be explained that these words were not actually used upon this occasion; this solitary deviation from strict accuracy has been introduced to show the whole tenor of Huss' teaching and one of the strongest reasons for his condemnation by the Council.

"Yes," he answered. " 'The helmet and sword of salvation.' No other arms."

But at last the lateness of the hour obliged the assembly to break up, and orders were given to the guards to lead the prisoner away.

Even this was not the end. D'Ailly rose and demanded that he should be brought back. Back again came the fettered feet, weary enough by this time. Having first taken care that the attention of the Emperor, which had wandered often during the long examination, should be fully aroused, D'Ailly began: "John Huss, I have heard you say that if you had not come to Constance of your own free will, neither the Emperor nor the King of Bohemia would have brought you here."

"Reverend Father, this indeed I said, that there were many lords in Bohemia who wished me well, and they could have so kept me that no person, not even the Emperor, or the king, could have constrained me to come here."

"Do you hear the audacity of this man?" cried D'Ailly, crimson with rage.

A fierce murmur ran through the assembly, and the Emperor's brow gathered thunder. But a noble from his own suite stepped forward, and stood undaunted between the angry monarch and the furious Council. It was that good knight and true, John of Chlum.

"John Huss speaks truth," said he, "and truth it is. I am the least of the barons of Bohemia, yet would I have kept him in safety for a whole year against king and Emperor. What, then, would those have done who are far mightier than I, and whose fortresses are impregnable?"

Had this been an assembly of knights and nobles, a burst of applause would have greeted the fearless soldier and the loyal friend. But in this conclave of priests the meaning of chivalry was unknown. Still, they could not outrage the belted knight and baron, as they had done the hapless heretic.

"Enough said," replied D'Ailly ungraciously. Then, turning toward the accused, he admonished him solemnly to submit himself to the Council. "Do so, I recommend you," he said. "Your person and your honour will fare well therefrom."

Now at last from the lips of the Emperor came the words which all men knew were words of fate. Friend and foe hung upon them breathless. Yet he began with an air of uncertainty and indecision — almost he seemed to be apologizing to the prisoner. "It has been pretended," said he, "that you were already in prison a fortnight when you obtained a safe-conduct from me. Nevertheless — I allow it, and many are aware of the fact — this safe-conduct was granted you before your departure from Prague. It guaranteed you the liberty of explaining frankly before the Council, as you have just done, your doctrines and faith; and we have to thank the cardinals and prelates for the indulgence with which they have heard you. But, as we are assured that it is unlawful to defend a man suspected of heresy, we give you the same counsel as the Cardinal of Cambray. Submit yourself, therefore, and we shall take care that you withdraw in peace, after a slight penance. Should you refuse, you will arm the Council against yourself; while as for me, be sure that I would rather burn you with my own hands than endure your obstinacy. Therefore, be advised, and submit unreservedly to the authority of the Council."[13]

So failed the last human hope — so gave way the last inch of solid ground beneath the feet of the hapless prisoner. The Emperor abandoned him to his fate. It was a bitter moment; and it may be that the many hostile eyes fixed upon him so keenly saw the anguish of his soul. But they saw no sign of weakness.

"I thank your highness," he began calmly, "for the safe-conduct which you graciously vouchsafed to give me."

More he might have said, but some new clamour interrupted him. When it ceased, he still stood in silence, as one whose thoughts were elsewhere. For the moment he seemed to forget that he had not said all that was needful. It was his first, and last, lapse of memory while he stood before the Council.

The ever-faithful Chlum called out to him, "Master John, answer the second part of the king's speech."

Then he said firmly, in his quiet voice, "I did not come here, most serene prince, in order to defend anything with obstinacy. Let anything better, or more holy, than what I have taught be shown to me, and I am perfectly ready to retract."

By this time it was very late. The Council was adjourned until the next day; the prisoner was led back to his dungeon, and everyone went home.

---

[13] The perfidy of Sigismund toward Huss did not consist alone or chiefly in his violation of the safe-conduct. What both Huss himself and his friends felt far more keenly was that Sigismund, after having himself invited him to come to the Council, with the express promise not only of protection but of assistance and cooperation, condemned him with his own lips, and said before the Council that he deserved to be put to death as a heretic.

XIII

THE THOUGHTS OF MANY HEARTS

Unto the judgment-seat of Him who sealed me with His seal,
'Gainst evil men, and evil tongues, I make my last appeal.

The next morning Hubert came as usual to his lord for instructions. Dismissing his chaplain, Charlier, with whom he had been in conversation, the chancellor turned toward him and said, "I have no need of you today."

The colour mounted quickly to the brow of Hubert. Could he have heard from someone of what he had done on Wednesday? Yet he read no added sternness in that always stern and sorrowful face.

"Am I not, then, to write in the Council for my lord?" he asked.

"No, my son. That is otherwise provided for. Do not attend today."

To Hubert this command seemed impossible to obey. Never before had he questioned the chancellor's lightest word, but now he inquired with a look of great distress, "And why? Have I offended my lord?"

"You have not offended," returned the chancellor kindly, and his sad eyes rested, with an expression almost of tenderness, on his eager young disciple. "But you look tired. To such as you, the toil and confinement of these last days has been hard to bear. Where is now that pleasant-faced young brother who used to come and bear you company? Go to him today, and amuse yourself, as young men love to do. I command it."

His tender thoughtfulness touched Hubert to the heart. But he scrupled to accept it while there lay between them unconfessed the thing that he had done. He murmured a word of thanks; then added boldly, though with an effort, "My lord, I have somewhat to tell."

The chancellor, occupied with many affairs, thought this some mere matter of business, and said rather indifferently, "Speak on."

"Somewhat — that I fear may have been a wrong-doing," pursued Hubert with hesitation.

The chancellor looked at him more attentively and with growing uneasiness.

"Have you done wrong?" he asked quickly. He knew at least that Hubert was no tale-bearer; if he told of wrong, it would be of his own.

"My lord, that is what I know not."

"You know not? Have you been so ill-instructed?" asked the chancellor sharply. "This is a wicked city, full of snares; especially for the young," he added. "What have you done?"

"It is not so much a deed which I have done as words which I have spoken."

The chancellor's brow cleared. A youth of Hubert's impetuous character might well have spoken unadvisedly with his lips, and no great harm done after all. A wise master takes care not to know too much of what is said by his servants.

"Have you, by deed or word, committed a mortal sin?" he asked gravely.

"I have — not," said Hubert after a pause, during which he ran over in his mind the familiar list of the "seven deadly sins."

"Then I do not wish to hear what you have said or done. If there was wrong toward me, I forgive it."

"There was not, my lord," said Hubert, quickly, and in a tone which made the deep lines of the chancellor's face relax into a grave smile.

"If there was wrong toward others, or toward God, tell your confessor, and take the penance he allots with patience — in any case, tell your tale to him. Now, go in peace and enjoy your holiday."

He waved his hand, and Hubert was dismissed, his heart very grateful for the chancellor's trust in him, but his mind and conscience still unsatisfied. It was not that he cared the least for the severe penance he was sure to undergo, Charlier, his rival in the chancellor's favour, being confessor to the household. But he was intensely anxious about the prisoner who was to stand again that day before the Council; vibrating between sympathy and admiration for the man, and fear of incurring sin (or was it of displeasing the chancellor?) by making common cause with the heretic. *Was* he a heretic after all?

Hubert passed from the chancellor's cabinet into the outer room, where he was accustomed to write. There, on a desk, lay the chancellor's copy of the Vulgate, a huge, weighty volume. Hubert went over to it, and, having found with some difficulty the place he was in search of, stood reading.

He was still absorbed in his occupation when the chancellor came out. Thinking, perhaps, that he had been too sparing of spiritual counsel to the young soul committed to his charge, he laid his hand on the lad's shoulder and said kindly, "It is a good day which begins with the perusal of Holy Scripture. Do you understand what you are reading?' "

"No, my lord," said Hubert, as he turned and bowed.

"How do you read it?"

Hubert read aloud in Latin, " 'Blessed are you when men shall revile you, and persecute you, and shall say all manner of evil against you falsely, for My sake.' "

"That is a passage which presents no difficulty even to the unlearned," said the chancellor. "A child could understand it. You ought to know that it was meant for the holy saints and martyrs, who lived in the early ages of the faith."

"Might it come true of any man even now, my lord?"

"Doubtless. Of Christians who dwell among the heathen, in *partibus infidelium*."

Hubert's heart sprang to his lips, and found utterance before he knew.

"Oh, my lord, God forgive me if I sin; but I shall never hear or read those words again without seeing the face of that man who stood so calmly before all the angry Council!"

The chancellor started, not visibly, but inwardly. He had not liked the look in his young secretary's face the day before, especially when the prisoner was mocked or insulted; yet he had not feared anything so dreadful as this.

"You speak idly, and as one without understanding," he said, with grave displeasure. "Read the passage again: 'Falsely for My sake.' "

" 'Falsely' was it not, when never a word was proved against him?" cried Hubert, growing bolder. " 'For My sake!' That appeal of his to our Lord Jesus Christ seemed to make those Italians — of course it *must* be the Italians, my lord, and the Germans — more angry than anything else he said. Except, indeed, that word about Wycliffe. Was that wrong, my lord?"

"He would have his soul with his," said the chancellor with a deep sigh. "In truth, his soul — unless he repents — will likely be before long with the lost soul of John Wycliffe."

Hubert shuddered. All that was within him rose in revolt against the terrible word.

"But, my lord," he cried, "he holds Catholic doctrine; he loves and studies above all things the Holy Scriptures; his life is without spot or stain, his enemies themselves being judges; is he not, then, 'in the grace of God?' "

"My son, I perceive you are much in need of instruction. We must distinguish between graces of God, which are given to many (and to this unhappy man, I must own, in large measure), and the grace of God, which only the faithful have, and which even they have only as long as they are faithful. These, however, are among the deep things of God. Even the wisest of us cannot understand how it is that He denies many things to those who are thankful and would use them well, and yet gives them to the unthankful who yet fight against Him." He sighed again, and remained for some moments absorbed in thought; then continued, partly to Hubert and partly to himself, " 'It is undeniable that upon some who, like Judas, are to perish everlastingly, He bestows the grace of diverse virtues.' "

Hubert gazed at him with eyes full of wonder. "I thought," he said, "that to be good was to be in the grace of God."

"My son, 'there are faithless children and wicked servants, to whom, nevertheless, the Heavenly Father sometimes gives of the fat of wheat, and satiates them with honey out of the rock; even as some kings have sent to persons condemned to death meat from their own table.' Great spiritual gifts are to be found sometimes with the cursed and reprobate children, either to the increase of their damnation, or as a sort of transitory reward for their labours, as false and unprofitable. So they hear the Gospel, 'Take what is yours, and go your way.' But be not cast down, my son; these mysteries concern not simple souls like yours. Leave them alone, and occupy yourself with the duties and the pleasures befitting your condition."

He turned to go, but Hubert cried impetuously, "May I speak but one word more to my lord?"

"If you wish," he said, pausing, but half reluctantly.

"It is some three years now since a poor boy, overwhelmed with guilt and shame, stood before you. He had neither gift nor grace, nothing to recommend him save perhaps that he scorned a coward's lie. Yet you deigned to say that he was worth saving" (Hubert's strong voice quivered at the words), "and you saved him. Of how much greater worth in the eyes of God and man is he who is to be judged today, and who need not stand where he does now if he could lie or feign?"

The chancellor was moved. It was some moments before he could answer, then he said gently, "What I did for you, my son, that I have never regretted. As for the other matter, leave it in wiser hands. Think no more of this man, who is a dangerous heretic, and would turn the world upside down. Moreover, do not fancy that *I* can do anything for him. No man can save a heretic, if he will not save himself by timely submission and repentance. All that remains for us is to save others from the deadly infection of his teaching and example."

He went out, and Hubert presently followed him with a heavy heart. He spent the day wandering idly here and there, deriving neither pleasure nor profit from his enforced leisure. He would not go to Armand, not caring in his present mood to be talked to about the queen's ladies, or the Emperor's hawks, or to be taunted with the misdoings of the Holy Council. However, toward evening Armand came to him, as he was walking about the Stefan's Platz, in order to be at hand when the Council broke up, and to hear the earliest tidings.

Armand had with him a little old man dressed in a sad-coloured gown trimmed with rich fur, with a four-cornered cap, starched ruff, and sword by his side, and carrying a cane with a large golden head.

The brothers greeted, and Armand spoke of the eclipse. He had been at Petershausen at the time, and he gave a vivid picture of the terrors of Queen Barbe and her ladies.

"Surely it portends some great calamity," he went on. "But if it is the Emperor's glory which is to suffer eclipse, I know not. Or, more likely, that of the Holy Council, which *you* think is the sun in the heavens — eh, Hubert?"

"Hold your peace about the Council," said Hubert shortly.

But here the stranger struck in.

"I am a man of no account with you, gentlemen," he said. "Yet, if you listen, I can tell you that which will allay your idle fears. See your own shadow there, master squire; yesterday, just such a shadow fell, not on the sun, but on the earth, and that was what you saw. It had no more to do with the Emperor or the Council than with this cane in my hand."

Hubert looked at him in amazement.

"Good master," he said, "you are jesting with us. How can you expect anyone to believe such folly? It was the sun which was darkened, not the earth — I saw it with these eyes. There was a black veil drawn over the face of it."

But Armand, when the old man was not looking, glanced at him and touched his own forehead with a rapid, but very significant gesture. So Hubert heard his answer with pitying tolerance.

"You are not the first, young sir, nor will you be the last, to put the darkness in the heavens when it is at your own feet." Saying this, he raised his cap and moved away.

Then Hubert asked, "Who is that mad fellow?"

"That is Queen Barbe's Jewish physician, Dr. Nathan Solito. He used to belong to the pope, but he came to Petershausen after his flight. Oh yes, he is certainly a little crazy, but very clever and immensely learned — learned, too, in some things which are not quite lawful, you understand? The queen's court is a strange place, Hubert, and one hears strange things there. I have met people who do not believe in heaven, or hell, or purgatory, no, not in God Himself, nor even" — added Armand, as a carefully-reserved climax — "nor even in the devil! Our little doctor says there are many people in the world like that — Italians especially."

"I marvel the sky does not fall on them," cried Hubert indignantly. "Talk of heresy, indeed, after that! Why do you listen to such wickedness?"

"Oh!" said Armand complacently, as he arranged the lace ruffles on his wrists, and threw back his short velvet cloak to show his doublet of violet satin to advantage. "One listens to everything. Still, I don't want to scandalize a good churchman like you."

"I am not a churchman," said Hubert, for the hundredth time, "and I never will be!" he added, a new resolve taking form and shape within him at the moment.

"Now you are jesting. What is to become of you if you throw away the chancellor's patronage, after all? And yet, brother, you are far too good for that trade. But let that be; I have other hawks to fly now. Listen, there has been a letter from the duke."

"Of Burgundy?"

"Who else? He is coming here, not exactly to the town, but to yonder forest, where he will set up his tents, and live in camp like a soldier during the pleasant summer weather. He says he longs to hear the stags belling at night. But I think the music he really longs to hear is the voice of the Holy Council acquitting Jean Petit."

"He will never hear that," said Hubert. "On the contrary, Jean Petit will soon be solemnly condemned."

"I thought the Council had far different affairs on hand. But I need not tell you that we Burgundians rejoice greatly at these tidings of the duke. I have special grounds for joy, as my lord has sent me a kind message, intimating that he will need my services near his person. But, Hubert," he added, lowering his voice, "there is a matter on which I have often wished to ask your opinion. It is for one of my fellow esquires, who has put the case to me; he is dreading, for reasons of his own, the coming of his lord. Suppose now you had done your chancellor a disservice, which yet he never knew of, should you feel bound to reveal it, at the risk of losing his favour? And if — if an innocent person had been compromised, but could not now be righted, nor the wrong undone in any way — how would you act?"

At any other time Hubert would have said, "Tell the truth boldly." But now he was in a bitter, perverse mood, in which it seemed to him as if even truth availed not, either with God or man.

He answered briefly, "I cannot tell."

Armand, instead of pursuing the subject, observed that the place was filling rapidly, and remarked on the crowd of servants leading richly-caparisoned horses, and waiting for their masters to come forth from the Council; there were even some costly litters, draped and curtained with silk, for the older or more luxurious prelates.

"It will soon be over now," he said, "and time it was too. I am here to learn what has been done today, not of my own will, but as in duty bound, fulfilling the commands of a lady. Our Burgundians are bitter against this John Huss, though not the Bishop of Arras so much as that bass-born varlet, Pierre Cauchon, who I verily believe wants the man burned just that he may see it done. At Petershausen are some who wish him well, especially yonder little Jewish doctor, who cured him of a fever, and one fair lady whom I know. Thanks to the Jew and his stories, Demoiselle Jocelyne is as tender over this heretic as though he were a falcon with a broken wing. She says she would rather confess to him than to any bishop in the Council. Our friend Robert would be well pleased to hear her. By St. Catherine, there is Robert himself, I think, standing over yonder in the crowd! But he is in plain cloth hose and jerkin like a townsman."

It was Robert. Armand caught his eye, and beckoned him to join them as they stood on the steps of St. Stefan's Church.

"How is your Nänchen, good friend?" he asked, greeting him with far less constraint than did Hubert. "But what has become of the abbot's badge on your sleeve? Are you no longer with the Black Monks on the Island?"

"I am not, Sir. I have a boat now, and fish on the lake or the river. You see, it is but an idle way of life to bear arms when there is no real fighting to do; and the other calling, at least, is one of honest toil, whereby a man may help himself and his fellows."

Then, turning to Hubert with an anxious look, and pointing to the Franciscan House: "Master Hubert, have you been in there today?"

"I have not," said Hubert sadly. "But yesterday gave small hope of any end save one for the man you love so well."

Robert looked at him intently, with keenly inquiring eyes, which were soon lit up with a gleam of satisfaction. But he only said, "Then, Sir, you were there yesterday?"

"I was, and on Wednesday. Yesterday I heard, but did not see him. On Wednesday I saw, but scarcely heard him."

"How did he look, Sir?" asked Robert eagerly.

"Like a soldier sent on a forlorn hope, who is weary and sore wounded, yet will die unflinching where he stands," said the soldier's son with deep feeling.

There were tears in the eyes of Robert, and his hand moved instinctively toward that of Hubert. But the difference of rank — in those days so marked and definite — made him draw it back again. He only said, "Ah, Sir, I knew that good heart of yours would speak, if you only saw him. And I have never seen him since they took him to Göttlieben. On Wednesday morning they brought him back; and now he lies in the dungeon yonder. Good care they take that none of us shall come, even into the court outside of it."

Having said this, Robert moved away, with a brief farewell to the brothers, to speak to someone whom he saw in the crowd.

He had told Armand the truth, yet not all the truth, about his present calling. There was but one service which friends outside could render to the lonely prisoner, and in this they had not failed. During the greater part of his long and cruel imprisonment they had succeeded in keeping up communication with him, had supplied him with writing materials, had sent him letters, and received answers from him. But the task had been difficult and dangerous. More than once it happened that, in spite of the most anxious precautions, a letter was lost, or fell into hostile hands. A servant of Chlum's, named Vitus, had been the innocent cause of some misadventure of this kind. Chlum was very angry, and Vitus himself sorely discomfited; all the more because he knew that the story of his failure had reached the prisoner.

"I would not care for anything," said he, "if only Master John does not think I failed him in his need."

But Robert, who knew every man and woman in the town and about it, proved an active and efficient helper. He could do much that the Bohemians, as strangers, could not attempt. During the past three months his new fishing-boat had found constant employment on the Rhine, near the Castle of Göttlieben. And now that the prisoner was removed to the Franciscan House, it proved that Nänchen also could help in the work which they both had at heart. Among her acquaintances were certain poor, obscure women, "the keepers' wives," of whose lowly ministrations a hint has come down to us across the centuries.

At last, very late in the evening, the Council broke up. There was a great stir and confusion in the Stefan's Platz, as bishops, abbots, and doctors poured forth from the doors of the Franciscan House, many of them calling loudly for their servants, who with horses or litters, tried to get near them, and pushed and jostled one another in the crowd. Charlier, who, much to his own satisfaction, had been doing Hubert's work that day, saw Hubert and Armand standing together watching the scene, and crossed the Platz to speak to them. He rather liked Armand, and his sense of a petty triumph gained over Hubert made him more amiably disposed even toward the favourite, whom he considered as his rival.

"He is doomed!" he said without preface or comment. "All that remains now is to pronounce the sentence."

From Hubert there was neither word nor sign, but Armand cried out, "Doomed? What for?"

"Heresy," said Charlier. The one word was enough; speaker and hearers knew it meant death.

There was a moment's silence; then Armand asked in a mocking tone, which nevertheless it cost him an evident effort to assume, "*What* heresy, if you please, Sir Chaplain! That is, if an ignorant layman may presume to inquire."

"Diverse and manifold heresies. I cannot remember all, nor even half of them. Nor, if I did remember, could you understand, Master Squire; being, as you say, a layman, although doubtless not ignorant."

"Still, you might give me a specimen. Just for my own instruction."

"Ah, but where to begin? The business was interminably long; sooth to say, we were all tired out. Yet wait — I will try. Yonder man has said that 'Jesus Christ, not the pope, is the Head of the Church;' that 'the pope who lives not the life of Christ is no vicar of Christ, but a forerunner of Antichrist;' that 'the Church could subsist, if God willed it, without a pope at all, and still be governed by Christ, as indeed it had sometimes done.' This I do remember, perhaps the best of all, for the man's look and gesture come back to me as he added, 'But what do I say? Is not the Church even now without a visible head? And yet Jesus Christ does not cease to govern it.' "

"Wrong! Wrong there, at least!" Hubert broke in impetuously. "Jesus Christ cannot be governing the Church *now*, or such things could not be done in it."

Charlier turned and looked at him, all the bitterness of jealousy reviving in his heart. "You had better take care of yourself, Master Hubert Bohun," he said, and Armand added, "Hush, Hubert; let him go on."

He went on accordingly. "Another scandalous proposition was that about heretics, that they should not be corporeally punished. How grievous a heresy this is, the chancellor has proved long ago. Our heretic had the grace, or the prudence, to qualify it a little, though his meaning was plain enough throughout. Then a blasphemous article from one of his books was read aloud, in which he compared churchmen who caused heretics to be put to death to the wicked scribes and Pharisees in the Bible. At this, as was natural, the Council waxed furious. Never heard I such an outcry! I thought the roof would come down on us. The shout rings yet in my ears, 'Who — who are like them! Whom do you compare to the scribes and Pharisees?' 'Those that deliver over an innocent man to the secular arm,' said he in answer, more calmly than I speak now to you. Can you conceive such audacity?"

"*I* can," said Armand, with a dangerous quiver in his voice. "For I have heard how my father stood alone, and kept the bridge against a troop of Armagnacs. But go on, Master Chaplain. What followed?"

"Much that I cannot tell you now. For instance, his heretical proposition that popes and priests in mortal sin are not true popes and priests at all. But this, through the will of Providence, turned to his own undoing. For he must needs go on: 'Nor is a king in mortal sin a true king.' Whereat we all shouted, 'Call the Emperor!' for his highness being weary — and no wonder — had gone out upon the balcony. When he came in, John Huss was ordered to repeat what he had just said, which he did with his unfailing hardihood. I rather suspect we shall hear no more, henceforward, of the Emperor's protecting him.

"At last they had finished with reading the evidence; and the Emperor himself, the Cardinal of Cambray, and many others, began to urge him to abjure, and throw himself on the mercy of the Council."

"Did he?" asked Armand eagerly.

"Not he! With the greatest humility of manner, but the utmost arrogance of soul, he said that he could not abjure, as he had not held any heresy. He spoke so meekly, you would have thought he would yielded everything; yet he yielded not one hair's breadth. Moreover, by this time he was deadly pale, and shaking with ague. Though he is a heretic, someone in charity thought to give him a live spider, wrapped in a piece of linen, to bind on his arm."[14]

"So they had to let him go, I suppose."

"Not they. A great deal was done after that. He underwent a long examination about some doings at Prague, and other matters, which I cannot call to mind in detail. That clever Bohemian, Palec, came well to the front, and pressed him hard — I hope the bishops will remember to give that man a good benefice, or some other gratification. Our cardinal, too — rightly is he called "the hammer of heretics.' "

"And your great chancellor," asked Armand, "did not he take some part in the matter?"

"Strangely enough, indeed," Charlier confessed, "he was silent the whole time. He sat still in his place, looking grieved and weary. I believe he is wearing himself out; of late, I know he has slept but little. But there were plenty to speak instead of him, though few, or none, as able as he. John Huss was beset on all sides; one taking up the word as soon as another was answered — often before it. Such a cross-fire of accusations, questions, reproaches, I think no man ever stood before. How he stood it, and found an answer for all — ill and suffering though he plainly was — only the Evil One, whose servant I suppose he is, can explain. However, the thing is settled now. He abjures or he dies."

"Not that last, I hope," said Armand in a low voice.

"I should have better hopes of him," said Charlier, "if he were scornful and defiant, or proud and boastful, as heretics are wont to be. But what can be done with a man who is at once so quiet and so immovable? Even the Emperor could make nothing of him; though he condescended to argue. 'I pray and conjure of you,' said our heretic, 'not to constrain me to do what my conscience forbids me. As I have never held several of these articles, how can I abjure them? While as to those I have acknowledged, if any man will teach me better, I will readily do what you require.' "

---

[14] He was very ill all this time, and had passed the preceding night without sleep, in much suffering from toothache and headache.

"Then why don't they teach him better?" said Armand. "There is the whole Council, with all the collective wisdom of the Church, to do it."

"Under favour, Master Squire, you speak now as a layman. The Council has done all you ask, and all that beseems it. The Council has *informed* him that the articles are heretical, and that he must abjure them."

"What? Those that he has never held, along with those that he acknowledges?"

"That is only a subterfuge," said Charlier hastily. "He has held them all — and worse."

"I suppose the Council, being infallible, knows what a man holds and believes better than he does himself," returned Armand.

Not detecting the sarcasm, Charlier answered approvingly, "You are right, Master Squire, and your understanding puts to shame others who have had larger opportunities" — with a glance at the angry face of Hubert. "The decision of the Holy Council is final, and cannot be questioned without mortal sin. For, being the sacred depository of the light and guidance which has been promised to the Church, it is infallible, as my lord the chancellor has so ably proved."

"Infallible, and all-powerful too," pursued Armand. "There is the secular arm, the Emperor and all his hosts, behind it. Strange indeed will it be if the Holy Council — with all the wisdom of the Church and all the power of the world — cannot vanquish this one poor priest, alone and helpless, ill and in chains!"

"Of course it can vanquish him, and will. If he is converted — and God knows I hope he may be — it will triumph in his salvation, if not, in his condemnation and punishment. Thus, as the holy doctors say, God is glorified, even in the wicked. Bohun, are you coming home to supper? It was late enough on Wednesday before you saw fit to make your appearance. But, indeed, you do for the most part what you please."

Hubert granted him no answer.

As soon as he was gone Armand turned to his brother and said, "As to this man's opinions, I cannot profess to judge of them one way or another. Though I own that, to a layman like me, it seems passing strange that the Council should fall upon him for attacking the power of the pope, when they have just deposed that same pope themselves; yes, and could find nothing bad enough to say of him. However, I admit their triumph over *him.* Now they want another, over this poor priest. He too must lie in the dust at their feet; he must say and swear that black is white at their bidding. Being a brave man, it will go hard with him. But he will have to do it — Hubert, what ails you?"

"This," Hubert broke out fiercely, "that I think there is no more justice or mercy anywhere on earth or in heaven. It is not the Council only — say what you will of the Council now, Armand, I stand silent and ashamed! But the chancellor even — the chancellor himself — thinks that all this is right and necessary, and according to the will of God! Yes, the will of God, Armand — think of that! He says that God deals thus with men — that He is hard and pitiless, and what *we* at least would call unjust! And who should know God if he does not — holy doctor and saint as he is? I can make nothing of it; it is all dark — dark to me, like that strange darkness yesterday morning."

Armand was terrified at the strong passion that surged through his brother's soul — a passion he was incapable of sharing, or even of understanding, although in his own way he was angry enough with the Council. He said, "Perhaps, after all, the chancellor does not know God any better than you or I, or even than yonder man they call heretic knows Him. But, Hubert, I pray of you take care; you will get into trouble with this wild, reckless talk of yours."

"Take care of what? I wish I was done with it all! I wish I was a soldier like my father, or like you, Armand; I would go back to France and fight. They are fighting there now, it seems. That, at least, would be something a true man might do. But, I suppose," he added sorrowfully, "I suppose the darkness would be there too."

XIV

A MONTH OF PEACE

The Saviour stood by him in pain,
Nor left him in sorrow forlorn,
And mitred blasphemers and tyrants in vain
Heaped on him their hatred and scorn.
He was meek as the innocent child,
He was firm as the storm-stricken rock.

— Song of the Hussites.

I bless Thee for the light that dawns e'en now upon my soul,
And brightens all the narrow way with glory from the goal.

Now let Thy good word be fulfilled, and let Thy kingdom come,
And in Thine own best time, O Lord, take Thy poor servant home.

It has been said that a great calamity — and the same may be true of a strange, unique destiny — "stains backward through all the leaves we have turned over in the book of life; all omens pointed to it, all paths led to it." He whom the Council that day judged worthy of the death of fire had borne on his hand, probably for more than thirty years, a scar of fire.

One winter evening, in Prague, a group of boyish students were gathered around the hearth where the logs were blazing. A "poor scholar," the widow's son from Hussenec, who earned his bread by singing in the church choirs, sat among them. As usual, he was absorbed in his book, which told of the martyrdom of St. Lawrence. Suddenly he stretched out his hand to the flame and held it there unmoved and silent, until a companion pulled it away by force. Questioned as to the reason of this extraordinary conduct, he answered simply, "I was only trying if I could bear any part of what St. Lawrence did."

The ardent boy grew to manhood, as strongly moved by heroic deed or purpose, as careless of self, sometimes perhaps as impulsive. Amidst abounding iniquity, he wore "the white flower of a stainless life." His contemporaries have drawn his portrait for us in words that deserve to be remembered for their beauty as well as their truth, "His life glided on before our eyes from his very infancy, so holy, so pure, that no man could find in him a single fault. O man, truly pious, truly humble — who was conspicuous by the lustre of such great virtues — whose desire was to despise riches and succour the poor, even to the experiencing of want yourself — whose place was by the bedside of the unfortunate — who invited by your tears the most hardened hearts to repentance, and soothed rebellious spirits by the inexhaustible mildness of the Word! Yours it was to extirpate vice from every heart by the old remedy of the Scriptures, which sounded new from your lips."[15]

But these labours, in which he delighted, were not the only ones to which God called him. Along with His word, which He put into his lips, He laid upon his heart a great burden; it was the same burden which He laid upon His prophets of old — upon Isaiah, upon Jeremiah, upon Ezekiel, when His Spirit "lifted him up," and took him, and caused him to behold the "wicked abominations" which were done in the house of the LORD. These men had great honour, but they had also great sorrow; to them the word of the LORD was "like a fire" which burned within them, bringing agony as well as illumination. The cry, "Woe is me!" was often on their lips. So has it ever been, so will it ever be, with those who are called to look down into the awful depths of human iniquity, and to confront the world's sin with God's message of "righteousness, temperance, and judgment to come." The sin against which John Huss was especially raised up to protest, sat enthroned in what called itself the Church, though in reality it was the world. To have exposed the avarice and the licentiousness of the clergy was the real crime of this man, of whom they said in their cruel hate, "When you saw a thief, you consented with him, and have been partaker with adulterers." "Woe, then, to me," he cried, after one of his scathing pictures of the evils that were eating out the heart of the Church — "Woe, then, to me, if I do not preach against these abominations! Woe to me, if I do not lament; woe to me, if I do not write!"

The sight of horrible and hideous evil is apt to awaken a fierce wrath and indignation, a passion of rage and scorn. Even the tenderest heart (and the rather because of its very tenderness) may be lashed

---

[15] From the letter addressed by the University of Prague to the Council of Constance.

into fury, tossed with wild storms of anger, by this bitter "hate of hate." It was not Dante alone who

> *Hated well because he loved well,*
> *Hated wickedness that hinders loving.*

The Bohemian Reformer "hated well' — not the sinners, indeed, but the sin. In his fiery and vehement denunciation of the evils which wrung his soul, he may perhaps have sometimes forgotten that the wrath of man works not the righteousness of God.

But, with the burden laid upon him, a great gift was given him. It is the best and greatest gift that God has for any of us — that for which all other gifts were well and wisely counted loss. He "knew Christ, and the power of His resurrection, and the fellowship of His sufferings." "For in writing these things," to use his own words, "I confess nothing else to have moved me thereto but only the love of our Lord Jesus crucified, whose wounds and stripes (according to the measure of my weakness and sinfulness) I desire to bear in myself; beseeching Him so to give me grace that I never seek to glory in myself, but only in His cross and in the most precious ignominy of His passion, which He suffered for me." They who have seen this vision of the cross of Christ cannot choose but turn away from all else and gaze upon it; and as they "gaze they advance, and are changed into His likeness, and His Name shines through them, for He dwells in them."

Those advance the farthest, and draw the nearest to Him, who follow Him in the path of suffering. Or rather He draws nearest to them. John Huss (innocent though he believed himself of the charge of heresy) had come to Constance, not knowing what would befall him there, and prepared to suffer for Christ's sake "temptation, reviling, imprisonment, or death." Only praying, and asking his beloved congregation to pray for him, that he might abide steadfast, and be found "without stain." But even the stainless crystal may take a finer and yet finer polish from the master's hand. During those long months of cruel imprisonment, all that there might have been in earlier days of mere human wrath and passion more and more passed from him; and "love, joy, peace, long-suffering, gentleness, goodness," grew and strengthened day by day.

When, after the final examination, he was led forth from the Hall of Council, one man from the Emperor's suite arose and followed him out. He was John de Chlum. Putting the guards aside, he drew near and grasped the fettered hand of the prisoner with a few brief words of hope and comfort. It was only a little thing to do — a moment's work — yet will it not be forgotten when the King shall say unto them on His right hand, "You have done it unto Me." It was tenderly and gratefully remembered, as long as the tired heart he sought to cheer could feel any earthly joy or pain. "Oh, how comforting was the touch of the hand of the lord John de Chlum unto me!" wrote John Huss. "He who was not ashamed to reach forth the hand unto me, the miserable heretic, in fetters of iron, cried out upon by all men."

Nor, indeed, could any earthly lot have been more "miserable" than that of the condemned heretic when, weary and exhausted, and so ill "that he could scarcely stand," he reached his gloomy dungeon once more, and was left there alone, face to face with his awful doom, the terror and anguish of the death of fire.

What the first hour of conflict and agony may have been we do not know, and we will not guess. Let silence hide, and darkness veil it. Yet very soon, the darkness passed, the silence was broken. After a brief interval, we see the prisoner again, and the pen is in his hand.[16]

Already thoughts of self had gone from him, and the concerns, the interests, the welfare of others occupied that large and tender heart. All he had suffered, all he had yet to suffer, had faded into distance. He saw no more the furious Council, the dungeon, the flaming pile; he saw instead that dear "chapel of Bethlehem" where he had so often preached the Word of God, and the well-known, beloved faces of the flock to whom he ministered. Believing, then, that his time was very short, that the next day, or the day after, might bring the end, he hastened to write to them his parting words of counsel and farewell. In that letter "no one was forgotten; great and small, poor and rich, priests and laymen, masters and servants, teachers and scholars," each had some special word of kindly remembrance, of exhortation or encouragement. All were entreated to serve God faithfully, each in his own vocation; and to keep and "stick fast to" the truth he had taught them out of the Holy Scriptures. But they were only to follow him in as far as he followed Christ. He was keenly conscious that he saw "through a glass darkly," that

---

[16] The letter quoted above was written, probably, on June 10. Of the letters of Huss in general, L'Enfant, the able and impartial historian of the Council of Constance, speaks thus: "neither Catholic nor Protestant, nor, I dare to say, neither Turk nor Pagan [could refrain from] admiring the grandeur and piety of his sentiments, the delicacy of his conscience, his charity toward his enemies, his tenderness and fidelity toward his friends, his gratitude toward his benefactors, but above all, a greatness of soul, accompanied by a modesty and a humility quite extraordinary."

others might understand the things of God more perfectly than he did. "I desire," he said, "that if any man, either in public sermon or in private talk, heard of me anything which is against the faith of God, that he do not follow the same. Albeit I do not find my conscience guilty of any such thing. I desire of you, moreover, that if any man at any time have found in me any levity in words or acts, that he do not follow the same, but pray God to pardon me." He asked their gratitude for the Bohemian lords who had stood by him so nobly, especially for Duba and the well-beloved Chlum. He beseeched their prayers for their king and for their queen (whose confessor he had been), and also for the King of the Romans (Sigismund, who had just abandoned him so basely), "that God in His mercy would abide both with them and with you, both now, and from now on in everlasting life."

He added, "I write this letter in prison, with my fettered hand, expecting my sentence of death tomorrow, but with a full and entire confidence that God will not abandon me, nor suffer me to deny His truth, or to confess what false witnesses have maliciously alleged against me. When, with the help of Jesus Christ, we shall meet again in the most sweet peace of the future life, you shall learn how merciful God has been to me, and how He has supported me in all my temptations and trials. I know nothing of Jerome, my faithful and beloved disciple, except that he, too, is held in cruel chains, awaiting death, like me, on account of his faith. Alas! It is by our own countrymen that we have both been delivered into the hands of our enemies. I ask for them your prayers. Remain, I entreat of you, attached to my chapel of Bethlehem, and endeavour to have the Gospel preached there as long as God will permit. I trust in God that He will keep that holy church as long as it shall please Him, and in the same give greater increase of His word by others than He has done by me, a weak vessel. Love one another. Never turn anyone aside from the truth of God, and watch that the good be not oppressed with violence."

But the next day did not bring the sentence of death that he expected; it brought instead a form of retractation which he was invited to sign and live. This was studiously mild and favourable: it had evidently been drawn up by a friendly hand — we know not whose, but it must have been by one of the leading members of the Council probably a cardinal.[17] Ever sensitive to the least touch of kindness, Huss began his firm though gentle refusal with these words,

---

[17] Supposed, with good reason, to be the Cardinal de Brogni, Bishop of Ostia, the nominal president of the Council, a man of amiable character, who evidently felt for Huss, and showed him what kindness he could.

"May the most wise and righteous Father Almighty deign to grant eternal life and glory to my 'father,' for the Lord Jesus Christ's sake. Reverent Father I am very grateful for your pious and paternal favour."

The "father," whoever he may have been, responded by a really tender and beautiful letter, in which he addressed the condemned heretic as his "most loving and beloved brother." He sought to remove his scruples by every argument he could devise; even saying that if his retractation were a perjury, the sin would not be his, but that of those who required it. And he concluded with these remarkable words, "Still greater contests will be given you for the faith of Christ." Those three days before the Council evidently had not been without fruit.

Everyone, friend and foe alike, was anxious now to save him. The Emperor, more solicitous perhaps for his own honour than for the life of the heretic, made repeated efforts to induce him to retract. Even those who had been most bitter against him sent or came to him with arguments and earnest entreaties. Many, no doubt, were really touched by his courage and patience; others were concerned for the credit of the Council to which, as they truly foreboded, the execution of the cruel sentence would not contribute.

He answered all with the same calm firmness — unboastful, unassuming, unwavering. He made no display now of the eloquence, the intellectual acuteness, the argumentative powers that had "electrified a nation." His gentleness and absence of self-assertion might almost have made him seem weak, only that he showed himself very strong. Even in his inmost heart he never appears to have hesitated. This was the more remarkable from the utter loneliness of his position. Not merely the loneliness of the dungeon, where iron bolts and bars shut him out from all human aid and sympathy, but the far more terrible loneliness of spirit in which this one solitary man stood out against the Church of his day. It should be remembered that he was not a Protestant, who could regard that Church as apostate and anti-Christian, and fall back for sympathy upon a great cloud of witnesses who had resisted her tyranny in the cause of a purer faith. He knew no other visible Church on earth; he had never dreamed of separation from her; no, he counted it his greatest honour to be one of her priests, he prized and administered her sacraments; he had never consciously departed from her teaching. He regarded the Council that condemned him as her highest authority, speaking with her voice, "a power ordained of God." But two things with him were of higher authority yet — conscience and the Word of God. The voice of God in the heart of man, the voice of God in the written word, must take precedence even over the voice of the Church. When this bade him do what those clearly forbade, he did not hesitate; looking beyond the Church, he grasped the hand of Christ Himself, and went forth with Him "outside the camp" — although he esteemed it the camp of God's Israel — "bearing His reproach."

Thus, without knowing it, John Huss became the champion and the martyr of those two great principles of Protestantism — the supremacy of Holy Scripture as the rule of faith, and what is rather inadequately called the right of private judgment. Like all rights, it is duty on the other side, and may be defined in the words of Huss himself, "Faithful Christian, seek the truth, hearken to the truth, learn the truth, hold the truth, defend the truth, even unto death."

It was doubtless with the hope of shaking his resolution that the Council allowed four weeks to elapse between his condemnation and the end.[18] The long, slow days as they came and went found him always firm; yet it may be not always joyful. Hours there must have been when the shadow of death lay heavy on his heart, when fearfulness and trembling took hold of him. But he found refuge then — where in our own hours of anguish we find refuge now — beneath the cross of Christ. Thinking of the bitter cup which Christ had drunk for him, he found strength and patience to take his own. "Certainly," he writes, "it is a great matter for a man to rejoice in trouble, and to take it for joy to be in divers temptations. A light matter it is to speak and to expound it; but a great matter to fulfil it. For our most patient and valiant Champion Himself — knowing that He should rise again the third day, overcoming His enemies by His death, and redeeming His elect from damnation — after His last supper was troubled in spirit, and said: 'My soul is heavy unto death,' of whom also the Gospel says that He began to fear, and to be sad and heavy. Who, being then in an agony, was strengthened by the angel and His sweat was like drops of blood falling on the ground. And yet He, notwithstanding being so troubled, said to the disciples, 'Let not *your* hearts be troubled, neither fear the cruelty of them that persecute you, for Me you shall have with you always.' Whereupon these His soldiers, looking upon the King and Prince of Glory, sustained great conflicts. They went through fire and water, and were saved, and received the crown of the Lord God. Of this crown I trust steadfastly that the Lord will make me a partaker, with all those who love the Lord Jesus Christ, who suffered for us,

---

[18] Huss was himself surprised at this delay: he says in one of his letters, "And as touching death, God knows why He defers it, both to me, and to my well-beloved brother, Master Jerome, whom I trust will die holily and without blame; and I do know also that he does suffer now more valiantly than I myself, a poor sinner."

leaving us an example that we should follow in His steps. O most merciful Christ, draw us weak creatures after Thee, for unless Thou draw us we are not able to follow Thee! Give us a strong spirit, that we may be ready; and although the flesh is weak, let Thy grace go before us, go with us, and follow us, for without Thee we can do nothing — much less encounter cruel death for Thy sake. Give us a bold heart, an upright faith, a firm hope and a perfect love, that we give our lives patiently and joyfully for Thy Name's sake. Amen."

His prayer was heard, and before long the cry of joy broke forth from his heart — "The LORD is my light and my salvation; whom shall I fear? The LORD is the strength of my life; of whom shall I be afraid?" And again, "The gracious Lord God has been, and is, and I hope will be, with me to the end." Yet the light and joy that came from heaven did not exclude a tender longing for human sympathy. To his dearest friend, John of Chlum, he proffered the request that he would be with him at the end. "Oh, you, the kindest and most faithful friend! I entreat of you to grant me still this, not to depart until you have seen everything consummated." It was the excess, not the defect of friendship that he feared from Chlum, so he wrote to his other friends, "Do not permit the lord John of Chlum, that loyal knight, my dearest and best friend, my other self, to expose himself to danger through love for me." And once more, in the last letter he ever penned, "For my sake, although perhaps dead in the body, do not allow any loss to happen to the lord John, the faithful and worthy knight, and my good benefactor." Then, as if he thought this plea not strong enough, "I entreat of you, for the Lord's sake."

His letters were full of loving, tender thoughtfulness for all his friends. Each was mentioned by name, and had some special message of counsel or comfort, and very often of gratitude for kindness received. A great number of names — many of them obscure and humble — which otherwise would have been hopelessly engulfed in oblivion have been carried down to us in this way, embalmed in the fragrance of words like these: "Dear and faithful Master Christian, the Lord be with you."[19] "Petr" (Mladenowic), "my most faithful and constant consoler and comforter." And again: "Petr, dearest friend, keep the

---

[19] This was a priest named Christian Praschatic, who well deserved a loving message. For he actually came from Prague to Constance at great risk to himself, though Huss had entreated him not to encounter the peril, on the desperate chance of a farewell interview with his friend. Fortunately this was during the imprisonment in the Dominican House, and, probably through the kindness of Robert, he attained his object. As may be guessed, the meeting was a very touching one. Praschatic was cited before the Council and imprisoned; but his friends succeeded in procuring his liberation.

fur coat for a remembrance." His few possessions he shared thus among his friends, carefully considering the needs or the tastes of each. His last letter is a series of such messages, with no word of himself in it but this: "I also entreat all to entreat the Lord God and His holy grace for me; we shall meet together before long in His holy presence. Amen."

At rest about himself, he found rest also about those aims and hopes which to men like him are far more than life, since they are "the things that life lives for." He had striven, and toiled, and suffered to lead men's souls to Christ, and to cast out evil from the House of God; for the reformation of the Church, and for the triumph of the Gospel of Righteousness and Peace. Yet, *as a Reformer*, he had wrought no deliverance in the earth, neither had the inhabitants of the world fallen. His "half-day's work" was done now: he was to die, and to die in a lost battle with the forces of evil. Standing face to face with death, he meekly accepted the lesson of his life,

I shall pass, my work shall fail.

"I have laboured in vain, and spent my strength for nought, and in vain." It was God's will for him, and it was well.

But "heaven is for those who have failed on earth — *failed so*." Will heaven even for them, have a greater joy than to stand by the side of the triumphant Christ, and to see Him do, by others, the work that dropped undone from their own feeble hands? To John Huss there was given so sweet a foretaste of this joy that in after times men came to think

there were prophet words on those lips in death.

It has been often said that he foretold the coming of Luther, and the dawn of the great Reformation. Yet he was no prophet, as he said himself, save in so far as he heard the mystic voices of those three great and true prophets, Faith, Hope, and Love — which bear continual witness within us of the final victory of truth and right, and the glorious manifestation of the sons of God. This was all that he foresaw, and it was enough.

"I ask you," he wrote to Chlum, "to expound to me the dream of this night. I saw how that, in my church at Bethlehem, they came to raze and put out all the pictures of Christ, and did put them out. The next day, I arose and saw many painters, who painted and made more fair pictures, and many more than I had done before, which pictures I was very glad and full of joy to behold. And the painters, with many people around them, said, 'Let the bishops and priests come now, and put out these pictures.' Which being done, many people in Bethlehem seemed to me to rejoice, and I, awaking herewith, laughed for joy." This vision he himself expounded afterward, "I am no prophet, and yet I firmly hope that this image of Christ, which I engraved in men's hearts at Bethlehem, where I preached His word, will not be effaced; and that when I cease to live, it will be far better portrayed, and by far mightier preachers, to the great joy of the people. And I, too, when I awake in the Resurrection, shall rejoice thereat with exceeding joy."

Christ "measures nearness to Himself by the keeping of His commandments," Huss had written in earlier days; and now he found His commandments "not grievous" — even that one which says, "Love your enemies."

All the insults and injuries of Michael de Causás, who, not content with accusing him falsely before the Council, set spies about his prison to cut off his communication with his friends, and boasted to his keepers in his hearing how soon they would burn him, drew from him no harder word than, "Poor fellow." He could forgive him heartily, and pray for him "most earnestly." But Palec, his own familiar friend in whom he trusted, had caused him far more bitter pain. Not all at once did this pain pass into the perfect peace of a Christ-like forgiveness. At an earlier period of his imprisonment Palec came to his dungeon, when he lay very ill and in great suffering, and began to reproach him cruelly with his so-called heresies, and especially with that one which he had really never held, the denial of Transubstantiation.

Huss turned upon him with a flash of natural indignation, "Oh, Master Palec, is this your greeting unto me? Truly, you sin grievously herein. Behold, tomorrow I shall die, or perhaps when I arise I shall be led forth to be burned; and what thanks, think you, will they give you in Bohemia for this?"

But afterward he feared "lest he should seem to hate him." Yet in this too, before the end, God gave him the victory. He forgave Palec entirely; and he found a unique and characteristic way of showing it. The Council, with strange inconsistency, allowed him a confessor, and he made choice of Palec for the office. He was willing to kneel at *his* feet, and to take from *his* lips the assurance of God's forgiveness of himself.

Palec, very naturally, declined the task: but he came once more to the prison, and not now to taunt or to threaten. This time the "greeting" was very different; it was Huss who spoke first.

"Palec," he said, using the familiar address of the old days, "I have said some things that must have given you pain. Especially, I called you a 'fictor' or 'concocter.' Will you forgive me?"

The heart which had been hardening itself so long was touched and melted now. Palec burst into tears. As soon as he could recover himself sufficiently to speak, he began to implore his injured friend to retract, and to save himself.

Huss explained to him with great gentleness the reasons for his refusal, saying to him, "I pray you, tell me your mind. Put yourself in my place. If you were called on to abjure what you had never held, or what you knew to be true, would you do it?"

"It would be very hard to do," Palec acknowledged. What further passed between them we cannot certainly say. All we know is, that Palec left the prison utterly broken down, and weeping bitterly.[20]

The last day Huss spent in prison, July 5, witnessed another parting, which stirred far deeper springs of feeling. An unexpected joy came to him; but it tried his self-command more terribly than much pain. He was brought from his dungeon to the refectory, to meet a deputation from the Emperor, sent to him, as a last hope, with a still easier form of retractation; he need only abjure those articles which he confessed to be his own. On entering the hall he saw four bishops, members of the Council, and with them — Duba and Chlum. The Emperor had begged these Bohemians to go and try what they could do with their countryman.

He could scarcely restrain his emotion when Chlum drew near and spoke to him, no doubt with a warm pressure of the fettered hand.

"Dear master, I am not learned; I cannot help you by my counsel; you must therefore decide for yourself. You know whether or not you are guilty of the things of which the Council accuses you. If you are conscious of any error, do not hesitate, be not ashamed to yield. But if not, I cannot advise you to sin against your conscience. Do not leave the path of truth from any fear of death."

Not the hostile eyes of the bishops, not the long, long habit of self-control, which had stood such cruel tests, availed to keep back the tears these words drew forth. His heart recognized the true nobleness

---

[20] Upon the refusal of Palec, the Council sent Huss a confessor of their own choice, a monk and doctor. This man, whose name we do not know, heard his confession with great kindness, and gave him absolution at once, without requiring him to retract, or even imposing any penance upon him.

of his friend, who trusted him so utterly, and would not add to his burden one appeal or entreaty which might make it heavier.

"Generous lord — oh, my noble friend!" he began; but his voice failed, and he broke down completely. When be regained his composure, he said, "If I knew myself to have taught anything erroneous, I would humbly retract it, God is my witness. I always desire to be shown better reasons from Scripture, and if they are shown me, I will retract what I have held until now."

Encouraged, no doubt, by what they took for a sign of weakness, the bishops began to press him. "Do you want to be wiser than the whole Council?" they asked.

"I do not want to be wiser than the whole Council," he answered meekly. "I pray you, give me one of the least of the Council to instruct me with better and stronger Scriptures, and I will yield at once."

"See how obstinate he is in his heresy!" said the bishops as they withdrew. Between the friends no farewell seems to have been exchanged; but no doubt they looked in each other's eyes, and silently gave each other tryst beyond the grave and gate of death, in the kingdom of the Father.

The farewell words, which he could not or did not speak, Huss had already written in the solitude of his prison to his dear friends and "gracious benefactors," the Bohemian lords. It was his last charge to them that they should give their service "to the Eternal King, Christ the Lord; He casts off no faithful servant from Him, for He says, 'Where I am, there also shall My servant be.' And the Lord makes every servant of His to be the lord of all His possession, giving Himself unto him, and with Himself all things; that without all tediousness and without all defect he may possess all things, rejoicing with all saints in infinite joy. Oh, happy is that servant whom when his Lord shall come He shall find watching. Happy is that servant who shall receive the King of Glory with joy. Wherefore, well-beloved lords and benefactors, serve you that King in fear, who shall bring you, as I trust, now to Bohemia at this present by His grace, in health, and hereafter to an eternal life of glory. Farewell, for I think this is the last letter I shall write; who tomorrow, as I suppose, shall be purified in the hope of Jesus Christ."

Not far were the golden gates, and the vision of the King in His beauty, from the man who wrote thus. But no one can be too near heaven for "a work of lowly love," so he added, "I pray you have no suspicion of faithful Vitus."

XV

A MONTH OF CONFLICT

The black night caught me in his mesh,
Whirled me up and flung me prone.

— R. Browning

Meanwhile the perplexed, angry heart of Hubert Bohun sought for rest and found none. All his ideas of right and wrong, all the beliefs and principles upon which his soul rested, had been rudely shaken. He might, indeed, have endured the dethronement of the great Council from the rather fictitious eminence to which it had been exalted by his youthful enthusiasm. But what pained his heart far more deeply was his unacknowledged, yet most real, disappointment in the great chancellor. He would still have died for him, have refused to listen to the slightest word against him, have borne any torture rather than speak such a word himself. And yet — what would he not have given to find in him some movement of Christian charity, or even of human relenting, toward the hapless prisoner in the Franciscan House?

Yet, terrible as it was to Hubert to think the chancellor could be wrong, it was far more terrible to him, in this instance, to think he could be right. The words which he had spoken to him on the morning of the last audience, haunted him like a hideous dream. Was God indeed what he described Him then? Did He deal so with His servants? Surely a man so good and so learned must know. But if those dreadful words were true — why, then Hubert despaired within himself of ever being really religious. That is to say, in the chancellor's own sense of the word. He could be religious enough in Charlier's sense, or in that of the monks of Rouen; he could say prayers, and fast, and do good works by the score. But the chancellor often said that without the love of God there could be no true religion; and Hubert did not think he could ever love God if God was like that!

He had always thought of the Son of God as the Judge, rather than as the Saviour. Once, and once only, had a gleam of light, shining from the chancellor's words, revealed for a moment the Redeemer — the loving and merciful One, who, though He was his Judge, had paid the great debt for him. The revelation had so far influenced him that from then on he had tried to do right, to be pure and good, and noble, chiefly, indeed, for love of the chancellor, yet dimly comprehending a higher aim and purpose. If anyone had asked him, he would have said in the language of chivalry — far more congenial to him than that of the Church — that he meant to be true man and loyal servitor to the Lord Christ.

But why then did the Lord Christ keep silence when an innocent man, suffering cruel wrong, made solemn appeal to Him? Hubert now no longer doubted the innocence of the alleged heretic. He had reached this conviction — as we usually reach our deepest and strongest convictions — not following link by link a single and definite chain of reasoning, like the proof of a proposition in Euclid, but drawn irresistibly by a hundred cords of evidence. The man's stainless life and conversation, his devout and holy words, his noble bearing, above all, his courageous truthfulness, pleaded for him both with the heart and the reason of Hubert. He knew that all this time he was calmly facing a horrible death, from which one word would deliver him, rather than stain his lips with that one word — a lie. He thought that in his place he might do the same, if strong enough. But then he would do it in pride and scorn, hardening his soul to a temper of fierce defiance. This man was not defiant, but — so he heard on all sides — gentle, patient, forgiving. Much did Hubert wonder what upheld him thus. Much he wondered, too, what he thought about himself and his own doom. What did he expect when all was over and his enemies had done their worst upon him? The Council condemned him; the Church cursed him and would soon cast him out solemnly; and Hubert could not conceive of any spiritual help or comfort coming to a man apart from the Church. Worse and more terrible still, Christ Himself was silent toward him. Did he, then, see nothing before him after death but a great blank, a land of darkness?

There were men in the world — Armand had told him so — who thought there was nothing else to see. Hubert began to turn this thought over in his mind. The longer he did so the more natural and probable it seemed to him. At first he had rejected it with horror; but the horror passed, and the thought remained. In his weary wanderings of soul in search of rest, he began to draw perilously near what looked like a place of rest, but was in truth only a shifting quagmire, which has swallowed many a wanderer up quick, and the pit has shut her mouth upon him forever. It is a mistake to think that only in our own age, and under the pressure of our own perplexities, has "the ever-breaking shore, that tumbles in the godless deep," sounded its dirge in the ears of men. The dark doubt of everything, beyond that which we can see or touch, which comes to souls whose innermost beliefs are shattered and nothing given them in their room, is as old as Job and the prophets, as old as Pharaoh and the pyramids, as old as human strife, and sorrow, and agony. From the beginning, the great mysteries have been there, encompassing all mortal life; yet for the most part it is, and ever has been, some special personal anguish, some violent perverting of justice seen or suffered, which arouses men to face them, and to explore their depths.

While Hubert, all unknown to those around him, was sinking deeper and ever deeper in the Slough of Despond, Armand's life was in marked contrast. He came one day to see his brother, and with an air of great mystery, which covered, though it could not conceal, an almost unbounded exultation, asked him to come with him into the fields. When they had reached a quiet spot, he told his story. Demoiselle Jocelyne had "broken gold" with him.

"I have sworn to be her true servitor forever and ever," he said, "and she does not scorn my homage. Of course, I am yet but a simple esquire, but the duke will find a way for me to prove my manhood and win my spurs. And then — we shall see."

He did not breathe a whisper of that shadow of the past which lay between him and his betrothed, invisible to her, but not to him. Indeed, it was fast fading from his own sight, by dint of not choosing to look at it. He was cultivating, and with good success, the convenient power of forgetting. He would never have been allowed to forget, if he had once told his story to Hubert. Perhaps it was as well, so he thought, as things turned out, that he had not. Still he felt that Hubert might have sympathized with him more heartily, and congratulated him more warmly on his good fortune. But to rejoice with those who rejoice, when we ourselves are perplexed and sorrowful, is a very difficult attainment, and it was far beyond poor Hubert's reach just then.

So the time wore on, until Friday, July 5. On that day a hush of expectation seemed to brood over the town; people stood about in groups, talking low and eagerly and doing little business, save in and near the cathedral, where there were great stir and excitement. Carpenters and other tradespeople were hurrying to and fro, bearing costly stuffs for decoration, or carrying boards, planks, and seats. As one of the officials told Hubert, "the whole place was being turned out of doors, and made over again." For the next day was to witness a solemn general session of the Council, rendered illustrious by the presence of the Emperor, and by all else of pomp and state and glory that the world could bring to lay at the feet of the Church.

Outside the Göttlingen Gate, in that part of the Brühl where Hubert had witnessed the eclipse of the sun, other preparations were being made that day; but of these, men did not greatly care to speak.

Hubert received his orders that evening from the lips of Charlier. It afforded great satisfaction to the senior chaplain to act as the chancellor's mouthpiece for the benefit of the insolent young favourite, who had sometimes passed into the chancellor's presence when his own kinsman had been excluded.

"You are to attend the session tomorrow, Master Hubert Bohun," he said; "but you are not required to take notes. You are to remain quiet in your place until the sentence of the Council is read upon the affair of Jean Petit."

Hubert started; he had not supposed *that* business would come on tomorrow. He said so, and in a tone that showed his great surprise.

Charlier was rather pleased that he did not affect any superior information, but frankly acknowledged his ignorance. So he graciously condescended to enlighten him. He said that the vague and general condemnation of the doctrines of Jean Petit, which was to be pronounced the next day, was perhaps as much as could be expected from the Council; but it was very far indeed from being as much as the chancellor desired.

"The Duke of Burgundy has been extremely free with his gold, and many of these prelates," he added with a shrug of his shoulders, "well — well, what would you have? You know, Bohun, there are plenty of fat benefices changing hands here every day; and the fingers must be well oiled to let them slip through with ease. But all these things grieve our good chancellor to the heart; as *I* can see, who am his kinsman, and know him really. Indeed, of late, though you doubtless have not observed it, he has been very sad. However, to return to your business. Here is what you have to do, and see that you make no mistake. As soon as the judgment is read, one of the notaries of the Council will hand you a copy. You must then immediately leave the place and come here; take a letter which you will find ready on the table in my lord's cabinet, seal it up safely, together with the paper you have received, address the packet to the Rector of the Sorbonne, and hasten with it to the house of Lebrun, the French goldsmith, opposite the Rhine-Thor-Thurm. He has a confidential servitor just going to Paris; and he has promised me, to oblige the chancellor, that the man shall wait, and take with him this packet. It is of great importance; so you must be sure to give it into the hands of Lebrun himself, and to get a written receipt from him. Do you understand?"

"I understand well enough. What shall I do if Lebrun is not there?"

"He will be there. You must not give the packet into any hand but his."

"Can I see the chancellor tonight?"

"No, you cannot. No one can see him — not even I. Today, as you know, has been a fast; and tonight he gives himself to prayer and meditation."

Hubert said no more. He understood quite well that the chancellor wished to make it impossible for him to go to the Brühl. But it grieved him that he should think this precaution necessary.

"He ought to have known me better," he thought.

Two men, that night, were kneeling in earnest prayer, within a few paces of each other, and very probably at the same time. If only by some strange chance they could have knelt *together*, they would have made a marvellous discovery. They would have found that the same words fitted both their needs, and the same faith and hope animated both their hearts.

"O Divine Jesus, draw us to Thyself," the martyr prayed in his dungeon.

Less confident, perhaps, yet with as true a longing for the light and joy of His presence, the great chancellor took up the word, "Let the holy will of God be done. If He wills it, let Him give me here a foretaste of His sweetness; if He wills, let Him deny it; my heart is ready for either."[21]

But not on earth were those two noble souls to recognize each other. One of them not only took his place among the judges of the other, and gave his voice against him, but added a keen affliction to his bonds by the severe sentence of condemnation which he passed on those articles of his which had been submitted to him.

"If I live," said John Huss, "I will answer the Chancellor of Paris; if I die, God will answer for me at the Day of Judgment."

But God did not wait until the Day of Judgment to answer for His servant.

---

[21] From Gerson's *Treatise on Spiritual Prayer*.

XVI

DESPISING THE SHAME

He stood transfigured there
In the smile of God.

In the gray dawn of the next morning Hubert rose and went forth to watch and wait for the opening of the cathedral; for he knew the crowds would be enormous, and the session was to begin with High Mass, as early as six o'clock. An intense longing possessed him to see again the face, to hear again the voice of the man who had stirred his soul to its depths. He entered the church among the first, and, being strong and agile, climbed into the embrasure of one of the windows, which afforded him a seat commanding an excellent view. Presently he discerned in the crowd below him, and much pushed and jostled thereby, Master Ulrich Schorand, the priest of St. Stefan's, who had married Robert and Nänchen. He offered him his hand, and with some difficulty helped him up to the window, where by close sitting there was room for two.

Now they could both survey the cathedral at their ease. At the upper end, near the high altar, which was duly prepared for the celebration of Mass, there was a stately decorated seat or throne for the Emperor, and lesser seats for those great princes of the empire who were to accompany him. Lower down, there were chairs for the cardinals, archbishops, and other princes of the Church; behind these, benches for the bishops and abbots; and lower still, in what was called the third rank, places for doctors, delegates of universities, and other members and officials of the Council. About the middle of the nave there was a kind of scaffold with a table or altar upon it, where the vessels used in the celebration of Mass were laid ready; and beside them, upon a post, hung the full canonical vestments of a priest.

While Hubert was wondering what these things could mean, cardinals, bishops, and doctors were pouring in rapidly and taking their places with haste and eagerness. With and after them came a crowd of spectators, filling the church to suffocation. Then at last came the Emperor with his splendid following. Schorand plucked Hubert by the sleeve, and bade him observe the Elector Palatine, who occupied one of the lower seats beside the Emperor; a stately figure in his electoral crown and ermine, with the golden apple and cross of the Holy Roman Empire in his hand. "His highness represents the Civil Power," said Schorand, "to whom, by the ecclesiastical sentence, the heretic is to be made over for execution. You will go, of course, to the Brühl, and see the end?"

"I will do no such thing," said Hubert, shuddering. "I have seen the like in Paris, on the Place de Grève."

"As for me," said Schorand, "I shall see all that is to be seen. But let us betake ourselves to our prayers. The Mass is beginning."

"But they have not brought in the — the condemned."

"Don't you know the Canon Law? The presence of a heretic would pollute the Holy Sacrifice. They are making him stand outside the door until the Mass is over."

The organ pealed out, and the white-robed choristers began their chant. Music, incense, the elevation of the host, the bended knees and heads of the worshipping crowd, all lent impressiveness to the scene. But one at least did not worship, though he went through the outward forms. Hubert never prayed now; what was the use of it? he thought. He spent the time in looking around him at the grand and solemn assembly, and trying to read the faces of the men — the foremost men of the age — who composed it. He saw a few noble, ascetic, spiritual faces, like Gerson's; many keen, intellectual faces, belonging to learned doctors and schoolmen; plenty of astute, clever faces, the faces of men of affairs, statesmen and diplomatists, so numerous among the great churchmen of the Middle Ages. There were faces which were commonplace, scarcely arresting the eye; faces which were kindly, even benevolent and others which were not kindly at all, but hard, cruel, sensual. Some of these, especially among the Italians, were beautiful in form and feature, though with a dark and evil beauty. Others were coarse and brutal, and in these today there was a hateful joy. As typical of the rest, Hubert singled out that of the Burgundian, Pierre Cauchon. The look of eager, delighted anticipation in his small, cold, cruel eyes, the smile on his sensual lip, made him hate and curse him from his heart. He could not have cursed him with a more bitter curse than that which actually came upon him — the execration and loathing of all future ages. For we know him now as the infamous Bishop of Beauvais, to whom the betrayed innocent Maid of France put up her piteous cry, "Bishop, I die through you."

At last the *Ite missa est* pealed through the cathedral. The door was opened, and, guarded by four men-at-arms, the prisoner was led in. Every eye in that vast assembly was fixed upon the man who stood face to face with death. His pale features wore a firm and resolute air, like that of a soldier going forth to battle, but also a look of hope, as if the soldier knew the battle was his last, and after it would come victory and rest. He was dressed in a long black gown or coat, with a doublet of the same beneath it, fastened at the waist with a girdle having a silver clasp. The chains had been taken from his hands, but his feet were fettered still. He came up the middle of the nave, where the scaffold was, and stood, calmly facing his judges. The spot where rested those fettered feet is still remembered, still pointed out in the pavement of that old church. It is "marked evermore with white" — always white, always dry, the legend says, however dark or weather-stained the surrounding stones may be. There are things which keep the glory of their whiteness undimmed through the centuries, and will keep it still when years and centuries shall be no more.

Presently he was commanded to ascend the scaffold; and having done so, he knelt upon it in silent prayer. Meanwhile the Bishop of Lodi occupied the pulpit, and was delivering a long, and, as most of his hearers thought, an eloquent sermon. Hubert did not listen, until Schorand whispered in his ear, "My Lord of Lodi wants to have the anti-popes burned, and not John Huss." In truth, the sermon was little else than a diatribe against the schism and its authors, and a panegyric of the Emperor.

A significant proceeding followed. A solemn proclamation was read, threatening with the major excommunication and an imprisonment of two months anyone, from the Emperor downward, who should dare to interrupt, by word or act, or by any sign, even the slightest, of applause or disapproval, the proceedings of this assembly, "convoked by the inspiration of God."

Then rose up in his place the papal auditor, and demanded the condemnation of the works of Wycliffe, from which a very long series of propositions sentenced as heretical was read aloud. This tedious business over at length, he proceeded to demand the condemnation of the works and the person of John Huss. He read out all the evidence which had been brought by witnesses against him, and all the articles which had been extracted, either truly or falsely, from his books, with the addition of thirty quite new ones never heard of before.

. . . the Bishop of Lodi occupied the pulpit, and was delivering a long, and, as most of his hearers thought, an eloquent sermon.

At first Hubert's attention wandered, but all his soul sprang up to listen when he heard the prisoner ask leave to answer for himself. "Now," thought he, "I shall know all. Now I shall learn the secret of his strength."

He bent forward so eagerly that Schorand caught and held him fast, lest he should lose his balance and fall. But — could he believe it? — could it be true indeed that permission to speak was denied him? Hubert could hardly accept for this the evidence of his senses. Yet he could not be mistaken, for he heard the prisoner ask for this last grace, plead for it earnestly — even passionately, saying with uplifted hands, "Only hear me now — and afterward — deal with me as you will."

"Hold your tongue!" cried the cardinals. "We have already heard you sufficiently;" and one of them, turning to the guards, bade them silence him by force.

"This is horrible!" said Hubert to himself. "To speak out once before he dies is the last right of every man, though he may have no other right left him upon earth. At least his fellows owe him this — to listen to his voice, to let him tell them, if he can, the meaning of his life, before they send him away from their midst into the great silence of eternity."

Schorand touched him again, and whispered, "Was not that proclamation at the beginning well thought of? Look at those angry faces down yonder! Look at that knight with his hand on his sword! I'm sure, but for the 'major excommunication' and the strong guard beside, we should have had trouble here today."

Hubert's eyes followed those of Schorand, and rested with momentary surprise on the flushed and angry face of his brother, who stood with other gentlemen in the crowd near the door. But he soon forgot him.

Meanwhile the work went on. Hubert now tried only *not* to listen; save when the prisoner — forbid him as they might — still threw in a trenchant word of comment or contradiction. One of the new "articles" never heard of before laid to his charge, on the authority of a certain doctor, the blasphemy of calling himself a Person of the Godhead. No wonder Schorand muttered, "If they knew *that* of him, why did they seek for anything else?"

Never while he lived could Hubert forget the look of pain and horror in the face of the slandered man, and his quick, indignant cry, "Name that doctor! *Who* said that of me?"

His appeal to Christ was again brought forward as a crime. He clasped his hands, raised them solemnly to heaven, and said, "Behold, O blessed Jesus, how Thy Council forbids what Thou Thyself hast ordained and practiced. Thou didst commit Thy cause into the hands of Thy Divine Father, leaving us an example, that we might have recourse to Him and to Thee. Yes," he added, turning to the audience, "I have maintained, and I maintain still, that the best and safest appeal is to Him who cannot be corrupted, over-reached, or deceived."

He was accused of despising the excommunication of the pope.

"I did not despise it," he said. "I sent my procurators to Rome, where they were ill-treated and cast into prison. It was therefore that I determined, of my own free will, to appear before this Council, under the public faith and protection of his majesty the Emperor here present." As he spoke thus, he looked steadfastly in the face of the Emperor, and a crimson blush mounted to the imperial brow. That blush was well remembered. "I should not like to blush as Sigismund," said another Emperor, when pressed to violate another safe-conduct a hundred years later. So Luther lived — to do the work we know.

At last they came to the reading of the two sentences — the first condemning his books to the flames; the second delivering over his person to the secular arm. Against the first he protested; to the second he listened patiently, kneeling and looking up to heaven. He rose when it was ended; but, after a brief pause, knelt down again.

"Lord Jesus Christ!" he began.

He will appeal to Him once more, thought Hubert, or perhaps, he will summon his judges to meet him at His bar.

He did neither. "Lord Jesus Christ!" he said. "Pardon all my enemies, I pray Thee, for the sake of Thy great mercy. Thou knowest that they have falsely accused me — pardon them, for the sake of Thine infinite mercy!"

Hubert's strong frame quivered with a choking sob. But the tears that might have followed it never came; for the burst of laughter and mockery with which the prayer was greeted dried them at their source. The cup of his indignation was full now.

"I must go," he said, "I can endure this no longer." He had quite forgotten his special business there.

But Schorand laid a detaining hand upon him. "What are you about?" he asked, in an earnest whisper of remonstrance. "Don't leave your place. The best of the show is coming on now."

"What more is there to see or hear? They have condemned and sentenced him unheard. He will take his secret with him to the grave."

"What more? Why, the degradation, of course. One does not see every day the degradation of a priest. Although, God knows, one sees priests enough who deserve it."

Now Hubert saw the meaning of the sacred vestments laid ready on the scaffold. As directed, the martyr put them on, gravely, reverently, and with some sadness in his look and manner, as one who fulfils for the last time a dear familiar office. When he took the alb, he said some words, beginning "My Lord Jesus Christ . . ." but Hubert could not hear the rest.

Then he stood erect upon the scaffold, a tall and noble figure, robed in priestly white, and holding in his right hand the sacred chalice. And now, once more, he was summoned to retract; and mercy, on these terms, was offered to him. He looked away from the prelates who surrounded him, and addressed himself to the crowd beyond. His voice at first was low, and broken with emotion, but gathered strength as he proceeded. "These lords and bishops," said he, "exhort and counsel me to confess that I have erred. But I stand here in the presence of the Lord God, without whose reproach and that of my own conscience I can by no means do it. For how then could I ever lift up my face unto God? Or how could I look upon the faces of that great multitude whom I have taught and instructed in His word, if, through me, those things which they thought most true should have become uncertain and doubtful unto them? No; I will not thus offend my brethren by esteeming this vile body more than their health and salvation."

At these dauntless words the soldier-blood of Hubert's knightly ancestors mounted to his brow. He scarcely heard the cry of the bishops, "See how obstinate he is in his malice, how hardened in his heresy!" But he waited breathless for what was to happen next.

The martyr descended from the scaffold, and was led up the church to the high altar. As he passed along, Hubert saw with wonder that a change had come over him. He looked like one whose warfare was accomplished; who had done forever with conflict and with strife. From now on no man could trouble him. In his face there was the shadow of a great peace.

Seven bishops had been appointed to the task of degrading him. The first of these, the Archbishop of Milan, came forward, and took the cup out of his hand with the words, "Accursed Judas, who has forsaken the covenant of peace, we take from you this cup of the blood of the living God, which you have profaned."

A gleam of light — such light as never came from star or sun — illumined the pale face of the martyr as he answered, "Yet shall I drink of it with Him this day, through His grace, in His kingdom."

"Christ *has* heard him, then!" Hubert cried in rapture.

"Hush!" said Schorand and others near him; but in the extreme tension and excitement of the moment the slight interruption passed unheeded. To Hubert a new thought had come, flooding his soul with impassioned hope. This man, abandoned and cursed by all, because he refused to utter a falsehood, had reached up beyond Council and Church and pope, until his hand touched the right hand of Christ Himself, in the heaven of heavens. Christ had answered his appeal; and in some strange, incomprehensible way was with him even now.

Meanwhile the painful scene went forward. Alb and amice, girdle and stole, all the insignia of the priestly office — things in his eyes infinitely precious and sacred — were taken from him, each one with separate curses and revilings. Even the worn fingers were scraped, where the anointing oil had been put at his consecration. Once he said, "For the sake of my Lord Jesus Christ I willingly bear all these mockeries;" but for the most part he stood in patient silence, still with the same radiant calm upon his face.

At last came the effacing or "violating" of his tonsure. A strife arose between the bishops whether for this purpose they should use a pair of scissors or a razor. As they wrangled long and angrily, the martyr said, turning to Sigismund, "See, they cannot agree, even in their cruelty." Finally the advocate of the scissors gained the day, and the thin hair was roughly cut in the form of a cross.

"It should have been the razor," observed Schorand. "Nevertheless, that will do. It cannot efface his Orders, for Orders are indelible; but it renders him infamous forever, and incapable of performing any ecclesiastical function."

"*Infamous*?" Hubert repeated. "Well, at least it is done now!" And with a sigh of relief he buried his face in his hands.

It was *not* done yet. Once more the martyr's voice rang through the crowded church. "For the sake of my Lord Jesus Christ, who wore for me the crown of thorns, I wear with joy this crown of infamy."

Hubert looked up. A hideous paper crown, an ell in height, and covered with horrible pictures of devils, had been put on his head. To Hubert it only seemed a crown of glory. No throb of indignation, no thrill of pity stirred his heart. He felt nothing, save that he was looking in the face of a man who saw the face of Christ.

Then came the final words of malediction. "And now the Church has nothing more to do with you. We give over your body to the fire, your soul to the devil."

"Into Thy hands, most merciful Christ, I commend this soul, which Thou hast redeemed." As the martyr said this, with his eyes raised to heaven, Hubert thought he must have seen there what the first martyr saw in the far-off ages of faith.

"Go, take him," said Sigismund to the Elector Palatine; and he, laying aside the golden apple, came forward and received the prisoner at the hands of the Council. Then he gave him over to the chief magistrates of Constance, who were present, with the words, "Take John Huss and burn him as a heretic. Take from him neither coat, nor clasp, nor shoe, but burn him as he stands, with everything that is upon him."

More than a century after this, the descendant of that prince lay dying, childless, the last of his race. He said it was God's judgment for that day's work; the curse had never departed from their house since his ancestor delivered God's servant to death.

And yet, neither Council nor Emperor, neither prince nor burgomaster, had hurt God's servant at all. Nothing more could hurt him now.

Hubert, with his eyes still on that calm face, thought of the Brühl, and the deed that presently was to be done there. For one instant a horror of great darkness blacker than the eclipse he had witnessed on that very spot swept over him. But it was gone before he knew, and instead, like the rays of the returning sun, there flashed across his soul, "The LORD is my light and my salvation; the LORD is the strength of my life." He understood those words now. And he

131

learned, in them, that "secret" he had longed so passionately to hear from the lips of the dying.

Thus the martyr passed from his sight; going forth to his doom with a joyful countenance and a firm and steady step. Absorbed as Hubert was, he scarcely noticed that the auditor of the Council had ascended once more to his place, and had begun to read something aloud about the "troubling of states," and "the killing of tyrants." It never dawned upon him that this was the expected sentence upon the affair of Jean Petit; until, when the reading was ended, he saw someone trying to attract his attention and holding up a folded piece of paper. Finally this paper was passed to him, with much difficulty, over the heads of the crowd. Thus he was recalled to the sense of his duty, which, in fact, he had utterly forgotten until then.

"I must do it this time," he said to himself, "for I was trusted. This time, but never, never again!"

"Where are you going?" asked Schorand, seeing him move.

"I have business; but I will be back in time to the Brühl."

"To the Brühl? I thought you said nothing would induce you to go there."

"All is changed now. I have no fear left for him. I must look on his face again."

He slipped quickly down from his place in the window, but Schorand called after him, "Wait an instant, and give me a hand, I will go too. So shall I be in time for the burning of his books in front of the bishop's palace. I want to see how he will take that."

Hubert turned again, with a sudden flash of indignation in his eyes; but he restrained himself, and without a word helped Schorand down. His strong young shoulders pushed a way for them both through the crowd.

Moreover, as the paper which he held up, conspicuously showed that he had real business, people gave place to him, and some of the guards helped him out. At last he stood once more in the bright July sunshine, under the cloudless sky. But he only paused for a moment to make a rapid calculation from the position of the sun that it must now be about ten, or perhaps "eleven of the clock." Then he dashed at full speed across the Münster Platz, and through the crowded streets to the chancellor's house. One thought alone filled his soul; to despatch his necessary work, so that he might go to the Brühl in time to see what the end would be, and how God would deal with His servant who trusted Him.

XVII

A LIFE SAVED

So (he) did not see the face
Which then was as an angel's.
— *Idylls of the King*

In a few minutes Hubert emerged from the chancellor's house with the sealed packet in his hand, and, seeking the least frequented streets, tore madly along, caring little whom he jostled or thrust aside. Never, even in Constance, had such crowds been seen before. The whole population of the city seemed to be out of doors, as well as the vast concourse of strangers the Council had brought together. The men were mostly armed, and there were troops of soldiers everywhere, beside the guard of nearly a thousand appointed for the safe-keeping of the prisoner. The phantom of a wild hope flickered across the excited brain of Hubert. Were the Emperor and the Council afraid of a rescue? Was a rescue possible? Might it be attempted? What were those gallant knights with whom he had gone to the Emperor a month ago doing? If only he might stand once more beside them now and strike one blow in this cause, welcome then the death of a soldier!

He might have known that, against such overwhelming odds, the desperate courage of a handful of Bohemian knights would have availed nothing. But he could not know that the best and bravest of them all was keeping down his indignant heart that day with his "dear master's" words of counsel and of peace. Chlum knew well that he would not have him fight; his last charge to him had been, "Serve the Lord Jesus Christ quietly at home — whom to serve is to reign."

At last Hubert reached the goldsmith's shop opposite the Rhine-Thor-Thurm, but he found it shut and barred; indeed, most of the shops in the town were shut that day. It seemed deserted also. Not until he thundered angrily three times at the door did a young apprentice, who looked as if he had been asleep, open it suspiciously a little way and inquire his business.

Hubert explained, and said he must see Maître Lebrun himself.

"That you cannot," said the lad. "For the Queen — a plague on her whims and fancies — had to send for him this morning to Petershausen, to show her some new trinkets from Paris. As if they would not keep until another day! He took with him all the men he could muster to guard the jewels. So, for my sins, I am shut up here to keep watch and ward, while all the town is making holiday."

"Thank God, brother Frenchman, that you have neither act nor part in such a holiday as this," said Hubert. "When do you expect your master?"

"He ought to be back by this time. Can you not give me the packet? He said he thought you might come during his absence."

"I wish I could; but my orders are absolute. I will go across the bridge and meet him."

Hubert was so far fortunate that when he reached the head of the old wooden bridge he discerned the man he sought on horseback, and already half-way across. A reasonable person would have stayed where he was and quietly awaited his coming; but Hubert that day was not reasonable. He could not keep quiet anywhere. He pushed his way through the dense crowd upon the bridge — all going toward the town — in the hope of thrusting his packet into the hands of Lebrun, and telling him he would return later for the receipt.

It was a difficult task, but at last he succeeded. The master was on horseback, the stout serving-men who guarded him and his treasure with their staves were on foot. Hubert, who was naturally mistaken by them for a daring robber, got more blows than one before he could attract the attention of Lebrun. But at last he showed him the packet, and entreated breathlessly that he would oblige the Chancellor of Paris by forwarding it, as he had promised to do.

"One would think it was a matter of life and death," said the goldsmith, vexed at being stopped at such a spot, and in such a way. "Yes, I will do the chancellor's pleasure, and with goodwill, for I and mine have been ever good Armagnacs, as he knows. But my lord had no need of such headlong haste. My man cannot go until tomorrow. Never was the town in such a state; the Duke of Austria's tournament, when the pope ran away, was nothing to this Burning."

"Nevertheless, take the packet; I will come back later for the receipt."

Lebrun took it hastily, his horse growing restive with the crowd and the noise. "Stand aside, Master," he cried to Hubert, "there are other horsemen coming after us." Then to the crowd, "Have a care, good people. Keep quiet, or there will be mischief done here."

Relieved at having so far performed his errand, Hubert sprang aside. As he did so, he felt the timbers of the old bridge shaking beneath his feet. There was a low parapet, against which he leant for an instant. Just then a little boy, in a gray jerkin and flat cap, leaped up, and stood upon it close to him, apparently to get out of the crowd. "Take care, my lad!" cried Hubert, though without turning around to look at him. "Take care, or you will fall over!"

Too late! The boy lost his balance, and with a great cry fell down into the river. Hubert was after him in a moment. He threw himself from the parapet sheer into the water, seized the boy with one hand by his stout cloth jerkin, while with the other he clung to one of the many crossbeams which strengthened the wooden supports of the bridge.

The child at first struggled in his grasp; but Hubert called to him — in German — to be quiet; and he made a really brave effort to obey. But meanwhile the beam to which Hubert was clinging, being rotten with age, gave way. He slipped into the water — caught at another beam — with a great effort reached and grasped it, but in so doing gave his arm a violent wrench. In a voice choked with pain he called again to the boy, "Hold on to me — for I can hold you no longer. Clasp me around the waist."

The boy did as he was told; and Hubert just managed get his sound arm around the beam. But, disabled as he was, it was hopeless to think either of swimming to the shore with his burden, or of climbing up again to the bridge by the woodwork. All he could do was to hold on, and shout for help. Surely, in that crowded place, help would come to them immediately. He called aloud, with all his might, and bade the boy do the same.

No help, no answer came. All were moving toward one spot, absorbed in one purpose. Probably no one heard; certainly no one heeded. Once and again Hubert raised his voice — in vain. The current was strong — the beam to which he clung was slippery with wet and slime — and he was in terrible pain. The drops of anguish were on his brow, and his strength was failing. Would no one hear, would no one answer? Was his last hour come — his and this child's? He tried to look up — the blue sky was over him, he could even see the shadowy white of the distant Alps. The well-known words of the Psalter surged through his brain — "I will lift up mine eyes unto the hills, from whence comes my help." No — not from the hills — from above the hills, from above the stars and sun — from Christ Himself. Christ — to whom His martyr called, and He heard him — " 'My Lord Jesus Christ,' that was what he said," thought Hubert. "Christ heard him; He will hear me too." So a strong cry went up from his heart, "Jesus, Lord — My Lord Jesus Christ, help and save us!"

Still praying thus he grew fainter. His mind began to wander; he thought himself in the Brühl, and even confused the anguish he felt with what was being suffered there by another. But still he held on. To himself it seemed that he was holding on thus with failing strength, but steadfast purpose, to the Lord Christ, the martyr's God, who would save them yet.

Suddenly the boy called out to him, "Master!"

"Yes — I hear," said Hubert, with an effort.

"Master," said the boy again, in broken words of imperfect German, with quick, short gasps between, "we will both be drowned. Better save one. I will let you go. I am not afraid to die. The water does not hurt — oh, *not like fire!* Only tell my father . . ."

"No — no!" cried Hubert, roused effectually by this. "Hold on bravely still. God will hear us."

Another silence — then the boy cried out joyfully, "A boat! A boat!"

Hubert heard, as if in a dream, the splashing of the oars; but there was a mist before his eyes; he could not see. Presently he was conscious of relief: the boy's weight no longer dragged him down; and yet he was not afraid for him; he knew he was saved.

Then he was aware of a voice, a woman's, almost a girl's, which said to him, "Oh, Master Hubert, do not faint! There is no one here to help but me and Fritz, my young brother."

"No — no! I am strong," said Hubert, with the new strength of hope, as he tried with his feet to find the boat, which was now close to him. He soon felt it beneath him, though as yet he dared not let go his hold of the beam. However, the slight sinewy arms of a lad of fifteen gave him effectual help, and at last he lay safe, though exhausted, in the little boat. The boy he had saved was there already, lying at the other end. The lad Fritz held one of the oars; the other was in the small but capable hands of Robert's Nänchen. Already they were pulling to the shore, and until they reached it no one spoke a word.

Then the rescued boy rose up, and stood shaking out his damp, dark locks.

"I thank God and you, Sir, for saving me," he said to Hubert; "but I fear you are greatly hurt."

Hubert opened his weary eyes and looked at him. Surely he knew his face — where had he seen it before? Nänchen he knew well, and stretched out his hand to her with a murmured word of thanks.

"Where is Robert?" he asked, without thinking; but the next moment he was sorry for the question.

All the great joy of having saved a life — perhaps two lives — went at once out of Nänchen's face, and she answered very sadly: "Oh, Sir, you know!"

He did know.

"How many — how long have we been in the water?" he asked. He was about to say, "How many hours?" but checked himself.

"Not many minutes, Sir, I think; but I cannot quite tell. I heard your cry, for I happened to be at the waterside. I ran everywhere to get help; but all the men who live near us are away, and those from beyond the bridge would not stop, or listen to me. So at last I found Fritz; and we put out in the little boat. Thank God, Sir, that we were in time. Will it please you and the little lad to come to our home to rest and to get dry clothing? It is close at hand — just within the gate."

Hubert thanked her, but said he would rather go home. His soul was still bent on his purpose; and he hoped, from her words, that he might reach the Brühl in time, after all.

But when he stepped on shore he found he could scarcely stand.

"Master Hubert, you must come with me!" said Nänchen. "Your face is white as marble. Where are you hurt?"

"My shoulder — but it is nothing."

He was glad, however, to lean on Fritz, and to follow Nänchen through the gate, and across the broad path by the river to the modest lodging which she and Robert called their home. She led her guests up a steep and narrow staircase into a comfortable room, with furniture of plain, unpainted wood, but spotlessly clean. A fire was burning on the hearth and apparently some cooking was going forward. But she would not let Hubert linger here; she brought him at once into a smaller chamber beyond.

"Will it please you to change your clothing, Sir?" she said. "This room belongs to our lodgers, two English priests, who are out — like the rest. But plenty of their spare garments are lying yonder; and they would make you kindly welcome to the loan of them. Sit down upon the bed, Master, and Fritz shall come and help you, while I attend to the boy elsewhere. Fritz, come here, and wait on Master Hubert."

The help of Fritz was very necessary. However, with his assistance, Hubert managed to get his dripping garments exchanged for dry ones; then he came, or rather staggered, back into the keeping-room, and sank on the seat Nänchen had placed for him by the fire. He was ready to faint, and his arm was very painful. But just then he only cared for pain and weakness because they spoiled his purpose.

"Too late! It is too late!" he moaned, bowing his head in bitter disappointment. "I shall see his face no more!"

On the table there was a flask of wine, which Nänchen had just fetched from the nearest hostelry. She poured some into a cup and was about to give it to Hubert; but the rescued boy, who was lying on a settle, dressed in clothes much too large for him, sprang up and took the cup out of her hand, saying, "Please let me do it; he saved me."

Then he presented it to Hubert. "Dear, kind friend," he said, "you must drink it. It will do you good."

Hubert experienced the curious impression, so familiar to most of us, that exactly the same thing had happened to him before. But it is not given to most of us to find it rooted in fact, as he did.

"I was offered a cup of wine somewhere," he said dreamily, "and it was by *you*. Where was it? Who are you? Let me think!" Then the whole scene flashed back upon his memory. He stood awaiting the Bohemian lords in that house in St. Paul's Street, with Fidelia, and Petr Mladenowic and an eager, dark-eyed boy.

"Panec Václav, the son of Chlum!" he exclaimed aloud. "I know you now. Thank God! Thank God!" He covered his face in deep emotion. "Thank God!" he said again. "He knew I would have given my life to save His servant. It could not be — but instead, He has let me risk it, to save the son of his dearest friend."

Then there came a mist before his eyes — all things grew dim and dreamlike, were about to vanish from him altogether. No! Once more, for a moment's space, all things grew clear again. He was standing in the crowded church, gazing on the grand, calm face, lit with that "joy, strange and solemn, mysterious even to its possessor," which he had seen in it that day. And as he gazed the martyr turned to him, and bent on him an expressive look of recognition and of thanks.

"For the sake of my Lord Jesus Christ, and for me, you have done this," Hubert thought he said. Then he neither thought nor knew anymore. He was unconscious.

XVIII

CROWNED

They that have seen thy look in death,
No more may fear to die.

When Hubert recovered consciousness, he was lying on the settle. Nänchen, Fritz, and Václav were beside him; an older woman, Nänchen's mother, was there also. They had drawn up the settle near the seat where he was, and managed, not without much difficulty, to get him laid down upon it. A mixture of strong and most disagreeable odours showed that they had been trying to restore him by various methods in vogue at the time, though neither very pleasant nor very efficacious. When at last she saw him stir and open his eyes, Nänchen murmured a fervent "Thank God!" and put wine to his lips. He drank a little, and felt revived; the colour began to return to his face.

"Good, good," said the old woman encouragingly. "Now is the time for your strong soup, my daughter. Give him some of that, but carefully, little by little."

Nänchen brought the soup, which was excellent, in a pewter cup, so well polished that it shone like silver. But Hubert turned from it with a shudder. By this time he remembered everything.

"I cannot eat or drink today," he said.

"So said my Robert this morning before he went forth. 'Don't be vexed with me, Nänchen,' these were his words, 'but I cannot break bread today until I know that he is eating bread in the kingdom of God.' That is why I made the soup for him, that when he comes back . . . but when will that be, I wonder? Woe is me, but it is a long, long day! It seems like half a lifetime. And no one comes to tell us what is happening yonder."

"What hour is it now?"

"That I cannot tell you, Sir. Most days I can guess the hour right easily. But this is like no day I have ever known before. I know not if it be midday, or afternoon, or nearing the sunset."

"It is sunset already," broke in Václav, who was standing at the window. "Look yonder, over the houses! The sky is red."

Nänchen went to the window, and looked, but turned away with white face and quivering lips, "*That* glow is from no setting sun," she said.

Hubert raised himself, stood upright on his feet, then, in spite of pain and weakness, knelt down. "O God," he prayed, "have mercy on Thy servant. Be with him now in his agony."

Nänchen, her mother, and Fritz knelt with him and prayed; but little Václav stood still by the window, looking from one to another with awestruck, wondering eyes. He did not understand. The old woman told her beads, and said Paters and Aves aloud, the others prayed silently. Václav would not interrupt them. He looked out again, and watched the strange, fitful red that came and went in the sky. As he watched the truth dawned on him. With a child's piteous, broken-hearted wail he turned away. That cry startled them all, and they rose up.

"Poor child!" said the old woman compassionately. "Nänchen, we ought to take him home to his parents."

But Nänchen, who knew who he was, shook her head, and murmured, "Not yet."

Václav came over to Hubert, who had sunk on the seat again, and, putting his arms around his neck, leant his head against his shoulder, and wept bitterly. All the others kept silence, scarcely even stirring hand or foot. Fritz stood at the window and looked out, but Nänchen had turned her back on that dreadful light, and the old woman seemed only to be thinking of the weeping boy, whom she watched with pitying eyes.

Some time passed thus; then a quick, strong step was heard on the stairs.

"Robert!" cried Nänchen, and everyone turned to the door.

Robert came in, very pale, but with his head erect, and his eyes shining with a strange new light. He looked around on the group in silence, showing no surprise at the presence of Hubert and Václav, indeed, hardly noticing them. He seemed struggling to find words for what he wanted to tell. At last he said, very calmly and simply, "He is with Christ."

Then from the lips of Hubert burst the one question that was burning in his heart. "Was Christ with him to the end?"

"Was the Son of God with those three who walked unhurt in the furnace?"

"Ah, but nowadays He does not quench the violence of fire," sobbed Nänchen.

"That is not the *best* that He can do. Wait — give me but a moment's breathing space — and I will tell you all. The time was long — hours seemed to pass while we stood watching and waiting there by that Ring in the Brühl — and still he came not. There were many delays. First, they stopped him before the bishop's palace, that he might see the burning of his books, at which he smiled, for he knew that they could never burn his words out of the hearts of men."

"Who told you that?" asked Fritz.

"One of the men-at-arms, who had been with him all the way, told us everything afterward. The crowds were great, so great that they feared the little bridge outside the Göttlingen Gate would break down, and they made the whole eight hundred soldiers pass over it singly, man by man. And they kept back the townsfolk at the gate, and would not let them go on at all. They did wisely there. For so noble was his bearing, so devout and earnest were his prayers, that the hearts of the people were moved. There were angry cries and murmurs among them, because they saw no confessor with him — a boon not denied to the vilest. So he was offered this grace, and our Master Ulrich Schorand, who chanced to be close at hand, was brought to him."

"Schorand so near! Ah, why could I not have kept beside him?" cried Hubert.

"But Master Schorand refused to hear him," pursued Robert, "unless he would retract. 'A heretic,' he said, 'could neither give nor receive the Sacraments.' "

"Master Schorand has heard his last confession from me, then," said Nänchen's mother. "What ailed him to be so pitiless?"

"Well, it mattered not; he could not hurt him," Robert said gently. "He prayed often and chanted Psalms, especially the fifty-first and the thirty-first. As he drew near we heard his voice, and caught the words distinctly — 'Into Thy hands I commend my spirit, for Thou hast redeemed me, O Lord God of truth.' Having come into the Ring, and going up to the stake, he knelt and prayed, 'Lord Jesus Christ, help me to bear this death of pain and shame, which for Thy name and Word's sake I willingly encounter. And forgive my enemies for this their sin.' Then he rose up, and — oh, Nänchen, he spoke to us!"

"So they let him speak to the people at last — at last!" cried Hubert. "And I not there!"

"No, master, they did not. They only just let him say that he died for no heresy or error, but because he had preached the true word of God. A word more than that they would not let him utter. But, Nänchen" — he turned to her with eyes full of light — light that shone through tears — "*I* have his farewell, his thanks, to keep forever."

"You? Did he speak to *you*? Oh, Robert, how I envy you!" said Hubert.

Robert bowed his head.

"He saw us as we stood there, Jacob and Gregory being with me, and the men from the other prisons. In his gentle, courteous way, he asked leave of the executioners to speak to us. So they led him near to us, for we could not enter the Ring. Oh, Nänchen, the face that I have often seen so full of pain and weariness was bright with joy. He said to us, 'Dear brothers' — yes, those were his very words — he called us *brothers*. 'Dear brothers, I give you great thanks for the many kindnesses you have shown me during my long imprisonment. Not my keepers have you been, but my brothers. Know also that this very day, as I steadfastly believe, I shall rejoice in heaven with my blessed Saviour, for whose Name's sake I suffer this death.' "

A sob checked the voice of Robert, and he covered his face. He knew well that though the martyr's thanks had been for all, as indeed all had deserved them, his last farewell look, and the last touch of his hand, had been for the best and dearest friend God gave him in the prison, still known to us as "one named Robert."

"Go on, Robert," said Hubert at last, in little more than a whisper.

Robert went on, speaking very quietly, and without looking up.

"During the long, slow, horrible preparations, he stood unmoved and calm, holding communion with God in prayer. Once he smiled — when in scorn and mockery they brought a foul and rusty chain to bind his neck to the stake.

"'My Saviour,' said he, 'was bound with a far more cruel chain for me, and shall I be ashamed of this one? No, I will bear it gladly for His sake!'

"When at last all was done, all was undone again, and changed, at the bidding, of someone who said that a heretic ought not to die with his face to the east. So again they bound him to the stake, this time with his face toward the setting sun. Better so! The wicked city was behind him — God's pure sky, and in the distance His everlasting hills, before his eyes. Then, once more, he had to put aside the cup of life which was offered to his lips. Two great princes, sent by the Emperor himself, came spurring in hot haste to the Ring. The executioner, who was already standing torch in hand, paused while they prayed him, with earnest and pitying words, to retract.

"He answered them with a glad voice, 'I call God to witness that I have not taught anything contrary to His truth, but in all my preaching, teaching, and writing I have endeavoured to turn men from their sins, and to bring in the kingdom of God. The truths that I have taught in accordance with the Word of God I will now maintain, and willingly seal with my death.'

"The princes wrung their hands and withdrew. I saw the executioner raise his torch, and then — my strength failed me. I hid my face — but still that fearful glow came through my clasped hands. Presently I heard his voice — brave, clear, and firm — and then I looked again without fear — God's peace was with him still — 'Christ, Thou Son of God, have mercy on me!' This he chanted twice; but at the third time the flame rose up and caught his face, and no sound reached us save the Name he loved so well — 'Christ — Son of God' — his last word to us. For a little while, in which you might have said two or three Paternosters, his lips moved as if in quiet prayer. Then he bowed his head, and went home to God."

There was a great silence. At last the voice of Václav broke it, "Then it was not dreadful after all?" he said.

"It was not dreadful, so far as we could see. Whatever it was to him, already he has forgot it all.[22] Now, while we speak, he is looking on the face of Christ."

"It is *we* who will not forget," cried Václav, the youngest there. "Never, *never*, so long as we live!"

"Nor our children, nor our children's children," said Robert.

But Hubert thought of the words of that glorious Psalm which the martyr sang on his way to death. Half unconsciously he said them aloud, "Oh, how great is Thy goodness which Thou hast laid up for them that fear Thee, which Thou hast wrought for them that trust in Thee before the sons of men!"

So closed over the town of Constance that eventful sixth of July — "a day to be much remembered." Much remembered in truth it was in the after years. Well spake the boy Václav: "Never, never," did the faithful in Bohemia forget their saint and martyr, who for their sakes laid down his life so willingly. His name remained a word of power, a spell to stir the deepest chords of feeling. "With a quenchless love profound" they kept his death-day sacred, alike in the halls of nobles and the lowly huts of peasants. Warriors kept it by many a watch-fire, on the eve of many a well-fought field and it made them strong to strike for vengeance and for freedom. Martyrs — and of these there were a great multitude, truly a noble army — remembered it in their agony, and prayed for grace to follow in his footsteps. After the lapse of nearly five centuries it is not forgotten yet. The noble "Church of the United Brethren" which sprang from his ashes still observes her martyr's memorial day throughout the whole world, wherever her hand has held up the standard of the cross. And where has she *not* uplifted that saving sign? In the snows of Greenland and Labrador, among "Negroes, Hottentots, and Esquimaux," in the lazar-houses of lepers,[23] in the wilds of America

---

[22] Most readers will recall the martyr's epitaph in Robert Browning's beautiful poem, *Easter Day*.

> *I was some time in being burned,*
> *But at the close a Hand came through*
> *The flame above my head, and drew*
> *My soul to Christ, whom now I see.*
> *Sergius, a brother, writes for me*
> *This testimony on the wall;*
> *For me, I have forgot it all.*

[23] The patient, unobtrusive, self-sacrificing work of the Moravian missionaries among the lepers deserves special remembrance at this time, when so much attention has been called to the subject. The Church of the United Brethren can boast of a noble succession of men who, unknown, unnoticed, and unpraised by their fellows, seeking only the praise of their Master, Christ, took up their abode among those afflicted outcasts, and gave up their lives to cheer and help them.

and Australia — lands of which he never knew — the "painters" of his prophetic dream, ever painting the face of Christ, pause on each sixth of July to remember his conflict and his victory.

Nor has his native land, the land he loved so well, ceased to cherish his memory, even though the light he kindled in her has been once and again all but extinguished in the blood of her best and bravest children. Every true Bohemian, whatever his creed may be, still loves and reverences Bohemia's martyr-hero; while the faithful remnant, inheritors of those who have held fast the truth from his time even until now, keep every year on his death-day the birthday of their Church.

Does he know all this now? Would he rejoice in it if he did? Not in the earthly fame; no doubt he "little recks who wreathes the brow" that Christ has crowned already; but certainly in this, that through him Christ is, and has been, and will be preached. As it was given him to be made like unto his Lord in suffering, so, as we dare to think, he tastes also of His joy. Of the servant as of the Master it is true that "he shall see of the travail of his soul, and shall be satisfied." "I too," said he, "shall rejoice with exceeding joy, when I awake in the resurrection."

Amen, so let it be! Waiting in hope, we also are satisfied — satisfied for him, and for the other saints and heroes of the olden days. What is harder, we are satisfied for our own beloved ones who are with them now within the veil, in mysterious, but most blessed communion, as to each we hear the charge and the benediction — "Go your way until the end comes, for you shall rest, and stand in your lot in the end of the days."[24]

---

[24] All the particulars of the trial, condemnation, and martyrdom of John Huss have been carefully taken from history; nothing has been added, though much has been omitted and curtailed. Very full and reliable information has come down to us from contemporary sources, especially from the narrative of Petr Mladenowic; nor was he the only eye-witness who placed on record what he saw. All later histories borrow from these, and all agree. I have used L'Enfant's *Histoire du Concile de Constance*; Bonnechose's *Reformers before the Reformation*; Foxe's *Book of Martyrs*; Marmor's *Conzil zu Constanz*, and others; but I desire to express my special obligations to the Rev. A. H. Wratislaw, whose *Life of John Huss*, published by the Society for Promoting Christian Knowledge is, I believe, the only work on the subject in English which takes account of the recent investigations and publications in Bohemia. It should be added, that Roman Catholic as well as Protestant historians bear witness to the heroic courage and fortitude of the martyr. One of the most remarkable of these, Eneas Sylvius Piccolomini, afterwards Pope Pius II, is said to have been an eye-witness. Since writing the above I have also read with much interest an excellent *Life of John Huss*, by Dr. Gilleatt, an American writer.

XIX

OUTSIDE THE DOOR

You have made the dead
The mighty, the victorious.

At nightfall Robert brought Václav home to his father; but he begged Hubert to remain until his return. When he came back he said to him, "Let me look to your arm, Sir. It would go ill with us poor folk if we had to run to the barber[25] every time we got a sprain or a bruise. We learn to help ourselves, and one another. And I think we mend as quickly as our betters."

Hubert consented; he probably would have consented that night to anything proposed by Robert. He allowed his arm, by this time much swollen, to be bathed with some cooling lotion of which Nänchen's mother knew the secret. For a while, indeed, he remained quite passive in the hands of Robert, who waited on and tended him with a zeal and carefulness which was a welcome relief to his own sore heart, while it greatly touched his patient.

"Your hand is as gentle as a woman's," said Hubert. "Not," he added rather sadly, "that I speak from experience, for woman's care have I never known since I was five years old." Somehow, the new influence that had come into his life was beginning to soften his whole nature.

"Ah, Master Hubert," said Robert, with quickly-falling tears, "you know where I learned this gentleness, and whom I served when he lay ill in yonder prison. God knows how often since then I called His ways in question, wondering why He did not take him home in peace, out of their cruel hands. But He knew best. He had more work yet for His servant to do for Him. *Now*, I can say truly He has done all things well."

Then he sat down beside the settle on which Hubert lay and they talked together. Through the long night that followed neither

---

[25] Barbers used to act as surgeons.

thought of sleep. Out of his full heart Robert told the story of those days in the Dominican House; how the patience, gentleness, and holiness of his captive had first gained his wondering admiration, and prepared his heart for the teaching that had changed all his life. Hubert was eager to know what that teaching was. Robert not only told him many of the words which had been stored lovingly in his memory, but brought out for him from its safe hiding-place the simple tract upon the Lord's Prayer, which, like that on Marriage, had been written expressly for himself.

Neither in the oral nor in the written teaching was there anything positively opposed to the creed of his day. Probably Hubert might have heard before, from the lips of the chancellor, most of the great truths which that night came to his soul for the first time in power and in majesty, as if spoken by a voice from heaven. No, were they not almost literally spoken so?

They were very old and very simple truths. Clearly and strongly was the love of the Divine Father set forth, and this not for great saints alone (as Hubert used to think), but for the humblest and lowliest of His creatures. "Our Father, who art in heaven" (so wrote John Huss), "Our Father, powerful in might, who art our Creator, our Father, sweet in loving; Our Father, rich in inheritance; Our Father, merciful in redemption; Our Father, able to protect; Our Father, always ready to listen! See what manner of Father is ours, who is in heaven!"[26]

"And see, moreover," said Robert, as he looked up from the page, "what manner of Father and of Friend was with him, to sustain and strengthen him through those eight long months in the lonely dungeon."

"Yes, well for *him*," said Hubert. "But for us, who have all our sins on us, we must fear and tremble before the great and dreadful Lord God."

"No, Master Hubert, for God is reconciled to us, and forgives us our sins, for the Lord Jesus Christ's sake, if only we believe in Him and follow Him."

" 'My Lord Jesus Christ,' that was what he said," mused Hubert. "And Christ stood by him all the time."

"Oh, Sir, he loved Him so! That love of Christ was his very life. I wish I could tell you how he used to speak of Him, but no — I cannot — I cannot, the words go from me. And to think they are all

---

[26] In giving this and what follows from the writings of John Huss, I have not confined myself to those which Robert had, but have used extracts from his Bohemian works.

lost now, those beautiful words. Stay, though — Master Petr wrote out something for me in German one day, out of one of his books. It is like his talk, as the dried roses Nänchen wore at our wedding were like the fresh summer blossoms. Here it is. 'Therefore after (Christ) let us go, to Him let us listen, and in Him let us place faith, hope, love, and all good works; on Him, as into a mirror, let us gaze, and to Him let us approach with all our might. And let us hear in that He says, "I am the way, the truth, and the life,"— the way in example, wherein if a man goes he errs not; the truth in promise, for what He has promised, that He will fulfil; and the life in recompense, for He will give Himself to be enjoyed in everlasting bliss. He is also the way because He leads to salvation; He is the truth, because He shines in the understanding of the faithful; and He is the life everlasting, in which all the elect will live in bliss forever. To that life and by that way and truth I desire to go myself, and to draw others.' "

"Surely God has given him the desire of his heart," said Hubert. "God grant it to me to follow him to that life, and by that way and truth!"

"And to me also," Robert answered. "He used to say that he wanted us 'so to know the most precious Saviour as to love Him with the whole heart, and our neighbour as ourselves.' "

There was a silence; then he resumed, "But I wonder, will the priests now account us heretics and wish to cast us out?"

"Why should they?" asked Hubert.

"Why did they with him?"

"You have said it yourself before, Robert — only because he bore witness of their evil deeds. And yet," he added thoughtfully and with an air of perplexity, "the fact remains that the chancellor believes him a heretic — or did believe him so — until yesterday." He pondered for a while in silence, then he added, and the words came evidently from the depths of his heart, "Heretic or no, from this day forth I follow him. No, rather, I try to follow Christ, as he did."

About sunrise Hubert fell asleep. He was awakened by the sound of the church bells ringing for early Mass. It was Sunday morning. Robert was kneeling by his side in prayer, but rose up presently and said with a smile, "They cannot shut him out from the house of God today."

"No," returned Hubert. "Today it is we who stand outside. And the door is shut."

"Not quite, I think, Master Hubert. To me it seems as if the door was still half open, and the glory shining through."

Hubert rose. "I must go home," he said.

Robert brought him his own clothing, assisted him to resume it, and constructed a sling for his strained and almost useless arm. Fortunately it was the left one. Hubert shook hands warmly with him, thanked him for his and for Nänchen's kindness, and went out.

Early as it was, there were many people in the streets already; but they were unusually grave and quiet, and stood mostly in groups talking in low tones together. One such group had gathered near the great door of the cathedral, and were looking at something freshly posted on it. By this time the bells had ceased, and the service was beginning within. As Hubert approached, intending to go in and hear Mass, a bystander cried out, "Here comes a scholar. Make way for him, friends. Please, Sir, be so good as to read for us what is written there."

Hubert read accordingly, and translated from Latin into German the following words: "The Holy Ghost to the believers of Constance, greeting. Mind your own business. As for Us, being occupied elsewhere, we cannot remain any longer in the midst of you. Adieu."[27]

There was first silence, then a confused murmur among the hearers.

"What does it mean?" asked one.

"Its meaning is clear enough," said another. "Where the devil reigns, whose work is murder, God cannot remain."

"Take care, friend," interposed a third; "that which is done by process of law is not murder."

"Not murder!" cried the former speaker. "If you had seen the man, as I did, on his way to death, and heard him pray, you would have sworn he was a devout Catholic and a good Christian."

"Yet he was a manifest heretic."

"There are many that think otherwise."

"Ah, yes; he had friends enough. One of them, no doubt has put up this scandalous writing in mockery of the Council."

"I think not," said Hubert, as he turned and faced the group. "No true friend of the martyr would wish to avenge his cause by taking in vain the most holy name of God, as this writing does."

"Very fine words," said a French priest, who joined them at the moment. "Especially from you, Master Hubert Bohun. Oh, I know you well! I studied with you in the Sorbonne, or rather, did not study, but played the fool. I have a particular recollection of one notable prank of yours, and it was about a placard. Perhaps you are throwing dust in our eyes, and know more about this one than you care to acknowledge."

---

[27] This placard was actually posted upon the church doors during the night that followed the martyrdom of John Huss.

"I?" cried Hubert in astonishment; but he did not think it worth while to say more, and turned from them to go into the church.

The bystanders took up his quarrel.

"Hold your peace, Sir Priest," said one of them scornfully. "He who suspects another often deserves suspicion himself."

"No," interposed a second. "Let the priest either prove his accusation, or take it back and apologize like an honest man."

The bystanders took up his quarrel.

"I accuse no one, and I take back nothing," the priest returned. "But I know that this young man, albeit he is secretary to the excellent Chancellor of Paris . . ."

But Hubert heard no more. He passed on and entered the church, where he knelt down in a quiet place, and was soon absorbed in solemn thoughts of the scene of yesterday, and in earnest prayer that the martyr's God would be his God also, even forever and ever.

On coming forth he walked slowly, and it must be said unwillingly, toward the chancellor's house. As he passed through the Ober Markt someone touched him on the shoulder. He turned, and saw one of the town guard, who informed him that he was obliged to put him under arrest in the name of the burgomaster.

"What have I done?" Hubert asked in surprise.

"That I cannot say, Sir. I can only say what you are charged with 'Contempt of the Holy Council,' " answered the man, who was very respectful, though firm. "You had better come with me quietly. I have a comrade at hand, and these," just showing a pair of manacles. "But I should be very sorry to use them, and shame a scholar like you."

Hubert's cheek flushed crimson.

"*Shame*?" he cried. "As if the sting had not been taken out of all that, for those who saw what I did yesterday! Put them on as soon as you please."

But the official only shook his head, and without more words brought Hubert to St. Paul's Tower, in what is now called Hieronymus Street, led him to a cell, and locked him in.

Hubert felt considerable surprise, but no alarm. If "contempt of the Council" meant holding the Council and its doings in supreme contempt and detestation, he certainly could not deny the accusation. But then the Council could not read men's hearts, and he had not, as yet, manifested his sentiments by any overt action. Unless, indeed — and here he suddenly remembered the words of the French priest — others might suspect him, as he had done, or pretended to do, of having written that placard. His boyish levities would give colour to the suspicion, if, indeed, there was any man now in Constance who happened to know of them, or cared to recall them. If there was, he would be sorry; not because of any punishment which might come upon himself, but because he thought the act of which he was suspected unworthy of the martyr's glory. It was not *thus* that he ought to be avenged.

He would be more than sorry; he would be stung to the quick, if by any possibility the chancellor could think him guilty. The chancellor!

At the thought of him his soul was troubled. Between them a great gulf seemed to have yawned suddenly. The pain and the passion, the hope, the joy, and the triumph of yesterday had borne Hubert far — much farther than he dreamed at first. It was only on looking back at his old self that he saw, or rather felt, the change that had come over him. How would those keen, deep-seeing eyes — whose approving glance had until now been his highest recompense — how would they look on that change?

It was the strongest love of his life which rose up within him at the question. From his infancy, until he found his brother in Constance, he had known no family ties, no sweet household charities. Only through the chancellor had the shadow of fatherly care and pity been cast over him, to help him to understand the fatherhood of God. He clung to him with equal admiration and affection, at once worshipping him as a disciple and loving him as an attached and grateful son.

He would not own, even to himself, that henceforward he must stand alone — no mere echo of the chancellor's word, no mere reflection of his thought. He preferred to hope, with the ardent hopefulness of youth, that what had moved his own heart so deeply had influenced the chancellor also. How, in fact, could he resist it!

That day, indeed, Hubert could not long continue troubled about anything. The peace into which the martyr had entered seemed to overshadow him. For the first time in his life his heart went forth to God in childlike love and in perfect trust. He knew he was in His hands, and he rested there.

The long, solitary hours wore on; but they did not seem to him either long or solitary, he had so much to think of and to remember. Once a warder came to him with food; and more than once he heard — or thought he heard — through the thick prison wall, the voice of a strong man's bitter anguish. He longed to console the sufferer, whoever he might be; perhaps some unhappy man who was sentenced to death. Since he could do nothing else, he prayed for him, very earnestly, yet not half so earnestly as he would have done had he but known him to be one for whom even then another martyr-crown was preparing, though it was not ready for him yet, nor was he ready for it.

Before Hubert thought it possible the daylight faded, and his cell was in darkness. The two preceding nights he had scarcely slept at all; so now he was glad enough to lay his weary limbs on the straw that had been provided for him, and to sleep in peace until the morning.

XX

SUNDERED BONDS

Come back, young fiery spirit,
If but one hour, to learn
The secrets of the folded heart,
That seemed to thee so stern.

In the morning, one of the town-sergeants entered the prison, and with a cheerful, congratulatory air desired Hubert to follow him. "I may wish you joy, Sir," he said, for I think your troubles are over now. A fine thing it is for a man to have a good lord, to stand by him and to take his part! The Chancellor of Paris has spoken for you as a scholar of fair repute, and one of his own household. At his request, you are to be put into his hands to deal with as he thinks fit. That means, that you will be let off with a 'do so no more,' just for form's sake."

"Such kindness is worthy of my noble lord, who has ever used me far better than I deserve," said Hubert, as he put on his gown, and prepared to follow the friendly sergeant. He was brought by him to the chancellor's house, and there formally delivered over to Charlier, who received him in the name of his master, and gave the sergeant a written acknowledgment for his person.

No sooner were they alone, however, than Charlier turned on him angrily, "You troublesome, rebellious young fool!" he said. "It was an ill day for my lord when he took you out of the prison of the Sorbonne, which your own misdeeds had got you into. So you must needs disgrace him and his household in the eyes of the Holy Council, and of all the world! It was a light thing for you to lose his letter, and neglect his work — in your eagerness to run off to the Brühl and see the Burning. Bad enough, indeed, but a light thing, I say, compared with the affair of the placard. One would think your narrow escape at the Sorbonne might have taught you the danger of lampooning your betters. But to some men there is no teaching anything. Nevertheless, the business will have had one good result. My lord knows you now, Master Hubert Bohun; and we shall see an end of the partiality and favouritism that so wronged his excellent judgment."

The hot young blood sprung to Hubert's forehead, but he kept silence, as he thought of the scene in the church, and the insults endured with patience there. He simply asked Charlier, "Will my lord be pleased to see me himself?"

"Perhaps he will, at his leisure, though it is more than you deserve."

But the chancellor did not make Hubert wait on his leisure. He sent for him immediately; and Charlier, as if he was still a prisoner, led him into his presence. Hubert made a lowly reverence, and then looked up sadly in the face of his lord. Very full was that face of care and sorrow, but it was also very stern. Even since Hubert saw him last, the furrows on the broad forehead had deepened, the lines around the firm lips had hardened. If Jean Gerson had borne his part in offering up a burnt sacrifice, at least it had not been a sacrifice that cost him nothing.

Still, before he spoke to Hubert, his eyes rested for an instant, with a softened expression, on the wounded arm. But the softness passed immediately, and he said, slowly and sternly, "Hubert Bohun, you stand accused of two faults; I am fain to begin with the slighter. What has become of the packet which on Saturday was entrusted to your care?"

It was well for Hubert that Charlier, in his anger, had reminded him that he would be questioned on this subject; otherwise, so thoroughly had it passed from his mind, that he might have had to pause and think before he answered, and the hesitation would have told against him.

Now he said clearly and simply, "My lord, I brought it to Lebrun. He was not in his house; but I found him on the Rhine bridge, and gave it into his own hand."

"Where is the receipt?"

"I said, being hurried, that I would return for it later. In that, I own, I did wrong.

"Being hurried, I suppose," broke in Charlier, "to go to the Burning." His master gave him a look that awed him into silence; and then said, turning again to Hubert, "Why did you not return for it?"

"Because, my lord, I saw a boy fall into the river from the bridge. I tried to save him; we were long in the water, and I was hurt. I was taken to the house of one named Robert, a citizen whom I knew; and there I spent the night. At the hour of matins yesterday, I was returning home after hearing Mass in the cathedral, when they arrested me."

154

The chancellor's countenance showed the surprise he felt at this unexpected reply; and Charlier indulged in an incredulous murmur, but did not dare to speak out. The chancellor resumed, more gently, "You were better employed than we thought for. Did you succeed in your work of charity?"

"The child was saved," said Hubert.

He will believe anything that boy tells him, to the very end, thought the exasperated chaplain. If Hubert Bohun said he had slain the seven champions of Christendom, the chancellor would only ask him which he began with.

"Are you seriously hurt?" pursued the chancellor.

"Oh no, my lord; it is nothing."

"Nothing, I can believe you think it, weighed in the balance with a life. My letter was important, but had you lost it in saving life I should never have reproached you. Even culpable carelessness I could easily forgive. But if indeed that placard, which appeared yesterday on the church doors, is from your hand, it is not against *me* that you have offended."

"My lord, I never even heard of it until the people called me to read it to them, as I was going into church yesterday morning."

The chancellor looked at him steadily, and in silence.

Charlier could contain himself no longer. "My lord, may I speak?" he said.

His master's tone was the reverse of encouraging as he said, coldly, "If you will, but be brief."

"For the past month and more, my lord, Bohun has done nothing but take the part of that heretic. I myself heard him say — and I crave your pardon for repeating such words — I heard him say that he did not believe Jesus Christ could be governing the Church, when such things as that man's condemnation were done in it."

"I did say it," Hubert broke in. "On the evening of June 8, after the meeting of the Council. But I was wrong — I know it now — and he was right who said that day, 'Christ reigns now and always, and, albeit there is no pope, He does not cease to govern His Church!' "

The faith that breathed in those noble words lit up in the chancellor's sad face a momentary gleam of pleasure. But it passed instantly for he remembered who had spoken them, and felt indignant with Hubert for daring to quote the heretic, and still more with Charlier for provoking him to it.

"Have you anything more to say?" he asked his chaplain, with an air of irritation.

"One thing more, my lord. What Bohun did in Paris — the affair of the placard, I mean — may have escaped your memory."

155

"My memory is not so treacherous. It is because I remember so well that I know how to deal with this matter, and a few words will suffice for it. Hubert Bohun, look up. If your eye shrinks from mine, it will be the first time since I knew you. You told the truth in Paris, you will tell it now. Have you done this thing?"

"No, my lord."

"Have you contrived or counselled, or had act or part in it, in any way?"

"No, my lord."

There was a brief pause. Then the chancellor said, "I knew it, my son."

Hubert breathed again. With the great throb of relief at his heart, eager words sprang to his lips. "My lord, I could not have done it! Once long ago, in my folly, I feigned idle words for the King of France, and men called it treason. But this — this would be blasphemy! Moreover, I can prove my innocence. It will be easy to send for Robert, who was with me all the time, and can make oath that I never left his house."

"There is no need for it. When I trust, I trust wholly. The matter is ended. It shall be named no more, by anyone." This with a glance at Charlier.

"Hubert, the Council sits tomorrow. You shall attend, and write for me."

The tone in which he said that one word, "Hubert," had a tenderness Hubert could hardly bear. But he steeled himself, with an effort, to the inevitable task before him.

"My lord," he said sadly, "I cannot write for you in the Council."

The chancellor looked at him in surprise; then a half smile played about his stern, sad lip. "Because you have been suspected?" he asked. "You poor, proud, foolish boy! Have I not said that I trust you?"

"It is just that; it is the trust, the goodness beyond words, my lord has ever shown me, which makes it so hard for me now. How can I speak? And yet how can I hold my peace? No, come what will of it, I must speak. I can write no more in the Council because of that thing which the Council did the day before yesterday."

Charlier uttered an exclamation of horror.

The Chancellor started, and his countenance changed perceptibly. "What do you mean?" he asked sharply. "Do you presume to judge the Council?"

"My lord, I judge no man. But this I know; he whom they slew the day before yesterday died like St. Stephen, and is gone where St. Stephen went. And with those who slew him God will reckon."

"Blasphemy!" cried Charlier, taking a step forward; but no one heeded him.

Sorrow, anger, and amazement, struggled in the look the chancellor bent on Hubert. "How dare you speak thus?" he asked.

"I dare anything *now*," answered Hubert. "I have seen enough to take fear away from me forever. I have seen how no shame can touch, no horror can daunt, no agony can hurt the man who trusts God, and stands on His side against the world."

"If this be not sheer raving, it is rank heresy," began Charlier again.

But the chancellor turned on him suddenly, and in that voice of anger he so seldom used bade him, "Go, leave my presence!"

His anger was unreasonable, or rather, it was vented on the wrong person. But Charlier dared not disobey; he went out trembling, and at the same time vowing vengeance against Hubert.

When they were alone together Gerson addressed Hubert, more apparently in sorrow than in anger. "You are in the snare of the devil. It is not the first time that he has taken on himself the form of an angel of light. But that he should have so deceived you as to make you plead the cause of a heretic, almost passes belief."

"My lord, I do not plead for him — God will plead. Safe with Him is His martyr's cause."

"*Martyr?*" All the emphasis of wrath was flung into the word. Still, the chancellor controlled himself, though with an evident effort.

"I must have patience," he said. "You are but a boy — a foolish, ignorant, conceited boy, and I own there was that in the man which might well — Child, you mistake the tinsel for the gold, the counterfeit for the true coin. Did not Judas bear himself devoutly before men? Did he not cast out devils and work miracles? Did he not say, 'Master, Master?' "

"Yes; but that he suffered patiently for the Master's sake — forgiving his enemies and praying for his persecutors — that I have never heard," said Hubert.

"You have heard, 'Though I give my body to be burned, and have not charity (that is, the grace of God), I am nothing.' The man you speak of shut upon himself the door of grace. He died in disobedience to the voice of the Church, which is the voice of God. His doctrines would have spread rebellion and disorder; and they, and he, have been justly condemned. Enough of him; he stands now before his Judge. His name I care not to hear or utter; it will be, I suppose, forever accursed among men. Though it might have been far otherwise — God gave him noble gifts, if he had but used them for His glory.

"Hubert Bohun, think of yourself. Do not turn from the light, and mistake the way to heaven. Do not wander out of the true path and follow vain shadows, or perhaps one day your feet will stumble on the dark mountains, and you will look for light, and behold darkness and the shadow of death. Hubert, Hubert," his hard face softened, and his voice grew tender, "do not cast yourself away."

"My lord, when you speak thus to me, I can scarce endure it; your wrath even were easier to bear than your kindness. But it avails not. I see only one step before me, yet that step I must take. I must go from you."

"Go from me? I am not sending you away. No, not even for your wild, reckless words."

Hubert shook his head sadly. "Yet I must go," he said. "It were better for me to die than by the lifting of a hand, by the stroke of a pen, to have act or part or share any more in the doings of the Council."

"This is a fit of midsummer madness. One would think you were a cardinal, or a bishop at the least! *Your* part in the doings of the Council is but the part of this pen in my hand, as humble and as safe. And yet, Hubert, still I say, do not go from me. Time and good instruction will dissipate your delusions. I myself will instruct you in the Catholic faith with more care than I have. Perhaps, indeed, I have been wrong in this matter. God forgive my sins of omission! I thought you more fitted for the active than for the contemplative life. I must amend this negligence, of which the enemy has taken advantage to sow the tares of heresy."

"No, my lord, not so. I am clear of heresy. I believe all I have been taught, only with better understanding than I have ever done before. I maintain no false doctrine; I only protest against a crime. If I were to hold my peace, the very stones would cry out. And I have no way of protesting save by refusing any more to serve those who did this thing, or those who approved of it."

That last word, "*approved*," carried a sting with it.

"Go your own way, then!" said the chancellor, at last thoroughly indignant, and turning his face away from him. "We part here, and forever."

"Yes, we part," Hubert answered mournfully. "Only once more, for this last time, let me thank you for the kindness of the past — let me pray your forgiveness."

"No, not one other word," the chancellor interrupted sternly. There was a silence: Hubert stood still; the chancellor sat motionless, with his face turned away. At last he looked at Hubert again, and said in a voice that trembled audibly, "Hubert Bohun, you have bitterly disappointed me."

"Oh, my lord!" cried Hubert, his own voice full of pain.

158

"You are only like all the rest. Ingratitude is the world's way. It is a bitter, evil world — would to God I were done with it! I thought — I was weak enough to think that you — you . . ." Then, with a sudden change of tone and manner, and half-unconsciously extending his hand, "Hubert, I thought you loved me."

Hubert was at his feet in a moment, pressing the hand to his lips. "God knows I love you, better than any living man." Quick tears choked his voice, but he resumed presently, "Only say that we do not part in wrath!"

"We part in sorrow and we part forever," said the chancellor, withdrawing his hand, though not ungently. "Go from me, Hubert Bohun; go, and God forgive you!"

"God bless my noble lord, the best friend I ever had! God give my lord the blessing of peace!"

Hubert turned sadly away, and the door closed on him. Could he have witnessed the pain of the strong heart he left behind, it would almost have brought him back again.

"Cease ye from man, whose breath is in his nostrils," said the chancellor. He had many lessons just then of the untruth, the unfaithfulness, the malice, the cruelty of men. Those he was contending for often pierced his soul with sharper arrows than those he was contending against. While fighting bravely against many adversaries for what *he thought to be* right and truth, he had received a wound from another quarter, which, jealously concealed, unacknowledged even to himself, still bled inwardly. For many a future day that trouble would "not pass, but grow." John Huss had never said, what his more impetuous fellow-martyr said afterward to his judges, "In dying, I will leave a sting in your hearts, and a gnawing worm in your consciences." Yet the memory of that patient, heroic death can never have left any man who had a share in it; and the noblest least of all. From then on not even earthly prosperity and success were given to the chancellor — "All things grew sadder to (him) one by one." He could say truly, as he often did say, "I am a stranger on earth;" yet the end of the pathetic prayer, "Hide not Thy commandments from me," did not seem to find an answer *then*. It rather seemed as if, while the earth was iron, the heavens above him were brass. We know this by a sure sign and token. Then, and for some time afterward, there was in his speech and writings, in his actions even, a great bitterness and hardness. In one memorable instance this hardness reached a point which we must need call cruelty, nor was he free from the reproach of "a virtual breach of faith." These are not the fruits which bear witness to a heart in communion with God, or a soul at peace with Him.

XXI

FOR THE LOVE OF THE LIVING AND THE LOVE OF THE DEAD

Flung to the heedless winds,
Or on the waters cast,
(His) ashes shall be watched,
And gathered at the last;
And from that precious seed,
Around us and abroad
Shall spring a plenteous host
Of witnesses for God.

— Martin Luther

Hubert went out from the chancellor's house without one thought that he was a "masterless man," homeless, friendless, alone in the world. Such thoughts would come afterward. At present he only felt the bitter pain of parting with the man he had so reverenced, loved, and followed. It was intensified by the thrill of a keen disappointment. How could it be that the great chancellor — so good, so wise, so noble — could not see what was so plain to *him*, could not feel what had appealed with such overmastering power to *his* heart?

Where was he now to bend his steps? He did not know: to his present mood all places were alike. For some time he paced idly up and down the street; but at last it occurred to him to tell his brother what had happened, so he bent his steps toward the Burgundian house in the Ros-Garten. He met Armand coming out of it, and was hailed by him with evident pleasure.

"I was just going in search of you," he said. "I have much to tell you. Come, and let us talk. Where shall we go? By the Göttlieben way?"

"Not *there*," said Hubert, shuddering.

"You are right. Let us go to the river-side."

Before they were out of the town, however, Armand began to pour forth his story. The first part was hard to tell; so he wished to get over it quickly — yet still hesitated — lingering on the brink, as it were.

"There was a thing," he said, "which happened to me in my boyhood, and which, from one cause or another, I never mentioned to you, Hubert. Perhaps it was not all my fault. I tried more than once; but, somehow, at the right time I could never get your ear. The day after the pope's flight I came determined to tell you, but I could get you to think of nothing, save the triumph of the Council over him."

"Ah!" said Hubert, sadly. "That idol at least is shattered now. What a fool I was!"

"Another time," resumed Armand, "some other thing withheld me, no matter what. And, I suppose, the tale not being much to my own credit, I was withheld the more easily."

Then, plunging at once into the middle of his story, he told Hubert in a few words the story of his boyish transgression, of the loss of the duke's despatch and its consequences.

Hubert could hardly contain his indignation. He would have thought beforehand that nothing just then could have moved him. But those are commonly mistaken who expect "a great grief," or a great emotion, to "kill all the rest." More often, it only leaves the nerves of feeling bare and quivering, doubly sensitive to new pain. So his bright, kindly, open-hearted young brother, whom he so loved and trusted, had all the time been keeping a secret from him! Far worse, he had been maintaining a cowardly silence, and letting others suffer the consequence of his own misdeeds! As if it were not enough to lose his faith in the chancellor, he must lose his faith in Armand too! Who, then, was left him to trust? But even in that bitter moment his heart answered softly, "*God*." With the sacred name something like calmness came back, though the sharp pain was with him still.

"Oh, Armand, Armand!" he cried sadly, "how could our mother's son have ever done so?"

Armand blushed, hung his head, and murmured, "I knew you would take it thus." After a pause he resumed, "And if I feared to tell you, how was I to tell the Demoiselle Jocelyne, whose brother Godefroi de Sabrecourt was? Think of that, Hubert, and pity me. I own I played the coward — but I was tempted sore. God knows, I was tempted sore. After we broke gold together it became impossible to tell her."

"But you ought to have done it before."

"If I had, would she ever have heard my suit? Afterward, I quieted my soul with the thought that she need never know, and that if she did not know, where was the harm?"

"Where?" cried Hubert indignantly. "To yourself, of course. You were destroying your own soul. I scarcely recognize my brother in you, Armand. But," he added with a touch of self-reproach, "I ought to have known — I ought to have guessed before this that there was something wrong with you."

"I suppose," said Armand meditatively, "*you* might have moved me if you had tried. I would have done — I would do now — almost anything for you, Hubert. But at last, after all, it was not you, but a man I never saw before, and never exchanged a word with, who opened my lips and set me free."

Scarcely able to accept the relief his last words brought him, Hubert turned and looked at him eagerly, surprise and hope dawning on his face.

"Yes," said Armand, answering his look, "I have told all now. Now I fear nothing which any living man — indeed, or the dead either, if the dead could rise and speak — could bring against me."

"My brother has come back to me, then, thank God!" cried Hubert joyfully. After a pause, "But to whom have you told it, Armand?"

"To the one to whom I owed it, and to whom of all others it was the hardest to tell."

"And she?"

"There was a bitter hour that I care not to recall. She said she had lost her faith in me; that if all the world beside had said it of me she could not have believed me false. 'Never false to *you*,' I faltered in my pain. 'He that is not true to truth, cannot be true to love,' she answered. What use is it to tell you how I prayed and pleaded? Enough — it was in vain. We parted — she in wrath, I in bitterness of soul. That was yesterday morning, at Petershausen, in the Pleasaunce, where we had been walking among the flowers. I lingered there the whole day; I could not leave the spot. At last — at last she deigned to hear me plead once more; and you know, when you are heard, you are half forgiven. Now I am forgiven wholly. Never have I been so light of heart — never in all my life. Demoiselle Jocelyne is the noblest as well as the fairest lady for whom true knight ever drew a sword."

"And you will be worthy of her," said Hubert; "it was well done — right well done of you."

"We are to be faithful to one another, and to wait for better days," pursued Armand.

"Why better days?" queried Hubert.

"Don't you see that one confession entails another? This morning I wrote a full account of the whole matter to my lord the duke (I wished I had your ready pen to help me, Hubert!). I can scarcely expect him to keep me in the service after that."

"Armand, you are better off at this moment than I am."

It was Armand's turn to be astonished now. "I don't understand you," he said; "you always have the chancellor."

Then he asked, rather irrelevantly, "How did you hurt your arm?"

"I'll tell you by-and-by; I also have many things to tell. Armand, do you remember a promise I made you, in jest, soon after our first meeting?"

"Yes, I do!" said Armand, with sudden earnestness, his eyes sparkling. "If your chancellor committed a crime, more especially a murder, you were to leave his service, and to tell him why."

"What you think then, of the deed done on Saturday?" asked Hubert in a low voice.

"That is just what I want to ask you," cried Armand eagerly. "I saw you in the cathedral."

Hubert bowed his head. There was a silence; then he said, very gently and sadly, "Armand, I have kept my word. I shall see the face of the great chancellor no more. I have told him that he whom they burned as a heretic died like St. Stephen, and is gone where St. Stephen went."

"Then a braver man than you have I never seen! You ought to be a good knight; perhaps you will one day. And, Hubert, I know you are right about that man."

Armand's voice now grew low and gentle, he looked and spoke as one who stands in a holy place.

"Strange it is to tell, but he it was who made me speak the truth, and cast lies and falsehoods behind my back forever. Demoiselle Jocelyne persuaded me to go to the cathedral on Saturday. I could refuse her nothing, but it was much against my will. I hated the whole affair; the heat was terrible, and to stand five hours in a crowded church, and hear Latin spoken, was no slight penance. Heaven knows what it was all about! You, I suppose, understood it all — but I, of course, never a word. There was something, however, which I did understand, and will never forget, as long as I live: the man's look and bearing, so dauntless and so calm; his steadfast refusal to purchase life by one word which was not true. And he — a poor priest; while I — a gentleman born, and the son of a knight. But, no doubt, God was with him, and gave him strength. For that he was a heretic, that of course will I never believe, nor my lady.

"But, Hubert," with a sudden return to his ordinary manner, "what will you do now? Have you determined?"

"I do not know; nor, at present, do I greatly care," returned Hubert.

By this time they had strolled back again to the town, and were turning up the Rhinegasse. A tall man in a notary's gown crossed the street, apparently to speak to them. Hubert had just time to say to his brother, "That is Mladenowic, the Bohemian scribe whom you saw with me that day at the Leiter House," when Petr came up, and grasped his hand with a warm greeting.

"God bless you, good Master Hubert!" he said. "You share our sorrow."

"And your glory," answered Hubert. "Were I a Bohemian I would hold my head high today."

"I have been seeking you," continued Mladenowic. "The chancellor's people told me you were gone they knew not where."

"What did you want with me?"

"My lord, the knight of Chlum, has charged me with a message for you. He bade me make his excuse to you for not visiting you himself. Indeed, these were his words (if you will pardon my repeating them, Master Hubert), that he could not 'set his foot inside that murderer's den,' meaning the chancellor's house."

"I shall account it an honour to wait on the knight of Chlum," said Hubert. "I esteem him very highly."

Then, turning to Armand, "Where shall we agree to meet?"

"No place so good as *The Golden Lion*, where we met first, as I may say," answered Armand. "You can fetch your baggage from the chancellor's, and have it left there. Meantime, I will order supper. Mine host has the best wine in Constance, and the best cook too."

"Do as you like," said Hubert, indifferently, as he turned to accompany Mladenowic to the house of Fidelia in St. Paul's Street.

Václav met him at the door, threw his arms around him, and embraced him with boyish fervour. Then, still, holding his hand, he led him in. "Father, here is good Master Hubert, who saved my life," he said.

Hubert looked in the strong face of the noble Bohemian. It was calm and firm, but full of grief — "a grief as deep as life or thought" — the face of a man whose heart is crushed, and with whom nothing stands unshaken still except his faith in God.

Then, gently disengaging his hand and laying it on the boy's shoulder, he said, "And this, Sir Baron, is the brave young knight who, when he thought we could not both be saved, bade me let him go and save myself, for he did not fear to die."

The sad features relaxed, and the father's eye rested on his son with tender pride.

"You never told me that," he said.

Then, turning to Hubert, "Do you marvel that I prize what you have given back to me? But for you, brave Frenchman, the same hour would have brought me two sorrows, each enough for a man to bear. How shall I show you I am grateful?"

Hubert's eyes kindled. "Would you but take my hand in yours," he began, "I should esteem it . . ."

He was not allowed to finish his sentence. The good knight took his hand, and pressed it in a strong, cordial grasp, well worth an embrace. At the same moment a younger man, handsomely dressed, and with a hawk on his wrist, came forward, saying, "Is this your gallant Frenchman, Uncle? Make him known to us."

Hubert recognized Latzembok, and looking around him for the first time, saw Duba also, seated at a table, clad in a doublet of quilted silk, a sort of knightly undress. His face and attitude showed deep sadness. He rose, however, and came forward, extending his hand.

"We know you already," he said. "It were ill done to forget the honest-hearted scribe who came with us that day to the Leiter House. As well for that deed as for the one before yesterday every Bohemian in Constance owes you a debt. But we only know you as Master Hubert, the French Chancellor's secretary. What is your surname, brave Frenchman?" (This Mladenowic, as it seemed, either had not heard correctly or had forgotten.)

"I am Hubert Bohun; my father was an Englishman."

"Bohun? Bohun?" Chlum repeated thoughtfully. "And an Englishman? Strange if my father were a friend of yours — strange indeed! Yet no, it is not possible; your father would have been too young. Is he living, Master Bohun?"

"No, Sir Baron, I lost him in my infancy. He was taken prisoner in France, and while in captivity married my mother. I know scarce anything of him or his kinsfolk."

"Was he, or was his father, perhaps, a friend of Master John Wycliffe's?"

"As to my grandfather, I cannot tell. As to my father, I fear it is but too true. At least, I possess a book which he, being then, as I suppose, very young, had received as a gift from the heretic."

"We Bohemians do not call Master John Wycliffe a heretic, although we do not follow him in everything," said Chlum gently. "Yes, it must be so. My father went to England in the train of Queen Anne, and formed friendships which he prized, none more greatly than that with the noble knight whom I have heard him name with honour as Sir Simon Bohun."

"True indeed," said Hubert eagerly. "I have heard that my grandfather's name was Simon; my father's, like my own, was Hubert."

"Now, in truth," said Chlum, "the grandson of my father's friend, and the preserver of my son's life, has a double claim on my friendship."

"But how came you, the son and grandson of good English knights, to be the French Chancellor's scribe?" asked Latzembok.

Hubert's answer was an indirect one.

"I am the chancellor's scribe no longer," he said.

"Why so?" asked Duba and Latzembok together.

Hubert looked at both of them in silence, then turned to Chlum, and looked longest and most earnestly at him.

"You can guess, Sir Baron," he said.

"Do you mean," asked Chlum, "that the manly words you spoke to the Emperor in our presence a month ago cost you the favour of your lord? I fear, indeed, it is probable enough."

"No, Sir Baron, it was not that," said Hubert eagerly. "My lord — may God be with him — was ever gentle and forbearing toward me. But how could I write any more for him, or for the Council, after what the Council did before yesterday?"

Latzembok and Duba uttered exclamations of surprise and admiration; Chlum's sad, earnest eyes seemed to read Hubert through and through as he asked, "And is that why you are the chancellor's scribe no longer?"

Hubert bent his head.

"But how came he to know what you thought of the Council and its deed?" asked Latzembok, drawing closer to him.

"I told him," said Hubert quietly.

"No man does one brave deed, and only one," said Duba. "Few men stop at the second. Here already is your third, Master Hubert; and God knows it is the bravest of all."

Then Chlum said gravely, "I confess I do not understand you, Master Hubert. We *Bohemians* mourn today, for our master is taken from our head. 'Alas, my father, my father! The chariot of Israel, and the horsemen thereof!' That is the cry of our sorrow; but with this the stranger does not meddle. The men of other nations who are assembled here do not know us, just as they knew him not. How is it that you, a Frenchman, and a pupil of his enemy and ours, know more than all the rest?"

"Yes, there is the wonder," broke in Latzembok, "that you should do all this — you, not a Bohemian."

"Not a Bohemian, but, as I hope, a Christian," answered Hubert. "The better Christian, all my days, because I have seen *him*. Sir Baron" — he turned again to Chlum — "I was in the church on Saturday — and I believe that God has *not* taken from him the cup of His salvation; but that even now he drinks of it in His kingdom."

With a sudden quiver of the firm lip Chlum turned aside.

It is often so. Thus calmly can a stranger speak of the joys those who have left us share in His kingdom; while to us, whose very life has gone from us with them, there comes only the desolating sense that the kingdom is very far away.

But Latzembok, Duba, and another knight named Leffle, who entered just then, atoned for the silence of Chlum. Never did a new convert receive a more cordial welcome than they gave Hubert.

"See how God is with us, after all," cried Leffle. "Already He is causing fruit to spring from our martyr's grave."

"His *grave*?" repeated Duba, with bitter emphasis. "Can we forget for an instant that even a grave has been denied him? His very ashes they would not allow to rest on God's earth."

"Is that true?" asked Hubert.

"Did you not know it? Coat and girdle and shoes, everything he had on him, was burned to ashes, lest anything should remain which we might recover and keep as a precious relic. Then all the ashes they gathered carefully together, and cast them into the Rhine."

Chlum, who had scarcely seemed to listen, now turned toward them again, and said abruptly, "They, and we, and the world, have not finished with those ashes. What will spring from them yet, God only knows. But it will be neither curse nor bane, but blessing. Blessing for us and ours, and our children after us. Blessing for Bohemia — but when and how — what more and what further — I do not see yet. It is hidden in the hand of God."

At that moment, a servant appeared at the door, bearing a letter. But instead of bringing it in, and giving it to his master, Chlum, he slipped it into the hand of Václav, and was going quickly away, when Chlum called him back.

"Come here, 'faithful Vitus,' " he said. "Before these knights, who heard me reproach you — too hastily — I take now your hand. There rests on you no shadow of blame. One of the last words *he* wrote was to exonerate you: 'I pray you, have no suspicion of faithful Vitus.' "

Vitus kissed the extended hand of his lord, then broke into passionate sobs and tears, and hurried out. It was some time before anyone spoke again.

Chlum at last opened his letter, and while he and the others examined its contents Hubert withdrew a little and stood by the window. Václav joined him, with the air of one preparing to make a confession.

"My father says," he began, "that I was much in fault on Saturday, and that it would have been my sin if we had both drowned."

"Was he angry with you?"

"Angry? No," said Václav, with a child's keen sense of the dignity of sorrow. "People in great trouble are never angry. Only he said I had done wrong. He sent me on Friday to Petershausen, there to abide for three days with Stanislaus the Pole" (Hubert had no difficulty in guessing *why*). "But I wanted to see the face of Master John again. How could I help it, Master Hubert? You know we all love him so. Better to die, I thought, than not to see him any more! They told me he would pass through this street, by this house. So I meant to come back here. I changed clothes with a young *flat-cap*, Hänschen, the baker's son at Petershausen, that I might not be known in the crowd. I got as far as the bridge, when that happened which you know. When I go home I will tell my mother and Zedenka what you did for me. They will thank you."

"The Lady Zedenka is your sister, I suppose?"

"Yes. Zedenka is much older than I; she is quite grown up. She does all manner of things for me. She is good — very good, and very wise. I had a brother, Johan, but he died last year, while my father was in Italy. Then Master John came to us and comforted us. Who will comfort us now?"

Presently Chlum came over to where they stood. "I suppose you will now return to your kinsfolk?" he said to Hubert.

"I have none to return to," Hubert answered, rather indifferently than sadly.

"Then what will you do, my friend?" the knight asked kindly.

"God knows," returned Hubert.

"I suppose," he added, "I shall find another service. I have always the scholar's weapon, the pen."

"The chancellor's secretary, very likely, might one day become a priest. Was that your mind, Master Hubert?"

"In this matter I am in a strait," Hubert answered candidly. "To be a good priest would be very good; but to be a priest like some I know here, a priest like those in the Council who did this thing — I would rather die! My father was a good knight, and fought for his country and his king, and gladly would I have followed in his footsteps."

"An honest wish for a gallant lad like you! Each should go after his own kind. What say you, then, to changing thy scholar's gown for a soldier's cloak, and your pen and inkhorn for a sword?"

"So would I right gladly, if I had a cloak and a sword, a captain to fight under, and a cause to fight in."

The shadow of a smile played over the sorrowful face of Chlum.

"I can find the sword and cloak at least," he said. "And if for the present you will take esquire's service under me, I can promise you such training in knightly exercises that you will be ready for the captain and the cause when they come."

For the instant Hubert was dumb, not with hesitation, but with wondering joy. Nothing better, nothing half so good, could he have dreamed of for himself. To serve this noble-hearted knight, the martyr's brave defender and dearest friend, seemed to him the happiest lot on earth. Moreover, his boyish aspirations would be realized now. He would be knight and soldier after all.

Two people mistook his silence for hesitation.

Václav broke in with an eager entreaty, "Oh! You will come to us, Master Hubert; say you will come to us!"

Chlum said modestly, "But I would not urge you, or hold you bound, should anything offer more suited to your wishes. For, as I said before the Council, I am one of the least of the barons of Bohemia; I have neither vast estates, nor great wealth, nor a fine retinue. I have only, like every other Bohemian knight, a fair skill in knightly exercises, which I shall use right willingly for your instruction."

"I am but too fortunate," said Hubert with a beaming face. "The renown of the Bohemian chivalry fills the world and I have often heard how esquires and pages from the farthest lands of Christendom resort to Bohemia for training. Sir Baron, I take your offer with heartfelt thanks, and I will be true man to you from now on, so help me God!"

Václav's shout of childish joy rang out unawares.

"That is glorious!" he cried. "Now you will come to Pihel! Now you will see my mother, and my sister Zedenka, and everybody! You shall be my grown-up brother, and Zedenka . . ."

"Hush, my son," said his father gently. "Today we speak low and soft, as those who sit beside their dead. Have you forgotten?"

Then to Hubert, "It is done. Come to us at once; for as soon as we can make ready we ride back to Bohemia, shaking off from our feet the dust of this wicked city."

The other knights, who heard the concluding words, expressed their approbation.

"Come tonight," they said to Hubert. "Come to supper. You are one of us now."

XXII

TWO STREAMS PART ONCE MORE

Yet the earth he left is holy,
Sacred every step (he) trod,
For (he) came a starry preacher,
Dedicating all to God;
Telling that a fair tomorrow
Shall come after this tonight.
Oh, the earth for us is holy,
Oh, the other world is bright!

Hubert repaired to *The Golden Lion*, where he found Armand awaiting him, seated at a table covered with snowy damask. His head was resting on his hands; but when he heard Hubert's step he looked up, and his face brightened.

"I have ordered supper at five o'clock," he said; "a *croustade royale*" (highly-seasoned game-pie) "*brouets* of almonds and cream, some trifle of a 'subtlety' in sugar to follow, and a flask of the best wine of *Beauçe* our host can find in his cellar."

"That is a repast for royalty," said Hubert, "not fit for a poor squire or a poorer scholar."

More he might have said; but he did not like to blame his light-hearted young brother, especially on the eve of a parting which might well be forever.

"I thought we should sup royally together for once, like honest gentlemen in place," Armand returned, "before we take staff and wallet, and go out on our travels like pilgrims and saunterers."

Hubert came near, and laid his hand on his brother's shoulder, looking down at his upturned face.

"I am no more a saunterer," he said. "Even already God has provided for me. That good knight of Chlum has offered to take me to Bohemia. He will make me his esquire."

"Give you success!" cried Armand, springing up overjoyed. "Or, rather, you have it already. Were I not a Frenchman, I should like to be a Bohemian. Don't you know the proverb, 'There are a hundred devils in every Bohemian soldier.' "

Hubert smiled. "A strange taste of yours," he said.

"Tush! You know what I mean. They are such splendid knights and soldiers. Do you remember hearing tell of the old King of Bohemia, who was slain at Creçy? Old he was, and blind, yet no braver warrior ever found a soldier's bed on the battle-field. But then you deserved your good fortune; you saved Chlum's son."

"Not knowing who he was, or what I did. The cry of terror called me, and I followed. That was all."

"I wish some princeling would fall into the river conveniently for me. There are enough here, and to spare, to do an honest lad that slight service among them. Still, I am not to be pitied. An esquire always has his sword and his cloak. Should my lord of Burgundy dispense with my services when he hears my story, I have reason to think Queen Barbe would accept them gladly; and I should be near my lady."

"I had not thought of that for you, Armand."

"No; and I will not have it," said Armand, with decision. "There would be no chance of fair fighting; and it is to that a squire must look who has to carve out his fortune with his sword. Moreover, I like not the manners of the court. Sorry enough I am to leave my lady there, yet *her* it will not harm. She is like a sunbeam gliding stainless through it all. But a sinful man like me! Not to talk of other foul things, which her faithful knight and servitor must abhor, and ought not even to name, yesterday I chanced upon a Hungarian gentleman of the bedchamber, who made me wroth with his profanity. Priests and prelates may be as bad as he says, and in truth I think they are. There may be bishops sitting in that Council who believe neither in God nor the devil — and certainly they act as if they feared neither. Still, all *good* men everywhere believe in God, and try to serve Him, and so would I."

"Yes," said Hubert, "and I believe knights and squires can serve him just as well as churchmen and scholars."

"Better, at least, than churchmen," said Armand. There was a silence, during which he meditated, very profoundly. At last he announced the results of his meditation after this fashion: "Every man has to fight, one way or another; or else he is a coward, and goes under, scorned of God and man. One has seen how a churchman even, fighting against lies and falsehood, can be braver than any soldier

171

sent on a forlorn hope. *He* believed in God with all his heart, and in Christ our Lord. That is what I mean to do; not, of course, to be a scholar, a heretic, or anything like that. What is a heretic, Hubert? I cannot understand it. I should have thought my Hungarian yesterday was more of a heretic than John Huss. Don't think I mean anything wrong, or contrary to the Catholic faith, Hubert. I only mean that I should like to stand *so* for truth or right, and God; even if it were against all the world."

"Wrong! Or contrary to the Catholic faith!" cried Hubert, his face beaming with joy. "No, it is now you are in the Faith, brother. I thank God for you."

After a pause he went on, in a tone of emotion, "The LORD was his light and his salvation. Then the light shone, and was reflected on you, and on me too."

"Ah! You are a scholar, and have fine words at will, Hubert."

"Finer words than deeds," said Hubert, sadly. "See what a fool I have been about the Holy Council — which I believed could do no wrong! You thought more rightly about the Council than I did. Still, in spite of all, I thank God I have seen the light. I hope to walk in it, God helping me. You will, too; and perhaps some day the light may shine reflected from you on others."

Armand took up his sword, which he had unbuckled and laid beside him. Raising the hilt to his lips, he kissed the cross on it reverently, and murmured some low words that sounded like a solemn vow.

He had scarcely finished when no less a person than the host of *The Golden Lion* drew near, bearing in his hand a small, very weighty packet, sealed and tied with silk, which he gave to Hubert.

"You are Master Hubert Bohun?" he said. "I was to give this into your own hand. Moreover, there is a chest outside, which has just been brought here for you from the house of the Chancellor of Paris."

Armand explained, "I knew you would hate to go there; so, while you were in St. Paul's Street, I just honoured my lord with a visit, and bade his people send all that belonged to you to *The Golden Lion*."

"You did not see him?" cried Hubert, eagerly.

"No, of course. But I saw that reptile Charlier, as I hope for the last time. He told me you had become a heretic."

Hubert was opening his packet with a thrill of passionate hope. He never heard Armand's conclusion, "So I answered that if he had been a *man* I should have made him swallow his lie at the sword's point, but since he was only a priest it did not matter — he might say what he pleased. What have you got there, Hubert? Gold?"

Gold it was indeed; but that was not what Hubert had longed to see. The parcel had been addressed by the chancellor's own hand, and sealed with the chancellor's own seal; and a wild hope had sprung up in the heart of Hubert that it might perhaps contain some message of pity or of pardon. Was he wholly wrong? A folded slip of paper lay beneath the little pile of good French crowns. With a trembling hand he unfolded it, and read in Latin these two words: *Abi Cito* — "Go quickly." A sudden paleness overspread his face, and he leaned his head on his hand.

Armand drew the paper toward him and read what was on it.

"A significant warning," he said. "No doubt our friend Charlier will say to others what he said to me. The Council is dangerous just now; it has tasted blood, and, moreover, it has been baffled. The victim has proved the victor. Not even the chancellor himself could protect you if some scoundrel priest, like that Paletz — Oh, the very notion makes me shudder! Go as fast as you can, Hubert. And until you do, keep close to your Bohemians, for with them no man will dare meddle."

But Hubert was as one that heard not. He sat still, with bowed head, gazing sadly on the gold, and on the far more precious slip of paper that lay beside it. There were tears in his eyes.

Armand touched him on the shoulder.

"Are you afraid, Hubert?" he asked, in a tone of surprised remonstrance. "My brave brother! I do not believe it of you. Rouse yourself! Look up!"

Then Hubert raised his bowed head, looked up, and smiled.

"No," he said, "I am not afraid, I am only grieved to the heart — for the chancellor, whose face I shall see no more. As to fear — Armand, I spent last night in prison, though you knew it not. And never did I feel more safe or more near to God. For I can say — even I, too — the Lord is my light and my salvation."

Much more did the brothers say each to the other that evening. Their paths, divided for so long, had run side by side for "one brief hour of crowded life." Now they were about to separate again, perhaps forever. But the six months which they had spent together in Constance had stamped on them both a character which neither time, nor change, nor any experience life might hold for them hereafter, could ever obliterate. To both there had come a real change, a turning from the darkness toward the light. It was a turning — not a translation. It did not transport them from earth to heaven, nor even from the fifteenth century to today. Each had still to tread his own path, to serve his own generation, amidst all its errors, ignorances, superstitions, and delusions.

To one of them, at least, it would never be possible to emancipate himself from these. Armand de Clairville would be to the end only a knight of the Middle Ages, and no

King Arthur, like a modern gentleman.

But he would be a true, pure, loyal-hearted knight, full of pity to the poor and gentle to the vanquished; and to the very best of his limited knowledge, he would serve and honour "Messire Jesus Christ."

To the larger and deeper nature, other and more difficult tasks might be appointed. Until now, Hubert Bohun had made more mistakes than his brother, perhaps only because he had loftier ideals. In the future, also, he might make mistakes. Certainly he would think much — do much — suffer much. It might even be appointed to him to tread the Reformer's difficult and perilous path, and at last to breathe the pure air of truth on heights which the Martyr of Constance had never trod. But wherever his footsteps might lead, according to his faith it would be done unto him. The LORD would be his light and his salvation, and in His strength he would walk in that light even to the end, and follow it to the very furthest and the very uttermost.

PART II

A STORY OF BOHEMIA

View of Prague

AT LEITMERITZ

Sad and slow,
Home they go.

— Old Spanish Ballad

In Northern Bohemia the fair summer sun shone brightly over waving cornfields and verdant pasture-lands, through which the broad waters of the Elbe were flowing in a swift, strong current. Green rounded hills, often crowned or girded with trees, diversified the landscape, and more than one of them bore on its summit a grim, square tower, the abode of some warlike knight or baron. But the central object of the scene was the town of Leitmeritz, its gray walls and crowded houses, its turrets and church spires rising upward in steep ascent from the banks of the Elbe to the higher level of the plain beyond.

A band of horsemen was approaching one of the gates of Leitmeritz, the St. Michael's Door. They wore rough travelling cloaks, furnished with the ample hoods often found so useful in those troublous times to conceal the faces of the wearers — but not needed now, and thrown back accordingly, for these wayfarers were in a friendly country. They were going home, and in fact had well-nigh reached it, since Leitmeritz, their last halting-place on their journey, was but two or three leagues from its termination.

Yet they showed little of the gladness men usually feel at the home-coming, especially after a long absence and many toils and dangers braved or borne. Their look and bearing were those of men who come back sad and slow — not, indeed, from a lost battle, but from one which has been all too dearly won — from a field from which honour and victory have been brought, but on which their best and bravest have been left behind, to return again no more.

Most of the little band were servants or retainers, but three were of higher rank. The leader was a tall, gray-haired knight in a crimson mantle, with a sad, firm, quiet face. He wore no plume in his cap, but a medal fastened by a golden chain, and he rode a beautiful black horse, which he managed with grace and dexterity. At his right hand rode a young man in a scholar's gown, at his left a handsome boy of twelve, on a stout palfrey.

As they drew near the gate the knight turned to the scholar.

"We must tarry here and sup, Master Hubert," he said, "though my men grudge the delay, and so does Václav. But our horses need a halt, and must be thought of — especially Rabstein," and his gloved hand rested caressingly on the sleek and shining coat of the noble horse. "Moreover, the townsfolk, among whom we have many friends, expect this much of me."

"No doubt you are right, Sir Baron," answered Hubert Bohun. But he spoke with a sigh; for the tidings which the Knight of Chlum brought back from Constance to Bohemia were not as the song of one that plays well on an instrument and has a pleasant voice. Rather were they words that rang like a trumpet-call in the ears of all who heard them. Such words are apt to cost the speaker dear.

The gate was open, and the knight and his followers rode in unchallenged. But not unwelcomed. First one, then another of the loiterers in the narrow street recognized the well-known face and figure. A cry of greeting was raised; people poured out of the shops and houses to join in it, and with shouts and eager exclamations to give God thanks for the safe return of their good friend and protector, whom they called Pán Jan z Chlum — or Chlumsky — or Kepka.

In the eyes of Hubert, the stranger, they looked like a motley crowd. Most of them were poorly clad, in jerkins of undyed wool or untanned leather, sometimes merely in coarse frocks fastened around the waist by a thong or a piece of rope. But among them were citizens of a better class, arrayed in seemly fashion, with good cloth doublets and hosen; there were women, too, both young and old, some of them in bright coloured skirts, laced bodices with silver ornaments, and white kerchiefs on head and breast. Nearly all had the dark hair and complexion and the oval faces of the Czech, with the eager, intense expression of their passionate race. The cries and greetings were mostly in the Bohemian tongue, though now and then a hearty German *Willkommen*, *gnädiger Herr* (Welcome, gracious lord) or *Gott sei Dank* (Thanks be to God) fell pleasantly on the ear of Hubert Bohun.

But even the shouts of joy seemed to have in them an undertone of sadness. The words were not all of welcome. There were murmurs of another kind among the constantly-increasing crowd that gathered around the band of horsemen, as they slowly ascended the steep and stony street which led from the gate to the market-place. The thought that surged in many hearts found a voice at last.

An old woman, bent, gray, and withered, sprang forward, and at much risk to herself seized the bridle of Chlum. "Where is he who was given in charge to you, Kepka?" she cried, in shrill, high tones of passion that rose above the clamour of the rest. "Answer that to God and us! How do you *dare* to come back to us without him?"

"How do *you* dare to insult my father?" cried the boy Václav, half unconsciously raising his hand, which held the riding-whip.

With one of his Chlum put it aside, with the other he soothed his startled horse. Then bending over the gray-haired woman, he answered gently, "Mother, be comforted for him. He walked with God, and he was not, for God took him."

"Took him to heaven in a chariot of fire, like Elijah," said one of the bystanders. "Sir Knight, we pray you tell us all about it."

Chlum bowed his head.

"Not *here*," said another. "Come to the market-place, good people; let them move on. Don't block the way."

At last the market-place was reached. They rode by the pillared town hall, and paused before the door of the principal inn. Someone immediately hurried out with a "stirrup-cup" of wine, which he presented to Chlum, saying in German and with much respect, "Welcome back to us, noble Kepka!" Hubert, Václav, and the attendants were served also.

While they drank, the crowd in the square settled into a dense solid mass, mostly men, packed as close as they could stand together — their strained, eager faces upturned to Chlum, where he sat on horseback. A strange silence held them all, as they waited breathless for his words. When at last he spoke, his voice, in its deep sadness, was calm and firm. So David, had he been there to see, might have told afterward how Jonathan was slain on his high places. Or rather, had David been the one to die for God and Israel, so Jonathan, in the after-days, might have told the story.

Hubert, of course, could not yet understand the Bohemian tongue. He sat still and watched the faces of the men who were hearing from the lips of Chlum how the noblest life they and he had ever known "went out in fire" in the Brühl meadow in Constance. Many times during their hasty journey he had done the same — in the market-places of other Bohemian towns, or in the great rooms of the village inns, often "as large as churches." The men of Leitmeritz were like the rest. They heard the tale in profound stillness; if any sought to interrupt even with a cry, the others silenced him promptly. But, as soon as the last word was spoken, with one accord they "lifted up their voice and wept."

Hubert's eye singled out among the throng one representative hearer — an apprentice lad, whom the crowd had pressed so close to him that his leather jerkin rubbed against the scholar's gown. The young Czech, a tall dark-haired athletic youth, wept and sobbed as unrestrainedly as a babe of four, the tears streaming unchecked down his manly face. But presently he dashed them aside, and looked up to heaven with some strong resolve in his face, while his lips moved as if in prayer. Hubert wondered what he was thinking — what he was saying to himself, doubtless in that strange Bohemian tongue.

Soon a portly and imposing personage, wearing a handsome fur-trimmed gown and a long gold chain, came out upon the steps of the adjoining town hall, and apparently exhorted the people to disperse. Then he approached Chlum, and greeted him with extreme deference, bowing low, and holding in his hand his three-cornered cap while he spoke with him. After a short colloquy, Chlum dismounted and went into the inn, directing the others to follow him.

They did so, leaving their horses to the care of a crowd of zealous attendants, who were ready to contend for the privilege of serving them. Before long they were all seated together at a plentifully spread table, Chlum, Václav, and Hubert being above, and the rest "below the salt."

Chlum looked weary, and had soon ended his repast. As he leaned back in his seat he observed in German to Hubert, "That was the burgomaster who spoke to me at the door. He is a German; a merchant of cloth and silk, and very rich, but in his heart opposed bitterly to our cause, though just now he thinks it well to speak me fair. Perhaps he thought I would have asked him to supper, but I could not bring myself to do it."

Hubert had observed Chlum's lack of cordiality, which he attributed — in this instance quite falsely — to the contempt of the knight for the merchant. So he was far from pleased to see the portly burgomaster enter the hall, and with an air of deprecatory humility struggling with a self-importance which he could not wholly suppress, approach the knight, and request the honour of a few minutes' conversation.

"I am ready to hear you, Herr Burgomaster," said Chlum, with the uneasy air of a naturally courteous man trying hard to behave as he ought to a person he dislikes.

An attendant brought a stool, which, however, the burgomaster declined to accept, until Chlum had formally requested him to do so. Then he drew out of his ample furred sleeve an open letter, and presented it to Chlum.

"I have had the honour of receiving this from your noble lady at Pihel," he said.

"I think," said the knight rather haughtily, and declining a gesture to take it, "I think it can scarcely concern me. Doubtless it has reference to some mercery, or other gear for the ladies."

"Pardon me, Sir Knight, if I take it on myself to say that it has reference to a very different matter. Condescend to glance over it, and you will see for yourself. I shall only venture to observe that your noble lady has been pleased to grace me and mine with an honour beyond our deserts, and for which we shall be forever grateful."

Chlum looked much surprised, not to say annoyed, but he no longer refused to take the letter. He read it very slowly and deliberately. It was written in a fair and delicate hand and in good German.

The burgomaster, like most fussy people, was impatient of silence.

"You perceive, Sir Knight," he began, "that your noble lady has had the great goodness to offer my daughter — though unworthy of such favour — a place in your illustrious household. This letter, in her own hand, testifies her gracious intentions."

"It is in the hand of my daughter," said the knight. "Nevertheless you are right. My lady wishes to receive your daughter as a bower maiden."

He paused a moment and stroked his beard, then added frankly, "My lady's wishes are my law, and my lady's pleasure is my pleasure. This being so, there is no reason for this matter to be referred to me."

"But pardon me, Sir Knight, your lady is good enough to propose that the maiden should ride to Pihel under your escort."

Chlum looked again at the letter, and could not deny it, though the suggested arrangement added to his evident vexation with the whole business.

"Doubtless the maiden is not ready," he objected. "We shall send for her by some other opportunity, for we are in haste to get home, and must set forth on our way immediately."

"The maiden is full ready, Sir Knight. She can go with you. We expected your coming today."

Chlum uttered an inarticulate sound, not understood, nor meant to be, by those around.

"Very well, Herr Burgomaster," he said. "As I observed, my lady's pleasure is mine. Get the maiden to horse as quickly as you may; and if we give her not all due and honourable care, she will be the first maiden toward whom the House of Chlum has failed in knightly devoir."

"I well believe it, good Sir Knight," said the burgomaster, bowing low. Then, receiving no sort of invitation to further converse, he withdrew to get his daughter ready for her journey.

As soon as he was gone, Václav turned to his father, and said in a tone of great annoyance, "Now what has possessed my lady mother, the good saints only know! To take for bower maiden and companion to my sister the daughter of a German — a lying varlet who sells cloth and silk at twice their value! Moreover, everyone knows old Peichler for a bitter Papist, and a hater of all that is good . . ."

"Hush, my son," interrupted Chlum, who looked, however, every whit as much annoyed as he did. "We cannot doubt for a moment your mother has some good reason. She has always excellent reasons for what she does. Keep her ever with you, Václav, and guide yourself by her counsels. She is far wiser than I."

"I do not hold with having a German girl hanging around Zedenka, talking German to her, and getting in the way when I want her," grumbled Václav. "Everyone at Pihel must speak Czech.

"Pihel, Pihel! We shall be at Pihel in two hours, or three at the latest," he cried, springing from his seat with a sudden change of mood. "Halloa there! To horse — to horse! The daylight will be gone before we are half way, if we do not hasten."

As the party sat on horseback before the inn, ready for their start, the same apprentice Hubert had noticed in the crowd led to the door of an adjoining house a quiet-looking horse, bearing one of the side-saddles that the Bohemians are said to have introduced into Western Europe. He knocked with his hand on the door, which was opened.

"Now," thought Hubert, whose station happened to be close by, "now we shall see this burgomaster again."

He did not see him, however. Two women, or rather a woman and a girl, stood just inside the door. The woman, who seemed to be of lower rank, was straining the girl to her heart in a passionate embrace, and both were weeping bitterly. But at a word from the apprentice they tried to bring their farewells to an end. The girl sorrowfully disengaged herself, the woman kissed her fondly and repeatedly, and led her, still sobbing, to the door. There she gave her a last lingering kiss, and, murmuring some words of sorrow and endearment, drew the hood of the travelling cloak so closely over her face as almost entirely to conceal it. The apprentice then took in his the passive hand of his master's daughter, led her to her horse, and assisted her to mount, which she did with no little difficulty.

Chlum, in spite of his prejudices, looked at her compassionately.

"Fear nothing, fair maiden," he said, "we will take good care of you." Then to one of his attendants: "Clodek, take the reins and lead the maiden's horse. She is, no doubt, unused to riding."

Clodek obeyed, and they set off at a good pace, for all were anxious to reach the journey's end. But the apprentice still ran beside the maiden's horse, with his hand on the mane, keeping pace with the riders seemingly without exertion.

"You are a brave lad," said Clodek, admiringly, after a long and brisk canter. "But go home now to your master. Your duty is well done. You can see for yourself the maiden is safe, and will be well seen to with us."

But the apprentice shook his head. "I shall see Mistress Aninka safe to Pihel," he said. "We lads of the ell-wand know what beseems us as well as you men of the pike and the cross-bow."

Chlum meanwhile was saying a few earnest words to Václav, Hubert having dropped behind. He had rather fallen into the habit of speaking to the boy as he would have done to an older person.

"It is not only because she is a German, and, as I fear, a papist, that I am as sorry as you are for the coming of this maiden to Pihel," he began, but corrected himself quickly — "or rather, that I would be sorry, only for the excellent reasons which no doubt have moved your mother to receive her, and which she will tell us in due time. There is another reason, which you are old enough to understand, but which I could not speak of before Master Hubert."

"You might — in Czech," said Václav.

"What sort of courtesy would that be? Besides, Master Hubert is fast learning our tongue, and will soon understand what is said before him. We must be careful not to let him know our affairs are so embarrassed that even the addition of one to our household is scarce to be desired."

"Is it for fear he would think himself unwelcome? But how could he, Father? King or Emperor would be glad to have our Hubert, if they knew him! Do you not think so, Knight and Father?"

"I like him as well as you, my son. Had I liked him less, I would not have ventured to ask him just now to cast in his lot with ours. But I think his heart is not set on this world's wealth or glory. Nor, I hope, is yours, Václav. For you are the son of a poor knight, and likely, when your own time comes, to succeed to a greatly impoverished estate."

"My father, I scarcely understand you," said Václav in some bewilderment. "We are not poor; we are rich. We have broad lands — Pihel and Janovic, and Kashimbock, Palmoky, Palkovany, and Chrudim, and I know not how many more. We could never come to lack meat and clothing — like beggars and minstrels, and poor scholars who go about singing, and people of that kind. We are *noble*."

"Can you not see, my son, that though a man may have a long purse, still, if he owes more than is in it he is a poor man? Yes, we are noble; but that does not always mean having broad lands and castles, and gold and silver. It means having ancestors who were loyal and brave in the fight, and gentle and courteous always. Nothing can rob us of *that*. Many things may rob us of the lands and castles. My affairs have lain unsettled since the death of your grandfather, so that I know not what is mine, and what is your uncle's, and from that has arisen confusion and loss. Yet it is not *that* which makes me a poor man today. Václav, I brought to Constance all the ready money I could raise; and while there I sent home once and again for more. It is all gone, like last year's snow — but the debts remain, and must be paid. I might say, indeed, that I went forth full and have come home empty, were that not too sadly true in another way, to say it of so poor a thing as gold."

"With the journeyings to and fro, we were well-nigh a year away," said Václav thoughtfully.

"And then there was that new boat you bought for Robert," he added, with a child's literalness and ignorance of proportion.

Chlum smiled. "That was a little thing," he said. "Quite little enough to do for Robert, and for Nänchen, who saved you and Master Hubert. Hard enough it was, too, to make them take the gift. No, Václav, it was for a yet more precious life than yours that our gold was poured out in Constance like water. And in vain. But I do not regret it. Tell me, do you?"

"No!" cried Václav passionately. "Never! Not if we gave our last groschen, and had to take the beggar's staff and wallet, and beg our bread through the land."

"Well spoken, my boy! You will not need to take the beggar's staff and wallet, but perhaps you may have to do instead something which will seem harder to you. I thought, as you know, of sending you as page to the lord of Hussenec, who noticed you so kindly in Constance, and who keeps one of the best households in Bohemia, and would give you such training in knightly exercises, and in all your devoir, as could not be surpassed in any royal court. But now I have not the means to equip you bravely like your comrades, and I would not let you go anywhere to be scorned and flouted, as a poor man's son. Will you, then, be content to abide at home, and to learn your devoir from me? Moreover, will you be content to forego costly armour, and fine horses, raiment of cloth of gold and velvet and the like, jewels to wear, and gold and silver to scatter at your will?"

"I want none of these things," returned Václav with decision. "Duba wants fine clothes and jewels, for he is going to be married, and Latzembok, for he has gone to the Emperor's court. But I shall not marry, because I have you, and our mother and Zedenka, and Master Hubert, and, certainly, I shall never go to the court and serve Sigismund the Word-breaker," said the boy, with kindling eyes.

"You are willing, then, for your part in our sacrifice?" asked Chlum.

"Knight and Father, I am heartily willing," Václav answered, with earnestness beyond his years.

"Well spoken! Now, my son, go and ride by that forlorn and sad-looking maid. Speak to her courteously, as a young knight should, that she may feel that she is welcome among us."

While the son and father talked together thus, Hubert had been conversing with the fleet-footed apprentice.

"Spring up behind me, when you will," he said to him. "My horse can well carry double."

"I thank you, Master Secretary, but this is my place, and I had rather keep it," returned the lad, answering, as he was addressed, in German. "But," he added immediately, "pardon me, Master, how is it that you speak German? Are you not Master Petr Mladenowic?"

It was not the first time that Hubert, in his scholar's dress, had been mistaken for the secretary of Chlum. Indeed, it was scarcely a mistake, for since they left Constance he had been acting in that capacity, at his own earnest request, and much to the relief and satisfaction of the good knight.

He said, "Master Petr has remained in Constance, to try if he can effect anything for the relief and solace of Master Jerome, who lies in a grievous dungeon — God pity him, and send him deliverance, if it be His will! But that we scarce hope for now. Did you know Master Petr?"

"No, he was never here. Pán Jan of Chlum found him in Prague, at the University. But I have seen some of his letters, written from Constance to the ladies at Pihel. Many of us in the town cared more for them than for meat and drink. But these things are not to be talked about too openly. Only, one is always safe with any man who eats the bread of Kepka."

"Which I do," returned Hubert. "But in the future I am to serve him as esquire, not as secretary."

"But tell me, Master," asked the lad, drawing near him eagerly, "tell me, were you also *there*?"

"I was not at the Brühl. I would have gone there if I could."

"Yes, gone there! So would I — so would every man of us!" cried the youth, his restrained emotion bursting forth at last. "But come back again? No, not if we knew it! Were there no more faggots in Constance, or no more executioners to kindle them? What hindered you all from crying aloud before the Council that you shared his faith, and sharing his suffering and his glory?"

"Would *you* have done that?"

"Yes, indeed, so I would! It is better to be a martyr for the Lord Jesus Christ than to reign over all the world and all the kingdoms of it."

"You are right there," Hubert answered. "Yet I think it becomes not common folk to raise their eyes to such high honour. God keeps it for His holy saints."

" 'It shall be given unto them for whom it is prepared,' " said the apprentice in Czech.

Václav, who meanwhile had been trying, with poor success, to win more than a monosyllabic "Yes" or "No" from the new bower maiden, now called out, "Master Hubert! Master Hubert! Pihel is in sight. There is the watch-tower, on the top of the next hill."

Soon the winding road brought the travellers to the base of the conical hill which was crowned by the towers of Pihel. Only a cross, a piece of broken wall, and a deep hollow (the former cellars) now remain to show where once the chivalrous lord of Chlum had his dwelling. But what Hubert saw was a frowning mass of dark gray stone with turrets and battlements and narrow slits of windows. Everything was for strength and security, nothing for beauty or for luxury, as was proper and fitting in a state of society where war was the rule, and peace and safety were the exceptions.

"Welcome to Pihel!" Chlum said cordially, as he turned to Hubert. "Did I not speak the truth before the Council that I could have kept our martyr here, and neither King nor Emperor could have torn him from us?"

II

EXPECTING

Oh! Are not meetings in this world of change
Sadder than partings oft?

Within the walls of Pihel, in a turret-chamber with narrow lancet windows, a lady lay on a couch. She wore a loose robe of violet silk, and her beautiful chestnut hair was partially hidden by a quilted coif and hood of the same colour, with long flaps. Her face was beautiful, too, with a kind of beauty which would have been rare at any time, but must have been rare exceedingly in the rough age to which she belonged, or rather in which she lived, for in every age there are anticipations of that which is to follow — flowers that bloom and fruits that ripen untimely, and are therefore apt to be fragile and short-lived. Páni Sophia z Chlum belonged to our age rather than to her own.

She was a confirmed invalid. Every feature of her pale, refined face bore the stamp of weakness and suffering. Those features in form and contour were almost perfect, and, lacking though they did the charm of health, they wore the higher charm of a deep and gentle thoughtfulness. The fact of her long-continued suffering set the lady of Chlum — the *Páni* — apart then, as it would be far from doing now. Then, as a rule, sick people got well — or they died. The day of life — which was usually briefer than ours — ended naturally, after a twilight seldom very tedious, in the night of death. It was a rare and exceptional thing to spend one's life in a kind of artificial twilight, shadowed and curtained in, protected from rough realities, but at the same time secluded from breezy open-air joys and excitements. Nor would such a lot have been Páni Sophia's, had not the tender family affection that surrounded and guarded her really prolonged her days.

By the side of her couch stood a tall and slender girl, in a bodice of blue velvet drawn together with a silver cord, and kerchief and sleeves of the finest and whitest cambric. Her hair, chestnut, like her mother's, but of a darker shade, was crowned with the high, cumbrous, peaked head-dress peculiar to her nation. Pure and buoyant health beamed from every feature of her face, and showed itself in every movement of her graceful, agile frame. Yet her likeness to her mother was unmistakable. It was a likeness such as might exist between a precious, frail exotic, with its pale, rare blossoms forced into artificial maturity, and the kindred plant, blooming freely in congenial soil, fed by the sunshine and nourished by the dew into full and luxuriant, because truly natural, life. Moreover, the girl's face had in it a hint of her father's, though rather in expression than in feature. There was something of his strength in the ample forehead and the firm outline of the well-formed mouth.

The lady lay supported by cushions, one thin hand pressed on her heart, the other playing nervously with a tassel of her robe. Her pale face was flushed — perhaps with fever, perhaps only with excitement.

"Are you sure all is ready, Zedenka?" she asked. "Have the bower women seen well to the chambers? Especially Václav's. Poor child! He will need to be comfortable now. Heaven knows how he has been faring all this time! Everything duly prepared for the new esquire?"

"Mother, I have just set the last stitch in the embroidery of his surcoat. I could not trust it to Ofka or Maria, they are not skilled enough in the dagging. And, indeed, I am glad to do it for him, since he saved Václav's life."

"Aninka will lighten your labours with the needle."

"No doubt she will, dear mother. Still, I wish we had not proposed her coming with my father; I fear he will scarce like it."

"My child, he is always so good to your poor weak mother that he will only need to hear she wished it. And when we tell him all the story, he will be glad to receive her. He will see that we could not leave the poor forlorn, motherless girl to the care of that most unfatherly of fathers. If we did, I think the Master might say to us one day: 'Inasmuch as ye did it *not* to one of the least of these.' "

"True, dear mother, and she *is* 'one of these,' I verily believe. She does not talk not much; but I think her good mother's lessons have not been forgotten, and that she loves the Holy Gospel. I *know* she is, like her mother, true *Bohemian* to the heart."

The Páni smiled. "I believe it comes never into your thoughts, Zedenka, that your own mother is of German race."

"Why should it, when she is of Bohemian heart?" asked Zedenka, kissing the thin white hand. " Mother, you are the best Bohemian of us all — and so thinks my father too. 'Learn religion of your mother, Zedenka,' was almost his last word to me before we parted a year ago. Ah, what a long, long year! Thank God, it is over now. Think, Mother, in one short hour, or two at the most, they will be with us!"

The hand which lay on the throbbing heart moved quickly with a nervous quiver, the flush on the worn features deepened. To the weak, great joy can never come unmixed with pain. There was a pause; then, as if with a sudden impulse, the Páni took her daughter's hand in hers.

"Dear heart," she said, "You are your father's child — like him, and dear to him as the light of his eyes. I say to you now, before he comes, do not grieve overmuch, do not lose faith or hope for him, if, at this sad homecoming, you find him confused and sorrowful — if even, perhaps, his trust in God is sorely shaken. Remember what he has seen and suffered in Constance. If his feet are almost gone, and his treadings have well-nigh slipped, can we wonder at it? It is not for us to judge; it is only for us to pray."

"Surely, Mother. And yet I think not to find my brave father confused and sorrowful. Rather I believe that tomorrow morning he will be counting up our pikes and cross-bows, and having every sword whetted, and every hauberk burnished well. For it is our country — our Bohemia — which has been outraged by the crime of Constance. And for these things women weep, but men *fight*."

"God forbid!" said the Páni, with a shudder. "Zedenka, such words are not good to speak. You know who has said, 'Vengeance is Mine, I will repay!' But leave me now, dear child. I would spend the time until they come in prayer. God grant I may be strong enough to go and meet your father at the gate!"

"Yes; rest while you can, dear mother. Meanwhile I will go and see to the setting forth of the rear-supper myself. My father likes a boar's head better than anything else, and so does Václav; but perhaps the young French gentleman may find the venison pasty more to his taste."

"I leave all to you, my daughter. Your skill in these matters is ever good."

When left alone the lady of Pihel was too much agitated to pray — *she thought*. Her mind wandered back unawares to the scenes and surroundings of her youth. The daughter of a Bavarian noble, high in court favour, she had received the same name as the infant Princess Sophia, on the understanding that the children, as they grew, were to be friends and companions. They became even more — they loved one another like true sisters. When — to the everlasting disgrace of those who should have been her natural protectors — the fair young Bavarian princess was given in marriage to King Wenzel of Bohemia, Sophia bore her company to her new home. But what a home for a young and innocent girl! Never — and this indeed is much to say — never did royal crown shadow the brow of a victim more worthy of compassion than the blameless queen of the dissolute, drunken, perhaps half-insane Wenzel of Bohemia. Her devoted companion sympathized in all the sorrows of her lot, and, unwilling to leave her, rejected several eligible suitors for her hand. But when at last the Knight of Chlum laid his hand and heart at her feet, she confessed that her own was won, though she knew not how or why.

Her married life was very happy. Her lord, like the Douglas of old, was "tender and true," and often did she contrast her own favoured lot with the sorrowful fate of her beloved queen. But when Chlum followed Sigismund to the Venetian war, she gladly returned — with her young daughter Zedenka, and her two baby boys, Johan and Václav — to the court of the queen, who found much solace in her company.

Queen Sophia then had a new confessor, who was exercising a remarkable influence over her. When the lady of Pihel saw him first, she did not credit him with any exceptional sanctity. He affected no austerity of bearing, no peculiarity of dress, but wore, with grace and dignity, the handsome fur-trimmed robes of a Master of Arts, with its wide, hanging sleeves or "wings," and cap edged with crimson. If he fasted often, it was certainly not so as to be seen of men. Gradually however, she became conscious of the strange atmosphere of purity that always surrounded Magister John Huss. She observed that he never wanted gift, benefice, or favour for himself or for any of his friends, nor indeed would he accept anything.

He was still young — as the queen was also — but no one seemed to remember that. Not the most evil of tongues, in that most evil age, ever ventured to recall it. It is well there have been some things in the world impossible to sully or to spoil. No slander ever rested for an instant on his name, but passed without leaving a trace behind, like a breath from a polished mirror of steel. No evil word was ever spoken in his presence. Those who were doing wrong avoided him instinctively with an awe akin to terror. It was rumoured, indeed, that he had the power of reading the thoughts of all who came within a certain distance of him, and might chance to reveal them in an

190

Reception of Huss at Nuremberg

inconvenient manner. Yet those who were in trouble were sure to draw near to him; he seemed to find them out by a sort of instinct and had a wonderful power of consoling them. The sorrowful-hearted queen was calmer, happier, stronger since she knew him.

Páni Sophia was not slow to seek the teaching that so greatly influenced her friend. Very soon a strange thing happened to her. She ceased to think of Magister John Huss at all. For there came on her soul, like a sunburst, the revelation of Another and a greater, even of Him who, once seen and known, forevermore has the pre-eminence in the heart of humanity, since "He has made it for Himself," and it "is restless until it finds rest in Him." Even the noble figure of the preacher of righteousness passed from her into shadow. Nothing remained visible but a hand, so holding a lamp that its rays illumined the cross, and the form that hung on it. That death on Calvary, that life in heaven, realized and appropriated by faith, transfigured all life and all death for her. From now on she would live, not unto herself, but unto Him who loved her and gave Himself for her.

She had no thought, no dream, of any opposition to the creed or the Church of her day. She and those around her who felt as she did, thought they had now learned the Church's real meaning, and belonged to her more truly than ever. She knew that wicked men called Magister John Huss a heretic; but she was sure it was only because he reproved their evil deeds, and because he exhorted everyone not to trust in rites and ceremonies, but to believe in God — the Father, the Son, and the Spirit — with their whole heart, and mind, and strength.

She began to evidence her faith in works of charity and mercy, as did many others at the same time and under the same influence. In this new and happy life the time went quickly by, until the return of her lord summoned her home. She left her little daughter Zedenka behind her in Prague. Even before the time of Huss, his chapel of Bethlehem had been a centre of Christian activity. The evangelical preaching of Stephen of Kolin, and of Conrad Waldhauser, and the self-denying labours of Milic among the poor and fallen, had already gathered around the Church of Bethlehem a band of men and women "whose hearts God had touched" before Huss entered that plain "pulpit of pine wood covered with cloth" which he was to make famous forever. "Honourable women not a few" had taken up their abode in the streets adjoining the church. They were not cloistered; for the most part they took no vows and belonged to no order. A few of them, indeed, were *béguines*, but the majority were widows or single ladies of rank living on their own means. They sought and found spiritual sustenance within the walls of Bethlehem, while they spent their time and their worldly goods in works of charity under the direction of the pastor.

The pastorate of John Huss brought a large accession to this pious community. The elder ladies used to receive young girls from all parts of the country, who waited on them and shared their charitable labours, very much as their brothers did pages' service with knights of good repute, receiving in return an excellent education and a share in the religious privileges of Bethlehem. In this way Páni Sophia placed the little Zedenka with her friend Pánna Oneshka, the daughter of the famous Bohemian writer and thinker, Thomas Stitny, who after her father's death had purchased the house immediately adjoining the chapel of Bethlehem. It was a great sacrifice for Páni Sophia to part with the child, but just then she was in the mood for sacrifices. It was the day of her first love, the "kindness of her youth." Everything seemed easy then.

She went home to tell what great things God had done for her, and to endeavour, by prayers, by tears, and by good works, to win others, and especially her dear lord, to share her faith. Then the first shadow fell on her. Chlum heard her with a mixture of indulgence and of reverence. He had always looked up to her; and now she was more than ever a saint in his eyes. That was all. He thought — or *she* thought he did — of his dogs, his horses, his armour, his hunting — of the affairs of the royal brothers, King Sigismund and King Wenzel, who were forever quarrelling — of the concerns of the peasants on his estates, to whom he was a kind, just, and considerate lord. For the rest, he went to Mass and confession, and gave of his substance to the Church, and what more had he to do with religion than that?

Once, at the earnest request of his lady, he went to Prague to see his little daughter, and to hear Magister John Huss. He came back laden with presents for the household, and full of a great triumph which the Bohemians, under the able leadership of Huss, had just obtained over the Germans, vindicating their right to their own university, and so reorganizing its constitution that henceforward Bohemians, not Germans, should rule in it. The Germans, he told the Páni, were very angry, and were leaving the city by hundreds, and — oh yes! He *had* heard Magister Huss, who preached a grand sermon in Bethlehem chapel on the eve of St. Michael and All Angels; it was all, so far as he remembered, about the misdoings of the cardinals in Rome. Páni Sophia could only pray and wait, and cherish a trembling hope that perhaps, after all, her lord was not far from the kingdom of heaven. Then came the troublous days when the angry pope fulminated an interdict against Prague on account of the presence of Huss. The pastor could not endure that his fellow-citizens should suffer on his account, and especially that they should suffer the deprivation of the ordinances of religion. He went therefore into voluntary exile, and Chlum was one of those barons who welcomed him gladly to their castles, and gave him opportunities of preaching throughout the country. At such preaching he was always present when it was possible, saying little afterward, but zealous in the duties of hospitality and in care for the comfort of the preacher, whom he regarded with unbounded veneration, not unmixed with awe. While Huss was preaching throughout Bohemia, Chlum was summoned once more to attend Sigismund in his wars, and he served him with courage and distinction. During his absence a great grief fell on his house. Fever visited Pihel — his elder son Johan died of it, and the Páni, who had nursed the boy devotedly to the end, was stricken down herself and brought to the gates of the grave. Her health, always fragile, never from that time fully recovered. Zedenka came home to tend her, and Magister John Huss himself, having heard of her sorrow and her sickness, journeyed to Pihel to comfort her. Perhaps it was owing to this visit that her spiritual life took new spring, and grew and strengthened in proportion as her bodily health declined.

Her lord returned to her, but only for a brief interval. For he brought the tidings that Huss was going to Constance, and that Sigismund had personally requested him, Jan z Chlum, with two other barons of Bohemia, Duba and Latzembok, to accompany "the Magister," and to guard him from all dangers, whether in Constance itself or going and returning.

Páni Sophia was overjoyed. This surely was the answer to all her prayers. This was that salvation of the Lord she had longed and hoped to see. She did not doubt that truth would win the day at Constance, that the Magister would vindicate his doctrines triumphantly before the Council, and come back to them, not only absolved from all stain of heresy, but surrounded with a blaze of glory. Surely her lord, seeing and hearing all, would grow strong in faith, and enter joyfully the gate of that kingdom from which for so long he had not been far.

She willingly allowed her remaining boy, Václav, to go in such company to Constance, as a better training than any she could give him. She had surety of her reward in a little letter written from Nuremburg, for Václav's education had been well seen to, and he was forward for his age. It contained the important information — "Magister John Huss has a beautiful black horse called Rabstein, on which he lets me ride sometimes;" and, what was in the writer's eyes far less interesting, "The other day, at Piberach" (the name being scarcely legible), "my father made a speech to the people in German, defending the doctrines of the Magister."

This was news indeed! That her silent lord, emphatically a man of deeds, not words, should speak in public at all was wonderful enough; that he should speak in German, a language he hated, was more wonderful still; but that he should do so in defence of doctrines which she scarcely dared to hope he comprehended, was most wonderful of all. What would she have thought, had she known that Huss said, "He spoke better than I did," and called him from then on in mild pleasantry, "the Doctor of Piberach?" At the end of Václav's letter the secretary, Mladenowic, added a few lines. Not all the deep respect of his formal ceremonious language could conceal the exultation of his soul — shared no doubt to the uttermost by his lord — at the favourable reception "the Magister" met with, and the honours paid to him everywhere. His entry into Nuremburg had been a veritable triumph. Very touching and significant was the love which these Germans — purely for the sake of the truths he taught — showed to the Bohemian patriot and reformer, who might have been expected to awaken all their prejudices. And very grateful and cordial was his response.

But this was too bright to last. The next letter chronicled the arrival at Constance, and tidings of evil omen followed all too quickly after. From the time she heard of the imprisonment of Huss, the life of the Páni was one long agony. Letters were few and rare, and, when they came, each seemed sadder than the last. What wonder if her faith was tried by the conduct of the Council — to her, as to others, the highest authority in the Church of Christ — and still more by the sufferings of the holiest servant of God she had ever known? She did not say it in so many words, even to herself, but she tacitly assumed that a shock which caused *her* faith to tremble must shiver that of her lord into fragments.

Moreover, she had many fears for his safety. Her doubts of his faith did not at all extend to his faithfulness. She was as sure as she was of her own existence that he would stand loyally by Huss —

In the dark prison-house,
In the terrific face of armed law,
Yea, on the scaffold, if it needs must be.

But at what possible cost to himself?

At last there came a letter which came near to breaking her heart. Not from Chlum — he hardly wrote at all; Mladenowic was the writer. It told of that mournful visit to the captive in the Franciscan dungeon, of which Robert had spoken to Hubert. The whole scene rose before her. She saw the holy teacher — the man she reverenced — lying alone, forsaken of all in his hour of need, the bolts and bars of his dreary dungeon fast shut upon him. *Forgotten*, left to die of hunger — he who had brought the Bread of Life to thousands! No one had intended the cruelty; it was only a chance that happened to him; he was only just — *forgotten*. But that was the sting of it. Over and over she said to herself, "Not one of them — not a sparrow — is forgotten before the Father of all. How was it, then, that He let His holiest servant be forgotten thus?"

"Sad was the meeting, sadder yet the parting," had Mladenowic written. She did not doubt that the next letter would tell how that noble life had gone out in silence and in darkness. No victory won, no deliverance wrought, no witness borne for God and Truth "in the face of the sun and the eye of light."

But it was not so to be. Tidings that Huss was after all to be brought before the Council reached her next. Then there followed quickly the mockery of trial, the condemnation, the martyrdom. She heard the bare facts, and but little more. The last letter from Constance just mentioned the rescue of Václav by Hubert, and then announced the speedy return of her lord. He would avoid Prague, he said, for fear of increasing the excitement there, and ride on in all haste to Pihel to see her, as he greatly desired to do. Later, he considerately sent a messenger, saying that he and his had crossed the frontier of Bohemia, and naming the day when they might be expected at home.

There were times when she looked forward to the meeting with thrills of joy, almost too much for her feeble frame. But more often it seemed as if the joy had gone out of everything for her. Would her lord come back to her even as he had left her? What hard thoughts of God and man might there not have grown up in his heart? What doubts, what desperation almost? And how could she help him to vanquish doubt and despair, while her own was quivering with the one, and almost trembling on the brink of the other?

At least she could pray for him; and that she did, daily and hourly. But it was now no more as in days gone by, when the candle of the Lord shone on her. Her prayer was not so much the trusting whisper of a happy, loving child, as the piteous wail of

An infant crying in the night,
An infant crying for the light,
And with no language but a cry.

Now, at last, the day was come — the day of that common thing on earth, a dreaded joy. That summer evening, as she lay and listened for the approach of the travellers, the tension of her spirit grew almost unbearable, until at last it produced a degree of bodily weariness which reacted upon it, and insensibly relaxed it. Thinking passed into aimless wandering of mind, which in its turn slipped unawares into a kind of half-dream. Finally, slumber stole over her.

A short, quick bark aroused her. Her lord's favourite dog, Bralik, also a great pet of Zedenka, had remained behind when his young mistress left the room. Now he rushed to the door — which fortunately was ajar — whined, scratched at it, dragged it open, then plunged or tumbled headlong down the narrow turret-stairs, making noise enough for a troop. There were noises in the house also — voices and hurrying footsteps.

"*They have come!*" said Páni Sophia to herself. With the strength born of excitement she arose, stood on her feet, and hastened to the door.

III

SILVER SPURS

We cannot speak, we seem to view
The hills we used to live in;
And feel our mother's smile press through
The kiss that she is giving.

— E.B. Browning

Amidst the gathering shades of twilight the travellers rode up to the castle gate. Hubert had a moment's vision of a form and figure framed in its quaint archway, and illumined by the light of a dozen torches, which came from he knew not where — a tall, slight form, and a face which to his unaccustomed eyes was a dream of beauty. Dogs rushed out on them with vociferous welcome, servants hurried forward helping the riders to dismount.

Hubert's eye followed Chlum as, springing from his horse, he folded the maiden in a fond embrace, saying but one word, *"Djerka"* — Daughter. A sense of loneliness stole over him with strange new pain; for him there was not the sweet welcome of a gentle voice, the tender touch of a loving hand. He alighted slowly, and came in, just in time to see Václav fling himself on his sister and half stifle her with his tempestuous embraces, while Chlum asked quickly, "Where is your mother?"

Two Bohemian words gave the answer. Chlum strode across the hall — but, checking himself suddenly, turned back again, and, taking the hand of Hubert, presented him to his daughter.

"My new squire," said he. "The brave youth who saved your brother's life. Besides, he is the grandson of Sir Simon Bohun of England, my father's friend, and has thus a hereditary claim on our friendship."

Deeply touched at being remembered just then, Hubert would fain have responded suitably, but, looking up, he saw again the fair vision — the stately head erect, the curved lips smiling slightly, the dark, expressive eyes fixed full on his face. A new sensation came over him: he lost his self-possession, blushed and stammered. He was thankful to his lord for adding, "You do the rest, Václav, I go to your mother."

"I am here, my lord," said a voice, low and musical, yet very penetrating in its tones. The lady of Pihel came forward with outstretched hands, her long silken robe sweeping the rush-strewn floor. Chlum bent his head over her hand, and kissed it reverently, with chivalrous duty and observance. Then he kissed her lip to lip, and the greeting was no whit the less tender for its quaint, old-world, ceremonious courtesy. Václav had his turn next, and then Chlum presented "Master Hubert Bohun, who is well known already to the mother of Václav. I believe my lady has been longing to thank him these many days past."

"Master Hubert Bohun is more than welcome to Pihel and to us," said the lady of Pihel, extending her hand. "We shall have time to show him we are grateful."

Hubert looked up. The sweet, worn face of the elder lady did not dazzle and confuse him like the radiant beauty of the girl. Rather, it gave him confidence and restored him to himself. Unused as he was to the society of ladies, he had the instincts of a gentleman, and his communication with the chancellor had taught him reverence. He dropped on one knee and touched with his lips the fair white hand of the Páni, then rising, he withdrew modestly into the background.

He was promptly seized upon by a servant who could speak German, and therefore had been deputed to wait on the new squire. "Shall I conduct you to your chamber, Master Squire?" he asked.

On Hubert answering in the affirmative, he led him to an upper room, neither large nor elaborately furnished — in fact, it contained nothing but a bed, a stool, and a carved chest, which lay open. But Hubert thought it a luxurious apartment, and it was certainly the best he had ever had.

"Who is to share it with me?" he asked.

"No one, Master. My lord has at present no other squire."

Hubert pointed first to various articles of apparel which lay on the bed, then to the open chest, where bright steel armour gleamed in the light of the torch his attendant carried. "Whose are all these?" he asked.

"They are your own, Master Squire. My lord sent us word that he was bringing a new squire from Constance, and bade us make ready for him all things suitable. The suit of armour is that which he wore himself when first he was made a knight, and he gave express directions about it. The apparel I hope you will find to your liking, Master Squire. The ladies embroidered the surcoat and the baldrick for you themselves, also the badge on your cap and on the sleeves of your tunic. They were glad to do it for you. And if I may make bold to say it, there is not one of us, gentle or simple, who will not be glad to serve him who saved our young lord's life."

So saying he turned to go, leaving his torch stuck in an iron bracket for Hubert's accommodation. But presently he returned, bearing a pewter basin of "fair water," that Hubert might wash his face and hands, as such conveniences were not usually kept in sleeping-chambers. He lingered to beg him, if he should need anything, only to call for "Prokop," and he would be promptly attended.

Hubert's heart was full. The thoughtful kindness he was receiving touched him deeply. Vague softening influences that he neither understood nor had a name for began to stir his soul. Who does not know such influences?

> We cannot see them go and come,
> We say, "Who passes?" — They are dumb.

And yet they are among the things that mould our lives. He took up the embroidered mantle and tunic, the cap and baldrick, and looked at them one by one. Those fine and delicate stitches, in many-coloured silks, in silver and in gold, had some of them been actually wrought by the frail white fingers of the beautiful lady who welcomed him so sweetly. But Prokop had said *the ladies*. Alone though he was, the hot blush mantled to his cheek and overspread his forehead at the bare idea of the Lady Zedenka having worked for *him*! Could he believe it? Could he deem himself worthy to wear what her fingers had deigned to touch? Doubtless the term included the bower women or bower maidens, whose labours the ladies of the castle directed and superintended. Yet not the less truly the gentle lady with the sweet face had worked, and thought, and cared for him. He could fancy he saw her bending over her embroidery frame tracing out those delicate flowers of white and blue which adorned the "dagged" or scalloped edges of the short crimson mantle.

This was odd enough, since, so far as he could remember, he had never seen the kind of frame ladies use for their embroidery. *Never*? Then what meant the picture that rose before him of somewhere, very far away — sometime, very long ago? He saw a lady bending over an embroidery frame, working diligently with bright-coloured silks, and a little child playing at her feet. He himself seemed to be sitting on a footstool by her side; and she looked down on him and smiled, gave him gold and silver threads and bits of silk, crimson and blue and white, to play with, and called him "*Mon fils*." Then he knew she was his mother, and the little child was his brother Armand. His memory had taken him back over fifteen years and more, to the old Norman castle.

In the midst of his vision his torch suddenly flared up, sank down again, flickered, went out. But the moonlight streamed through his narrow unglazed window, glittering brightly and coldly on the steel in the oaken chest. He took out the armour piece by piece, and as well as he could, examined and admired it. It was good plate armour, probably from the forges of Milan, of finely-tempered steel, and in excellent condition. Everything was complete, from the helmet with its vizor down to the "silver spurs" which were the badge and token of his new calling belonging properly to the squire, as "golden spurs" belonged to the belted knight. Then he drew from its scabbard the good sword, long and light, and of keenest temper, doubtless from the workshop of some famous armourer in Toulouse or Bordeaux. Once and again he turned it around and made it gleam and flash in the cold, clear light. Apart from its use and value it was "a thing of beauty," and he could not help but admire it. He wondered in what cause he was destined to draw it. But this he knew well — he could not draw it for a nobler lord, nor one more worthy of the service of a gallant squire than the good knight of Pihel.

There in the moonlight he arrayed himself in the squire's tunic, surcoat, and hosen. Thus equipped, he descended to the hall to proffer his first service as squire to his new lord.

So, for Hubert Bohun the old life ended and the new life began.

200

Then he drew from its scabbard the good sword, long and light . . .

IV

THE NEW LIFE

My lips were sealed, I think, by his,
To words of truth and uprightness.

— E.B.

The gold may pass through the furnace heated seven times — it cannot remain there. The white and blinding glare, the fierce glow of its fusion, if prolonged, would mean destruction. Everything depends upon what comes after. You can take it from the furnace and pour it, all fluid and burning still, into any mould you choose, easily as a child's hand can pour water from a pitcher. But this done, it hardens, and keeps for all time the form and fashion it took when first the fire-spirit made of it a living, liquid flame.

Hubert Bohun had passed at Constance through a veritable furnace of emotion and of passion. All the beliefs of his life had been shaken to their foundation. He had broken loose from the influence of the man who until now had been the anchor of his soul; the Great Council had proved a most bitter disappointment; his eyes had seen the red glow of the flames kindled at its bidding to consume the witness for truth and right. But out of the anguish there came to him light and hope. God had answered His martyr who appealed to Him "in the joy of his heart." That joy was reflected upon Hubert. He was as one who stood on the holy mount, and saw the glory of the Transfigured.

But what was to come after? The faith might last, and the peace, perhaps even the joy; the mood of exaltation could not. What would the return to common life — with its tasks, its trials, its temptations, even its pleasures and amusements — mean for Hubert?

It was well for him that the mould into which the metal was poured was — *a home*. Since the gentle lady of Clairville gave her last kiss to her little son, Hubert had never known a home. His first experience of life had been the hard discipline of the monastery — punishment, rebellion, then punishment again; and an entire absence of sympathy — not to speak of love, for which he pined immeasurably in secrecy and silence, never expecting to find it.

Then came the boundless licence of the Sorbonne: the wild freedom; the sense of young, vigorous life, overflowing in all manner of doing and daring; the fiery joys of conflict and victory — over wolves, over Cabochiens, over Doctors of the School, all the same to him, if only he might let loose his energies. But though he drank wine and changed jests fairly enough with his wild fellow-students in hall or cellar, these were as little like home as the refectory of the hated monastery.

The great chancellor found him just at the crisis when the reckless boy was changing into the lawless youth. He saved him from gross evil; to him Hubert owed the inestimable blessing of an early manhood without a serious stain. Yet the austere gravity of the chancellor's household, though it trained and fostered a pure and lofty character, was certainly not home-like.

In the age of chivalry, manners were considered of supreme importance; and as in new surroundings little outward things are usually the first to impress us, Hubert's deficiencies were brought home to him through these before there was time for other influences to be felt. He was painfully conscious that he had never been instructed — like his brother — in the behaviour and the observances due to ladies. He had a comfortable impression from the first that the Lady Sophia — the Páni, as she was called — would be kind to him, and judge him leniently as a poor scholar, unused to the ways of chivalry. But he stood much in awe of the Pánna — the Lady Zedenka. Her presence confused and embarrassed him, while at the same time he could never forget it. She did not often speak to him; but occasionally, in compassion for the stranger, when everyone around him was talking rapid Czech, she addressed to him a few commonplace words in German, and then he found it difficult to answer her.

His duties as squire included some slight attendance on the ladies, and one day at table, when he served her with bread, she said to him, "Our dark rye bread must seem strange to you, after your white and delicate Parisian *boules*, which we have heard of from travellers in France."

Half inaudibly Hubert murmured something, ending with "Very good."

"No doubt the French rolls were very good," she answered, affecting rather mischievously to misunderstand him.

Hubert, roused to say something, said too much, as shy people are apt to do. "Were they good or were they otherwise, Pánna, I know not, for they came never in my way. At the chancellor's table — save on festival days — we ate good black bread, and gave God thanks for the same. Moreover, we fasted often — more often than you do here." Here he stopped, overwhelmed with confusion at the thought that he seemed to be reflecting upon his hosts. By way of mending his mistake he capped it with another. "But then, of course, the chancellor was *religious*."

"I don't know about religion, or about fasting," broke in Václav. "Except it be a kind of fasting to drink ale instead of wine, which we do now, save on feast days, the wine being kept for the sick."

For once Hubert answered well: "Bad wine, such as we often had at Constance, was not half so good as this excellent ale. May I fill your cup with it, Panec?"

"Do so — but call me Václav, not Panec, else I will break your head presently in the tilting field."

Václav had formed for Hubert one of the boyish passions common to his age, and compounded of intense admiration for a senior and true camaraderie with an equal. At first, too, he enjoyed the pleasure of patronising him a little. The knight's son, at twelve, had already made considerable progress in knightly feats and exercises. He could fence a little; he could tilt at the ring; he could strike the "quintain" deftly, and avoid the avenging blow of the sandbag with which it was weighted; he could manage his steEd with ease and grace. All these valuable accomplishments, except the last, Hubert had to learn from the beginning. But he seemed to learn them by magic. So brilliant was his progress, that he soon bade fair to surpass Václav. When asked if he had ever been taught before, he answered, "My teachers were the Cabochiens in Paris. They taught me to keep a quick eye and a ready hand, on pain of getting a shrewd blow — and the rest comes easily."

The grave face of Chlum used to relax into a smile of satisfaction as he watched the two lads while they did their exercises in the courtyard of the castle; and grave enough, in spite of the joy of reunion with his family, was the good knight of Pihel, after his return from Constance. He found himself deep in debt, and with his affairs in much confusion. He knew not how to unravel or to set them straight; and he had no competent assistant, for his steward was illiterate, and his secretary, Mladenowic, was in Constance. He was even at this time without a chaplain. The priest who served him formerly, and who continued at Pihel during his absence, had shown tendencies opposed to the teachings of Huss. Consequently his services were dispensed with; and at present the household attended Mass and confession in the church of the neighbouring hamlet, though this arrangement left what Václav called "a lack of learning at home." But it is to be feared that the lack of gold and silver was more evident and more painfully felt.

Yet this lack was not Chlum's greatest sorrow. All around were mourning the martyr of Constance, as pastor, patriot leader, father in the faith of Christ. *He* mourned him far otherwise. The knight of that age was accustomed to choose another knight as comrade or brother-in-arms, to be loved with more than a brother's love, and defended with a fidelity which was held to supersede even the claims of parent, wife, or child. Such a brother-in-arms Chlum had never found, but he was destined to find much more in the priest whom his sovereign committed to his care. The long journey to Constance threw him into most intimate and close association with him. Afterward they spent three weeks together in a narrow lodging in the crowded city. "There is no one with me in the house but the lord of Chlum," wrote Huss; and we wonder what spell kept the gallant knight by the churchman's side while the city teemed with attractions which his companions, Duba and Latzembok, evidently did not disdain.

Nor in this friendship was there "one who loved and one who was loved." It was not gratitude alone which made Huss write of Chlum as "my best and dearest friend, my other self." They who bring most to other souls find most in them. It is clear that Huss found in that strong, silent soul of Chlum's something that responded to his own.

Chlum's transport of indignation at the treacherous arrest of his friend burst the bonds of his silence and made him eloquent. He hurled his fearless remonstrances in the face of the wicked pope; he hurried with appeal and expostulation from cardinal to cardinal; to be put off civilly by some, repulsed coldly by others, denied access to the rest. He even appealed to the populace, but the enemies of Huss had been beforehand with him, and he was mocked and insulted. Then he wrote his solemn protest, signed it with his name, and sealed it with his seal. Taking in his own hand the hammer and the nails, he went forth in the sight of all, and nailed a copy of it to the door of every church in Constance.

There followed for him seven months of conflict, of indignant pleading, with Emperor and with Council, the cause of the oppressed. During that time notes and letters passed to and fro, though with difficulty and danger, between the captive and his friends. Those words from the prison, written sometimes on torn fragments of paper, often in bodily weakness and pain, quickened faith, sustained hope, and deepened love.

But deeper and deeper still the shadows fell. That day when, with Duba, Latzembok, and Petr, he saw his suffering friend in the Franciscan dungeon, filled up the measure of his indignant passion. Then, like the others, he lifted up his hands to heaven, and with tears that did not shame his manhood prayed God to give him one day the power to avenge the cruelty.

He had still much to learn. The Great Teacher taught him, by letting him stand by, and look and listen while a scholar more advanced than he made perfect proof of his scholarship. He did not turn aside the ear, nor refuse to learn even the hardest lesson of all — the lesson of forgiveness. But it cost him dear. When he returned on the sixth of July from the field of the Brühl, he knew that the battle was over, and the victory won, and he gave thanks to God for his friend. But he knew also that the best part of his own life was laid in ashes by that fire. His work was done; as the Scotch say, "His weird was won."

He returned home to find the affairs of the country in confusion, and his own scarcely less so. Everything seemed without savour, without interest to him. It was no wonder, perhaps, that the narrow life of an impoverished baron at Pihel seemed little worth after the strong excitements of Constance. In spite of the solace he found in the company of his wife and daughter, the good knight sighed often, and looked gloomy and abstracted.

One day, soon after his return, he came into the stable as Hubert's willing hands were adding a fresh lustre to the glossy coat of Rabstein. It was part of a squire's duty to learn these offices, and Hubert loved to perform them for Master John's favourite horse, "My Rabstein, who surpasses all the rest in spirit and endurance."

Rabstein knew the footstep of his lord, and neighed his welcome. Chlum patted his arched neck, remarking to Hubert that he looked better than ever. "Hussenec," he added, " would fain buy him from me at any price. But only death shall part Rabstein and me. Hussenec would take my son too, as well as my horse; and it would be a good thing for the boy, as he would give him the best of education. Still — I doubt . . ."

"Sir Knight, may I crave a boon of you?" asked Hubert, as he paused.

"Yes, indeed, as many as you will. But my power to grant them may not be equal to my will."

"This is within your power, Sir Knight. Will you let me instruct Václav, with such small skill as I possess, in his Humanities? He is a very apprehensive boy, and quick of wit; it is pity if he should be idle."

Chlum stroked his beard. "It is a kind thought of yours, Hubert," he said.

"It is my pleasure, Sir Knight, and Václav, being somewhat fond of me, will learn the more readily."

"In truth, I know not what to do with Priest Sbynek gone from us, and no loss either. I can't send the lad from his mother just now, and so, Master Hubert — since you are so good. But remember, he must behave himself. Should he fail to learn his Latin, do drive it well into him with a good stout stick."

Hubert laughed. "I shall want no stick for Václav," he said. "My only fear is of another kind. You may apprehend, perhaps, that I shall make of him a Nominalist?"

"Make of him a — what? Do you mean a Frenchman?"

"I mean a disciple of the philosophy we Frenchmen were taught in the Sorbonne. We were taught, as touching universal ideas, such as faith, hope, virtue, that they have no abstract existence, but that they exist only when united to their particulars."

"If you can teach him faith, hope, and virtue, he may think what he pleases about their particulars. However, I remember now that controversy; as, had I not been dull, I should have done at the first. Master John was a Realist, and of course he was right. But by the time Václav is old enough for these subtleties, I may — if my estate permits, and he shows himself studious — send him to Prague, to keep his terms at the University. Meanwhile, Hubert, I thank you right heartily."

When Chlum went indoors, he sought his lady's bower. He found her alone, for her bower women were occupied elsewhere, and she had sent Zedenka to take the air, attended by her faint, pale shadow, the quiet little bower maiden. Aninka's hands were deft at the needle and the distaff, but her step and voice were so rarely heard that Zedenka used to say she always spoke in a whisper and stepped on wool.

The lord of Pihel sat down beside the couch on which his lady lay. He told her of Hubert's proposal, adding that it was a great relief, for he had not known what to do about the boy's education. "I think God put it into his heart," he said.

Páni Sophia felt bound to say something in reply that might strengthen the faith of her lord — that faith which she feared was

207

so sorely shaken, if indeed it was not destroyed. Her heart beat with a mixture of hope and fear, and an earnest prayer went up to heaven before she answered, "He *never* forsakes those that trust Him. We may think it sometimes, seeing the terrible things He lets men do, and sits silent in His heaven the while. 'His way is in the sea, His path in the deep waters.' But He will bring all right at last. Only we must not doubt Him."

"Doubt Him? I, of all men, could not. For *I have seen Him.*"

In great surprise, she turned, and looked at him wonderingly.

"Do you marvel, Páni, that such sight was given to a dull and simple man like me? Yet, if I remember right, it was a Paynim king who stood by the furnace and saw One walking there like unto the Son of God."

There came to Páni Sophia at once a thrill of rapturous hope and a shock of possible discovery, changing the aspect of all she thought she knew best in the world. What human being ever does know another really?

"Do you mean that you have seen Him thus, by faith?" she asked tremblingly.

"How could I help seeing Him, when He was there? It was only to forget the crowd, the Ring, and all the rest, and look at the face of the man He was upholding with His right hand."

"And I was afraid for you, my knight, lest that day's battle was too hard for you!"

"You know he asked me to be there. He wrote to me, 'O you the kindest . . .' I cannot speak of it — I will show you the letter."

He rose, walked to the narrow window, and stood looking out, down over the valley. Presently he asked, though without turning around, "Did Petr tell you in his letter that I saw him again — the day before?"

"No; did you?" she asked eagerly.

"The Emperor sent me with Duba, to entreat of him to retract and live."

Páni Sophia sank back upon her couch with a sigh. "And you accepted *that* charge?" she said.

"I accepted the chance of seeing his face and touching his hand once more."

"In the dungeon, as on that sad day?"

"No. There were with us the bishops, sent by the Council; and ill would it have liked their lordships to set foot in such a place. They had him brought to the refectory. At the sight of us he was much moved." His own voice trembled.

"Well? What did you say?" asked the Páni.

"I said, 'I am an unlearned and simple man, not able to give you counsel; but if you have erred, do not let shame withhold you from retracting.' "

"You said those words to him? I am sorry." Her voice was full of pain and of unconscious reproach. She went on in that tone of tender apology which from loving lips hurts often more than blame. "Not that it changed anything. It only must have made it a little harder for him. You could not help it. It was too much to ask from mortal man to stand and look in his face and bid him die."

"I did just — that thing. For I added, 'Do not leave the path of truth from any fear of death!' "

"Thank God!" said the Páni, with a throb of joy that was actual pain in its intensity. "My own true knight! But that was almost — martyrdom!"

"Almost? What was it else?" he added, turning around to her again. "He gave his life to God."

"I meant, for *you*."

"For me? I stood before him, and saw his tears fall, with my own eyelids dry. Yes, he wept. Why should he not? He loved us all so well. I think, too, that he understood my words, and felt beneath them what no words of mine could speak. But for me the worst was over then. With those words I gave him up to God. I knew that He called him to be His witness, and asked his life of him, and of me. After that there was no bitterness in the next day's agony. Something else came with it that was not agony, that was almost joy. I cannot understand — I can only wonder."

"And I, too, wonder but as the disciples did when they believed not for joy. Beloved, you have proved your knighthood in a nobler field than ever your fathers fought! I am proud of you — no, not *proud*, I thank God for you. He has come very near to you, my knight."

"He has put great honour on me, unworthy," he answered, coming over and standing beside her. Her words of praise were very sweet to him. "Páni," he added, "I have those precious letters written from the prison to show you. Until now I have feared to do it — feared even to give you his last message to yourself — knowing your tender heart."

"His message to *me*? Oh yes, you told me he saluted me with his other friends."

"His words are: 'Salute also your wife for me, whom I adjure you to love in Christ, for I hope she is of the number of the children of God, in the keeping of His commandments.' "

"How could it hurt? How could it do anything but comfort me to be thus remembered?" said the Páni, her tears falling. "Together we will read the letters, and also together we will read the Book he loved, and gave us in our own tongue, the Holy Scriptures. No doubt, on the journey, and in Constance, he expounded to you many things therein."

"Ah, but I was a dull scholar, and have forgotten much. Still, God knows, I like nothing so well as to read my Czech Bible, and gladly will I read it with you. You will help me to understand it."

"I think," said the Páni quietly, "it will be the other way."

Thus was broken down between those two that barrier which often makes the most tender and loving still in the inmost core of their being "strangers yet."

That evening the Páni said to Zedenka, "My child, your father is nearer God than any of us — far nearer than I, who idly dreamed that I could teach him. All this time God has been teaching him."

Sometimes our nearest and dearest are too near to be seen clearly, too dear to be judged impartially. Even because they are our own, a very part of ourselves, we extend to them that self-depreciation which we have cultivated so jealously. It takes us by surprise, it almost confounds us, when they rise up suddenly before us in the full stature of saints and heroes. But if it strikes us dumb it is with wondering joy. Hardly is there a greater joy than to see those we love reaching up higher and even higher even though we, who perhaps have given them the first upward impulse, are left immeasurably below them.

Páni Sophia did not say these things to herself, because in the fifteenth century these things were not said, or even consciously thought. But there sprang up within her a new gladness, which lent new strength for a while to her feeble frame.

V

UNDER THE SURFACE

We have steel in our hearts and our hands,
We are thousands that fear not to die;
And we'll faithfully keep to His latest commands,
And we'll follow His path to the sky.
— Song of the Hussites

A few days afterward Hubert gathered some berries on the hill, and brought them to the ladies in their apartment. When, in answer to his gentle knock, he was bidden to enter, he saw that they already had a visitor; if one so lowly as the apprentice lad, who stood cap in hand at a respectful distance answering their questions, deserved the name. The Páni sat in her straight, high-backed armchair, to our ideas very uncomfortable, yet the most luxurious seat the castle contained. Zedenka was bending over her embroidery frame. And the quiet bower maiden had her distaff in hand, but her fingers just then were idle: there was a very unwonted flush on her face, and her pale blue eyes actually sparkled. Frantisek had brought her tidings from home, and apparently she was listening to them with no lack of interest.

Hubert recognized the lad who ran beside them to Pihel, and gave him a friendly greeting.

The Páni explained, "This good youth has come from Leitmeritz to bring his master's daughter a message and a token. Please, Master Hubert, take him to the hall, and see to it that he is well refreshed with meat and drink. When he sets out again, Mistress Aninka will give him a message for her father."

Nothing loath, Hubert took the apprentice under his wing. Pihel contained far more servants than were necessary, especially in the present state of its lord's finances. A call to one brought at least half a dozen, who supplied Frantisek zealously with bread, meat, and beer, and hovered about him on the chance of hearing the news of the town. Václav came in also, to have the strap of his stirrup mended, as he said, but he did not go away again when the repairs were finished.

Hubert's acquaintance with Czech was improving daily; but he was still unable to follow a consecutive narrative, and only caught a sentence here and there of what Frantisek was saying.

The youth became presently very earnest, and his voice grew at once lower and more rapid. Hubert lost more and more of his words; but not one of them escaped Václav, as he leant over the table with both his elbows on it, looking intently at the speaker. The group of servants was now augmented by Vitus and Clodek, who, having been at Constance, and shared its experiences and its lessons, were much in advance of the others in knowledge and intelligence. As for passionate interest in religious questions, that existed everywhere in Bohemia, and in all ranks, from the highest to the lowest.

"There are many in the town that think so," Frantisek was saying. "If any of the knights and barons, like your noble Kepka here, would take up arms to avenge him, I believe they would have such a following as Bohemia has never seen. Every lad who could buy or borrow a sword would have it; and for the rest, a flail from the threshing-floor, a scythe or a reaping-hook, would do as well. Yet there are some of us who say it would be better to follow his teaching than to avenge his death."

"So say I," spoke Vitus. "Although," he added sadly, "*I* have little right to speak at all." He could never forgive himself for the accident others had so freely forgiven.

"Specially," pursued Frantisek, "should we remember how he spoke against Indulgences, and bade us beware of the cunning and avarice of the priests, who care for nothing but to rob us of our hard-earned groschen. They tell us, indeed, that a man should leave his living mother to starve, while he spends a kop of groschen getting his dead father out of purgatory. That is making void the command of God for the sake of filling their own pockets. Besides, how do we know there is any such place as purgatory at all?"

"Ah, there you speak rashly, friend Frantisek," said Clodek. "Everyone knows he must go to purgatory."

"Not *everyone*," said Frantisek in a lower tone.

"Your master would take his quarterstaff and break it on your shoulders if he heard such talk from your lips," remarked one of the older servants.

"My master knows I serve him well, so he will likely keep his quarterstaff to lean on when he goes to the Town Council," returned

Frantisek with spirit. "You have the Holy Scriptures here with you in the house," he added. "I pray you, what do they say about purgatory?"

"Master John never spoke against purgatory," said Clodek, with the air of one who settled the question.

"But against Indulgences much and often," returned Frantisek. "And I pray of you who were in Constance to tell me if from anything you heard of him you gathered that he thought to go to purgatory himself?"

Clodek was silent; but Václav cried out eagerly, "He did not, Frantisek, he did *not*! He said to Robert, 'This very day I shall rejoice with my blessed Saviour in heaven!' "

"By your leave, Panec, that proves nothing at all," said the old man who had spoken before. "A saint like him! While he was on earth he lived in heaven; how, then, could he go when he died, to a worse place?"

"I do not think the dying thief was much of a saint," said Frantisek. "Yet was it said to him, 'This day you shall be with Me in Paradise.' "

"I think," said one of the young men, "we ought to leave these hard questions to the priests."

"Yes, to *good* priests," said Prokop, "not to ignorant fellows like our Master Sbynek, who is gone from us back to Prague, and a good riddance too."

"There *are* good priests," answered Frantisek. "God be praised, who is raising them up among us to teach His people. There is one of them coming just now to Leitmeritz — a right learned and godly man — the priest of Arnoštovic."

"Where is that?" asked someone.

"Oh, near Prague. I know you are all honest lads here, seeing you wear the colours of Kepka. You will keep a secret?"

"Ah, that we will," said several voices.

"When I journeyed to Prague last April on business for my master, I heard that same priest Wenzel preach. *That* was something like a sermon! He spoke of the Lord and of His dying for our sins; and how we must repent and believe on Him, and love Him with all our hearts. He spoke, moreover, of the cup of Christ, which the wicked priests have been keeping to themselves, and forbidding us to touch, although He said when He gave it, 'Drink ye all of it.' "

"Hark to that, Clodek," said Prokop. "You can say nothing against *that*. Master John approved the giving of the Cup."

"And I take it," added Frantisek, "that all who love him will do as he said about that."

"Then all will Bohemia arise as one man, and demand it of the priests!" cried Václav. "And if they refuse, we will take it by force."

"Under favour, Panec, he never did counsel that," observed Vitus modestly. "He said that 'adult believers who asked for it devoutly, should receive it in the name of the Lord.' "

"So says Master Wenzel," added Frantisek. "Though I think he would not refuse it even to a child who had true faith and love."

"*I* am not a child," said Václav. "I can ride well, and tilt at the ring."

"Would we had such another as Priest Wenzel for our chaplain," observed Prokop.

"I would not mind hearing what he had to say," said the old man. "Though, in general, I do not like new ways."

"Then, Father, you may have your wish soon enough," returned Frantisek. "Master Wenzel is coming to Leitmeritz next week."

"Does our lord know that?" asked someone.

"You can tell him if you will. We are keeping the matter quiet, as there are some folk in the town — and my master, to my sorrow, is one of them — who bear no love to the Word of God. But Kepka is a good friend. Everything is safe with him."

"But where will Master Wenzel preach?" asked Clodek. "I think there is not a priest in the town who would give him his pulpit."

"He will have a better pulpit than any of theirs," returned Frantisek. "In a royal church, where Master John has preached many and many a time. It has a pavement of emerald, green and fair, and high overhead it has a glorious roof, blue as the sapphire."

"Hold your idle talk of emeralds and sapphires, which likely you have never seen," said Clodek. "If you have an honest tongue in your head, tell us in plain words where Master Wenzel is to preach. Perhaps some of us will go to hear him."

"In plain words, then — next Wednesday being a holiday, at noon Master Wenzel will preach in old Zuzikon's field by the river. It is just half a league from the town."

"And the Holy Sacrament? The giving of the Cup? Will he venture to do it?" asked Vitus, instinctively lowering his voice.

"What I do not know, that I cannot tell," returned Frantisek, with an air of mystery. "Though there *is* some talk of another meeting at daybreak in some private chamber in the town. But nothing is arranged as yet.

"But I must be faring homeward. Will any of you do me the favour to ask if Mistress Aninka has a token to send to her father?"

"Will you ask her yourself?" suggested Václav.

"That would I right gladly," the youth returned, flushing. "But it would be overbold in me to trouble the ladies again."

"Not if I bring you to them. Come along with me," cried Václav, suiting the action to the word. They disappeared together, and soon afterward were seen, still together, walking quickly down the hill, Frantisek talking as fast as he walked, and Václav apparently drinking in every word.

That evening Chlum observed to the Páni, "Now, God forgive me, Páni, if perhaps I have misjudged that varlet Peichler. The man must have some good in him somewhere, else would not his daughter love him so fondly. Never saw I such a change in a young maid as in her tonight. Almost she looks beautiful; and once, really I heard her laugh. All because, as they tell me, she has had a message from her father."

The Páni smiled. "It has not occurred to my good lord," she said, "that the charm might be rather in the messenger than in the message."

"I had not thought of that," he answered, "being dull of comprehension."

VI

A RASH RIDE

There's many a crown for who can reach.
Ten lines, a statesman's life in each!
The flag, stuck on a heap of bones,
A soldier's doing! What atones!
They scratch his name on the Abbey-stones, —
My riding is better, by their leave.

— R. Browning

The field-preaching was openly discussed at Pihel, like most other things, for secrecy was not the custom of the place. Chlum was reserved on the subject; he rather checked the eagerness of Václav. When the talk with Frantisek was reported to him, he said, "I like not to hear of new notions. Our enemies will say we had them from Master John, and slander him the more as a heretic. Nevertheless, if any man of mine will go and hear this Master Wenzel, I shall not say no to him."

Before the day came, however, the thoughts of most of the household were turned in another direction. In a little village some leagues away, belonging to the lord of Pihel, a German chapman, or peddler, had been attacked by the peasants, who, it was said, had beaten him severely and left him for dead. Chlum could not tell from the accounts that reached him whether the object of the outrage had been robbery or revenge — whether they simply wanted to seize the contents of his pack, or thought they had been cheated by him in the sale of them. Or perhaps the long-standing hatred between Czech and German might have had something to do with it. Chlum felt bound not only to protect the wounded man, but to do justice and judgment upon his assailants. The barons of Bohemia, at that time, had the power of life and death over their vassals, and power and responsibility are coextensive.

216

He took with him to the scene of the outrage his steward and several of his servants, all fully armed. He also asked Hubert to be of the party, not only for the sake of seeing the country, but because he was already beginning to lean on his young squire's quick intelligence and sound judgment. One of the horses was sick, and he did not wish to take Rabstein, as the road was rough and in parts only a bridle-path. So Václav's palfrey was put in requisition for the use of Hubert.

The boy grumbled a little. "I want to go to the field-preaching," he said.

"It can't be helped," his father answered. "Moreover, your mother will like to have you at home with her. Perhaps you may entice her to go out and breathe the air. She is so much better now."

Václav was disappointed at this reply. He hoped his father might have suggested — or at least have sanctioned — his using Rabstein, a privilege which had already been accorded him on rare occasions. His whole heart was set on going to the preaching. The more he thought of it, the more impossible it seemed to him to give it up. He made up his mind at last to ask his father boldly to let him take Rabstein; but it was not easy to find a convenient opportunity.

Wednesday, the day of the preaching, was the very day fixed on for the journey to Miloval. In the gray dawn the party mounted at the castle gate. Václav, with due observance, held his father's stirrup.

"Take care of your mother, my son," said Chlum as he sprang into the saddle and, gathering the reins in his hand, looked down affectionately at his son.

"My mother wished me to go to the preaching," the boy cried desperately. "Father, may I . . ."

At that moment Zedenka waved a kerchief from an upper window in farewell. Chlum saw it, and kissed his hand to her. Then his horse — a young one scarcely broken, and very fresh and restive — began to plunge and rear. A prompt start and a rapid canter were the best remedies; he therefore gave the word, and in another moment all were gone. Václav's request was never made. Had he made it, how would he have been answered?

This question might have perplexed an older casuist. Plainly, he ought to have referred it to his mother and abided by her decision. But his mother was not yet awake, and might not be for some hours. In those days people usually rose at five, breakfasted — if they breakfasted at all — where and how they could, dined about ten, noon being unusually late. But the invalid lady of Pihel was a law unto herself. She slept little at night; and though, since her lord's return, she had begun to make many exertions untried before, the long morning's rest was still a necessity.

Zedenka, however, was a very early riser; should he go to her? He was very fond of her, but he also held her in great reverence. She was so wise, so learned, so good; perhaps a little awe-inspiring in her goodness, and certainly less indulgent than his gentle mother. Before he went to Constance, Zedenka used to take him to task pretty sharply for his childish faults — when he tore his best jerkin; sent an arrow through the glazed window of the dining-hall; and, worst transgression of all, broke the goblet of Venetian glass the queen had given to his mother. No, he did not care to tell Zedenka; although he thought she would approve of his going to the preaching, and would certainly have gone there herself, had she been a man.

Vitus and Clodek would have gone, but they were with their lord. Prokop would go gladly; but the ladies needed him that day. The Páni had a fancy, much encouraged by Zedenka, to make a "pleasaunce" near the castle, like those the travellers told her of at Constance, where the burghers took the air on summer evenings. Zedenka saw the benefit to her mother of this new interest and occupation, so she threw herself into it heartily, and Prokop, with others, was to delve that day under her superintendence.

Václav, knowing this, thought his mother would be fully occupied, and have the less need of him. But then his father had told him to take care of her. Perhaps it would be better after all — perhaps, at least, it would be more right to give up his own will and to stay. What would Hubert say if he were here?

The thought of Hubert brought back the memories of Constance; and with these came the recollection of the peril into which his self-will had betrayed him there. His meditations were not unprofitable, and they led him at last to an excellent resolution.

He said within himself, and then he said out loud, to make it sure, "I will not go." Once the thing was settled, he felt strangely light of heart, and not a little proud. He knew that he had made a real sacrifice, and he tasted the joy that follows sacrifice.

Having been up since daybreak, he asked the servants, who were all devoted to him, for some breakfast. Prokop brought him the remains of a venison pasty and Václav, while he satisfied his boyish appetite, told rather grandly of his virtuous resolution to stay at home and forego the preaching.

"It is very right, Panec, that you should stay with your lady mother," said Prokop. "No doubt the days would be long to her and to the Pánna if you were away. But see here, Panec" — he drew

218

near him and lowered his voice — "Master Wenzel's preaching is not the *best* thing, after all. Do you mind what Frantisek said about the Mass at daybreak in the upper chamber, and the giving of the Cup?"

"No, Prokop, he said nothing of that. Only that perhaps somewhere, in some chamber, it might be."

"*It will be*, Panec. On Sunday there came to the church here, to Pihel, one who told me all. He is a friend of Frantisek, and it is in Frantisek's own mother's house this thing is to be done. In Prague, you know, Panec, they have been doing it these months past."

"Who is Frantisek's mother? Where does she live? I like Frantisek; he is a brave fellow. I wonder he is not a soldier."

"Do you know, Panec, that his father was of the town council, and very well thought of? A good Bohemian, and respected in his calling; — he was of the guild of armourers. It was through the default of certain barons, who had his goods and never paid him, that he came to poverty. Not every noble lord is like our Kepka, who would rather want himself than bring a poor man to want. The son has the good word of all, even of his churl of a master; and he is working hard that soon he may keep his mother in comfort."

"But dare they give the Cup anywhere save in the church?" asked Václav, with wondering eagerness.

"Dare not a priest say Mass anywhere, Panec, specially if it be a case of necessity? Did not Master John say Mass in your lodgings in Constance?"

There was a pause. Václav looked up with a brightening face. A thought had dawned upon him — a thought so grand and glorious that he scarce knew how to utter it.

"It would be *very* early tomorrow morning," he said.

"Certainly, Panec. At daybreak."

"There was a splendid moon last night," pursued Václav. Then, after a pause, "Do you think my father will come home tonight, Prokop?"

"Not likely, Panec. Those villagers are the very devil for bewildering a man with talk. Add to their tongues, which will wag fast enough, the glozing tongue of a German chapman, used to talking the maids into buying barragon for French taffetas, and you may guess how long it will take my lord to see daylight through the business."

"Would he might come tonight! I would crave his leave — yes, on my bended knees — to go to that giving of the Cup."

"And I am sure you would have it, Panec."

"Yes, *if* he comes. But then the horses, they will be all tired out."

"There is Rabstein, Panec."

"True — Rabstein. I think he would let me take Rabstein for *that*."

"Think? You may be well sure of it, Panec. And I would be proud to wait on you, and to see that he is properly cared for in the town."

"That means a second horse, though."

"Not at all, Panec. I shall run beside you, as Frantisek did that night," said Prokop, who was an active young fellow, quick and daring, though rather heedless.

"Well, I *hope* he will come. If not . . ." Václav did not finish his sentence; he rose from the table, and went upstairs to his mother.

Evening came, and night; yet Chlum had not returned. Václav held his young eyes back from slumber until midnight. He had dreamed all day of the night's ride to the secret meeting, until at last

The thought grew frightful, 'twas so wildly dear.

There was in his young heart a very real desire to do the will of the Lord Christ. Surely this taking of the Cup was His will, for all His faithful people; even for a boy like himself, if he truly believed and loved Him? Master John had written from his prison telling them it was right to do it. Then he *would* do it, even if it were to cost him his life. Here, no doubt, a secret excitement mixed with his graver thoughts. He would be the *first* in all his house to do it. Neither his father, nor Duba, nor Latzembok, nor any of the knights and barons he knew, had ever attained this high privilege.

Then there was the charm of the adventure; the long moonlight ride all alone, the visit to the town, the meeting with Franz. He did not choose to take Prokop. He told himself that he did not wish to give him the fatigue of keeping pace on foot with such a horse as Rabstein; but perhaps an unconscious pride in carrying through the whole affair without assistance had as much to do with his determination. Moreover, why should he need an escort?

No one was likely to be alarmed about him. Prokop would be able to tell where he had gone. He would be at home again, if not before his mother rose, at least in time for dinner. Should his father have returned in the meantime, he would tell him, what he was telling himself over and over again, with a vigour and insistence that testified to some secret doubt, that he had thought himself justified under the circumstances in taking his leave for granted.

A little after midnight he arose, threw on his clothing, and went downstairs. Within doors all was quiet and comparatively dark; without, a glorious flood of moonlight was making the courtyard bright as day. He could even see the hasp of the sliding bolt on the door of Rabstein's stable. It was scarcely an adventure to ride down to Leitmeritz on such a night, by the best and smoothest road in all the country. Yet the throbbing of his boyish heart as he crossed the courtyard told him not unpleasantly that he *was* "upon adventure bound," like a young knight-errant.

His next act was to saddle Rabstein, as he well knew how to do. The porter, with some ceremony, had brought to him overnight the keys of the castle; respecting, in the absence of his lord, the youthful dignities of the Panec. There was a postern gate, quite large enough for a horse to be got through. His fingers were hurt and his wrists strained in the effort to turn the heavy key in the great cumbrous lock, but he succeeded at last.

He led Rabstein — who seemed to understand what was wanted of him, and bowed his arched neck willingly to pass through the low doorway — softly out, mounted, and cantered gaily down the hill. Now indeed his heart was full of exulting joy. Clear in the moonlight gleamed before him the white line of the Leitmeritz road. Green fields were on either hand, with here and there a pool of water, which the moonbeams changed to liquid silver. Behind him was the village, wrapped in profoundest slumber; not one solitary light in the queer little windows, like half-closed eyelids, that pierced the high, sloping, wooden roofs.

Not a light anywhere, save the moonlight. Not a motion; not a sound of voice or step, save the rhythmic beat of Rabstein's hoofs on the hard, dry road. The good horse went with a will, as if he knew, thought Václav, that with every step he was bearing him on to the fulfilment of his dear master's dying command.

Not a motion anywhere? Stay; was there not some stir in the bushes yonder, where the shadow lay so black? What if near him there were — *robbers*? It is true that the district "had rest and was quiet," so far as might be in those troublous times; still, the thought of a danger to face, or a foe to fight, could never have been far from the mind of a child of the fifteenth century. Feeling himself a man in very deed, Václav laid his hand on the small, light sword Latzembok had given him in Constance, but only to see a "merry brown hare" dart across the moonlit road. He laughed gaily to himself as he sped along, free and joyous, like an arrow from the bow, like a bird in the air. Then he sang aloud in the gladness of his heart fragments of the old Bohemian songs with which his memory was stored.

Presently there came in view the swift, broad river, the moonbeams tracing on its bosom a pathway of living light. The battle-song he was ringing out died upon his lips. He thought that on that bright pathway someone might come to him — some angel, some saint with a golden glory around his head, such as, no doubt, Master John was wearing now. He felt no fear, only a kind of awful joy. Then he thought of what they were going to do yonder in the town — of that solemn, holy rite, so strange and new, yet so old. Master John had bidden them do it — the Lord Christ had ordained it in remembrance of Himself.

Then he sang softly Master John's own Sacramental hymn:

> *Jesus Christ, our Saviour dear,*
> *Brings us to the Father near;*
> *By His bitter pain and throes,*
> *Saving us from endless woes.*
>
> *That we may remember ever,*
> *And forget His kindness never,*
> *Gives He us His flesh for food,*
> *And for drink His precious blood.*
>
> *God the Father also praise*
> *For this gift of royal grace;*
> *Since He gave His Son for thee,*
> *From thy sin to set thee free.*
>
> *Doubt Him not, but trust Him still;*
> *He will all thy sickness heal,*
> *Quicken well thy fainting heart,*
> *Grace for all thy need impart.*
>
> *Let thy fruits thy calling prove,*
> *For His sake thy neighbour love;*
> *So the joy that thou hast found*
> *Shall flow out to all around.*

Before he ended the dawn was in the eastern sky. He could see the spire of St. Michael's Church above the dark, indistinct mass which he knew to be the roofs of the Leitmeritz houses.

When at last he knocked at the city gate, he was admitted with a promptitude that surprised him. The gatekeeper was in sympathy with the object of his visit, and already on the alert, watching for friends from the neighbourhood. At first he was surprised to see so young a communicant, but his surprise changed to admiration when he found that Kepka's son had ridden from Pihel to join them, alone and at midnight, on the very horse that had belonged to Master John Huss.

Both horse and rider received something like an ovation. An admiring, sympathizing crowd escorted them to the house of Frantisek; then Rabstein was led away, to be fed with the choicest provender Leitmeritz could supply, while the delighted Frantisek took Václav in charge, and presented him proudly to the pastor.

VII

RABSTEIN

Woe worth the hour, woe worth the day!

The lord of the soil found plenty of occupation in Miloval. The peddler, happily, did not prove to be so sadly hurt as was thought at first. He had certainly given the peasants some provocation. He was offering saffron for sale, and he told them that if it was not pure he would submit to the fate of Berlin and Wlaska, the two unfortunate merchants of saffron, who were burnt alive in Prague for the crime of adulterating their wares.

"They were almost as bad as heretics," he had added. "Though, of course, they fared better, since, being duly shriven before they died, they had only to burn once, whereas heretics, like him who died at Constance, burn twice — here and hereafter."

The poor man had made the mistake of supposing himself in a papist village — but he was quickly undeceived. It was only wonderful that he was left any life at all.

Still, Chlum could not pass over the outrage. Independently of the claims of justice, it would have been very bad policy to allow chapmen and peddlers to be maltreated on his lands. He could not fine the offenders, as they had nothing to pay; nor could he carry them off to the rarely-used dungeon of Pihel without cruelty to them and inconvenience to himself. So he bade his steward return to them in kind the treatment they had given to the chapman. They bore the infliction (which, moreover, was not very grievous) with true Slavonic stoicism; and afterward their lord said to them, "You see, my children, those who sin have to suffer. Furthermore, they make others suffer with them. I must take this German, whose words I like no better than you do, back with me to the castle, and have him tended there, lest he should die, and his blood should be upon us. Next time, think twice before you do what hurts all and helps none."

224

Other affairs, each a trifle, but altogether requiring time and patience, claimed the attention of the lord of the soil, who had not visited Miloval since his return from Constance. When night approached, a wagon-load of fresh straw was thrown down upon the floor of the largest room in the place, and the party slept on it in their cloaks. It was the evening of the next day before they could set out for Pihel, and the condition of the undesired guest, whom, "like good Samaritans," as Clodek observed, they were bringing with them, made their journey a slow one.

Everyone was in bed when they arrived; but the servants were soon roused, and Zedenka also made her appearance. All hurried to and fro, getting food for the travellers and finding accommodation for the wounded man. In the bustle, if anyone remembered Václav, it was only to think it quite natural that he should be fast asleep. Hubert, like the rest, soon sought repose, for they were all very tired.

Out of his first sound, dreamless sleep, he was awakened suddenly by a blaze of light. Prokop stood over him, torch in hand, his face white as marble. "What is it?" he cried, starting up. "Is the place on fire?"

"No, Master."

"Is anyone ill — dying?"

"Depends on what you call it, Master."

"Give me my clothes, then. Who is it?" He flung on his garments while he listened for the answer.

"The Panec never came home all day."

"Home? Where did he go?"

"To Leitmeritz. To the meeting."

"But that was at noon on Wednesday."

"There was another meeting — at daybreak. He went to that."

"And has not come home?"

"He has come home, Master."

"What has happened, then? Speak at once, Prokop. Must I shake it out of you?" cried Hubert in an agony, as he threw his gown about him and clasped his belt. This was easier to him in his haste than to don a tight jerkin, with close-fitting hosen.

"The Panec himself is safe, Master."

"Then what is all this disturbance about?" he added, in a gentler voice, for he saw that the tears were streaming down the honest fellow's face. "What is the matter, good lad?"

"Master Hubert, it is Rabstein."

"Rabstein?"

"Yes, Master. I would give my life for his this night. The beautiful horse Master John loved!"

"Your *life*? Is he dead?"

"Not dead — better if he were. Kepka will never ride Rabstein anymore. God forgive me — it was my fault. I encouraged the Panec to take him, that he might go to the giving of the Cup."

"How did this evil thing happen?"

"I scarce understand. The Panec was riding home by the level road in broad daylight. I suppose he was thinking more of what he had heard and seen than of his going, though the thing might have happened to any man anywhere. It was at that turning to the right, past the halfway stone by the wood where the charcoal-burners live. The Panec says Rabstein put his foot suddenly into a deep hole neither of them had seen, and fell — on both knees. He led him slowly to the forge of Martin the smith, who is well skilled about horses. He did all he could for him."

"Is he there yet?"

"No, the Panec has brought him home. He is in his own stable."

"Let us go to him. Where is the Panec?"

"With him. He will leave him no more than he would a man in such distress. What our lord will say or do God only knows."

Hubert hastened to the stable, Prokop going before him with the torch. Once he turned to say, "Master Hubert, I shall never have the courage to speak to my lord. I look to you to tell him it was I who put the thought into the mind of the Panec."

"How came no one to miss him all day?"

"I told the Pánna where he was; and somehow she contrived to keep the Páni's mind easy about him. I believe they thought he stayed in the town."

They reached the stable. The porter, the chief groom, and two or three other servants were there already, but there was nothing they could do. Václav stood in the midst, white and scared, a wooden bowl in his hand filled with oats, which with caresses and coaxing words he was trying to induce Rabstein to eat. It was not the best food for him at the time, and probably he showed his instinct by refusing. Evidently he had been sorely shaken and terrified, as well as badly hurt. The blacksmith, however, had bound up the wounded knees carefully with some soothing application.

Hubert had little skill to minister to Rabstein, and almost as little power to console Václav. He gave him what he could — a brotherly embrace. This broke down the boy's remaining fortitude:

flinging his arms around the neck of Hubert, he wept and sobbed like the child he was.

"What shall I do?" he cried. "Oh! Hubert, what shall I do?"

"Have you had any food all day?" asked Hubert.

"Frantisek gave me a piece of rye bread, for I would not stay to dine."

"Prokop," said Hubert, "fetch me a piece of wheat bread and a cup of wine."

Prokop went on his errand, and managed to procure both; though not without some delay, wine and wheat bread not being the ordinary fare of the Pihel household. While he was gone, Hubert persuaded the other servants to go back to their beds, since it was evident that nothing more could be done for Rabstein.

"Sit down on yonder chest," he said to Václav, "and eat and drink, before I hear another word from you."

Václav obediently took the bread; but before he tasted it he broke off a piece and offered it to Rabstein. Seeing that he ate it, he gave him more, and stood alternately eating and feeding the horse until the goodly portion brought by Prokop had disappeared. Then he drank the wine.

Seeing him restored to something like composure, Hubert said, "The thing you have to do, Václav, is to tell your father."

"Oh! I cannot. You tell him, dear Hubert."

"I will," said Hubert quietly.

A little comforted by this assurance, and worn out with fatigue and want of sleep, Václav presently began to doze. As his eyes were closing unawares, and he could no longer sit upright, Hubert induced him at last to throw himself on a heap of straw in the corner of the stable. The next moment he was fast asleep.

Hubert watched and waited for the morning. His vigil was not a long one. The lord of Pihel was an early riser even for that age; as soon, therefore, as the earliest of the servants came out into the yard Hubert went in.

Before long he returned; not alone. With white, wrathful face and hasty, powerful stride, Chlum followed. Václav still lay sleeping, and Hubert knew not whether to be glad of it. His awakening would be a terrible one.

Chlum did not even look at him. For Rabstein knew his master's step, gave a pitiful neigh, moved stiffly toward him, and held up first one and then the other wounded knee to him, with a mute appeal for sympathy in his great, soft, wistful eyes.

As mutely Chlum caressed him. Accustomed words rose to his lips, but something choked them back before they were uttered.

Meanwhile Václav awoke, struggled to his feet, came forward, stood before his father pale with terror, but unflinching. At last Chlum's eye fell upon him. He trembled from head to foot, and even Hubert held his breath, awaiting the inevitable outburst.

It never came. Chlum stood in silence, looking at his son as if he saw him not. The strange silence lasted — it seemed for an age — it might have been for a minute.

Then Václav could bear it no longer. "Father!" he cried, averting his face as he spoke.

"Speak on," said Chlum slowly, in a voice not like his own.

"Knight and Father, strike me! I deserve it."

There was no answer.

"Father, strike me!" prayed the boy once more. "Only — do it now."

"My son," said Chlum at last, and the voice, with all its sadness, was so gentle that Václav ventured to look in his face again. What he saw there made him throw himself sobbing at his feet.

"My son," said Chlum again, "I cannot look at Rabstein without remembering how great wrong may be borne — and forgiven. How, then, should I not forgive the lesser wrong, wrought only through want of thought and by one I love?"

"Yet the wrong is done," sobbed Václav, "and done to Rabstein! Father, I deserve to suffer. You cannot hurt me more than I have hurt Rabstein — than I am hurt already in my heart."

"That I well believe. Therefore, why should I strike you? Not in anger — I am not angry; nor yet for your profit, since you have been punished already. Rise up. Go and tell your mother you are forgiven."

"Father, it makes me worse — more sorry, a thousand times — to be forgiven," sobbed Václav.

"More sorry? — Yes. *Worse*? — Not so. But go now, for I must examine Rabstein's injuries myself. Hubert, you stay and help me."

Václav went, to sob out his story at his mother's side. "Mother," he said, "have you ever seen a knight so brave and kind and generous as my father?"

Páni Sophia's answer may be easily guessed. "I remember now," she added, "certain words of Master John's, which he spoke concerning patience and forgiveness. 'It brings a man nearer God,' said he, 'to take one contrary word,' or even one vexing deed, 'in patience, than to scourge himself with all the rods he could find in a forest.' "

VIII

ANOTHER RIDE

Oh, holy Teacher, could'st Thou rise and live,
Would not those pale lips murmur, "I forgive?"

"It is not so bad as I expected," said Chlum, a few days afterward. "True, I shall never ride Rabstein again. Still, the good horse shall spend the rest of his days in ease and plenty, like some brave old knight come back from the wars with his wounds and his glory. So do not grieve over him, Václav.

"Daughter, how goes it with your patient, the German peddler?"

Truth to tell, Rabstein had been a much greater object of interest and attention than the other invalid. Still, the peddler had not been neglected. Zedenka was well skilled in herbs and simples, and, accustomed to minister to the sick, was able to give her father a satisfactory answer.

"He improves daily, Father. Moreover, he seems very grateful for my care of him. I have had much ado to withhold him from giving to the serving-women all the bright-coloured kerchiefs in his pack, in thanks for their attendance. I think he is a simple man, who meant no harm, but only repeated the foolish talk of others. He likes to hear the Holy Scriptures read or recited, and says he sees now we are good people and not heretics, and he too will be a Hussite."

"I do not like that name, 'Hussite.' "

"He says that in all the towns and everywhere men are giving it to those who follow Master John. When I lived in Prague with Mistress Oneshka, we used to be called Johannites, since John was his name, and also that of Wycliffe. Why do you not like the new name, Father, if I may be bold to ask?"

"Because there are plenty who will take it on their lips while they do many foolish, and perhaps evil, things. It is too dear to me for that."

Just then Prokop entered with two letters in his hand. His share in Rabstein's misadventure had, of course, been forgiven, as it would have been unjust to pardon Václav and punish him.

"Who brought these?" asked the knight, as he took them from him.

"A horseman, Sir Knight; he is in haste to depart."

"Then, as quickly as you may, give him to eat and drink of the best, and feed his horse."

"Is he to have an answer, Sir Knight?"

"I shall speak with him myself."

He broke the seals of one of the letters, and read it through, slowly and carefully, pausing at every word. Then he said, looking up, "I am as glad of this as any soldier was of the trumpet that called him to battle. Indeed, I expected it, but not so soon. It is the call to Prague to join the knights and barons of our realm in solemn protest against the crime of Constance."

"You will go, my knight?" It was the Páni who spoke.

"If I were on my deathbed I would arise and go."

"How soon?"

"Immediately. Hubert, you shall come with me. You have never seen Prague, our noble city, one of the wonders of the world. Moreover, I need my squire — and my secretary!" he added with a smile.

"Master Hubert shall go," said the Páni. "With your good leave, my knight, so also shall Zedenka. Pánna Oneshka has been praying for a visit from her this year past and more."

"No, Mother," interposed Zedenka, "I care not to leave you now."

"You may well leave me, dear child. I am much better, and have loving attendance from all, especially from little Aninka, who is so good and watchful. I think that poor child, whom we took out of kindness, will prove a blessing in the house. You shall go, my daughter. I wish it."

Then, after a pause, "My knight, what of Václav? Were it not well that he too should go, and see that which is done?"

"No," returned Chlum with decision. "Václav shall stay with you."

Václav looked up. "Yes, Father," he said, with prompt acquiescence, "I will stay with my mother." It was in his heart to add, "I do not deserve to go," but something withheld him, perhaps akin to the feeling which kept the prodigal from saying *to his father*: "Make me as one of your hired servants."

Chlum said no more, but opened his second letter, which was far more elaborately sealed than the other, and tied with red silk, being, in fact, a private communication from a personal friend, while the other was a kind of circular.

It took him a long time to read it. His face, at first full of interest and satisfaction, gradually assumed a look of perplexity, even of annoyance. At last he handed it to Páni Sophia.

"From my good friend, Petr de Svoyshin," he said. "As you see, he is in Prague, with his lady. Heaven send the affairs of the Mint at Kuttenberg may come to no harm through the absence of the Master! He speaks nobly of the zeal of our knights and barons in the good cause. But what ails him to trouble *me* concerning the moneys I expended in Constance? You see he asks for the account of them. I do not know how it can concern him. Nor ever saw I yet that writing groschen down on paper brought one of them back again."

"Still, you better give it. The king may have asked about it."

"*The King*?" The tone in which the words were said spoke volumes. From King Wenzel men no longer hoped or feared anything.

"It is hard to tell what I know not myself — and what is the use? Unless," he added presently, "there are among the barons some who think I did not all I could have. It is likely enough. My good friend, the Master of the Mint, may wish to stop their mouths. As for me, I do not care."

So saying he left the room. Later, when he and the Páni were alone together, he said, "It is necessary to I consider the cost of taking Zedenka with us to Prague."

"It will cost you scarce anything, my knight. You and Master Hubert must lodge with Wenzel the cupmaker. But she will abide with Pánna Oneshka."

"So be it, then. If you wish it, she shall come. I can borrow what I need in the city. Daniel, Baruch's son, deals fairly for a Jew."

"No, my knight; to the Jews' quarter you shall not go. See here." She rose, took from the *chatelaine* that hung at her girdle a little key, and going to a cabinet of carved ebony that stood by the wall, unlocked it, and took out a casket. Then, bringing it to her lord: "Open that, my knight, and see if what is within will not serve your purpose better than a covetous Jew, who will charge you thirty-three percent on every ducat."

Chlum opened the casket, and saw a coronet, slight but very beautiful, its golden circlet set with rubies, amethysts, and sapphires.

"The queen's wedding-gift! No, dear heart, no! You shall not part with *that* for me."

"Why not, beloved? What are all other gifts compared with the one you gave me that same wedding-day? Keeping *that* I can let go the rest."

"Would I were rich to give you the fairest jewels from the mine — not poor, to take what you have, like a robber."

"For *whose* sake are you poor today, Kepka?"

In the end Chlum took the jewel, but with the earnest hope that he would not be obliged to part with it.

He set out on his journey accompanied by Hubert and Zedenka, and also, according to the custom of the time, by a retinue of armed and mounted servants, with which he could very well have dispensed.

During the journey they were joined by other knights and barons, going to Prague for the same purpose. These were naturally anxious to converse with Kepka, who had been an eye-witness of the events which were stirring the nation's heart to its depths. Thus it sometimes fell to the lot of Hubert, as her father's squire, to take care of the Pánna. Not that she needed his care — she rode her handsome palfrey quite as securely, and far more gracefully, than Hubert did his stout hackney. Still, it was his duty to ride by her, ready to obey her commands, or to shield her from intrusion or annoyance. He felt honoured, of course; but the honour, at first, was just a little overpowering. Yet there was a subtle charm in it, which he felt gradually more and more.

The Pánna had compassion on his bashfulness; now and then she conversed with him in German; she even condescended to point out, for his benefit as a stranger, places of interest which they passed by the way.

Once she bade him look at a ruined keep or castle, which frowned on them grimly from the brow of a rugged hill.

"That is Ostrodek," she said. "A few years ago it was the stronghold of a famous robber-chief."

"Then, Pánna, you have robber-chiefs in Bohemia also? In France there were many, because of the wars. There was in the land no law, nor justice. Moreover, a great plenty of barons, knights, and gentlemen, being ruined, and their dwellings destroyed, became robbers, having nothing else to do."

"Though we did not have the excuse of war, Master Hubert, the country certainly was in much confusion, and law and justice was sadly lacking. The robber-knights had gone so long unpunished, scarce a road in the land was safe from them, and happy was the traveller who was *only* robbed. However, our King Wenzel, in one of his rare fits of energy, took it into his head to rid the land of this plague. He sent Archbishop Sbynko with an army against the fiercest and most desperate of them all, this same Zul of Ostrodek."

"An archbishop, of all men!"

"I wish Archbishop Sbynko had never done worse. That time, at least, he did his work well. Yonder fort was stormed; the ruffians Ostrodek had collected around him were hanged, and he himself was brought in chains to Prague, to suffer the same doom."

"A dark story, Pánna."

"So it is. Still, I doubt not King Wenzel did right in refusing him a pardon. In vain he pleaded his noble blood, his knightly name. All the favour King Wenzel would grant him was to die on a gallows higher than the rest. And so he died."

"As he had lived, no doubt?"

"No, not as he had lived. While he lay in his dungeon in black despair, cursing God and man, one came to him bearing God's message of grace and peace. So tenderly did he plead, so earnestly did he pray, that at last, the heart of stone was melted. Ostrodek listened, wept, repented, and believed. He died; but he died in peace and hope, asking God's forgiveness, and desiring all faithful people to pray for him also."

"*Laus Deo* (Praise God)!" cried Hubert. "Do you know, Pánna, who it was that wrought such change in him?"

"One who has turned many to righteousness — our dear Master John."

Hubert bowed his head. "I might have known it," he said softly.

"But, Master Hubert, see what is strange — the robber and murderer, men rewarded with the gallows, the servant of God who brought him His grace and mercy, men rewarded — with the stake."

"It is strange, Pánna, when we remember that the Saviour of both, men rewarded — with the cross?"

Hubert struck a higher chord than Zedenka was in tune for just then. She was silent for a space. Then she said suddenly, "Master Hubert, you cannot feel this thing as we do."

"Can I not? I come from Constance."

"I know what you have seen and what you have done, and I honour you for that."

Hubert felt his heart throb joyfully, but her next words sobered him fast enough.

"Still, I say that *him* you do not know, and us you do not and cannot know. You come from another land, have other thoughts, and speak another tongue."

"I shall speak your tongue soon, and read it, too, Pánna. I want to read Master John's Bohemian writings."

"Yet, after all, you will but read them as I read Latin — strange thoughts in a strange tongue! For each race has its own, in which, or not at all, it must hear the wonderful works of God."

"But Master John also wrote books in Latin — especially *De Ecclesia*."

"Yes, for the scholars, for the learned. I have heard men say that they have in them more of the thoughts of your English Wycliffe than of his own. Not so the words he gave us in our mother tongue. They came from his own great heart, and they have gone straight to ours. Never man spake or wrote so before in our Bohemian. Yet, when we read, we think not of the words at all. When you look through a window, you think not of the glass — you see it not — you see the fields, the trees, lying before you as they are. So, through those words of his, crystal clear, we see that which he would have us see — the truth."

"I have always thought more of deeds than of words," said Hubert. "Yet there are words which are mightier than deeds."

"There are words which make deeds. Master John's words will make many a fearless deed of arms, if our Bohemian knights have not lost their ancient prowess."

"Not deeds of arms," said Hubert doubtfully. "At least, not arms of that kind."

"Of *all* kinds," returned Zedenka, her cheek flushed and her eyes sparkling. "*You*, Master Hubert, the son of a brave English knight, would you have the knights and barons of Bohemia sit down tamely in their castles, never raising a hand to avenge the crime of Constance, or to clear their country in the eyes of the world from the stain of heresy?"

"They are not sitting tamely down. They are protesting."

"With pen and ink. There are words mightier than deeds, Master Hubert, but there are words which are weak as water unless mighty deeds stand behind them."

"But," asked Hubert, much perplexed, "but, Pánna, what is it you would do?"

"Demand satisfaction for the past, and safety for the future."

"How?"

"If needful, at the sword's point."

"But that means — *war*."

"Does that word sound ill in the ears of an Englishman? I thought you loved it."

234

"Yes!" cried Hubert, his own eyes sparkling. "But, Pánna, in this cause one thing withholds me. War means *revenge*."

"Have I not said so?"

"He whom we love forbade that. You remember Pánna?"

"He was a saint and martyr of God, and did well to forgive. But it would not be well done in those who come after him! They have in charge his honour and their own."

"Not *his*; that is in other keeping," said Hubert in a low voice.

"Well, their own," returned Zedenka impatiently. "I looked for a more martial spirit in you, Master Hubert."

Hubert was overwhelmed with confusion. That the Pánna should be disappointed in him was too terrible! Still, he could not keep silence. With a faltering voice, but firm purpose, he answered her, "I hope, Pánna, that I should fight well in any righteous cause. For your noble father or for you, Pánna, if I may dare to say so" — he flung the words out tremblingly, with a curious mixture of fear and joy — "I would fight to the last breath, to the last drop of my blood. But I could not fight to avenge Master John. The sword would drop from my hand, for the seeing of his face, and the hearing of his voice, as I heard it that day in the church, praying God to forgive his murderers."

Zedenka was silent, but her face showed her disappointment. She had quite expected to find, almost as a matter of course, in the brave young squire the sympathy her father, much to her astonishment, had failed to give her. Nursed and cradled from her infancy in Bohemian song and story, patriotism was a passion with her. She worshipped Huss rather as the patriot hero than as the religious teacher. Nor had her education under Pánna Oneshka hindered this. She was her loving daughter, her obedient pupil; not for the world would she have donned a ribbon, or looked forth from a window, if forbidden by her guardian. Nonetheless did her young soul put on its own mental adornments, look forth from its own spiritual windows, quite uncontrolled by the authority that dominated the details of her outward life. She had watched with passionate interest the struggle between Czech and German in the university and in the town. She longed, no doubt, for the triumph of the Gospel, but she longed far more for the triumph of the Bohemian race and tongue. Her love to the Gospel was genuine, but it was not supreme.

She expected her father to come back from Constance full of indignant wrath, and thirsting for revenge. Much to her surprise he came back, instead, surrounded with an atmosphere of calm that almost awed her. Now it seemed that Master Hubert shared the same.

The silence lasted. What was the use of talking, when one was not understood? Hubert for his part had said enough, and though his heart every moment was sinking lower and lower, under the sense that he had offended, he had nothing to recall.

At last from those fair lips there came words which were very courteous, yet very terrible. In the gentlest way they put Hubert leagues apart from her. "We do wrong, Master Hubert, to trouble you with our Bohemian affairs, which, as is reasonable, you cannot understand."

He made no answer. He would not protest anymore; some day perhaps he might show her whether he understood or not.

An impulse of good nature made her continue, lest he should think she was angry, "Look ahead, Master Hubert, at those blue hills. There stands our noble city; you can see already the towers of the Hradschin. There is no fairer place in all the world. The Paynims have a proverb 'See Damascus and die.' I would say, 'See Prague and die.' But then, you know, I am a Bohemian." She smiled on him, even graciously.

Still the unreasonable youth was not comforted. "I am not of sufficient importance to offend her," he thought; and there was a shade of gravity, even of sadness, in the young eyes that looked for the first time on the distant towers of the Hradschin.

IX

THE CUP OF CHRIST

See, the feast of love is spread,
Drink the wine and break the bread;
Sweet memorials, until the Lord
Call us round His heavenly board;
Some from earth, from glory some,
Severed only "Until He come."

(Written in French.) *Hubert Bohun to the Sieur Armand de Clairville, greeting.*

MOST DEAR BROTHER,

At last I have found opportunity to send you a letter. Bertrand of Avignon, bachelor of the University here, desires to go back to the Sorbonne, from where he came. As agreed upon between us in Constance, he will give these presents to the rector for you. I hope that, through him, they will reach you in safety.

I am much disquieted by the rumours which are current here, of a great battle between the English and the French, fought at a place called Azincort — or some such name. It is said that the French have been utterly overthrown, and many thousands of them slain. I am sore troubled with fears for your safety, my Armand; since I know well that where fighting is, there would you be. Hard would it be for you to turn your foot from a lost battle, or your face from the foe. Still, I am fain to trust God for you, dear brother; and may He have you ever in His good keeping.

As for me, I may say indeed in the words of the Psalter, "The lines have fallen unto me in pleasant places." The good knight, Jean de Chlum, or as they say here, Pán Jan z Chlum, is as noble a lord as a squire ever had; and his household show me much kindness. But I pray of you,

237

Armand, if you hear anything from any man concerning the Chancellor of Paris, to tell me thereof in your letter; for his goodness unto me, a poor scholar, I shall never forget, but I shall pray for him daily, to the end of my life.

This Prague, or Praha, as the inhabitants call it, is a wonderful city. It has five parts: the Altstadt, which is the centre; the Neustadt, on the right bank of the river Moldau; and the Kleinseite, on the left; the Judenstadt, where the Jews live, of whom there are very many; and the Hradschin, on the hill, which is a very strong fortress, and has in it also the cathedral and the king's palace — but King Wenzel does not like it, and is seldom there. To go from the old town to the Hradschin and the Kleinseite, you cross the Moldau by a broad and fair bridge, wherewith the late Emperor, Charles, has adorned the town. In the Altstadt are the Town Hall and the University, also many noble churches; especially those two where the Word of God is preached faithfully — the Teyn Church and the Chapel of Bethlehem. In the Kleinseite the archbishop has a fine palace, and there are many other goodly buildings which I cannot tell you of, nor yet of the Jews' quarter, which is very singular, and strange to see. Never did I behold so many Jews together in my life; it is said that their ancestors came here from Jerusalem when it was destroyed by the Paynims, for their wickedness in crucifying our Lord. I saw their chief Rabbi, as they call their head priest, or bishop, the other day when I attended my lord to their quarter, where he had to go on some private business. He is an old man, having a long white beard, and a goodly robe, with words or sentences in some strange tongue wrought on the hem. I suppose they are cabalistic signs, unlawful for Christian men to wear or to read.

The city is full of unrest — there have been great tumults of late, partly, on account of that which has been done at Constance. Here Czech and German, Hussite and Papist, are as ready to fly at one another's throats as were Burgundian and Armagnac in the old days in Paris.

Thus far I wrote to you yesterday, but I could proceed no further, for my lord summoned me to attend him as his squire to the great meeting of the barons of Bohemia and Moravia, who were come together in the Bethlehem Church to protest against the counsel and deed of those who put Master John Huss to death.

Never have I seen such a sight! The great church — the same in which he used to preach — was filled from door to door with splendid, martial knights. You could not have kept your eyes, Armand, off the embroideries of gold and silver on their mantles and surcoats of crimson, blue, or violet, and the jewelled hilts and scabbards of their swords and poniards. And then the men themselves! Bareheaded they stood, for it was the house of God — some heads white with age, many more raven black, and the dark faces full of wrath and sorrow. As one spoke after another in words which, being Czech, I could not wholly understand, dark eyes kindled, hands flew to the scabbards of their swords. Sometimes steel clashed on steel so loudly as to drown the speaker's voice. Then someone in a long robe — clerk or notary — read aloud the great protest. It ended thus: "We will protect with our lives those true preachers who preach the Word of God, and we are ready to shed our blood in their defence." At this there arose a great shout, and all pressed forward to sign. I think they would have gladly signed it with their blood. A very aged knight with a snow-white head was the first. I think he was blind, for his squire led him up to the table where the great roll of parchment lay, and held his hand as he wrote. The others paused for him, but came up eagerly after, pressing one on another. My lord was in no haste; first or last was all the same to him. Enough for him to know that not one among them all loved Master John as he did. I believe there were sixty names and more, of the barons of Bohemia and Moravia, written there today. Had those of lower rank been allowed to sign, all the parchment in the city would not have sufficed. The University has its own protest — as well it may.

But enough of these matters. Dear brother, I desire earnestly to hear of your welfare. Should this letter reach you — as, through the favour of God and the kindness of Bertrand of Avignon, I hope it will — I entreat you to write by the hand of any you can find who is coming to Prague. See that you put upon the cover the name of my lord, the Baron of Chlum, for in Bohemia everyone knows him. Spare not, moreover, to tell me of the fair Demoiselle Jocelyne. No doubt you do wear her favour proudly; and if God spare you, you will wear it on many a well-fought field. It were easy, I think, to fight remembering those dark eyes and looking for your reward from those fair lips. Almost I could find it in my heart to envy you, Armand — no, rather, I wish you joy, and a good issue to your patient waiting.

Most of all I pray of you, dear brother, to remember what we said to each other before we parted; how we vowed to love the good God and to serve Him, and truly to follow the Lord Christ; so that, whether we meet again on earth or not, we shall meet with joy in His presence. God be with you, most dear Armand, now and forever.

So prays your loving brother,
HUBERT BOHUN

Given at Prague on the second day of September, in the year of grace fourteen hundred and fifteen.

As Hubert, having written the last words, carefully cleaned his good goose-quill, and replaced it in its case, his lord entered the room.

"Master Hubert," he said, "I have need of the paper, on which there are certain accounts of moneys, which I gave into your care when we were leaving Pihel."

"Here it is, Sir Knight," answered Hubert promptly, diving into a box which stood beside him. As he was secretary as well as squire, the charge of his lord's papers devolved on him. The document he produced was of formidable length, crowded with figures, and with writing in Czech. He knew that the writing was the Pánna's, and that she had taken enormous pains to straighten and set in order her father's very confused and fragmentary accounts. He stood amazed at the young lady's ability, learning, and industry; and it was with deep respect and veneration for all these that he handed the paper to his lord.

"My friend Svoyshin will have it of me," explained Chlum, "though I do not see not the need or the use. Master Jerome (whom God deliver, if it is His will!) received from us at Constance a document certifying that he had done all that he could in the cause of his friend. Would to God he had been content with it, and gone home quietly! I suspect they mean to give me some such document, lest hereafter men should question — but as for me, I do not care."

After a pause, he added, "Hubert, I would speak to you of another matter, of far greater importance. Tomorrow, being Sunday, the holy sacrament of the altar will be administered in both kinds in the Church of Bethlehem. You are one of us in heart already, as you well have

Jerome of Prague

proven. Will you, then, be one of us before God and the world, and partake with us of the cup of Christ, which He has given to all the faithful?"

Hubert bowed his head reverently. "If only I were worthy," he faltered.

Chlum laid his hand on his shoulder. "You are not worthy, but *Christ* is worthy," he said, and passed out without another word.

With a heart full of reverent awe, Hubert followed his lord and Zedenka the next day, and mingled with the dense, but singularly quiet, crowd that streamed into the Church of Bethlehem. It was soon packed full from door to door but great was the contrast between this and the last assembly there. A grave and solemn stillness brooded over all. Men and women sat or stood, absorbed in silent prayer, or with eyes fixed upon the altar, which had for them a new attraction, although it bore only the usual vessels and adornments. Many, too, there were who looked up sadly at the plain cloth-covered pulpit of pinewood, where one familiar face and figure would be seen no more.

Hubert looked up too; wondering how it must have been when that voice of power, now stilled forever, rang through the great church, thrilling the hearts of the "three thousand" assembled there. Then his eyes fell on the frescoes on the walls, where some hand, not very skilful, had painted those "pictures of Christ" of which the martyr dreamed in his dungeon. Were the "better painters" even now at work as he had foreseen?

Presently there was a movement in the crowd — a raising of bowed heads and turning of eager faces toward the pulpit. The preacher was ascending to his place. He was slight and spare, of small stature and insignificant appearance. Hubert ought to have expected this; he had heard him called Jacobel, or Little Jacob, as a kind of familiar name. But he had heard also that he was a great doctor, learned in the Scriptures, and passing eloquent, and somehow, though unreasonably, he was disappointed.

But he soon forgot the preacher in the sermon. Jacobel gave out as his text, "Drink ye all of it." So clearly and distinctly did he speak, filling the great church without apparent effort, that Hubert, imperfectly as he knew the language, scarce missed a single word. First came a piece of clear, close reasoning from Scripture, about the command and intention of Christ and the practice of the Primitive Church, illustrated especially by the First Epistle to the Corinthians. Then followed an able historical survey, showing that in the early ages all the faithful alike partook of the cup of Christ. Then life and fire came into the speaker's words when he told that in their own Bohemian Church the practice had been handed down for long ages from father to son, and in some places had been preserved even to within the memory of living men. But gradually the tyranny of Rome, the pride and selfishness of the priests, and the superstition of the people, had robbed the laity of this precious gift. Now, in God's Providence, it was restored to them. God had raised up among them faithful preachers, who shunned not to declare unto them all His counsel. These they might believe and follow without fear, accepting their word as the word of Christ. He who now stood before them was as certain of His will in this matter as of his own existence, and was ready to lay down his life in proof of it. But they had a better witness than his. The letter which he held up before them had been penned by a hand they knew — penned faintly, in uneven characters, for the hand was fettered and the dungeon dark — yet would those few brief words have more power with them than an archangel's eloquence. He read them aloud. "As touching the Communion of the Cup, you have my writing, in which I have given my reasons, and I can say no more, save that the Gospel, and the Epistle of St.

Paul, prescribe this custom, and that it was in use in the Primitive Church."

The preacher paused a moment. Here and there in the crowded congregation a sob was heard, and so intense, so breathless was the stillness that the low sound struck on the ear and seemed to echo through the church.

"Then draw near in faith," he resumed, "and take the cup of Christ without fear. It is no mortal hand, not even the hand of the sainted martyr, that gives it unto you, but the hand that was pierced for you, the hand of Christ Himself. Take, and drink ye all of it! But from now on let the hands that take it be sacred to Him, and used only in His service. Let the lips that touch it utter only such words as are pure and blameless in His sight. Let the feet that bear you to His table bear you nowhere He would not have you go. Let every member of your body, every power of your soul, be given from now on unto Him who gave Himself once for you on the cross, and gives Himself now to you continually in this Holy Sacrament, to the joy and comfort of your souls." The powerful voice ceased, and all was still.

Then a great wave of sound, strong and sweet and solemn, swept over the vast assembly, and rose up to heaven. Three thousand voices, as the voice of one, sang out with heart and soul the words of John Huss:

Glorious Priest, Eternal Son!
With Holy Ghost and Father One,
Our redemption Thou hast done
By Thy love.

Thou on earth with us hast dwelt;
Wounds and anguish Thou hast felt,
Souls to save, and hearts to melt,
By Thy love.

Thou dost deign for us to plead,
And in heaven dost intercede,
Thus supplying all our need,
By Thy love.

Dearly hast Thou bought us, Lord!
Forth for us Thy life was poured,
Keeping thus Thy faithful word,
By Thy love.

243

Brethren, let us cease from sin,
Take the boon He died to win,
To His kingdom enter in,
Through His love.

Let us praise Him, loving so,
Dying for us here below,
That we endless life may know,
Through His love.

The burden *z ve Milosti* lingered on the ear of Hubert, and in his heart the sweet sense of that supreme and boundless love. The office of the Mass began. A thousand times before had Hubert heard it, but this time was different from all the rest. At last the moment came for the crowd to approach the altar. Chlum and Zedenka went up hand in hand; Hubert followed them. Perhaps no words would have expressed the feelings of his heart so well in that solemn hour as those of the "prayer of humble access" in the beautiful English Communion Service. They were not written yet; but the faith and humility they breathe has been the heritage of believing souls from the beginning: "We do not presume to come to this Thy table, O merciful Lord, trusting in our own righteousness, but in Thy manifold and great mercies. We are not worthy so much as to gather up the crumbs under Thy table. But Thou art the same Lord, whose property is always to have mercy. Grant us, therefore, gracious Lord, so to eat the flesh of Thy dear Son Jesus Christ, and to drink His blood, that our sinful bodies may be made clean by His body, and our souls washed in His most precious blood, and that we may evermore dwell in Him, and He in us."

An assistant priest administered the wafer, but Jacobel himself gave the cup. In the order in which they knelt Chlum received it first, then Zedenka, then Hubert, with a hand that trembled and a heart that had no room just then for any thought, save that he was obeying the command of Christ. But as he listened to the solemn words, "The blood of our Lord Jesus Christ, which was shed for you, preserve thy soul and body unto everlasting life," another thought came, flooding his soul with joy. He was taking the gift of Christ. So the preacher said; but Hubert did not believe because of the saying of the preacher. He knew it for himself. Christ was there — there with him, Hubert Bohun. His voice spoke to him. His hand touched him in mysterious, but most sweet communion. He gave him the gift that includes all others — He gave him Himself.

That he thought the bread and the wine had undergone some miraculous change — had become something which they were not, and which Christ never meant them to be — was an evil and a loss, because all error means loss, and "no lie is of the truth." But no mist can greatly harm when the sun shines through it; and that was the true sun which shone that day in glory upon the bowed and trusting heart of Hubert Bohun.

He rose and gave place to others. Those others pressing around him were not strangers any more. They were friends, brothers; they drank with him of the cup of Christ, and were one with each other, as with Him, in that sacred bond.

Moving slowly down the crowded aisle, he at last regained his place. Still crowds were thronging to the altar, still the cup was being given. Often enough before had he seen it given, though never *thus*, and never to himself. Once, only once in his life, he had seen it *taken away*.

The whole scene flashed suddenly before his mental vision — the crowded cathedral, the Fathers of the Council, the Emperor and his princes in their pomp and glory. Alone in the midst stood the one grand, solitary figure, wearing for the last time the robe of priestly white. "The cup was taken from him, and through him it is given back to us to-day — our gain through his loss, our joy through his suffering," so Hubert thought. Then he heard again those brave words of faith and hope as they rang through the crowded church, "Yet shall I drink it with Him this day, through His grace, in His kingdom." "Even now he is drinking of it there, while we drink of it here," thought Hubert; "and his joy and ours alike have come through the loss and the pain of One whom in my heart I bless and thank this day." Then in gladness of heart he lifted up his voice with those who sang the *Gloria in Excelsis*, "Glory be to God on high, and on earth peace, goodwill toward men. We praise Thee, we bless Thee, we worship Thee, we glorify Thee, we give thanks to Thee for Thy great glory, O Lord God, Heavenly King, God the Father Almighty."

Could he, or any of the worshippers assembled that day in the Church of Bethlehem, have foreseen the strife and bloodshed, the woes and agonies, which the claiming of the cup of Christ was to bring on Bohemia — would he, or they, have lifted up their voice in that song of the angels? Indeed, would they have dared to raise to their lips that cup which was to be bought at such a price?

Perhaps not — perhaps even the boldest would have quailed, had the future been unrolled before him in prophetic vision. Yet if *now*, they know it all — those just souls and true in their place of waiting near the Throne — we think they are content. It may be, even, they are able to rejoice for and with their brethren, to whom was given the cup of the sufferings of Christ, as well as of His salvation and His glory.

X

A DEBT PAID

His (friend) my rank is among men.

A few days afterward some ladies were seated at work in a quiet room of the house adjoining the Church of Bethlehem. The room was large, and well furnished, though in a style which fashionable folk of the fifteenth century pronounced decidedly antiquated. It was hung with good, though faded, tapestry; while a spinet, and a case containing books, testified to the cultivation of the inmates.

Two of the ladies occupied a kind of dais, rather apart from the rest. One of them was advanced in years. Her long, close-fitting robe of black had no ornament save a rosary with a golden cross, and her gray hair was gathered up under a plain silken hood — to have worn the high-peaked Bohemian headdress would have been a sign of "worldly conformity." Pánna Oneshka was that phenomenon so rare in the Middle Ages — an unmarried lady of mature years, not a nun. Being one of that company of devout and honourable women who had gathered around the walls of Bethlehem, she was looked upon as a religious person — a kind of *béguine*, though of a higher social rank like an uncloistered nun without the vows. Her face, which showed signs of declining health, was strong and full of character. In youth it had been a hard face, perhaps, but the hand, not always an unkindly one, which added the wrinkles, had softened the stern, uncompromising lines. The keen gray eyes were keen enough still for seeing or for service — they could see a great deal more than the work on which she was engaged, a garment of canvas or coarse linen, intended doubtless for the poor.

Zedenka sat before her, similarly occupied. But her slender fingers drew the clumsy needle in and out of the coarse stuff with nervous rapidity, and her heightened colour and sparkling eyes showed that she was listening to the conversation of her aged friend with some strong feeling, apparently not altogether pleasurable.

Pánna Oneshka was saying, "It was well done of your father and the rest to protest against the deed of the Council, which was an insult to the whole Bohemian nation. But it is not well done of them to talk as if the Gospel began with Master John Huss, and will be heard no more, now he is gone. A great deal too much there is, even among the faithful, of the spirit St. Paul rebuked in the men of Corinth. 'Who then is Paul,' said he, 'and who is Apollos, but ministers by whom you believed?' Who then, I would ask, is Master John Huss, except the same? For that matter, I remember him myself, a poor boy singing in the church choir, and glad enough to eat his basin of pease porridge with a crust of rye bread for a spoon. It was said he did menial work for the professors in return for leave to attend their lectures. I know well he found it hard to keep himself at college; nor could he have done it at all but for the lord of Hussenec, the father of him that now is, who used to give him now and then a gown or a pair of shoes. So he got his learning — so much of it as he had, which I never heard was anything remarkable. I have known those who in acquaintance with the classic authors of antiquity, and also with the writings of the Fathers, were as far beyond him as he was beyond poor Archbishop A.B.C. — who burned Master Wycliffe's books, though he could not read them, and learned his alphabet after his consecration."

"There are plenty of doctors well learned in the classics and the Fathers," said Zedenka. "Yet not one of them can speak to the heart as he did. His words are life and fire."

"There are words of other men, however, likely to outlast them. There is more weight in one of the 'sentences' of my father, than in a whole treatise of Master John Huss. You think I say so because I am his daughter? No; of a truth I say so because so it is. Master Matthias of Janov, and Master John Milic, those holy servants of God, knew and loved well the Bohemian writings of my father, for he was the first to write with classic elegance the tongue of our people. They held him a master in the teaching of morality. Ah, those were men indeed! There were giants in the land in those days! Would we had them among us now! Truly, our Bohemia is in sore need of them."

"Only in that case we might be tempted to forget that Paul and Apollos are nothing," observed Zedenka mischievously.

"Your tongue is shrewd," said Pánna Oneshka, raising her keen eyes from her work and bending them on the face of her young companion. "But rest content, my child. I had no thought of speaking against Master John Huss, as indeed I could not, for he was ever a holy and blameless man of God. Only I would say, 'Call no man your father on earth.' "

"I suppose that means, except one's own father," said Zedenka, who well knew that Pánna Oneshka absolutely worshipped the memory of her father, the knight of Stitny, unquestionably a man of deep thought and great piety, whose works had much acceptance among the faithful in Bohemia.

"That which pleases the multitude is not always that which lasts the longest," said Pánna Oneshka. "However, I will not talk of these things to you. You are young, and the young like best that which shines upon the surface. Only this I say: I have left to you — for, of all who are left now on earth, I love you, Child, the best — the books of my father, which are written in his own hand. I meant Master John to have them after me — so much younger as he was than I — but God willed it otherwise. Now they are for you. When your hair is gray as mine, and you have borne as many sorrows, then, I think, if you live so long, you will begin to understand them."

Zedenka was touched. Laying down her work, she put her hand caressingly on the withered hand of Pánna Oneshka. "I shall hold them dear for your sake," she said.

"I know it, my child. But I would have you hold them far dearer for his sake; for, though men know it not, they have never seen his like since — nor will they. But I would ask you, Zedenka, what you mean to do about the queen? You can not surely disregard the wish she has so graciously expressed to see you?"

"I see not how I can go to the palace," said Zedenka, with some embarrassment.

"What should hinder you?"

"Dear Pánna, there are many things," said Zedenka hesitating.

"I cannot see them. Your father is here to conduct you, and his new squire, a very gentle youth, to wait on you both."

"I do not like to go, in any way, without my mother," said Zedenka, with much less than her usual frankness and self-possession.

"If that is your trouble, Child, you know I have access at all times to the queen, and I will present you. None, save your mother, has more right to do this thing for you."

Zedenka bent her face over her work, yet could not prevent its showing her perplexity. To decline the offer would have been impossible, to accept it reluctantly would have been ungracious. How could she confess to her friend that her real difficulty was the lack of the dress and the ornaments which the daughter of a baron of Bohemia ought to wear on such an occasion? Her mother had not known the queen was then in the Hradschin, and therefore had not foreseen the contingency; and she could not trouble her father about it in the midst of his present cares and embarrassment. At last she said, faintly enough, "I thank you, Pánna."

"I will speak to your father. No doubt he will be here soon to inquire after your health; or else he will send that likely youth, his squire, who seems to be well affected to the Gospel, though he is a foreigner. Tell me, has the knight of Chlum no other squire at present? What has become of the gentleman he took with him to Constance?"

"Vavrence and Bilek have entered the service of our cousin of Latzembok. As he was going to the Emperor, it pleased him well to have them."

"Your cousin of Latzembok is no credit to you or to us. Is it true that he has purged himself, on his knightly oath, of suspicion of heresy?"

"I have not heard of it," said Zedenka.

Pánna Oneshka bestowed a very keen glance on her. Before the journey to Constance there had been some talk of an alliance, for which, as the parties were cousins, a papal dispensation would have been required. But, although the young girl's face still wore an unusual flush, Latzembok was by no means answerable for it; nor did it cost her anything, save cousinly concern, when her friend continued, "If he has done that, I hope your father and your uncles will never speak to him again."

"But he might disown heresy," said Zedenka, "for we are not heretics."

"We must let men call us what they count us, Child. Did they not call the Master of the house 'Beelzebub?' As for me, I had as readily be called 'heretic' as Johannite, and far more readily than by the newfangled name of Hussite; yet that also I suppose we must bear. Ah, here comes your gallant young squire. He is welcome."

Hubert entered, looking very handsome in the crimson mantle and tunic which the ladies of Pihel had embroidered for him. The velvet cap with its single plume he held in his hand, as he bowed low and gracefully, making suitable salutation to all who were present, then standing respectfully before the lady of the house and the daughter of his lord.

"My lord has sent me to commend him with all respect and observance to the noble Pánna Oneshka, and with all affection to my lady, his daughter," he said. "I was also to inquire after the health of the noble ladies, and to receive their commands."

To this long sentence, spoken in very correct Bohemian, a suitable answer was returned by the elder lady, and Hubert continued, addressing himself to her, "My lord would know, Pánna, if he has your gracious permission to wait on you before vespers. He has something to communicate to you, and also to his daughter."

"A father is ever welcome to his daughter; and a true knight, like Pán Jan z Chlum, is ever welcome to me," said Pánna Oneshka graciously.

Here Zedenka put in a word: "Do you know, Master Hubert, if my father has had a letter from Pihel?"

"I think not, Pánna." He might have spoken more decidedly, since the good knight could have received nothing unknown to him, for he attended him all day, and at night slept at his feet on a truckle-bed. On the present occasion, he knew very well what his lord had to tell, but of course refrained from the slightest intimation that he did so.

His next duty, not a hard one, was to drink to the health of the ladies in a cup of good Gascon wine. This was served to him by a bower woman of mature age and staid demeanour, whom Pánna Oneshka summoned by a little silver bell.

He would then have taken his departure, but Pánna Oneshka detained him, ostensibly to question him about his impressions of Prague, but really to ascertain his religious opinions. To his surprise and admiration, she spoke to him in excellent Latin, having heard from Zedenka that he had been formerly a scholar of the Sorbonne. His answers pleased her greatly; although no indulgent critic, she was satisfied with their Latin, and more than satisfied with their theology. She looked on him with the kind of interest — half-wistful, half-pathetic — which the aged, whose days are well-nigh over, so often feel for the young, who have all the glorious possibilities and all the terrible perils of their lives before them. She ended by presenting him a gold ducat, a kind of gift which in those days was considered quite suitable and proper, even between equals.

Hubert made due acknowledgments, and said before he withdrew he would get Wenzel, the cupmaker and goldsmith, with whom he lodged, to put a clasp to it, that he might wear it in his cap underneath the badge of his lord. This rather surprised the practical Zedenka, who thought Master Hubert might have used the gold to buy some of the many things he must have fancied in the great city. But at least he was proving himself no inapt scholar in the ways and fashions of chivalry.

The story Chlum had to tell was like this. Among the many friends whom he met at Prague were Petr de Svoyshin, and his wife Páni Anna de Frimbuck. Svoyshin was Master of the Royal Mint of Bohemia, a position of great gain as well as of much influence and importance. The Mint was at Kuttenberg, in the neighbourhood of the rich silver mines, and Svoyshin usually resided there, in what was called "the Welsh Castle." He was a zealous Hussite, and his wife, Páni Anna, was yet further advanced. She was "a lady of excellent gifts," much hated by the priests. She felt for Huss that devoted personal love which no man ever evoked more abundantly. In the last letter which he wrote to his friends in Bohemia — if not the last letter he ever penned — he had made of her and of her lord a very earnest request, which had reference to "his best and dearest friend," the Knight of Chlum; he asked them, for the love of him, to defray the charges Chlum had incurred on his account in Constance.

Dying lips do not often ask in vain. But to fulfil *this* prayer Páni Anna would have pawned her last jewel, and her lord would have said to her, "Do all that is in your heart." Such sacrifices were not needed, however. Wealth was theirs; more than sufficed.

At their invitation, Chlum came to their lodging. Hubert, who attended him as usual, remained standing at the lower end of the room, where also a notary was present, with pens, ink, and paper.

Meanwhile Chlum and his friends conversed together. The state of the country would have provided them with an inexhaustible theme, if the thoughts of all had not turned rather to Constance and to what was done there. Svoyshin held in his hand the paper with the figures on it in the writing of Zedenka.

"Do you think, my friend," he asked presently, "that this is a true and faithful account of all the moneys you expended in Constance, and in going and returning?"

"Yes, so far as I know. But please give it back to me, or destroy it if you will, for it is worth no more than the paper it is written on. It is true that a year ago, when the Emperor gave the business in charge to Duba and to me, it was understood he would defray the cost of it. But would to God *that* were the only obligation he failed in!"

"Since he failed in the greater," said the lady, "I am not sorry that he has failed also in the less. Only those who loved the dear master should spend their substance for him."

Chlum felt the same, but he had small skill in saying what he felt. He only bowed to the lady, and turned to Svoyshin once more. "I can guess your reason for desiring it of me," he said, pointing to the paper. "You have heard, it may be, some idle talk among our knights and barons, as if I did not all I might have done, and you want to silence it, like the good friends you are. You may spare your pains. God knows if I kept back my gold, if I would have kept back my life! That is enough for me."

"Yes, Friend, enough for *you*, but not for us. Do you think there are none but yourself who loved him, and would fain spend somewhat for his sake?"

"Yes, *many*. But it was not given unto those many to do it. It was given unto me."

The lady understood him better than her lord. She rose from her chair, and laid her hand on his arm.

"Sir Knight," she asked, "will you be generous and give of your abundance — of the abundant honour God has given to you — a little share also to us?"

"I do not understand you, Páni Anna."

"Then read this," said Svoyshin, placing a paper in his hand. "You know the writing."

Chlum was much moved. "A letter of his!" he exclaimed.

He took it eagerly and read: "For my sake, although perhaps dead in the body, do not allow any loss to happen to Lord John, the faithful and worthy knight and my good benefactor. I entreat you for the Lord God's sake, dear Lord Petr, Master of the Mint, and Lady Anna."

The words of praise and kindness went straight to the strong man's heart. A mist rose before his eyes, the letter almost dropped from his hand — almost, not quite; it was too precious for that.

He said in a low voice, "Keep your gold, and let me keep *this*. I am repaid."

"You shall have both, Sir Baron," said the lady. "You have earned them. And take therewith the thanks of every true Bohemian, now and forever."

"That the business may be settled at once," said Svoyshin, "the silver is with us here; and the notary has it ready, kop by kop, in full account, to deliver to you."

Chlum did not answer. In his strong, silent soul, which had no voice for its own conflicts, a conflict was raging. His heart clung desperately to the sacrifice he had been allowed to make for the man he loved. For him, that sacrifice had become a possession, a sacred treasure. For him, giving had been changed into receiving; and it was receiving which would be a great and bitter giving up, a veritable sacrifice. Could he give up so?

But Master John willed it. It was *right*; right in all ways and for all reasons. Others, who were dependent on him, ought not to suffer for his sake, that he might please himself. Moreover, what was he, more than others, that he should want to keep the best things for himself? What was he? He was Master John's "best and dearest friend, his other self;" he was "that faithful and worthy knight, his good benefactor," who was thought of tenderly, whose cares and interests occupied him even on the very eve of martyrdom. That was enough. Gold and silver might come or go, they could neither give nor take away such joy as that. It had been easy to spend and be spent; it was harder, much harder, not to be allowed to spend anything at all; but with those words in his heart he could do it. All that Master John willed should be surely done.

At last he said, bowing his stately head as one who pays homage, or yields observance to some higher law: "My noble friends, I take what you offer, and — I thank you."

There was perhaps a little hesitation in the last words. Then, with that quiet suppression of all emotion which sometimes evidences the deepest emotion of all, he passed at once to practical detail.

"My squire, Master Hubert, who is also an excellent secretary, having served in that calling at Constance, can do the reckoning; or, if you will, I will send a notary."

So, in a few words, the matter was settled. But not thus lightly and easily, with so many "kops" of silver groschen, could Bohemia pay the debt she owed to "that faithful and worthy knight," John of Chlum. Well may her artist-son, in his great picture,[28] place near the pathetic figure of the martyr, as he stands for the last time before his judges, the martial form and noble, sorrowful face of the faithful friend, holding in his hand the historic hammer which nailed his fearless protest to the cathedral-door. Let no man deem that heroic protest against successful wrong is all in vain. Every such protest is recorded, not alone on high — where He that is higher than the highest regards — but in His book of remembrance here below, wherein are the things that make nations and mould the future of humanity. But for Chlum and his companions the story of the last days of Huss would probably have been very different; and almost certainly it would never have been fully known to the world. He succeeded in surrounding with a blaze of notoriety, which the moral grandeur of the victim changed into a halo of glory, the sacrifice he could not prevent.

---

[28] The picture of John Huss before the Council of Constance, by Brozik, now in the Staromestska radnice (the Municipal house) of Prague.

XI

THE USES OF PROSPERITY

For the heart grows rich in giving, all its wealth is living grain
Seeds which mildew in the garner, scattered, fill with gold the plain.
— Mrs. Charles

If that was indeed good fortune which had come to Chlum, it illustrated the saying that good, like evil fortune, does not come alone. His brothers had come to Prague on the same business as himself, and with the help of certain men of law a satisfactory arrangement of the family property was brought about. One of the estates which fell to Chlum he had no wish to keep, his possessions being quite large enough without it, and he was able to dispose of it in an advantageous manner. Thus relieved from pecuniary pressure, his first care was to pay his debts, and his next to provide a liberal store of things his household needed or could wish for, from embroidered robes and silken cushions for the ladies, to fustian and dowlas for the boys of the kitchen.

A more important matter was to re-organize the household itself. One chaplain and confessor at least was indispensable; most of the barons had two — one for themselves, and the other for the ladies of their families. Chlum thought himself fortunate in finding a priest of excellent character named Stasek, who had been turned adrift by his former lord for giving the Cup to some of his dependants. He did not need or desire any squire save Hubert, but two or three pages of gentle birth were a usual appendage to such a household as his. Henry of Leffle, who had been with him in Constance, wished him to take his son in this capacity, and he readily agreed. But he sought out the widow of a brother knight who had fallen in the Venetian war, and finding her, as he expected, poor and burdened with a numerous family, he took one of her sons also. He chose the third, a mere child of ten, and small and slight for his age, considering that he could easily find places for the two elder boys with some of the knights and barons then in the city.

According to our ideas, Luca z Leffle and Karel z Sandresky would have been companions for Václav and shared his sports and studies; but this was not the way of the fifteenth century. Knights took other people's sons, and ladies other people's daughters to educate, while, in compliance with the same custom, they sent their own to strangers. The worldly advancement of the young people seems to have been the thing most considered in these arrangements.

Judged by this standard, Václav was fortunate, or at least he might have been so. The man of most mark among the Hussites was undoubtedly the powerful lord of Hussenec. It speaks well for this proud baron that he was an ardent admirer and disciple of the Reformer, who had been one of his own villagers, and whom he may have known as a poor scholar, helped through college by the bounty of his father. Hussenec had even journeyed to Constance, in the vain hope of saving the "dear Master." He was now in Prague, taking a leading part in all that was done there for the vindication of his memory; and he renewed to Chlum the offer he had made him in Constance, where he had been struck by Václav's boyish grace and intelligence. They discussed the matter walking up and down under the colonnade of the Eisengasse, between the Rathhaus and the Carolinum, or University building. Chlum was attended by Hubert, and Hussenec by his son, a splendid, proud-looking young knight attired in the height of the then prevailing fashion. He was not too proud, however, to drop modestly behind with Hubert, and to converse with him very amicably. He made special inquiries about Pánna Oneshka, showing an interest in the daily life of that excellent lady which rather surprised Hubert. He supposed Hubert must be an authority on the subject, as he had such frequent occasions to go to her house. Was it not true that, although so devoted to Bethlehem Chapel, she and the ladies with her sometimes walked over to attend vespers at the Teyn Church, by way of taking the air?

Meanwhile Hussenec was assuring Chlum of his interest in Václav, and promising to fail in none of the duties of a father, if he would entrust him in his care. Chlum was certainly pleased; and, as he could now afford to equip his son suitably, he had no positive reason for declining. Still, he hesitated. He had two thoughts in his mind; one of which could, and the other could not, be avowed openly. How could he ask the Páni — frail and delicate as she was — to part with her boy again, now just restored to her after a year of absence? Moreover (this was the thought *not* avowed), he feared for his son the martial spirit of Hussenec, which would inevitably pervade his whole household. Hussenec and his gallant son were foremost among those who talked of vengeance for the past and security for the future; and thought that for both they must look to their own good swords in their own brave hands. Chlum, on the contrary, had Master John's last counsel forever sounding in his ears, "Serve God quietly at home." Finally, he asked Hussenec for time to consider the matter, and to take counsel with his lady. In any case, he thanked him heartily for the proposal, and would esteem any connection between their houses a great honour.

Hussenec cast a backward glance at his son, who was just then favouring Hubert, in excited tones, with his opinion on the doings of the Council. "Yonder goes a lad," said he, "who would not be averse to a connection of another kind, if you and I approved of it, Kepka."

"Your Panec? What do you mean, Sir Baron?"

"That I can scarce say yet. But of what my Klaus means there is no such doubt. Never Mass or sermon will he miss at Bethlehem."

"I am glad to hear that he is so piously disposed," said Chlum innocently.

"Most worthy friend, I fear your fair daughter has more to do with his piety than his confessor would care to know. Wild horses will not drag him from the Bethlehem Street, if there are but a chance of the young lady coming forth, or even showing her face at a window."

"My daughter!" exclaimed Chlum. Then he relapsed into silence, wishing heartily that he had the Páni with him in Prague. At last he resumed, "But then she is only a child."

"She is a young lady of great beauty and distinction; and I think that boy of mine has good eyesight and better taste. Still, as you say, she is young. So is he; and quick in love and hate, hot of head, and perhaps too ready of hand. Let the matter stand over, if you will, for future consideration. But I hope such consideration would not be unpleasing to you, or to the Páni herself?"

"It could not, to either of us, be other than an honour," said Chlum in reply; and the subject dropped.

Chlum was not sorry when at last his business in Prague came to an end. Prague was a bewildering place, where strange things were liable to happen; where a man might be asked at a moment's notice to speak his mind upon anything in heaven or on earth, from Purgatory and the Invocation of Saints to possible suitors for his daughter's hand. It was a very real trouble to him, also, that he found himself unexpectedly popular, and the subject of a good deal of attention. The knights and barons of Bohemia and the magnates of the University could not but do honour to the man who had stood so loyally by their hero and their martyr. To Chlum this was not only surprising, but absolutely painful. Why should such honour come to him only because he had *not* been a false knight and a faithless friend?

His party was now augmented by little Karel Sandresky, who looked very pretty in his new page's dress, and was much petted by Zedenka. Lucas Leffle was to be sent afterward to Pihel by his father. But Chlum was destined to receive another addition to his household, and an unexpected one. The day before his departure he wished to visit a friend in the Kleinseite. As he came forth from his lodgings — the house of Wenzel the cupmaker in the Grosser Ring — a wild-looking boy in a gray serge frock sprang forward, and, thrusting Hubert aside, seized the stirrup of his horse and held it for him ostentatiously.

Chlum mounted, and threw him a groschen.

The boy picked it up, but tried to give it back to him. "I do not want your silver," he said. "I am as good as you, Sir Knight!"

Chlum thought he meant that he was as good in the sight of God — for the religious earnestness of the time had reached even the street boys of Prague. "It may well be you are a better Christian than I," he said. "Yet a good silver groschen would do no harm, even to a saint."

"I am neither saint nor beggar, and yet I crave a boon of you, Sir Knight." The boy pressed closer, and looked up in his face, his dark eyes lit with a burning eagerness. "Let me serve you. I will work — fight — *die* for you, if you will but give me a chance. Only let me serve you!"

"Poor boy! What should I do with you? Yet stay — if indeed you want to eat honest bread of your own earning, perhaps I can help you to a service with someone."

The boy shook his head decisively, throwing back his shaggy, jet-black locks. "I serve no man but you, Kepka," be said.

Chlum was amused, perhaps even a little flattered by his persistence. "What could you do for me?" he asked.

"Sir Knight, I am noble as you are, and it is my birthright to serve you at the board, and in the field, as noble pages do. But take me — only take me, and I swear by every saint in heaven I will serve you as scullion, kitchen varlet, turnspit even — anything you will, and never will I say no to you!"

"Who are you?" asked Chlum, much surprised.

The boy raised himself on tiptoe, to get as near to Chlum as he could, and whispered one word — "*Ostrodek*."

Chlum repeated it aloud, not on the instant remembering the name or the story; upon which Hubert, who had been listening with much interest, struck in with a few rapid words in German.

Chlum turned to the boy. "You could scarce remember your father," he said. "Where have you passed the years since his death?"

"I remember my father well, Sir Knight. I was past seven years old *then*. Afterward my mother brought me to the Monastery of the Holy Cross there on the hill, and bade them take me and make a monk of me, so that with me our race might come to an end."

"I trust, Sir Knight, that as he grew he showed the monks he had too high a stomach to brook *that*," Hubert threw in, touched by the similarity of the boy's lot to his own.

But Chlum answered him in German: "A boy may be too good to make a monk of — or too bad," and turned again to the boy. "Why did you not stay there, and do as your mother bade?"

The dark eyes flashed, as visibly as the flint when the steel strikes it. "Because they used me like a dog," he said. "I hate them!"

"Why? What did you do to anger them?"

"What I will do again, if I have the ill-fortune to be caught and dragged back to their dungeon. Curse them!"

"Hush, Boy; those are wicked words."

"I warrant me you would say worse words yourself, Kepka, if they told you the man who saved your father's soul was burning in hell-fire, and then starved and beat you for telling them they lied."

"What do you mean?" asked Chlum, with awakened interest.

The boy turned half away, and kicked a stone which lay at his feet. He looked at Hubert, then at Chlum again.

"I don't know what that fine young gentleman said to you just now in German," he said. "But I take it for pretty certain he told you my father was hanged. For I think the very stones at my feet cry it out, and the walls and the houses — the trees even, if I go forth into the field. But then, he made a good end! Everyone says that; the monks say it themselves. I trust that by this time his soul has gone up to heaven; and he has been received by Messire God, and by our Lord, and by our Lady, as an honourable knight, purged from all stain of sin. What sort of a son would I be to him — and I *am* his son! if I brooked to hear ill words spoken of the man that saved him?"

For the first time Chlum's hand touched the boy — rested on his shoulder. "What did you do?" he asked, more gently than he had spoken before.

"Called them a pack of liars. Then they misused me — to cast out the devil, as they said. I ran away, and here I am."

"Why did you come to me?"

"Because, Sir Knight, I heard them say you were his friend, and almost as bad as he, craving your pardon. The sub-prior said the Council would have done right well to burn you too."

Chlum felt the trembling joy of some unknown poet who hears it said that he might have rivalled Shakespeare. Truly he

> *Had not sought in battle*
> *A wreath of such renown.*

"I was not worthy," he said, with a smile.

"Sir Knight, you will take me with you?" the boy pleaded, his wild eyes softening, and his hands clasped in piteous entreaty. "I will serve you so faithful! And oh! If ever you fight to avenge *him* — just give me a sword!" and the fierce look came back again.

"I shall never fight to avenge him. My poor boy, I cannot bid you from me, though I know not well how to order you. Go in there to my lodging." He pointed to the door of Wenzel's house. "My men will care for you until my return. Ask for Clodek, and say I sent you.

"Hubert, we must go. Time presses; and it is ill done to keep our horses standing so long. Perhaps it is well that we do not have Rabstein," he added with a sigh. "He would scarce have borne it so patiently."

He was very silent during the ride, but when they were nearly at home again he bade Hubert turn toward the Neustadt.

"To the house of Leffle," he said. "I must see him again. He may take it ill if his boy is put to serve with this young Ostrodek. If he should, I must give Lucaz up, though I should be sorry."

"Lucaz' father wished you to have him, Sir Knight," said Hubert. "It would be a pity to disappoint him."

"The Father of the fatherless wished me to have the other — and His will comes first. Poor child, there must be good in him, when he had the grace and the courage to stand up for Master John against them all. Mark me, Hubert, when he comes to Pihel he shall fare exactly like the rest. If anyone is base enough even to hint at a gallows in his hearing, you shall not spare the rod. As he truly says, he is of noble birth."

"Yes, he is, Sir Knight. The fire of it is in his eye and on his cheek. I trust he will need good guidance."

"And I believe he will have it. What with you and Master Stasek, and a soft word or a kind look now and then from my lady, who knows her way to all hearts, God bless her!"

They left Prague the next day, on a dull October morning, with the east wind blowing withered leaves across their path. This did not hinder a party of their friends riding with them for the first stage of their journey "to show them honour, and also for their good company."

Conspicuous among these was the Panec of Hussenec. As he rode beside the palfrey of Pánna Zedenka, Hubert thought it was no wonder his own sober, and, as she accounted them, timid counsels failed to find favour in her eyes. The young knight's fiery talk was all of Bohemia's ancient glories, from the days of Queen Libussa down to those of the great Emperor Karl; of her unconquered chivalry, her battles and her victories, of her ancient rights and liberties, and the giving of the Cup. To Hubert it had been the Cup of Christ, taken from His hand, with deepest humility and gratitude. To young Hussenec it was rather the cup of the people, claimed by them as a right, as something sacred indeed, but at the same time pre-eminently national and Bohemian. To the one it was a pledge to die for as martyr; to the other, a symbol to fight for as a soldier.

XII

PETR'S TIDINGS

But we on changeful days are cast,
When bright names from their place fall fast;
Oh, ye that with your glory passed,
We cannot mourn you now.

There were peaceful days at Pihel after the return of the travellers from Prague. In the chapel, on Sundays and holidays, Stasek preached the Word of God and gave the Cup of Christ, not only to the household, but to as many of the neighbours as wished to receive it. People often came from Leitmeritz for the purpose, Frantisek seldom being absent, and not discontinuing his attendance even when evangelical preaching and the Communion in both kinds were to be had in the town.

In this quiet interval Páni Sophia regained a measure of health, such as she had not known since the death of her son. She clung fondly to her remaining boy, and he was devoted to her. Her lord, seeing this, shrank ever more and more from the thought of sending him away, also because he worshipped Hubert, whose influence over him was very good. When, therefore, young Hussenec rode over to Pihel to know the final decision, Chlum, with much courtesy and many apologies, explained this to him. Still, Hussenec did not think his visit thrown away. It was likely, as he told his friends, to be his last for some time. He was going to England, to see the court and the country, and to stay for a term or two at the famous University of Oxford, where he might hold converse with the disciples of the great Master Wycliffe. He promised Hubert — whom he was disposed to patronize a little more than that young gentleman exactly liked — to look up his kinsfolk in England, and asked for a "token" from him to show them. There was another person in the castle whom he asked also for a "token," though in very different fashion, and Hubert knew not if she gave it. He did know that a knot of crimson ribbon she had worn at her throat adorned the young knight's cap as he rode away, but he shrewdly suspected it had been picked up without her knowledge.

When Hussenec was gone Páni Sophia observed to her lord, with a sigh of relief, "I hope he will be preserved from harm in all his journeys in foreign lands, and that he will continue there for a good space."

"I am glad that, as touching Zedenka, nothing is concluded absolutely," Chlum answered. "The child is full young; there is time enough. Still, we must remember there is no better alliance in all Bohemia; any maiden might feel honoured by the preference of the Panec of Hussenec."

Young Leffle came to the castle just after the departure of Hussenec. He was a bright, good-humoured lad, and he and Václav and little Sandresky made the old walls ring again with boyhood's "merry noise." Ostrodek contributed less to the general enlivenment. Although devoted to Chlum personally, and always obedient to his lightest word, he was moody, irritable, and liable to violent fits of passion. Truly, as Hubert said, he needed good guidance.

In November, when the first snow was on the ground, came another visitor, the Secretary Petr Mladenowic. Chlum, Hubert, and Václav welcomed him warmly; and their first eager question was about the unhappy prisoner still pining in the Tower of St. Paul, in Constance. Since their return to Bohemia they had not heard anything of him. "If he had been burned we would know," said Chlum. "Still, it is hard to guess why they have spared him so long."

Mladenowic, who looked more tall and gaunt than ever, and more melancholy, stood in silence, with downcast eyes.

"Perhaps he was so closely shut up you could hear nothing of him; that was no fault of yours," said Václav, noting his embarrassment. "You remember, Father, how Vitus saw him at the window, and managed so cleverly and bravely to get a word with him, though it was like to have cost him dear."

Vitus, who was present, flushed at the words of praise, and gathered courage to say: "I pray you, Master Petr, tell us all you know. Master Jerome is very dear to us."

Still Mladenowic hesitated, until Chlum said, "Whatever the truth is, let us hear it, Petr. Have they dealt worse with him than even with Master John?"

"Sir Knight, *they have*. With all their malice, Master John they never hurt; Master Jerome they have hurt, and sorely."

"What do you mean?"

Recantation of Jerome

"Sir Knight, he has retracted, denied his faith, slandered the memory of the man he loved, as we all thought, better than his life."

In the group gathered around him there was a dead silence. Bitter sorrow and mortification might be read in every face.

At last Ostrodek broke the pause with a cry of "Shame!"

"Silence, Boy!" said Chlum sternly. "It is not for us, who have borne nothing for our Lord, to blame him who already has borne so much. I suspect," he added, turning to Mladenowic, "it is a lie which our enemies have set on foot to discredit him and us. What proof have we of it?"

"Proof, Sir Knight? Only too much. I saw him with these eyes, and heard him with these ears, in the cathedral, praising the Council, and submitting himself wholly to its decisions. I read the letter he wrote to his friends in Prague, saying he had been deceived, and was now enlightened by the grace of God. Alas! Alas! How the gold has become dim and the fine gold changed! But," continued Mladenowic, the glow of a dawning smile illumining his sorrowful face, "there was one thing neither Council nor Emperor, neither hope of freedom nor fear of death, could make him do. Slander Master John as heretic

263

he might, but against him as man could no word be wrung from him. 'There never was a fault in him,' " he said.

"I cannot but think," faltered Páni Sophia, in a voice choked with tears, "what the strong man must have suffered to bring him down to that."

"This I will say indeed, Páni," said Mladenowic, "that he looked a wreck, pale, worn, and emaciated, scarcely able to stand."

"He that is without sin among us — no, he who thinks he would have done better in his place — let him cast a stone at him," said Priest Stasek.

"Is he released yet, Master Petr?" asked Vitus eagerly. "For if he is, and my good lord here present will give me leave, I would willingly go to him, and comfort him, and serve him. No doubt his heart is broken."

"He is not released, nor likely to be."

"And why? On what pretext can they keep him now?" was asked indignantly, by more voices than one.

"They say his retractation is 'suspected;' there are other articles against him — they are drawing up a new act of accusation."

"It is like them, the priests of Antichrist! Cruel — treacherous — cowardly!" cried Václav.

"There are many, even in the Council, who think ill of it, and say so as plainly as they dare," pursued Mladenowic. "The Cardinal of Florence has acted very honourably. When the Council refused to set the captive free, he resigned his place on the commission appointed to try him, and would have no more to do with the business. If all were like him, we might have to meet wrong and violence, but falsehood never. Also, the English Bishop of Salisbury spoke for him nobly, but in vain."

"When a man sells his soul he ought to get the price. Even the devil knows that," said Ostrodek, unabashed by his recent rebuff.

"I think the better part of the Council would have prevailed, and Master Jerome have been set at liberty," continued Mladenowic, "had not the whole influence of one of the greatest of the doctors been used against him. 'A man who has once been a heretic can never be trusted,' said the Chancellor of Paris. If, after all, Master Jerome comes by his death, his blood will be on the head of Jean Gerson."

"Untrue! *Untrue!*" cried the voice of Hubert, which had not been heard before. "Master Petr, you are mistaken. Jean Gerson never counselled a baseness."

"Under favour, Master Hubert, it is you who are mistaken. The chancellor's part in this matter is known by all men. I had it from those who heard his spoken, and read his written, words."

"Then they lied!" cried Hubert; and passion so far overcame him that he added, "Or you do!"

"*My son!*" said Chlum, with a look of surprise and pain. Look and word passed unheeded then, though afterward Hubert recalled them. But he recollected immediately that it was the act of a coward to give the lie to one who could not give it back to him at the sword's point. With quick shame for his discourtesy, he hastened to apologize.

"I crave your pardon, Master Petr; I know you only speak what you have heard, and believe. But this thing *I* can — not — believe — *never!*" So saying, he turned away and strode rapidly out of the hall.

The rest discussed the story with shame and pain, but with tender pity for "a good man's sin."

"Who would have thought it?" they all asked. Jerome had been a proverb for dauntless courage and impetuous daring.

"Just the man," said Stasek, "for whom we would have foretold the martyr's crown. Rather for him than for Master John, who was always tender of heart. I remember the time those three poor lads — one of them of my namesake and kinsman — were put to death for speaking against Indulgences — how Master John — who had begged hard for them, saying, 'Whatsoever you would do to them, do it rather to me' — took it so to heart that he could not preach the next Sunday in Bethlehem. But Master Jerome, who never feared the face of priest or friar — who burned the pope's bull — who defended Wycliffe and his doctrines in half the universities of Europe — Master Jerome to fail thus!"

Chlum went over to the table fastened against the wall, on which the great Czech Bible lay. His study had been so much in it of late that he was not long in finding the place he sought. With the slow and hesitating utterance of one unaccustomed to the exercise he read aloud —

" 'Rejoice not against me, O mine enemy: when I fall, I shall arise, when I sit in darkness, the LORD shall be a light to me. I will bear the indignation of the LORD, because I have sinned against Him, until He plead my cause, and execute judgment for me. He will bring me forth to the light, and I shall behold His righteousness!' Amen!" he added solemnly, as he closed the book. Nor was he heard to speak another word on the subject.

Afterward, in very deed, God did bring His servant forth to the light, and he did behold His righteousness. When, like Peter, he looked not to the face of Christ, but to the waves and billows, which were boisterous, he began to sink. But, like Peter, he cried, and the Lord heard, stretched forth His hand, and caught him, and held him fast. Not many months afterward a second martyr crown was won in Constance. "Strengthened with all might," the brilliant, impetuous Jerome recovered from his fall, witnessed nobly before the Council and at the stake for his "dear master," and for his dear master's Lord and King,

And made (himself) an everlasting name.

XIII

HUBERT'S AWAKENING

Untrue! Untrue! O morning star, mine!
That sitteth secret in a veil of light
Far up the starry spaces, say Untrue!
— E.B. Browning

Hubert Bohun went sorrowfully out on the hill. His heart, always tenacious in affection, clung with all its strong fibres to the idol of his youth. To have heard that the great chancellor was dead would have been easy for him to bear. Though he hoped and dreamed that somehow, somewhere, he would see his face again, he could not but know how very uncertain of fulfilment was such a hope and dream. He would have surrendered it with resignation, only saying to himself, "He is gone where he longed to go." But to think him guilty of a baseness, to be forced to believe that he had broken faith with a helpless prisoner — that was agony indeed. Alone though he was, the bitter pain and shame of it mantled his cheek with crimson.

The thought of all Gerson's goodness toward himself came back upon him. "As a father pities his children," so had he pitied the friendless, half-desperate orphan youth. With that almost unbearable reality with which a voice sometimes comes back to us unbidden (while, if we try to recall it, it will not come), he heard the chancellor say to him, "My son!" Perhaps the suggestion came, though he knew it not, from Chlum calling him so today for the first time. But in his ears no voice would sound ever again like the voice of the great chancellor.

Now they were all speaking against him; they were calling him cruel, false, treacherous. No! He could not say the words even to himself. He had left the hall that he might not hear them; yet he knew them, everyone; they seemed to be sounding in his ears. Petr was going on declaiming, and the rest were striking in with their comments and exclamations, in a tongue which was not his, uttering

267

thoughts and passions in which, after all, he had little share. They were very kind, very good to him; but, still, they were of other race than his. They told him so; the Pánna had said so very plainly, had made him conscious of a great gulf fixed between them. He was welcomed, he was trusted, he was thought for; but he was still a stranger in a strange land.

He was quite sure that, of all the voices raised against the chancellor, that of the Pánna would be, not the loudest, for loud it never was, but the most severe and uncompromising. He almost heard her speak the words of blame, and he could not bear them. Not from *her* lips. Why? How was it that her words had such power over him? What business had he to care — to care so much, at least, if indeed he was, as he said, "A stranger in a strange land?" He knew — and in that moment he recognized the fact, acknowledged it to himself, for the first time — *he did care*. He cared passionately — unutterably. What was the meaning of this folly?

Kepka was a good lord to him, but he was lord, and Hubert squire, and a penniless squire too. Such thoughts as Hubert's did not run in regular grooves, nor follow a logical sequence, else he might have been surprised to find himself the next moment, without apparent reason, thinking of the broad lands of Hussenec, of *his* stately castles, and *his* pomp and wealth.

What had he to do with Hussenec, except to treat him with due respect, should he ever cross his path? What had he to do with the Pánna, except to serve and honour her as the daughter of his lord? What wild fancies had been rising within him unbidden and unchecked? Now Petr Mladenowic had come back, and although he would still be squire, his services as secretary would, he supposed, be needed no longer. He knew not if he should continue to be governor of the pages. Already he felt painfully his inability to carry on one important branch of their education. Of the science of heraldry he knew nothing. For instruction in what was then considered as indispensable as Latin would be now, they had to go to the Pánna, who in this, as in all other respects, was a very accomplished young lady.

Gladly would Hubert have shared their lessons; but as this was of course impossible, he had to content himself with making Václav or Lucaz repeat them in private for his benefit. Václav's Latin was his strong point, but heraldry was that of Lucaz. Lucaz was nearly as old as Armand when he won his silver spurs and became squire to the Duke of Burgundy. Why should *he* not soon be squire to Kepka? That would be a very good arrangement, the connection would be excellent, and the friendship between the two families had been of long standing. Hubert could not hide from himself that tomorrow, if he pleased, Kepka could get a dozen squires for the asking — young men of good family, proud and happy to serve him, and with influential kindred who might stand by him in the troublous times likely to come on the land. What need, therefore, of him, the stranger?

The stranger — how could he call himself so, even in thought? How could he think it a strange land where he was, since the LORD, his "light and his salvation," was with him there? Who was it who had said to him, "You put the darkness in the heavens when it is at your own feet?" Thank God, it was *only* at his feet; above him in the heavens all was light. He would look up, and not down — look for the light, and not walk in the darkness. Since he was God's son and servant, was he not also everywhere at home? Had He not answered him once and again in the joy of his heart, and would He not answer him always?

As he turned back into the court of the castle he chanted softly to himself the words of the Psalm which was his own special and peculiar treasure: "Thou hast been my succour; leave me not, neither forsake me, O God of my salvation. When my father and my mother forsake me, then the LORD takes me up."

When he reached the house, Petr came up to him and said, "Master Hubert, I have a letter for you. There was no opportunity to give it to you before. It is from your brother, the Duke of Burgundy's squire. The duke has come to abide awhile in his tents in the forest which is near unto Constance, and his people are in great joy."

Hubert eagerly took the letter. Armand was not, like himself, a trained scribe: in fact, this was only the second epistolary effort he had made in his life. It ran as follows:

FAIR BROTHER,

I give you knowledge that the duke has come and is very gracious to me. At first I feared he had never had my letter, but it well appears that he has had it. He seems to think but lightly of my trespass. It even seems to him, as far as I can see, as if I were taking blame on myself only for the purpose of clearing Sabrecourt in his eyes, out of the devotion I bear to his sister. How he knows that I bear such devotion I cannot tell, for I am sure I named the damsel only once in my letter. However, he not only raised no question of dismissing me, but assured me of his favour, and condescended to say that he would soon so advance my fortunes that I might lay them at the feet of any fair lady I chose. He is mightily glad of the success of his allies, the English, in France, and fully content besides with the turn matters are taking in the Council. All of us who have served him here have had tokens of his favour. I am sure I did nothing with the Council, yet I am not left out. But, if it is not too bold to say so, I think these good things have come to me through the kindness of One greater than the duke.

God be with you, dear brother. I hope you are in health, and progressing as much as desired for you by your loving brother,

ARMAND DE CLAIRVILLE

One morning a few weeks afterward Hubert walked again upon the hill. Again the ground was covered with snow, but the morning sun glorified the pure and sparkling crystals beneath his feet, or hanging from the boughs of the leafless trees. He had come to seek solitude; for now the squire's chamber was shared by Mladenowic, and also by Ostrodek, whose quarrelsome propensities had necessitated his separation from the other boys.

Presently, however, he was joined by Mladenowic, his tall form wrapped in the "fur coat" which had been the dear Master's dying gift.

He said with a little awkwardness, "I hope I do not disturb your meditations, Master Squire?"

Hubert's answer was courteous — we may hope it was also true.

"I want to speak to you on the affairs of my lord — of our lord, as I may say. He has very special need of the services of a faithful secretary, since — for all he is a wise man and skilled in affairs, and one who has judgment and understanding above many — he has no great skill where ink and parchment and kops of groschen are concerned."

"Naturally," said Hubert; "he is a knight."

"Ah! I understand," returned Petr, rather offended. "Gentlemen like you, who are knights, or hope to be, think it beneath you to acquire such skill. Yet let me tell your honour that, for the want of it, many a noble knight leaves his debts unpaid, which I think ought to be further beneath him still. That is not our Kepka's way; but he may well be wronged and cheated, and come to loss."

"The more need of your good services, Master Petr," said Hubert kindly, anxious to soothe the sensibilities he saw he had wounded.

I hope I do not disturb your meditations, Master Squire?

"If my poor services were needful to him, of course he should have them," said Petr.

"But what better could you do than serve him?" asked Hubert, surprised.

"It seems to me that I am called to another service," said Petr slowly and with gravity.

"If for any other lord you would leave Kepka, you are not the lad who went with me to the Emperor that day in Constance," said Hubert, with a touch of displeasure.

"Nor would I for any lord save *One*. Nor at any bidding save His who said of old to His servant, 'Write the things which you have seen.' "

"Do you mean that you should write the things you have seen in Constance?" asked Hubert, with awakened interest.

"I do, Master Hubert. Just now they are so fresh in our memories, that we think they will never be forgotten."

"Forgotten!" cried Hubert. "May my right hand forget its cunning before I forget what I saw that day in the Church of Constance!"

"But who is going to make our children, and our children's children, see it too?" asked Mladenowic.

"Do you mean that you will *write* it, Petr? Do you think God has given that task to you?" asked Hubert, laying his hand on his shoulder and looking eagerly in his kindling face.

"Is there anyone else to do it?" asked Petr.

"None so fit, since you were with him from the first."

"And — *to the last*," said Petr.

"It is a high calling. Petr, I envy you."

"Will you help me, Master Hubert?"

"I? How could I? Do you not know, Petr, I had never word nor look from the man who showed Christ to me, and changed all my life? He never knew there was one called Hubert Bohun, who would have gladly died for him."

"Yet without the help of Master Hubert Bohun his story can scarce be written — by me. For see, Master Hubert, Kepka is a true lord to me, and it would not be the act of an honest man to leave his service if he were to suffer loss thereby. Besides, Master John himself bade me think for him, and help him on my return. You are squire now, and no doubt you do well all that pertains to the office. But when we were in Constance it was the pen, and not the sword, your hands were used to. Can you play the man with *both*, and be a skilful scribe as well as a fearless squire! It will be so much better in all ways than for my lord to seek a stranger. There will be work enough for your pen, with my lord's three brothers to write to and arrange affairs with. And, perhaps, also as regards the Pánna — was not that what the visits of the young lord of Hussenec meant? And, indeed, it is an alliance to which no one has, or could have, any objection. Did you like him, Master Hubert? Did you think him worthy of the Pánna?"

Hubert's cheek flushed, but he answered steadily, "I like him well enough, Petr; but you can not expect a good squire to think any man on earth worthy of the daughter of his lord."

"One thing is certain — even our Pánna could not take a better name than his. Then, Master Hubert, you will try to be to Kepka true squire and true scribe — yes, and true *son* — helping him and standing by him as the Panec would if he were older? So shall I go to Prague with a free heart, and write my book — and I think the book will be partly yours."

"And when the book is done, Petr?"

"That is to look a long way off, Master Hubert." He was silent for a while, then suddenly began again: "Why should I spare to tell you, who are so true a friend, all the thoughts of my heart? Master Hubert, I know myself weak, unworthy to do so great a work. So I have cried to the Strong for strength; and I have made my vow unto Him, that if He will be with me and prosper me, then I will give the rest of my days to His service."

"Do you mean as a priest or a monk?" asked Hubert.

"No monks for me, Master Hubert; I know too much about them. No, I desire, when my book is written, to serve God in His sanctuary, as one of the humblest of His priests."

"I too, have had such thoughts," said Hubert. "But — I must own it — the priests seem to me, for the most part, so unworthy."

"True, there are plenty of dumb dogs, which cannot bark. I pray God I may not be one of them, but a faithful shepherd to feed His people with the bread of the Gospel, and to give them to drink of the cup of Christ."

"Amen! Dear Petr, may God prosper you, and give you the desire of your heart!" said Hubert.

Petr, quite satisfied, went indoors, while Hubert still remained in the field. It was not long before they met again, and sat side by side in the chapel, at the morning service. Yet in that brief interval a wave of resolution, swift but strong, swept over the soul of Hubert. Perhaps some vain dreams, never definite enough to crystallize into words, and half dispelled already, were then crushed down with a strong hand. Let them go! Not dreams, but deeds, should from now on be his motto. He would be true squire and servitor to Chlum, and to all his house; not content to be *less*, not asking to be *more*, save in that sense in which the faithful servant is a son to the good lord. Already he was God's son, and Christ's servant — that was, and that should be, enough for him.

Of Mladenowic it may suffice to say that it was given him to fulfil his double purpose. Thirty years afterward he was still preaching the Word of God as a faithful pastor; while his great work, *The Narrative* of what he saw and heard in Constance, remains to witness for him until this day, and is the chief source of our information concerning the last months of the life of John Huss.

XIV

THREE YEARS AFTERWARD

Millions are learning their rights to discuss,
And heroes shall rise from the ashes of Huss.
— Song of the Hussites

On an August day in the year 1418 the busy streets of old Prague
were filled with a motley crowd: knights and squires in bright apparel,
on horseback or on foot; students of the University in cap and gown;
substantial burghers in gowns of good cloth or coats of curried leather,
bareheaded apprentice boys, ragged street urchins, all together thronged
the Carlsgasse, which led from the noble Karlbrücke to the Ring.
For the Papal Legate, appropriately named Dominic, was to pass
that way in his progress from the Hradschin to the Church of St.
Stephen, to hear solemn Mass, and to bless the bones of four men
who had lost their lives in a street tumult, and were accounted martyrs
by the priestly party. But, to judge by the looks, the gestures, the
cries of the crowd, the welcome awaiting him was neither reverent
nor loving. Yet no one could say it was lacking in warmth — of a
certain kind.

"Yes, so he likes it well," an honest merchant observed, with a
bitter smile — "him and his lord the pope. Blessings for dead bones,
curses for living Christians."

"Fools they are for that, Master Mercer," said an archer, who
stood beside him. "To dead bones, blessings and curses are all one;
while living Christians may possibly pay hard curses with harder
blows."

"How can they, if they are all burned up first?" asked a citizen
in a plain dress. "If I had my will, I would burn the legate himself
for bringing us such tidings, with the pope's bull to light the fire."

"No! No!" cried a student. "The pope's bull should be hung
around his neck and burned with him, as was done by the martyr of
blessed memory, Master Jerome."

274

Trial of Jerome

"Hold there!" said an older man. "Master Jerome did not burn the bearers, only the bull."

"True, and I would not burn him," cried another student. "I would set him astride on his own palfrey, with his face to the tail, and a halter around his neck."

"For my part," put in a third, "I would duck him in the Moldau, as Master Jerome did the priest who spoke against Master John Huss."

"Hush! Here he comes!" said the first speaker.

Outriders, in handsome liveries of scarlet and gold, cleared the way with their halberds. Behind them came the legate himself, ambling daintily on his showy palfrey, with shoes of silver, and housings stiff with gold and jewels, while a saddle-cloth of scarlet embroidered with gold nearly swept the ground. The cardinal's mantle was of scarlet velvet, adorned with the costliest lace, and clasped with rubies; but his red hat shaded a countenance by no means at ease, or happy in its expression.

As he came in sight, an apprentice boy struck up a song in doggerel German,

> Welcome! Welcome! Here they come,
> Dogs of Rome, the deaf and dumb
> Though they bark not, they can bite,
> They can curse, and burn, and smite.

"I'll spoil that fine red hat for him!" cried a student, catching up a stone.

"You shall not do such a thing," said a squire, in a *garboiseau* (doublet) of quilted silk, striking the stone out of the hand of the boy.

The squire was a tall young man of twenty-three or twenty-four, with chestnut hair and beard, frank blue eyes, and a handsome, manly face, singularly open in its expression.

"If it were anyone but you, Bohun . . ." grumbled the youth. "But you do as you wish with us all."

"Bohun? Bohun, did you say?" asked a personage in a furred and tippeted gown, with a three-cornered hat and a gold-headed cane. "Good Master Bohun," he continued in rapid French, as he turned toward the squire, "if you have any bowels of compassion, come with me, I pray you, and save a brother Frenchman, and an old acquaintance, out of the hand of these Bohemian demons."

"A Frenchman, and an old acquaintance! Who are you, and how do you know me?" asked Hubert, looking down at the little physician, unmistakably a Jew, old and wrinkled, with hooked nose, bushy eyebrows, and a very ample forehead. It passed through his mind that he had seen his face before, though he knew not when or how.

"I'll tell you that, if you like, Master, when you have done a good turn for your countryman. Do me the favour to come with me."

Hubert followed him under one of the colonnades behind the Rathhaus, where there were shops of various kinds. They stopped before a wine-shop, from where proceeded various discordant noises, shouts and cries, stamping of feet, and clashing of pewter vessels.

"What, *here*?" asked Hubert.

"Just so. The fool had to go and drink bad wine, lose his money and his temper, and peril his life among these ruffians."

276

Looking through the open door, Hubert beheld a sight that stirred his wrath — a heap of student caps lying on the floor. He strode in hastily. A group of lads, with disordered dresses and hushed faces, were sitting, standing, or lounging around a stool to which a priest, in a torn cassock, seemed to be glued by positive terror. His face was turned from Hubert, his head bent down, and his hands raised as if to shield it; he seemed to cower and shrink into himself before the storm let loose upon him. The riotous youths were mocking, taunting, threatening him to their hearts' content. When Hubert entered, one of them was holding a wine-cup to his lips, and bidding him drink to the confusion of Pope Martin, and Pope Martin's bull, and the health of all good Hussites.

"Good *Hussites*!" cried Hubert in indignant scorn. "Is that what you dare to call yourselves, you foolish, impudent boys? Shame on you!"

"Better than you are! What business is it of yours?" cried the lad who held the cup, dashing it with its contents at Hubert.

It fell short of him, on the sanded floor, already stained with similar libations. This did not prevent a dozen angry hands and voices being raised at once against the offender.

"Fool!"

"Blockhead!"

"Donkey!"

"How dare you?"

"Do you have eyes in your head?"

"Don't you see, it is *Master Hubert*?"

Evidently, for some reason or reasons, Hubert was a most popular person among the students; the thoughtless but impressible lads, far from resenting his interference, hastened to apologize and to excuse themselves, the chief offender setting the example, and explaining that he had not recognized Master Hubert in the dimly-lighted room.

"Leave him alone," cried Hubert to the rest. "He has not even touched me. But what has this priest done to you that you should use him so?"

A chorus of voices answered: "He is the legate's man!"

"He has come here with him to slay and burn us!"

"He praises the Council!"

"He calls Master John a heretic!"

Lastly with concentrated scorn, from the youth who flung the cup, "He is an accursed *Nominalist*!"

"And you are a great doctor of philosophy!" retorted Hubert, laughing in spite of his wrath. Then he addressed himself to the persecuted priest. "I pray you, Sir Priest, to pardon the insolence of these foolish boys. I will see to it that you receive no further harm, if you will allow me to accompany you to your inn. Or, perhaps, you lodge with the legate . . . oh! It is *Charlier*!"

For the priest, at the words of courtesy, had turned half around, raised his bowed head, and removed his hands.

"And *you*," he faltered, in much confusion, as he ventured to look up at his deliverer, "you — *you* are the last person from whom I might have looked for kindness. You are Master Hubert Bohun."

"At your service," said Hubert, coming toward him with a smile.

Charlier was greatly embarrassed. "If in the past I was — if I said . . ." he began to falter out.

But Hubert quickly took up the word. "We will not talk of that at present," he said. "The matter in hand is to provide for your safety." Then, turning to the students: "Brothers, this French priest, whom you have insulted, is an old acquaintance of mine. I will see to him. As for you, I counsel you, go to your homes at once, and for the future keep out of wine-shops and taverns. You call yourselves good Hussites?"

"Yes, Master Hubert, and so we are," cried several voices at once.

"Ready to die for our faith," added someone.

"Those who die for their faith have learned first to live by it," said Hubert. "Good Hussites are not found in wine-shops, drinking and quarrelling. They are found in churches and schools and libraries, serving God and minding their books."

"Right there, Master Hubert. But please do not report us to the rector this time. Master John Cardinal is not one who thinks the bachelors' sticks were given them for ornament."

Hubert promised good-naturedly; and then, beckoning Charlier to accompany him, walked out.

Charlier explained to him, in a confused, agitated way, that he had come to Prague in the train of the cardinal legate; but there not being room for all in the quarters assigned them in the Hradschin, he had come into the town in search of accommodation.

"You should have gone to the Kleinseite, where birds of your feather are apt to roost," said Hubert, "or at least to the Neustadt. You were not fortunate in trying the Altstadt, where the popular feeling is so strong."

"As I soon found to my cost. No one would take me in. At last I was tired out, and turned for refreshment into the wine-shop where I met the treatment you saw."

278

"Who was that physician who asked me to go to your help?"

"Solito the Jew, who was physician to Pope John; you may have seen him in Constance. He has also come with the cardinal, who picked him up somewhere on his way. He is at no loss for a lodging, having friends in the Jews' quarter. But for myself I know not what to do. Never have I seen a town in such a state."

"For the present come with me; my lodging is close by."

Charlier hesitated; he could not forget the enmity he had shown to Hubert in the days gone by; nor could he think it possible that Hubert had forgotten it. But Hubert, with kindly insistence, overbore his reluctance; if he had not forgotten, at least he had thoroughly forgiven. He led his guest to the house of Wenzel the cupmaker, where he lodged, along with Václav and Lucaz Leffle. Leffle was out; but Václav, now a fine lad of fifteen, happened to be within doors, and seeing that the stranger Hubert brought with him looked tired and hungry, at once fetched food and wine, and set them before him.

While Charlier refreshed himself, Hubert answered his inquiries, reserving his own for the present. He told him that he was still in the service of the knight of Chlum, and happy and prosperous. He was his squire, and dwelt with him for the most part in his castle at Pihel, though sometimes at the court, or elsewhere. At present he was with the Panec, and another youth, his companion, at the University, as their parents wished them to abide there for a season, under the special charge of the rector, Master John, Cardinal of Rheinstein, who was much esteemed for learning and virtue.

Charlier laid down his knife, took a parting draught from the deep tankard of light wine beside him, set that down also, and sighed deeply. "You did well to leave the chancellor's service, Master Hubert," he said. "Yes, very well."

Hubert looked at him eagerly. He had been thirsting all along for tidings of the chancellor. "It seems you have left him also?" he asked.

"Left him? No, I was dismissed. That is to say, we were all dismissed. He called us together, before he left Constance, told us he had no more occasion for our services, and no means of rewarding them, and bade us shift for ourselves."

"And you took him at his word!" said Hubert indignantly. "I, at least, would have stayed with him to the last."

Charlier shrugged his shoulders. "What would you have?" he asked. "We were sorry enough; indeed, there were few dry eyes among us when he bade us farewell. But he said truly he had no means of advancing our interests, or even of maintaining us. He — the great chancellor — left Constance alone, on foot, with a staff in his hand and a pilgrim's wallet on his shoulder."

Hubert bent his head sadly, and shaded his eyes with his hand. "And was *this*," he said, "the reward of his splendid services to the Church and to the Council?"

It was not until after an interval of mournful silence that he was able to ask, "How came it all about, Charlier?"

"Master Hubert, everything turned against him. You know well that all the foes of Reform in the Council hated him, and so did the faction of the Duke of Burgundy. England and Burgundy always go together, so the English victory of Agincourt has made Burgundy supreme. Since Agincourt, neither Council nor Emperor dared lift a finger against him, or say an ill word of the doctrines of Jean Petit."

"And *such* were the influences that ruled the deliberations of the infallible Council!" said Hubert with sad, slow scorn. "How bitter must have been the chancellor's disappointment! And the hopes he built upon it of the Reform of the Church — they, too, have been rudely shattered!"

"They have indeed, Master Hubert. Perhaps you in this far country never heard the particulars of that affair? The question of Reform was very cleverly managed, that I must say; and in the end it was very skilfully shelved. The Emperor, the English, and some of the Germans were as keen on it as our chancellor; they talked forever of the corruptions of the Church and the sins of the churchmen. Sermons were preached on it — and before the Council itself — which would have made your hair stand on end with horror. No heretic could have said more, or worse. Everyone agreed there must be a Reform. But the Italians and some of the Germans, and even our own Cardinal of Cambray, laid down the law: 'During the schism the Church is a body without a head. It is dead — it cannot act. First let us give it a head; let us elect a pope; and then let him reform the Church.' "

Hubert laughed — a bitter, joyless laugh. "Let the wolf protect the sheep," he said.

"So some were inclined to say," Charlier answered, with surprising candour. "But everybody's mouth was stopped — most of them, agreeably enough, by fat benefices. The Bishop of Salisbury, who stood like a rock for Reform, and whom no man could have bought or silenced, very opportunely departed this life. He had been long in failing health; so long, indeed, that it was commonly reported — such folly do men talk sometimes — that he was never the same man since the death of John Huss. There were plenty of bishops not so scrupulous as Robert Hallam. The Archbishop of Riga, for example, got the rich bishopric of Liège."

"If he got a hundred bishoprics, he would still be a miserable man," said Hubert. "It was he whose cruelties aggravated the sufferings of our martyrs in prison."

"Others, according to their degree, got various gratifications," pursued Charlier. "So his Holiness Pope Martin V was duly elected, and fine doings we had over it, as all the world knows."

"We have heard of them here," said Hubert. "Little joy they brought, or are likely to bring to us."

"Banquets were magnificent," Charlier resumed, "and Indulgences plentiful for his holiness is most eminent in the grace of liberality — when it costs him nothing. But as for reforms, we may consider them postponed until the Greek Kalends. Postponed they are assuredly during the pontificate of Martin V. He is in the saddle now; and well he knows the use of bit and bridle. 'Humble cardinal — haughty pope,' as the saying is."

"But all this," said Hubert, "would go near to break the chancellor's heart."

"There was much more than this. His enemies, hounded on by the Burgundians, never ceased to thwart and worry him."

"I knew he had enemies, and bitter ones," said Hubert.

"Naturally. He is the best of men; but as you knew, good Master Hubert, he was somewhat austere and hard, not to say just a little impracticable. He could never understand that churchmen, after all, were *men*, and their little frailties no such great affair."

There was an angry gleam in Hubert's blue eyes as he answered, "He only expected others to be pure and noble, as he was. If they hated him for *that*, it was as the darkness hates the light. Such hatred could not injure him!"

"Not much — had it not been for the English victories in France. These it were that ruined him. He has lost everything — place, power, emoluments. If he is still called Chancellor of Paris, it is only by courtesy, for Paris is in English hands. Thus his enemies in the Council were emboldened to redouble their attacks upon him. At last they accused him of heresy."

Hubert almost sprang from his seat. "They accused *him* of heresy?" he repeated, with incredulous wonder.

"It is true — amazing indeed, but true. He whom men called the light and soul of the Council, the Council itself turned around on, arraigned at its bar as a heretic. But what is this, Master Hubert?

Your face is full of triumph; you rejoice, you exult in it! I would not have thought it of you. I thought you loved him."

"God knows I love him," said Hubert with emotion. "And yet I say, thank God!"

"For the humiliation of your benefactor?"

"For his *glory*. For the honour the Lord Christ has put upon him, in giving him to drink of His cup."

"I do not know what you mean," said the bewildered Charlier. "I cannot understand you."

"What fault could they possibly find in him?"

"Certain articles were drawn up against him, the particulars of which I do not remember now. Most of them related to the power of the pope. One I do remember, because he did indeed utter the words ascribed to him, and in my presence. 'I would rather,' he said, 'have Turks and Pagans for my judges than the Commissioners of the Council.' Another, also true enough, as I think, claims that he said John Huss would not have been condemned if he had had proper advocates."

"*Ah*!" said Hubert, drawing a long, deep breath of satisfaction. "What was his answer, Charlier?"

"To that article? I do not know. To the whole series, this is what he answered: 'Notwithstanding that I possess ample means to reply to calumny, I should think it shame for me, who am but dust and ashes, if, like Jesus Christ, the Master of us all, I did not pass over the personal insults directed against me, to occupy myself with those relating to the Faith. I shall let the Holy Council judge for itself which is truth and which falsehood. To take the trouble of refuting all that is false, to give bite for bite, is a brutal, frivolous, insane struggle, unworthy of Christian gravity.' "

"A noble answer!" said Hubert, touched to the heart. "John Huss could not have spoken more nobly."

"You think to honour the chancellor by comparing him to a convicted heretic!" said Charlier. "About that man your infatuation, and that of these Bohemians, passes belief. All the world wonders at it. Even that Jew is scandalized by it. Do you know what he says blasphemously? So the first Christians reverenced our Lord; and then, by degrees, they began to worship Him."

"A Jew who was physician to Balthazar Cossa had no need to come to Bohemia to be scandalized," said Hubert. "But the chancellor, Charlier? He was acquitted, of course?"

"He was acquitted; for his enemies meant insult, not injury. Still, the insult stung him to the quick. Yet I think his disappointment with the Great Council was worse than any personal pang. I think that, for himself, he could have gone to the very stake rejoicing, had the Holy Council only fulfilled his dream, and accomplished all he expected from it. But, Master Hubert, I have beheld the anguish of his soul — I have heard him say, 'I have seen with my own eyes what the prophet Isaiah said, "Judgment is turned away backward, and Justice stands afar off, for truth is fallen in the street, and equity cannot enter. Yes, truth fails, and he that departs from evil makes himself a prey; and the LORD saw it, and it displeased Him that there was no judgment." ' "

"No wonder his great heart is broken," Hubert said. "But," he added, as if to himself, " 'He heals the broken in heart.' " After a pause he asked, "Where did he go when the Council ended? Back to France?"

"No; the France of England and Burgundy is no place for him. The Duke of Austria, who respects him greatly, has offered him hospitality in Vienna; and there he has gone, as I told you, on foot, in the guise of a pilgrim."

"Would he had come here instead!"

"Are you mad, Master Hubert? Your 'Hussites' would tear him in pieces."

"God forbid! We tear no man in pieces, Master Charlier, not even your legate, who brings us so black a message."

"You speak fairly, Master Hubert, but your companions breathe fire and slaughter. What do these angry cries mean that greet us everywhere, these threats and insults?"

"They mean *this*, Master Charlier, that the nation's heart is roused. Can you wonder? The Council began with that great crime of which all the world has heard. It added to its iniquities the cruel murder of a second innocent man, only for defending the memory of his friend. 'I stand here,' said Jerome at the stake — and before God he spoke the truth— 'I stand here only because I would not approve the counsel and deed of those who put John Huss to death!' And," added Hubert, "its next step was the citation of a great number of Bohemians, all of them distinguished men, many of them learned doctors and teachers in the University."

"Not one of them appeared," said Charlier. "Was not that a proof of their guilt?"

"Rather," said Hubert, "of their common sense. With such samples before their eyes of the entertainment provided for them, was it any wonder the Bohemians declined to come to the feast? The Council finally — and to pass over other insults, such as the letter sent here by the blood-stained hands of the Bishop of Lytomissel — has responded by the Act, or Decree, which you know. And now the new pope sends us his bull, affirming and confirming the same."

"As is meet and right," said Charlier. "In this matter Council and pope are at one."

"Well you say, 'in this matter,' " said Hubert bitterly. "Let the Council ask the pope to restrain his avarice, his luxury, his simony, and they might as well speak to the winds of heaven. Let them ask him to kindle faggots for innocent men; then indeed he is 'servant of the servants' — I will not dare to say 'of God.' "

"Master Hubert, you are unjust."

"Am I, Charlier? Do you know the meaning of the message you and your lord the cardinal legate have brought to Bohemia?"

"Of course — generally speaking. The papal bull has for its object 'the suppression of heresy.' "

" 'Suppression' is a fair-sounding word, but of evil import. In this bull all the people of Bohemia, from the barons in their castles and the doctors in the Carolinum down to the apprentice lads and serving maidens, are commanded to renounce the Communion of the Cup, the free preaching of the Word of God, the supremacy of the Holy Scriptures, and, in general, the teaching of Huss and Wycliffe. More, they are called on to affirm that Huss was a heretic, justly put to death. Rather than do this last, thousands and tens of thousands would die."

"It is likely that their constancy, or their obstinacy, may be tested," said Charlier.

"It is *certain*, if pope and Council can work their will. Decree and bull are abundantly plain on that point. Every man, woman, or child who will not renounce or affirm as they ordain, must be delivered over to the secular arm. That means — burning alive."

"Well?" said Charlier quietly. The thing was a matter of course; what was there for anyone to say?

"*Well*," echoed Hubert, as he rose and stood by the window, looking down at Charlier. "If you think of it, it is horrible. Suppose *yourself* in such a case. Suppose they bade you declare the chancellor a villain, stained with all the crimes of Balthazar Cossa — or die tomorrow in the fire?"

"But he was not guilty of one of them."

"Is *that* your logic? No; nor was John Huss a heretic."

"But the pope and the Holy Council . . ."

"Charlier," interrupted Hubert, speaking with deep earnestness from the very depths of his heart — "Charlier, we cannot believe as they bid us. It is impossible. Some of us now and then may say that we so believe, for it is no light and easy thing for shrinking flesh to dare the anguish of the death of fire. If you doubt of it, put your finger in the candle lighted for your need tonight."

"All the greater reason for submission," said Charlier, though rather hesitatingly.

"What?" cried Hubert, with kindling eyes. "The greater reason for falsehood, for denying that which we *know* to be the truth? Have you never read the Vulgate — 'We ought to obey God rather than man' — or the saying of those who 'changed the king's decree, and gave their bodies to be burned?' — 'Our God whom we serve is able to deliver us, but *if not* . . .' Yes, Charlier, mark that '*if not.*' That is the word of power. The men who dare to say it will change the world. Men will be burned; women, also — such things have been done before. But you cannot burn a nation. Sooner or later, men will fight for their lives."

"And take up arms against their lawful sovereign?" threw in Charlier.

"Their sovereign may side with them — I do not know. But suppose, though it is scarce possible, that all that multitude lay down their lives in silence, or with prayers on their lips for their murderers — like Master John — still they have kinsfolk, they have friends. Men have fathers, brothers, sons; women all these, and lovers and husbands too. If someone you loved were taken before your eyes . . . No, I cannot think of it, cannot utter it, even for the sake of argument." His manly cheek flushed and paled again, and he turned his face away. At last he went on brokenly: "But you are a priest — you cannot understand. However, there are things which may not be endured by living men. God has set bounds to the anguish human hearts can bear, as He has set bounds to the sea that it may not pass. Perhaps — if He gave me grace — I might die for Him myself; but I should be a poor and desolate man this day if His world did not hold a few whom I would fight to save until the sword clave to my hand and I had no more power to lift it. And then I would lay my body on the ground between them and anything that would come to harm them."

Charlier was awed by his vehemence. He shrank, as it were, into himself. "Yet you showed me kindness," he said. "You rebuked the rudeness of the students."

"Why not? Are you to blame for all this? Even if you were — you shall see we shall not harm a hair of the legate's head. We desire to harm no man. We would be peaceful, law-abiding."

"Yet I *have* heard of tumults and bloodshed in this good town of Prague."

"Yes; such as used to be, and no doubt are still in Paris. There are hot heads everywhere; and the youths of the University are nearly — not quite — so wild and reckless as those of the Sorbonne. But our chiefs, whom we look to as our leaders, repress disorder and violence as far as they can."

Here their eager colloquy was interrupted by a knocking at the door. "Come in," said Hubert. A man of respectable appearance, fully armed, but looking weary and travel-stained, entered the room.

"Vitus!" exclaimed Hubert in astonishment. "God save you, good friend. But why in Heaven's name are you here? Is there anything wrong at Pihel?"

"Ah, Master Hubert, would I could say *No* to that. But in truth I bring heavy tidings . . ." He stopped and hesitated. But it was not hard to guess them, for it was well known now that the health of the lady of the castle was failing.

Hubert, therefore, was much more sorrow-stricken than surprised when Vitus continued: "Every day the dear Páni grows weaker. Not that there has been any great or sudden change, but she herself has asked her lord to send for you. So I have come to bid you return at once with the young gentlemen, whom she desires greatly to see. It was her own word that they should all come without fail; our Panec, and Panec Lucaz, and — she herself bade me tell you expressly — young Ostrodek."

"Alas!" thought Hubert, "Where am I to find him?" For Ostrodek, during a temporary absence from Pihel, had fallen in with a band of zealots of extreme opinions and warlike propensities, and had joined them in an attack on a monastery, in which some of their friends were imprisoned. Since then he had either continued with them or had been in hiding; and all the efforts Hubert made to trace him during his stay in Prague had proved fruitless. He said to Vitus, "I fear that last is impossible. But I pray you, good Vitus, eat and drink, for you do need it sorely. Meanwhile, I will summon our Panec and the other, and we will get to horse as quickly as we may. Ah! Woe is me for the dear Páni!"

"No, not for *her*, Master Hubert, but for our dear lord. And, indeed, for us all."

A thought came to Hubert on the instant. Catching at a straw of hope, as we are all apt to do in such a case, he turned to Charlier. "Do you know where that Jew physician may be found?" he asked him. He remembered that in Constance the skill of Solito was highly esteemed, not only by those about the pope, but also at the court of Queen Barbe.

Charlier, who was really grateful for the undeserved and unexpected kindness he had received, said at once and cordially, "Happily, I can tell you that. I heard him say this morning, as we passed the shop of a seller of drugs in Green Street, that the owner was a friend of his, and he was to dine with him. If I knew the way I would fetch him to you willingly. The name of his host was, was . . . but who could ever hope to remember these barbarous Bohemian names? Wait! It was something like Smyrna, which is spoken of in the Vulgate."

"Smyrksic?" said Hubert. "I know the man, and will send to him at once. It is close by. As for yourself, I will speak to Wenzel the cupmaker, who is our host here, and he will send with you one of his apprentices to find you safe quarters."

Then all was haste and hurry. The Jew was soon found; and, what was more, he was easily persuaded to come to Pihel. In fact, he had only consented to accompany the legate because he wished to visit friends of his own race in Prague. He knew the legate's stay would be very short, and he had no desire to bring his own to an end as quickly. He was therefore not sorry to shake himself loose from him by retiring into the country until after his departure. For the wrath and disappointment of the legate he cared nothing at all. He thought the patronage of a powerful Bohemian baron, such as he supposed Hubert's lord to be, would be far more likely to advance his interests. He might even through him obtain an introduction to the King of Bohemia, whose health was greatly shaken by his life of excess, and who might therefore welcome and reward the services of a skilful physician. So he went willingly with Hubert Bohun.

Václav, his boyish heart full of a great deep sorrow, Lucaz Leffle, Vitus, and the other attendants, made up the party. Ostrodek could not be found.

XV

SAFE TO THE LAND

Safe to the land! Safe to the land!
The end is this!
And then with Him go hand in hand,
Far into bliss.

— Dean Alford

For some time past all the busy, active life of Pihel had revolved around the quiet room where the lady of the castle lay. The great state bed, with its pillars of oak, carved elaborately by skilful hands, its coverlet and cushions of embroidered silk, its hangings of rich tapestry was surrounded by screens and curtains, making a chamber within a chamber, which excluded draughts and ensured privacy. Loving hearts and gentle hands were always there to minister to the sufferer. Her own bower women, and her daughter's bower maiden, Aninka, were assiduous and devoted; so, indeed, were all the household, down to the little page, Karel Sandresky, not yet thirteen, who was made supremely happy by being allowed to do trifling services for the Páni, or sometimes to watch beside her for an hour while she slept.

But the post of honour belonged to Zedenka. She was not only her mother's head nurse, she was also her physician. She administered the herbs and simples which were her only medicines, and watched her night and day with all the devotion of a daughter.

Beside the great bedstead was a tall, straight, high-backed chair, carved in oak with the same pattern. On that chair not one of the household ever sat, not even Zedenka, though her favourite dog, Bralik, was wont to lie crouched before it, watching all that went on with looks of half-human interest. But the Páni's dark eyes, large and bright in the wasted face, were forever turning to that chair. Even when it was empty it seemed to soothe and comfort her. When it was occupied, her heart was at rest.

At the first sound of the familiar step upon the stairs the white cheek on the pillow used to flush, and a quiver of expectancy pass through the wasted frame. Then Bralik would prick his ears, rise up, go softly toward the door, Chlum would come in, and, as he pushed the screen aside, the Páni never failed to raise herself to greet him, while, not so much over her face as into it from some depth within there came a light, like the flame newly kindled in a lamp of translucent porcelain. He would bend over her frail hand and kiss it — sometimes with some low word of tenderness, sometimes in silence. Then he used to take the chair beside her. Often he read to her from the Czech Bible, or from the writings of Master John; oftener still, as the days went by, he was content to sit there silent, while she, if only he was there, was more than content. His presence was enough for her.

Now and then there were interludes of quiet talk, usually begun by her, such as this, "My knight, do you know that Frantisek is no longer an apprentice, and his master, who could not well do without him, pays him good wages?"

Chlum started, as if aroused from a reverie. "I did not know it, dear heart," he said. "It happened, I suppose, while I was with the king."

Chlum, during the past three years, had been often at the court of King Wenzel — assuredly not for his own enjoyment.

"It was more than six months ago. My knight, he loves our Aninka. What do you think?"

"I think she is a fortunate maiden. But, my Páni, we cannot part with her."

"Not yet. But this is what I think. Frantisek and Aninka may strike hands at once, and pledge their troth to each other."

"What of the father — that wrong-headed, stony-hearted Papist?"

"I think he can be managed, with your good help, my Kepka. There are some things Peichler loves better than the pope's bull. He is ambitious, and he is covetous. If you would promise to dower Aninka, and give her in marriage yourself, as one of your household, with some little honour and observance, I suspect Master Peichler's consent might be won. Especially if he is made to understand that his daughter will wed none other."

"He may take her from us, and force her to do it. He is an evil man, my Páni."

"Force her? Neither king nor Emperor could do that."

Chlum shook his head, and looked incredulous. "Poor child!" he said.

"My knight, do you not understand her. Look at that cup of water. Could anything be weaker — more yielding to your touch? Yet its drops will wear the hardest rock, and no man living could squeeze it into a smaller space than it would allow."

Chlum's eyes followed hers to the cup.

"I see your meaning," he said. "All shall be as you want it. We will dower Aninka and in due time give her in marriage."

"*You* will, beloved."

Then on both a silence fell, for both knew what neither cared to say. *Not yet.*

By and by the Páni resumed, "Strange if the maiden were to wed before the mistress. Our Zedenka's future is not clear to me, Kepka."

Apparently it was not clearer to her father. He bent down and stroked Bralik before he answered, "If I had known young Hussenec was going to stay in foreign parts these two years and more, I may have given him fewer fair words before he went. Still, for some things, it is well that he is away. When the father levies armies, and lets men say of him that he is likely one day to be King of Bohemia, the son stands in slippery places. Do you think that Zedenka favours him, my Páni?"

"Truly I cannot tell. If not, why would she not even hear the suit of the young lord of Austi, whose father was Master John's chosen friend, and whose mother is one of the best and noblest women in all the land? If yes — but that I cannot think. It is all dark to me. God will guide."

So the conversation dropped.

Another day she said, "My knight, it were well, I think, to send Vitus to Prague for Václav."

Chlum's strong heart quivered with a new pang. But he gave no sign.

"It shall be as you say," he answered quietly. "Vitus shall go at once."

"Let them all come," she went on. "Dear Hubert, who is as a son to us, Lucaz, and Ostrodek."

"Ostrodek is not there. Would I knew where he is! Sorry enough I am now that I sent him on that errand to Hussenec. His is a wild nature, like Ishmael's in the Holy Scriptures."

The Páni lay silent, with eyes half-closed. Presently a tear stole from under the drooping lids, and her lord heard her murmur, "Oh, that Ishmael might live before Thee!"

"Dear heart, you were ever tender over him. You did pity him," he said.

"No; I loved him. I *love* him. Let Hubert have him sought for everywhere, and tell . . ." She stopped there.

"Tell him what, dear heart?"

"That I want to see him, to say goodbye." Without a word Chlum went out and did her bidding; with the result we know.

The coming of Václav and the others cheered both the invalid and the watchers, and even produced a temporary rally. This was in no way owing to the physician; for Zedenka was positively angry with Hubert for bringing him, and would by no means allow him to undertake the case. She had a horror of physicians, not at all surprising, considering the remedies they were accustomed to use in those days. From time immemorial the ladies of their house had attended the sick and dying, and done for them everything that could or ought to be done. Why should they change the customs of their fathers and their mothers, and bring in Jews, infidels, and heretics, only to add to the sufferings they could not cure? She appealed to her father; and Chlum decided in her favour, for he knew now that God was taking from him the desire of his eyes, and he only wished that she might be taken gently and without pain.

"Do you make it right with the Jew, dear Hubert," he said. "Give him a handsome guerdon, and tell him we do not doubt his skill, but we like not to change the customs of our house."

Hubert undertook the task, quite expecting the physician to go away in a rage; for the physicians of that day seem to have had their full share of professional sensitiveness. But the Jew took the rejection of his services with unexpected philosophy. He was a man wise in his generation; and he determined that no slight, real or fancied, should drive him from the safe retreat of Pihel until he was quite sure that the legate had left Bohemia. So he stayed in the castle, using all his tact and cleverness to make himself acceptable to its inmates. By-and-by, as Hubert observed with surprise, the Pánna began to talk with him about her simples and decoctions, and he even ventured to offer suggestions for the comfort of the invalid, which she did not disdain to consider.

Time and strength were given to the loving mother to "speak to the heart" of her boy in words of wise and tender counsel. Nor was Hubert forgotten, nor Lucaz, nor Karel, nor anyone. Zedenka was so constantly with her that while she had, and needed, fewer formal conversations than the others, she enjoyed more real communion than any, save *one*. With the hopes, the fears, the future of each, the

Páni's mind was much occupied. Not sadly; certainly not untrustfully; only like one who has to leave half-read some tale full of interest — he knows the artist may well be trusted to "perfect the work as planned," still he cannot refrain from eager guesses of the how, the when, the where. Moreover, unlike the reader she could contribute to the conclusions she desired by counsel and by prayer.

One day she said to Zedenka, "I know not how it is, my child, but I cannot read God's will for you as plain as for the rest."

"Can you not, dear Mother? It seems plain enough to me." She was standing at a small table near the bed, and mixing a draught as she spoke. "It is His will now that I should prepare this for you, and that you should take it from my hands."

The invalid obeyed, as she always did, but presently resumed, "I was thinking of the days to come, my child. As I lie here and wait, I have many visions of that which will be. I think God sends them. He knows I must go on still caring for those I love. I see Václav and Hubert — for Hubert is a son to me — true knights of God, fighting for His cause — I am sore afraid the fight will be a hard one. 'Every battle of the warrior is with confused noise, and garments rolled in blood.' And dark, dark is the cloud that overhangs the land."

"Dear Mother, how do you know?"

"From many signs and tokens. But chiefly from this: your father will not now speak to me any more of what is going on in the land."

"He was never a man of words," said Zedenka.

"He thinks I should look now toward the land I am going to. But I did wrong to say to you that I am sore afraid; for, though I see conflict, I see victory too — for them. 'There shall not a hair of your head perish!' It is for you I am perplexed, Zedenka."

"Is not that true for me too, Mother?"

"Surely, for the end. It is the way that is dark to me. A maiden is not as a youth."

"She is the handmaid of the Lord, as he is His servant," said Zedenka.

The large eyes, bright with fever, looked wistfully into those other eyes, bright with youth and beauty. "My child, my daughter, could I only read your heart!"

Zedenka shrank a little from her gaze. "I have my father to live for," she said.

"Not forever, Child. When the time comes you must not grudge him to me."

"Mother, I think — I *know* — that Pánna Oneshka means me to have, not her books only, but her house also when she is gone. I am, as she is, the daughter of a knight. I can live there, as she has done, and serve God in His poor. Not bound by vows — for with these I hold not; not even as a *béguine*, but free."

Never once had Páni Sophia thought of such a life as this for her beautiful and gifted daughter. But to the place where she was now shocks of joy, or sorrow, or surprise came faintly, as did the household noises through the thick tapestry that curtained her around. She lay still, trying to take in the new and surprising thought. At last she said slowly, "Good, if God wills it for you, since all He wills is good. Good, but to my earthly thoughts, not best. My child, I have known great sorrows, but greater joys. I would not live over again; yet can I wish you no better lot for this world than just such a life as mine."

Zedenka's cheek, a little pale from watching, flushed suddenly. She was silent for a space; then she took up a silken cushion which lay near her on the bed.

"Do you see, dear Mother, the cushion the queen made for you with her own hands, how sadly it is torn?" she said. "The feathers are almost falling out. It will be quite spoiled. I must fetch a needle and silk, and mend it at once."

The Páni turned her face away, with a slight, half suppressed sigh. Evidently, to the end, the heart of her child was to be to her "a fountain sealed" — probably because that heart did not as yet understand itself. Well, she could trust for her as for all the rest.

Of herself she spoke not much, but accepted thankfully the ministrations of Stasek, took great delight in the Holy Scriptures, and was often in prayer.

One day, when the chair beside her was occupied, and no one else within the screen, she asked wistfully, "My knight, do you think that there is any such place as purgatory?"

Chlum hesitated; it was hard to meet her look, and refuse the answer he knew she expected. But he that would use faithfully the talent of truth must never trade with borrowed capital; the truth that has not first been made his own will bear no interest when lent to others. He said tenderly, "Not for such as you, my saint; but there may well be those that need it. Master John believed *in* purgatory."

"No, dear heart, not in purgatory. His word, while he was yet with us, was this: 'We may believe of many things, but we should believe *in* nothing but God — Father, Son, and Spirit.' That being so, I believe in the Father who loves, the Son who redeems, the Spirit who makes holy. The rest matters not so much."

Chlum murmured something about "the prayers of the faithful."

"Yes, I know you will pray. But do not grieve more than you can help. There will be trouble enough without that. I know more than you think, Kepka. You do not tell me the tidings that come to you from Prague or elsewhere, or talk of them before me."

"That is only because . . ."

"Because you think they would trouble me? It was always so with you. You would keep all the trouble for yourself, and share all the joy with me, or give it to me wholly if you could. Kepka, I am not going from you to less love than yours."

"God forbid!"

"We talk of 'infinite' love, but we do not understand it. I thank God for giving me, in that I know, a measure for that which I know not. I have only to think of His love, 'It is *more*.' Of what He will do with me I have no fear. Enough, I go to Him. But I think that if He lets us suffer here, it is that we may grow like Him. *There* 'we shall be like Him, for we shall see Him as He is.' It is seeing, not suffering, that will do it."

After this the ebbing tide, which had seemed to come back a little way, again retreated. When weakness increased the mind sometimes wandered — always a sad experience for the watchers. We gaze on the beloved face, our eyes dim with tears, but no answering look comes back to us. We touch the lips, the hand; yet are farther away than if continents divided us. The saddest part is that "the things seen" remain with us, while "the things not seen," in which we delighted, seem to have gone from us.

The Páni, in her wanderings, often spoke of, or to, the beloved pastor, whom previously she seldom named. Chlum and Zedenka were both present one day when her fancies shaped themselves in words like these: "Dear Master John, I entreat of you to pray for my children. 'Tis true they are but babes; yet ask God to make them His own, and to keep them from this evil world. Yes, name their names before Him — Zedenka, Jan, Václav. He remembers names — keeps them written in His book and on His heart. Dear Master, I beseech you, pray most of all for my lord, my own true knight. He is kind and brave, but — 'if any man love the world, and the things of the world.' Pray for him that he may give up all for God, and be content to do it."

Upon the fevered hand that lay outside the silken coverlet Chlum placed his own. "He is content," he said gently. "But God help me!"

he cried, a strong man's suppressed anguish struggling through the words. "I cannot tell her now."

"Father, she knows," said Zedenka. "She says you are nearer God than any of us. That we are to learn of you, and follow you — until we meet again."

"You have misunderstood her, Child. She must have been speaking of Master John's teachings, and of his words."

"Not so, Father; she has said it often."

The days wore on, those days so slow and sad, which, while they are passing, seem interminable; yet, when they are past, seem like a watch in the night. While they last we say in the evening, "Would God it were morning!" in the morning, "Would God it were night!" Yet often in the after-years we would give half our lives to have the worst and darkest of them back again.

At last that day came which is unlike all the rest, that day which for one has no ending, while for others (most often, perhaps, for *another*) it seems the end of all things. It stole on insensibly, as such days are apt to do; the long-expected when it comes is the unexpected.

Since the dawning of the day the dying lay for the most part in a kind of stupor. Those she loved watched around her, while she slipped gently and insensibly, like some fair barque, from the deep, broad river of the lesser into the tideless, shoreless ocean of the greater love.

Already she had had those "rites of the Church" which pious Hussites at that time continued to receive. Stasek stood beside her, now and then offering prayers or repeating words from the Holy Scriptures. At intervals she seemed to know the dear faces around, and smiled, or pressed the hand that held hers so constantly, but made no efforts to speak.

Toward the going down of the sun a servant, approaching noiselessly, beckoned Hubert from the room. He was absent for some minutes. When he returned, he went up to his lord, who sat all day in his accustomed place. "Sir Knight," he said, in the low voice that befitted the time, "Ostrodek has come back."

"Let him come here," said Chlum, without taking his eyes from the white face on the pillow.

Ostrodek entered the chamber of death. His dress was dusty and travel-soiled, but he had flung off his heavy, mud-stained boots, and his step was noiseless as a girl's. The prodigal's confession was in his heart, but the solemn presence in which he was sealed his lips, and he stood in awestruck silence, close by the screen.

But Chlum stretched out his hand, and beckoned him forward. "Come here, Ostrodek," he said.

"Ostrodek!" another voice repeated — a voice they had not thought to hear again. The dying eyes opened wide, first with the dawn of returning consciousness, then with full recognition; they sought the face of the wanderer, so anxiously yearned over, so earnestly prayed for. "Ostrodek — thank God! Welcome home — *home*;" the last word was repeated twice.

The light faded as quickly as it came. Over the white face there stole a subtle change; but there was no sound nor sign of suffering.

"*In manus tuas, Domine*" (Into Thy hands, O Lord), Stasek began. Before the brief prayer was ended a song of praise had begun in another place.

But out of sight, out of hearing! That is the trouble. That is the mystery over which throughout the ages our poor human hearts have been breaking — are breaking still. *There* is music and rapture; *here* is only silence.

Speak Thou, availing Christ, and fill this pause.

XVI

CONFIDENCES

"Nothing easier," said Talleyrand, "than to found a new religion: You have only to be crucified, and to rise again the third day."

Hubert's three years in Bohemia had matured him greatly in mind and character. The Divine law, "Give, and it shall be given you," proves its truth in many unexpected ways. The youth who pours at the feet of some noble leader a wealth of genuine devotion is educating himself thereby to deserve and receive a similar tribute, and to become God's instrument in moulding and fashioning young souls after His grand design. And thus he inherits the promise, "Instead of your fathers you shall have children, whom you may make princes in all the earth."

To Václav, Hubert was a dear elder brother; and also, scholar though he had been bred, "the very pink and mirror of chivalry." The other youths followed suit; and during his brief stay in Prague the students in the University caught the infection and made a hero of him; the rather, because his experiences at the Sorbonne enabled him to enter into the frolic and excitement of their lives, and to sympathize with them in all innocent enjoyments.

In the sad days that followed the death of the lady of Pihel, Hubert was needed, in one way or another, by almost everyone there. Stasek, good man and faithful pastor though he was, had been denied the crowning gift of sympathy. He was a priest, so he had never known for himself the sweetness of domestic ties; and he lacked imagination, which sees the unseen, and knows the unknown, by the grace of God. He thought it was a good thing for Páni Sophia to be taken from the changes and chances of a world just then exceptionally "troublesome," and he said so to her silent, uncomplaining lord, and to her broken-hearted children. It was very true, and they did not dispute it. Only Chlum was sometimes heard to murmur, with a heavy sigh, "Oh for Master John!"

It was to Hubert that Václav poured forth his boyish sorrow, weeping passionately and reproaching himself bitterly — as those who have least cause for it so often do — with every fault, real or imaginary, of which he had ever been guilty toward the best of mothers.

To Hubert came Ostrodek also with his burden of remorseful sorrow. "I never intended," said he, "to forsake my lord's service and become a masterless man. But fate was too strong for me."

It was the day after the Páni's funeral, and they were standing together in the great hall, now silent and deserted.

"But what is a man made for but to conquer his fate?" asked Hubert, looking earnestly at the tall youth, with his long, black hair and bronzed, resolute features. "If you had been true man to your lord, and returned at once from the errand he sent you on, all would have been well."

"You know my lord sent me to Hussenec."

Hubert knew, and had often regretted it. He knew also that it was Ostrodek's evident restlessness and longing for change which had induced Chlum to make him his messenger, under the impression that a little action and adventure would do him good.

"I had to go and seek him in the South," Ostrodek resumed, "down there in the neighbourhood of Austi. In all those parts there was nothing to be heard but the clash of armour, the drilling of men, and preparing for war. Still, I was coming back — really, Master Hubert, I was coming back — having done my errand well and truly, when I fell in with a band of peasants, sturdy lads, armed with their flails, at the end of which they put iron spikes or balls. Two or three gentlemen were with them, and a few pikemen and archers, properly armed. But, after all, I think the flails are the best. They were singing songs and hymns, as they marched along on their way to that rook's-nest of a monastery where, they told me, the monks had shut up some of their friends, and were starving and torturing them. Now I ask you, Master Hubert, what was a man to do? — But you know the rest." A fierce light gleamed in his black eyes, and his dark cheek glowed crimson. "If we routed the rooks and made a bonfire of the nest, let those look to it who kindled that fire in Constance."

"With that," said Hubert, "the Franciscans of St. Joseph's, whom you harried, had nothing to do. And if they had . . ."

"If they *had*, do you think we would have said to them, 'Go and find shelter where you may, you birds of evil omen?' Not so, by all the saints! There would have been another tale to tell, and not a mother's son of them left to tell it! But you see, Master Hubert, that I could not return to Pihel after that. It would have been in everyone's mouth that Kepka was harbouring disorderly folk who burned monasteries; no, that he let his own folk do it, and received them back again. Even the king would have heard of it; and, Master Hubert, the king respects Kepka more than he does most men, and it would be a pity to spoil *that*."

"Where, then, have you been?" asked Hubert. "While I was in Prague I tried hard to find you, and could not."

"I can scarce tell you. I have been in many places, and with many men. At Tabor, at Austi, at Pilsen, with Hussenec, with Zdenko, with . . . But when I heard in Prague ten days ago that the Páni was sick unto death I tarried not an hour, as you know." There was a silence. Then he said, in a gentler voice, "Master Hubert, I pray of you to be a suitor for me to my lord, that he may pardon me."

"He has pardoned you already, Ostrodek. The dear lady's dying words assure you of that. Strange that *you*, of all others, should have had her last word, and her last conscious look!"

"Yes, strange that *I*, so unworthy." He paused a moment; then drew from beneath his vest a lady's glove of Spanish leather, soiled and worn. "I found this yesterday," he said. "Do you think my lord will let me keep it? If he will, I shall wear it always in her honour, for she was like our Lady in heaven — kind and gracious unto all, and especially unto me, the outlaw's son. So was Kepka, and so were you, Master Hubert. You would fain have made a gentle Christian knight of me among you, if it was to be! But fate and the devil were too strong for you. I have but to see the flash of a sword, and the colour of blood, and, God help me! I know no more until I am knee-deep in it, with the sword done to shivers, and the hilt of it glued to my hand. I can stop, and consider, and hold myself in, just as much as the wind can. I must fight, and slay, and burn. It is all I am fit for, and I verily think it is what God made me for, if it was God who made me at all. There, do not speak to me: it is of no use. I know all you would say; and I would live so as to please you and Kepka, and — and the others — if I could; but I cannot. There is one thing more that I have to say to you, Master Hubert. I know, as well as you, that I am the last of a doomed race. What is there for me, after all, but fighting and bloodshed? Gold I shall never care for. I could have had as much as I could carry out of the treasures of that monastery. As for other joys — such as woman's love — they are not for the son of Zul of Ostrodek. I made up my mind to that while I was still here with you. We boys — Lucaz, Karel, and I — we all worshipped the ground Pánna Zedenka trod upon, and I dare say Lucaz and Karel do still. It began almost from the first; but it grew more and more when she used to teach us heraldry. It did not matter for the others, who were children; but my childhood came to an end forever when I kissed my father and bade him goodbye in the prison at seven years old. I know, of course, that I was the veriest fool that trod on God's earth — that Pánna Zedenka was as much beyond my reach as the stars of heaven — but I could not help myself. I loved. And with Ostrodek, love or hate once is love or hate always. You are laughing at me, Master Hubert!"

"I? No, dear boy; *no*! God forbid!"

"Our race, which ends with me, was ever foremost in love, as in war. But all that is over now. She shall never know. No one shall ever know, save you."

Hubert made one step forward, took Ostrodek's hand, and pressed it with a mighty pressure, as if in a vice. But something which rose in his throat prevented him from speaking.

"You are hurting me," said Ostrodek, with a smile; "but I like it. Now you understand. I shall never have a living lady to fight for and to win, as others do. Therefore, if Kepka will let me keep this token of the lady who is dead, I will wear it right loyally, and worship her memory, and do brave deeds in her honour so long as I live. But I dare not ask him — at least, not yet — not until I know he has forgiven me."

"He has forgiven you," Hubert assured him once more. "You will return to your duty, serve him faithfully, and learn to be a true knight, as he is."

"He would not have me."

"No, he will welcome you. Was not that the dear lady's last word — 'Welcome home'?"

"I would disgrace him."

"Disgrace him! And you talk of wearing his lady's favour!"

"When it comes to fighting, I shall not disgrace any man, Master Hubert. If Kepka would only fight! But seeing he will not, I may perhaps some day give place to the devil — as you would say — and lose his favour forever. But that is not all. There are things no man may bear in silence day after day. If the Pánna had wedded Hussenec, and gone away to the South, I might have stayed with Kepka and with you. As it is, it is best I should go. But please ask him to give me first his forgiveness and his blessing."

"Where do you plan to go?"

"Oh, as for that, when I was at Pilsen I happened to render a small service to the lord John of Trocsnov, the king's chamberlain — he whom men call Zisca. No doubt you know him by report; have you ever seen him?"

"As far as I know, I have not."

John of Trocsnov (Zisca)

"If you had, you would know it well. A man with one eye has something to be remembered by; but, besides, his face is like no other man's. He has a deep line down the midst of his forehead, a nose like an eagle's, and a great head closely shaven. Have you heard what passed lately between him and King Wenzel?"

"No."

"The Knight of Trocsnov was walking in the court of the palace, sad of cheer and lost in thought. The king saw him from a window, beckoned him, and asked what ailed him. 'I am thinking of Master John Huss,' said Zisca, 'and of the grievous insult the nation has received in his death.' 'Neither you nor I can help that,' said the king. 'But if you can do anything, take courage, and avenge your countryman!' I think, Master Hubert, that if the Emperor tries to enforce the Bull of Pope Martin upon Bohemia, the world will hear more of John of Trocsnov."

"I think," said Hubert, "the Emperor will hardly dare so far."

"At least, he is trying all he can to cajole, or threaten, or persuade King Wenzel into doing it," said Ostrodek. "In the end Wenzel will have to yield to his imperial brother, who is by far the stronger; and then look out for martyr fires."

"Neither king nor Emperor can burn half the nation," said Hubert.

"Let them try!" said Ostrodek, with a grim smile. "In the meantime, this same Knight of Trocsnov has offered me my silver spurs, and I am inclined to think I will go to perdition a little less quickly in his service than in that of Kepka, although, God knows, I love Kepka well. Therefore, will you ask him to forgive me, and to let me go?"

At this point in the conversation the little Jewish doctor came bustling in. Strangely enough, he had fallen ill himself the very day of the Páni's death, and only now was he well enough to leave Pihel. He came to ask Hubert to provide him with the means of departure.

Hubert, of course, shared the prejudices of his age, and looked down upon the Jew from an immeasurable height; though, in common with the other inmates of the castle, he treated him with half-pitying kindness. This kindness was recognized and felt by the physician, who had not met with it too frequently.

"You have been good to me, Master Hubert," he said. "For my part, I think Hussites are better than Christians."

"*Better* than Christians!" said Hubert. "What do you mean? I hope we are *good* Christians."

"I beg your pardon, Master Squire, if I have said something wrong. I do not comprehend the religions of the *goyim*" (Gentiles).

"There is but one religion that I ever heard of," said Hubert: "the true religion of our Lord and Saviour Jesus Christ, which I wish you believed, Master Nathan."

"To be frank with you, Master Squire, I have been considering the matter, and with much attention."

Hubert's face showed the pleasure he felt. "I wish you would read our Holy Scriptures," he said.

"I have read them," said the Jew.

This conversation was carried on in French; and, as Ostrodek did not understand a word of it, he presently whistled to Bralik, who was lying half asleep before the empty hearth, and they went out together.

The Jew looked after him in silence for a minute, then turned to Hubert once more. "Your Christian custom of paying adoration to images is a great stumbling-block to us," he said. "We think it a breach of the second commandment, which God gave to our fathers, and which you also acknowledge."

"We do not adore them," said Hubert. "Master John was very careful to avoid mistakes upon that point, and to teach everyone that God — and God alone — is to be believed in, worshipped, and adored."

"I have heard what your learned doctors say upon the subject," returned the Jew. "And I do not in this matter speak for myself, for I am, if you will know the truth, a disciple of Averrhoës."

"I know the truth no better than I did," returned Hubert, "for I never heard of Averrhoës."

"He was a great philosopher, Master Squire. But pardon me for speaking of these matters, which do not generally interest knights and gentlemen, and indeed are considered beneath their attention. Nevertheless, as I know *you* to be also a good scholar, there is one question I would fain ask of you, if you will not think me over bold."

"Speak on."

"I see not yet in your churches, among the images of those whom, let us say, you *venerate* — that of your founder. And more, your lady, who was most devout, hardly spoke of him during the last days of her life, so far as I know. How is that?"

"Our *founder*?"

"Naturally — he whom they burned at Constance. And let me tell you, Master Hubert, that I know he was a good man — unjustly slain. It was for envy that council of priests delivered him up — you see, I *have* read your Scriptures. I have been in two places which make me think the Christian faith has some power in it that as yet I know not — the palace of Balthazar Cossa and the prison of John Huss."

"About the last I understand you," said Hubert; "about the first — I do *not*."

"That the Christian faith *survives* such scandals as the one seems to me as strange as that it sustains such miseries in the other. One thinks it must be choked by the tide of corruption, and perish out of the world; but behold! it springs up again in men's hearts, here and there and everywhere, fresh as the first day."

"The faith *must* survive," said Hubert, "for it is from God."

"In a sense, though not in the sense you think. For it is from Nature, and Nature is God, and God is Nature. You can see how it grew up, aided by what is going on here, under your very eyes. Its Founder whom you adore as God, was a just man, who went about doing good, preaching truth, love, and mercy. He was hated — as the darkness hates the light — betrayed, delivered up, slain. This burned the love of Him into the hearts of His followers, who preached His doctrines, kept a solemn feast in His honour, were called by His name. Because they had a great memory, a great love, a great passion to animate them, they grew and prevailed and waxed strong, until they changed the face of the world. That is how new religions grow up. Do you understand me, Master Hubert?"

Hubert understood him just well enough to be horror-stricken at the comparison he hinted. It was given him to make the right answer. "But Christ rose again the third day."

"His *spirit* rose again, and lived in His followers. Presently, when I walked through the village I heard someone sing,

"He is dead; but his spirit lives on
In the quenchless devotion we feel."

"No! no! no!" cried Hubert, passionately, and now fully awake to the tendency of all this. "No; not His spirit — His body rose again. I think, Master Nathan, it is a mortal sin to listen to you, and I am putting my soul in peril."

"Pardon me," said the Jew, "I have no wish to offend — what would I gain by it? You and the others here have showed me more kindness than our race often gets from the *goyim*. What I say is by way of a proposition for discussion — a thesis, as you call it in your schools — for you are a scholar, Master Hubert. Doubtless, as time went on, the followers of your Christ came to believe that His body rose again."

"They did not believe," cried Hubert. "They *saw*, and they saw that very day."

"So, of course, you have been taught to think. All depends on the proofs; and, for my own part, I confess that never yet have I fairly studied them. In the meantime, I have seen what the self-sacrifice of a great martyr and the love and loyalty of his disciples can do. And I ask — not of you, but of myself — *Is there more than this?*"

"More, a thousand times."

"It is natural, it is right, that *you* should think so. In Constance you thought the sun was darkened, and would not believe when I told you it was but the earth. It was no more a miracle than the falling of your shadow on the grass. I knew beforehand it was going to happen, and could have told you."

"I doubt if such knowledge be lawful," said Hubert.

"It is quite lawful, even in the opinion of your own doctors and teachers," returned the Jew. "There is a priest now in Prague, and one whom you esteem a good Hussite, Master Christian Praschatic, who is learned in the science of the heavenly bodies. He will foretell eclipses for you, both of the sun and of the moon."

"Can you, Master Nathan?"

"I know of them from the calculations of the wise men who lived before us."

"Please tell me some, that I may know of them also; if indeed you can," said Hubert, rather incredulously.

"I have not my books with me here. I wish I had — just to convince you."

"No, never mind, Master Nathan," said Hubert, courteously, but with an involuntary smile, which the Jew did not fail to remark. It piqued him, and moved him to an effort to show off his learning.

"I remember something at this moment, which I will tell you," he said. "You know that the year which follows next year will have a day in it more than that, or this?"

Hubert thought a moment, then said, "Yes; it will be leap year."

"Then wherever you are, in the night that follows that day, a little after midnight, look at the heavens, and you shall see the moon darkened, as the sun was in Constance; that is, of course, if the night be clear."

"I shall remember," said Hubert. He inclined to the opinion expressed in Constance by Armand, that the clever Jew was a little crazy. Still, he longed to win him for the faith in Christ. "I wish," he said, "that when you return to Prague you would go and hear Master Christian preach."

"I have no objection," said the tolerant Jew, at heart a freethinker. "Certainly I shall visit him, for I want to converse with him upon the science of astronomy, in which we are both so much interested. For a time I shall abide in Prague — but perhaps not long; for I am a wanderer to and fro upon the face of the earth. It is the doom of our race. You and your friends have dealt well with me, Master Hubert, and wherever I go, if it be in my power to do a good turn to any of this house, from the lord of Chlum to the dark lad that left us just now, my will shall not be lacking."

"The best turn you could do for us," said Hubert kindly," would be to let us have the joy of hearing you believed in Christ our Lord. We will pray for you."

"I thank your good will. Such faith as yours is not ill to live by, or to die in. But you think you have all the truth, when you have but a fragment, and that you misunderstand. Well, Master, you will speak for me to your lord, and arrange about my departure? Give him also, I pray of you, my hearty thanks for his generous treatment of me."

Hubert's honest heart was troubled by the words of the Jew. How indignant Master John would be, he thought, could he hear such a blasphemous comparison! Surely it would hurt him more than all the insults and mockeries of his enemies. He remembered his look of grief and horror that day in the cathedral, when slanderously accused of having made himself as God. It had given him, most likely, the last pang he knew upon earth. Were those who loved him exposing him to this by the very wealth of their hero-worship? So much Hubert could see; but he failed to see that the Jew had caught the end of a clue of thought which, if honestly followed out, might lead him to the feet of Christ. Comparison shows differences, and there is a difference as wide as that which sunders earth from heaven, between the wisest teacher, the holiest saint, the most self-sacrificing martyr, and the Man who was crucified on Calvary. Other men have been holy and beloved, have made disciples, taught them, died for them. What more did He do — what more *was* He — that, centuries after, men and women who had never seen His face should die for the love of Him, with His name upon their lips?

Hubert's mind soon turned from the perplexing arguments of the Jew to the more intelligible concerns of Ostrodek. Yes; under all the circumstances it was well that Ostrodek should go. He would speak to Kepka, and, without betraying the poor lad's confidence, make all right with him. For his own part, he loved him, he even respected him, more than he had ever done before. Respected him! As he thought over his words, and the revelation they contained, a sudden shiver of pain and shame ran through him. Sometimes a moment flashes into consciousness the outcome of years of unconscious growth. Was Ostrodek indeed more noble, more straightforward, more honourable than himself?

Nearly three years ago Hubert set his foot upon the fair flower of love just beginning to unfold, and crushed it, as he thought, forever. But he knew now too well that he had only bent its stem. Since then he had let it raise its head again, and bloom and flourish unchecked. And now?

It was not so easy for him to efface himself — to go away and seek another service — as for Ostrodek. At Pihel everyone wanted him — at least, almost everyone — from his beloved lord, to whom his soul clave, down to the lowest menial. If there was an exception, it was that one whose slightest look and gesture had more power with him than the words of all the rest. The Pánna, so awe-inspiring when he came first, had grown frank and friendly as time wore on. But of late it seemed to him that she had frozen up again. At first, in her anxiety and watching — now, in her sorrow and loneliness — she was unapproachable. An invisible wall, like a sheet of glass, seemed to stand between them. Still, he was not going to be a coward, and to quit his post. What was right for Ostrodek would be wrong for him. He must do his work — where he was, bear his fate as he might, and trust God for the rest. As said the French proverb he had learned at the Sorbonne, *Fais ce que tu dois, advienne que pourra* (Do what you must, come what may).

XVII

SILVER SPURS AGAIN

Thou sufferest not the heart to freeze,
For Thou art with us all the days.

— Mrs. Charles

The past three years had not been idle or uneventful for the lord of Pihel. His temporal affairs had prospered; it seemed as if the money given back to him by the martyr's desire had brought with it a special blessing. The estates under his management now contained more than thirty villages, besides a great number of scattered dwellings. He was sincerely anxious to fulfil his duties to his vassals, but the state of the country rendered these extremely difficult and perplexing. The majority of his people were Hussites; and he had to protect them from the molestations of the neighbouring Papists, and not seldom to restrain their own ill-regulated zeal. Others, however, remained attached more or less strongly to the old order of things. These he sent Stasek, and other faithful pastors, to instruct. Why he did not go a step further, and, like some of the other Hussite barons, force all his vassals to adopt the Communion of the Cup, he could not in the least have explained. Only he observed to those who urged him to the use of severe measures, "The Cup of Christ is a gift. It seems scarce reverent to our Lord to force His gifts upon those who dislike them."

Not all his determination to follow Master John's counsel and "serve God quietly at home" could prevent his being drawn into the whirl of public affairs, and obliged often to go to court. He stood by the side of his friend Hussenec when that baron led into the presence of the king the deputation which claimed for the Hussites freedom of worship, and the restoration of the churches and schools of which they had been deprived. But while King Wenzel flew upon Hussenec in a rage, told him he was spinning a halter for his own neck, and banished him to his estates, he did not extend his anger to Chlum, whom he knew to be devoid of that personal ambition which, not altogether unjustly, he attributed to Hussenec. Wenzel liked and respected Chlum all the rather, perhaps, because in the affair of Huss he had been badly used by the imperial brother whom he himself so cordially detested. Recognizing the importance of keeping hold of that weak, vacillating nature, Chlum endured the penance of long visits to the lonely fortress where King Wenzel buried himself with his ignoble pleasures, hiding his eyes from seeing the miseries of his subjects, and his ears from hearing their complaints. It is worth while to a brave man, even at the risk of life, to hold and display in battle a worthless rag, soiled and torn, and fluttering in the breeze, if it bears upon it the royal arms. It was doubtless the influence of Chlum, and of a few like him, that so long withheld Wenzel from adopting a policy of persecution against the Hussites. In spite of the many acts of violence of which they were the victims, they believed, almost to the last, that at heart he was not unfavourable to their cause. His queen, they knew, was their friend, but she had little influence over him.

At the time of the Páni's death Chlum seemed to grow suddenly ten years older; and his hair and beard changed from gray almost to white. But that was all. He made no complaints, said nothing of his sorrow. He had the accustomed prayers and masses offered for her, though half the household thought them unnecessary, and Zedenka even ventured a word of remonstrance: "Dear Father, does it need all this? We know she is with Christ."

"Master John did not forbid it," he answered. "And what harm can they do her?" He paid for masses and made offerings for her much as we place flowers on the graves of those we love — not to benefit them, but to relieve our own hearts.

For the rest, he suffered, but not bitterly. For the pain that comes with peace is "not painful pain." There was in his heart no resistance to the will of God, but an utter and measureless content with it. Not in vain had he stood, even to the very end, beside that burning pile in Constance. There are some battles which need not be fought twice; some gains which never can be lost again.

He knew, too, that he had fallen on evil days; he could thank God that the one he loved was safe, delivered from those things which were coming on the earth. The door of her home had opened to receive her, and she had gone in, just before the breaking of the storm. Black with thunder, and heavy with rain, the clouds hung over them; already the first large drops, heralds of the coming tempest, were falling slowly one by one.

Not long could the weak and wavering Wenzel continue to protect his Hussite subjects, even if he would. His brother, the Emperor Sigismund, was alternately threatening and cajoling, but always urging him to take decisive measures against them. Even if, contrary to all probability, he should still refuse, the whole strength of Germany might be hurled against the little kingdom of Bohemia, to enforce at the sword's point the Bull of Pope Martin and the Decree of the Council. This was what the Papists threatened loudly, while with bated breath they whispered often another word of terrible import — *a Crusade*. Awful hints of a country desolated and a race exterminated lurked beneath the common taunt, "You Hussites are as bad as the Albigenses." There was in Bohemia at this time a colony of Waldenses, who had lived there for many years without molestation. They had fearful tales to tell of their native valleys, wasted with fire and sword by the emissaries of the Church in the days of their forefathers. "Served them right," said Václav, on hearing some of these. "What had they hands for, and weapons in them? In the name of God, we Bohemians at least will fight to the death for our hearths and our homes."

But this warlike temper Chlum dreaded also. He lamented the acts of violence into which the more turbulent members of their party were sometimes betrayed. His favourite aspiration, "Oh, for Master John!" was sure to rise to his lips when any of these were told him. "He knew the signs of the times, and what Israel ought to do. He could control, and calm, and guide. Without him, we are as sheep having no shepherd."

The same wish was prompted by the wide and ever increasing divergences of opinion which he saw around him. John Cardinal, the Rector of the University, and the other heads of the moderate party, had recently published a manifesto, condemning, though with mildness, the more advanced Hussites, who denied purgatory, and refused to pray for the dead, to invoke the saints, or to practice confession. Of this manifesto Chlum approved; but he had a mournful suspicion, deepening into certainty, that the members of his own household — Hubert, Zedenka, and even young Václav — were not one with him in this matter. He did not blame them; but it deepened his sense of solitude and isolation. There are two ways of following in the footsteps of a great leader. You may take your stand on the last "poor inch of ground" his dying feet have pressed, and defy heaven and earth to dislodge you from it. Or you may leave it and go boldly forward in the path that he was treading, until you too are called elsewhere and fresh runners take your place. Chlum followed in the first way, Hubert and the others in the second.

At this time Chlum took comfort in carrying out every wish his lady had expressed. He soon spoke to Peichler about the betrothal of Frantisek and Aninka. That worthy hung back for awhile, that he might extract better terms from the good-natured knight; but he yielded eventually, and the betrothal feast was given at Pihel when the first months of mourning were over. Aninka was to remain with Zedenka during the interval between the betrothal and the wedding. "For," said Chlum to his daughter, "it would be hard for you to be left alone so soon."

I am alone always, thought Zedenka, though she did not say it. In those days she said little; nor, indeed, did she weep much. Hers was a strong, deep, reserved nature — her father's mixed with her mother's. This sorrow went down to the roots of her being; first stunning, then agonizing, then almost hardening. It was quite unlike the sorrow for her young brother, out of which she had risen triumphantly to soothe and cheer her mother. It was yet more unlike the passion with which she mourned and worshipped the martyr of Constance. *That* kindled her imagination, this crushed her heart. The angel of death looks like an angel of glory; we see through our tears his grand, awful beauty, when he comes to those we reverence — to hero, king, or pastor — with the summons, "Come up higher." But when he crosses our familiar paths, and takes from us the desire of our eyes, the treasure of our hearts, we cannot see the glory — we can only feel the pain. It is so terribly real, so awfully near. Near? It is not near, but within us, crushing, burning, slaying. It is part of our very being.

We sometimes try to deaden the pain by the narcotic of outward activities. The youthful Chatelaine of Pihel was very busy in those days; her cares and duties were manifold. Life resumed its ordinary course. Ostrodek went away, with kindly farewells and good wishes from all; but Lucaz and Václav did not for the present return to the University, and Hubert remained with them. Chlum knew that in the interests of what he called "the Cause" he ought to go to the court soon again, but he could not well leave his household in its present state.

Zedenka understood his difficulties, and thought the best course might be to break up the household for a while. In that case she herself would go to Prague to visit Pánna Oneshka.

"I would like to be with her and to learn of her," she said. "It would be of much use to me hereafter. Besides, she has of late been ill again, and would take such a visit very kindly."

"No, my child, I do not like to part with you. Besides, what should we do with the lads? To take them to the court is not good; and if we leave them here, they will be running to meetings and gatherings all over the country. Already Václav has been asking for permission to go to Tabor, where some are preaching the end of the world, and other strange doctrines. Václav listens much to Frantisek — who is a good lad, *very*, and Aninka a fortunate girl; still, one can never guess the next thing he will take into his head. Do write a kind letter to Pánna Oneshka, and send her some gifts. You know what she would like. Say you will visit her soon — I cannot spare you now. I shall send Vitus to Prague next week. Have a packet ready by that time."

Zedenka knew her father meant, by the gifts her aged friend would like, things which had belonged to her mother. But it was not easy to find gifts suited for Pánna Oneshka. Dress and jewellery were out of the question, since she always wore a plain black robe without ornament. However, a rosary of olive-wood brought from the Holy Land by a Crusading ancestor of her mother, and a Book of Hours in a case of carved ivory, were put aside for the purpose. Lastly, she remembered a certain embroidered cushion, wrought by Queen Sophia's own hands, which her mother had loved to use, and Pánna Oneshka would prize for her sake.

But the castle was searched for it in vain: it had been mislaid, and none of the female members of the household knew anything about it.

The day before the departure of Vitus, Hubert came into the ante-room which the boys used for their studies and indoor sports, and saw Karel Sandresky lying fast asleep on the rush-strewn floor, his head pillowed comfortably upon that very cushion. He shook the boy awake with scant ceremony, and asked rather sharply where he had found it, and why he had not brought it at once to the Pánna. Karel, a delicate boy, who had grieved deeply in his childish way for the Páni, sprang to his feet flushed and startled. As soon as he understood what Hubert meant, he took up the cushion, held it out before him, looked at it critically, and ejaculated in a tone of contempt, "*That old thing!*"

"Do you not know," asked Hubert, "that the Pánna has been searching for it everywhere? It is the queen's own work, and our dear lady set much store by it."

Hubert saw Karel Sandresky lying fast asleep on the rush-strewn floor, his head pillowed comfortably upon that very cushion.

"She had many better ones," said Karel. "Look, Master Hubert, the tail of the falcon wrought on this side is all stained, and on the other the silk is torn — see here." He turned the cushion, and showed Hubert a long rent on the plainer side, which had been partly repaired, and the work left unfinished with a loose thread hanging from it. "How could I know *that* was the thing all the women were hunting for? I thought it was something handsome, fit to make a present of. I should be ashamed to offer this to a serving-woman."

"How did you come by it?"

"Oh, I don't know. It has been lying about forever so long. I just happened to take it up. Will the Pánna be *very* angry with me, Master Hubert?"

"Well, hardly," said Hubert with a slight smile, "but we must bring it to her at once."

"Dear Master Hubert, *you* tell her about it. She will not be angry then. She is so fond of you," said Karel, looking straight into Hubert's face with wide, innocent blue eyes.

"Nonsense!" said Hubert, turning quickly away.

Karel burst into tears.

Hubert turned back again and laid his hand caressingly on his shoulder. "Dear boy, what is it?"

"The Pánna will be vexed about the cushion, and now you — you are vexed too, Master Hubert. For all that, I am right. Ask Václav: he knows."

"I am not vexed with you, my boy. Only you should know that is not the way to speak of a lady. The utmost one should permit oneself to say is this: 'She does use you with much courtesy,' or, 'She holds you in some regard as her father's squire.' But listen to me, Karel — do you call yourself a Hussite?"

The blue eyes shone through their tears. "I am a Hussite," he said.

"Hussites may have to die for their faith, so they should learn in time to be brave and firm, and not fall to weeping like babes upon every slight vexation."

"I — *won't*," said Karel, biting his lip, and forcing back the tears.

"Good. Go out now to the lower meadow, where Lucaz and Václav are practising their exercises with Rabstein. When you can leap into the saddle, as they do, without touching the stirrup, I'll give you a pair of gloves. Stay, give me that cushion: I shall take it at once to the Pánna." Somewhat comforted, Karel went forth to join the older lads. They could not only leap fully armed into the

313

saddle, but perform many other feats, such as 'placing one hand on the saddle-bow of the charger and the other near the ears, taking him by the mane, and from the level ground jumping to the other side of the charger. Rabstein, gentle as a lamb, yet full of spirit, served them admirably in these exercises. He was the friend of the whole household and the playfellow of the boys. They often used to ride him; but it would not have been safe, after his fall, for his lord to do so, in the cumbrous and heavy equipments worn by the knights of that age.

Karel forgot his troubles for a while in watching the feats of the others. Both did well; but, to the delight of Karel, Václav excelled. There was one feat, however, which they waited for Hubert to join them before attempting. He would sit on horseback, and Lucaz or Václav would take him with one hand by the sleeve, and without other help leap from the ground upon his shoulders. Hubert did not like them to do this, even with Vitus or Prokop, if he was not present himself. This morning both were eager to try it, especially Lucaz, who had fallen the last time, and longed to regain his character for agility. Karel was beset with questions. Where had he left Master Hubert, and why did he not come out to them?

Thus recalled to his troubles and his fears, he said he would go in and look for him. When he came into the court he found the serving-women, with Aninka at their head, busy shaking out, brushing, and cleaning curtains, hangings, and bed-clothes. It was early November, and they were taking advantage of the last mild and sunny days of autumn.

The Pánna? Oh, she had gone indoors a little while ago. They thought she would come back to them soon, as she seemed very anxious about the work.

Karel went toward the "bower" where she often sat with her women. But he did not get there, for in passing through the corridor he saw her sitting in the deep recess of a window. She had the cushion in her hand, and Hubert was standing near her. As he approached Hubert moved quickly and took his place farther off. Both looked much disturbed; indeed, he thought the Pánna had been weeping. What was far more wonderful, Master Hubert, too — brave, strong Master Hubert — had unmistakable tears in his eyes. And that after his words to him! The Pánna's fingers were playing nervously with the loose thread of silk that hung from the cushion, and her eyes were dwelling on it, as if it was telling her some story of the past.

"She must be very much vexed about it," thought Karel. He went boldly up to her. "Dear Pánna," he said, "please do not be

314

angry with Master Hubert, it will make him so unhappy — and he had nothing to do with it. It is all my fault. I am very sorry."

This was too much, coming suddenly, as it did, upon the deep converse, sad and sweet, into which they had drifted unawares. In the momentary revulsion of feeling Zedenka laughed, and Hubert joined her. The gray old walls and the vaulted roof echoed the unwonted sound.

The first laugh after a great sorrow is seldom taken note of, yet it means a great deal. If those we mourn could hear it where they are (and perhaps they are not so far away), it would make them very glad. It would say to them, "No whit the less near and dear are you, beloved; you are in the very core and centre of our hearts forever. But we know that you would have us take up our lives again — not their cares and burdens only, but their joys. We take you with us into all; we are the better, the stronger, the richer, for what you have been — what you *are* — to us. When we meet again 'in the most sweet peace of the future life' we will tell you everything, for you have part in everything. Meanwhile, in this waiting time, the thought of you blesses our blessings, no less than it cheers and soothes our sorrows."

Something of this Zedenka may have felt, as the echo of the moment's laugh died away, and she looked "through a rainbow of tears" at the work her busy fingers touched last in her mother's room. Thus had she left it unfinished, that very thread hanging so, when called suddenly to do some little office for her, and she had never resumed the task. There it had lain forgotten — "an unconsidered trifle;" but what eloquence, what pathos it had for her now! As she drew together those frayed edges, and set those first stitches — a little unevenly — the dear voice that was silent now had been saying to her, "I could wish you no better lot than mine."

Hubert, meanwhile, went at once to the chamber where the lord of the castle sat alone, having just dismissed his steward, after a long and troublesome interview. Chlum sat idle, wrapped in his white mantle — the garb of deep mourning — his head resting on his hands. His mind was filled with perplexing, foreboding thoughts, for every day brought him fresh evidence of the troublous state of the country, and even his own vassals were stirring.

But never yet had Hubert come to increase his cares, while he had often lightened or shared them. Recognizing his step, Chlum looked up and smiled.

"Sir Knight," asked Hubert, "can you hear a few words from me?"

"As many as you will, my son. What is wrong, and with whom?"

Hubert's grave eyes and anxious face prompted the question.

"Nothing, Sir Knight, save with me alone."

"With *you*? If I can help you . . . But say on."

Hubert held in his hand his silver spurs, and now he laid them on the table before his lord.

"What is the matter?" asked Chlum, with surprise. "Is it a sudden summons to your native land? For nothing else — for nothing less, I think — would you leave us, Hubert."

His voice sank a little, and was not quite steady, as he ended.

"My lord, I would not leave you . . ."

"I begin to understand. You think, and with reason, that in due time these silver spurs ought to be exchanged for golden ones; and you see no chance of that while you are with me."

"Indeed, Sir Knight, I have no such thoughts. But hear me, my good lord, I pray you. Let me tell you all that is in my heart, and then, if you bid me from you, never to see the face of you and yours again, I will obey without a word."

"What is this madness, Hubert? One would think you had committed a crime! But speak on. You know I love you well and cannot think you have anything to tell that will not make me love you better."

"Sir Knight, your words are noble — as ever. I, too — God knows — I love you well. But the truth is, I love one who is near you far too well for my own peace. Now, Sir Knight, my tale is told."

A change passed over the knight's sad, thoughtful face but its meaning was inscrutable. There was a long silence. Hubert could hear the beating of his own heart. At last he ventured to say, "Forgive my presumption."

Chlum stretched out his hand to him, while the perplexed lines of his face softened into a smile. "There is no presumption," he said. "We are peers in rank, and the chance that made you an exile might as well have been ours. But there is another question — what is best for my child and for you? Does she know of this thing, Hubert?"

"My lord, just now we fell unawares into converse about our dear lady who is gone. And I think the Pánna knows I would give my life to comfort her sorrow. That is all."

"You are quite frank with me, Hubert?"

Hubert bowed his head.

"Let me think. I am slow of thought, and I have none to take counsel with now."

Hubert stood waiting patiently.

"How long has this thing been in your heart, Hubert?" asked Chlum at last.

"It began soon — very soon — after I came," Hubert answered candidly. "But when the young lord of Hussenec was here I crushed it down, set my heel on it, thought I had conquered it. For I knew his purpose, and I knew what I was, and am — a penniless squire, only fit to hold her stirrup and to bear her train. But it would not die. All unknown to myself it lived — it grew. Some chance words revealed it to my own heart, and now, I fear, I have betrayed it to her. Sir Knight, shall I go away?"

"Where would you go?" asked Chlum of him, as he had asked of Ostrodek.

"I must find another service, though never any so dear to me as yours."

"Do not go, Hubert. You are as a son to me. Until we know what to do you can come with me to the king's court; or Zedenka can go to Prague to visit Pánna Oneshka. Perhaps," he added, and even in the midst of his perplexity he could not forbear a quiet smile "perhaps, after all, she may not find that kind of life the most agreeable. Take back your spurs, my son. Silver may sometimes be better than gold. And pray God to guide us all, for in truth we need it."

"Father," said Václav, coming in, "Frantisek is here; and he has brought dreadful news."

This startling announcement did not produce the effect that might have been expected. People were used in those days to "dreadful news." Human nature becomes used to anything, even to living on the slope of a volcano. Chlum only said, "Let us hear it at first hand, then. Bring him here."

Presently there entered a very fine young man, clad in a doublet and hosen of good gray cloth, and having at his girdle a three-cornered purse of leather, probably well filled. He bowed low to the knight and squire, who greeted him very kindly, Hubert even placing a stool for him, though he declined this remarkable honour, and stood modestly, cap in hand, before his superiors.

A question from the knight drew out his tidings. "This morning, Sir Knight and Master Squire, one came from Prague to my master, who said there is a royal edict out banishing Master John Jessenec, and ordaining that the churches and schools of those who hold the Communion of the Cup shall be taken from them and given to the Papists."

Even the steadfast-hearted Chlum changed colour and looked moved. "It can't be," he said, half to himself. "The king would not *dare*. It is some lie of the Papists, Frantisek."

"It is too true, if my good lord will pardon me the word. Our man — he is a scholar — saw the edict posted on the gate of the Vyssehrad, and read it for himself. Moreover, he said the city is in an uproar about it."

"But 'tis only so much waste paper, after all," cried Václav. "King Wenzel can never act on it. He should have known that much, though he is a . . ."

"*Hush*, Václav: he is your king!" Chlum interrupted.

A little while longer they talked with Frantisek, drawing out any further information he had to give, which, indeed, was not much. Then Chlum sent him to Aninka, charging him, however, not to excite her fears, nor those of the household. "It is not the king who speaks in that edict," he said, "but the Emperor and the priests. And — there are stronger than they."

Left alone with Hubert, he laid his hand on his shoulder and said gently, "My son, this settles one question, at least, for you and me. We go to the king at once, to try if faithful counsel may yet do anything with him. For the rest, the Scripture says, 'The time is short.' "

This was indisputable; but the conclusion to be drawn therefrom was not equally clear. Hubert looked at him inquiringly.

" 'The time is short' — shall I therefore say to you, 'Wait long?' " he continued, with a smile. "And yet, my son Hubert, I bid you: wait. God will show us His will in all things — if our will is to see it. As for this thing, I am inclined to take for my guide the will of her whom it most concerns. But we must first be sure that she knows it herself. So I ask of you patience and silence; at least, until after our return from the court."

"What my lord asks of me shall most gladly be observed," said Hubert, bending down to kiss his hand.

XVIII

MOUNT TABOR

Hark! What a sound, and too divine for hearing,
Stirs on the earth, and trembles in the air!
It is the thunder of the Lord's appearing!
Is it the music of His people's prayer?

Surely He cometh, and a thousand voices
Call to the saints, and to the deaf are dumb,
Surely He cometh, and the earth rejoices,
Glad in His coming who has sworn, "I come."
— Frederic W.H. Myers

Six months had passed away since the persecuting edict of King Wenzel awakened the fears and the indignation of the Hussites. It was then November — now it was July; and we know that the earth wears a very different aspect in July and in November. But something more than the change from winter frost and snow to summer sun and air was needed to account for the alteration in the looks and the bearing of the men of Bohemia, and in the aspect of their country. Had we, who, peering through the mists of centuries, see but dimly "men as trees walking," been actually among the eager, joyous pilgrims who thronged the roads of Southern Bohemia in the summer of 1419, we would have found it hard to realize that we were in a land over which so lately the heavy thunderclouds were brooding, and which even then was full of wars and rumours of wars.

Young and old, rich and poor, men, women, and children, were streaming onward by every road and path, from every castle, town, and village, and from many a solitary hut or cottage, toward a single point.

The picturesque hill, a promontory near the fort of Luschnec — from that time on and forever to be known in history as Mount Tabor — was in the very centre of the district where Huss had preached most often during his exile from Prague. The neighbouring town of

Austi was the dwelling of his most attached disciples and most intimate friends. All around the living seed of his evangelical teaching had sprung up and borne fruit a hundredfold. When the edict of King Wenzel drove the Hussite preachers from Prague and other cities of the kingdom, many of them took refuge in Austi and its neighbourhood, sure of a welcome. A crowd of the laity of all ranks and classes flocked to it also, wishing to hear the Gospel preached and to receive the Communion of the Cup. The movement for some time was entirely spontaneous. But great open-air gatherings and field-preachings were becoming more and more the fashion among the Hussites. It was determined by the chiefs of the party to make Mount Tabor the scene of the greatest and most imposing one which had yet been held. So they sent messages throughout the length and breadth of the land inviting all good Hussites to attend an assembly, wholly for religious purposes, which was to be held on Mount Tabor on St. Magdalen's Day, July 24th.

The journey to Mount Tabor was in itself a festival and a holiday. A sky of "deep palpitating azure," flecked with bright clouds, bent down over the pilgrims, and seemed to bless them silently. The earth around them was green and glad, full of promise for the later harvest-time. The grass was jewelled with flowers, the birds sang in the branches of the fruit-trees by the way.

Pihel contributed a goodly band to the pilgrim host. Hubert was the acknowledged leader, and beside him rode Václav, now a tall youth of sixteen. They were followed by a company of retainers, with steel caps and corselets, and armed with pikes or swords. Some townsmen from Leitmeritz, in more peaceful attire, were taking advantage of their escort.

Chlum, whose visit to the king was ineffectual, had gone to Melnik, a fort at the junction of the Elbe and the Moldau, of which the queen had made him castellan, it being part of her appanage or dowry. He would gladly have had Hubert with him there, but he thought it of more importance that Hubert should accompany Václav, who was bent upon going to Mount Tabor, in order to keep him within the bounds of sobriety and discretion. Zedenka was in Prague, with Pánna Oneshka.

Half a day's march from Tabor the Pihel band overtook a little procession from a country village. They had already seen a hundred like it, and passed them with a friendly exchange of greetings and good wishes. This time the pastor walked at the head of his parishioners, having resigned his pony to a tired woman, who sat on it holding her baby fastened cornerwise on a pillow, as Bohemian babies usually are, while a neighbour led it for her. There were young men and old, there were women and little children. In the midst was a wagon, drawn by bullocks, containing provisions, cloaks, blankets, and a few simple cooking utensils. Perched high among the gear, on a kind of throne, sat two golden-haired children of six or seven, safe and fearless, laughing and playing with the flowers their companions plucked by the way and flung up to them.

"Stay, Hubert!" cried Václav, as soon as he caught sight of the pastor's face. "Yonder priest is Wenzel of Arnoštovic. I must speak with him."

"What Wenzel?" asked Hubert. "There are so many Wenzels. I do not remember him."

"Nor could you, Brother, since you have never seen him. But I could not forget him if I lived a hundred years. He it was who gave me first the Communion of the Cup in the house of Frantisek's mother, in Leitmeritz."

So saying, Václav drew near the priest, and brought his horse to a walking pace.

"God save you, Father," he said. "I heard you preach in Leitmeritz four years ago, and I hope I shall hear you again tomorrow."

Notwithstanding the great difference between the youth of sixteen and the child of twelve, the pastor of Arnoštovic soon recognized the eager-hearted boy who had taken the Cup of Christ from his hand with such evident and genuine emotion. He had been struck by his early piety, and was interested in him as the son of Chlum. He asked him now after his father.

"My father is at Melnik," said Václav. "He has the place in charge from the queen. I believe he hopes still to convince the king that there is no use in trying to crush us. Nor is there. The whole country is with us, Master Wenzel."

"God is with us, which is better," said the pastor reverently. "But tell me, I pray you, is Frantisek, the mercer's apprentice, in your company?"

"No, poor lad; to his sorrow he could not come. His mother is dying; and, moreover, his master is a pestilent Papist, and he cannot afford to anger him more than he must, for he is betrothed to his daughter."

"Is that so? Then he must be very unlike himself, or she very unlike her father. Which is it?"

"The last," said Václav heartily. "Aninka has lived with us since we came from Constance, and thinks just as we do. She is my sister's bower maiden, and is with her now in Prague."

"Prague has not been very quiet since the Hussite priests and schoolmasters were driven away," observed the pastor. "I would our friends there, and some also of those over there" — with a glance at the broad, low hill now rising in the distance — "would remember that the wrath of man works not the righteousness of God."

"True," said Václav; "yet there is such a thing as righteous wrath. We may be forced to fight."

"*You* may," the priest answered. "As for us, the weapons of our warfare are not carnal. Better so. It is better to suffer than to fight."

Shouts of laughter from the children interrupted this grave discourse. The little ones on the wagon had got hold of a basket in which some of the women had packed certain small articles of finery, chiefly knots of bright-coloured ribbon, intended to grace the next day's festival. They were throwing them down to their companions in exchange for the flowers, much to their delight. The owners, however, did not appreciate the sport, and tried to recover their property, which the children, half in fun and half in mischief, struggled to keep. Presently two or three smart cuffs and boxes on the ear exchanged as many peals of laughter into sounds of another kind.

But the pastor promptly interfered; the little disturbance was quieted, and order and good-humour restored.

"I marvel you should bring babes like these such a distance," said Václav, glancing at the pair on the wagon.

"How could their mothers come if they were left behind?" asked the pastor. "Babes though they are, they know what they are going to, and their little hearts are full of it. They will remember it all their days, and tell of it to their children and their children's children, when we are gone to rest. If we grow weary, or if any disorder begins among us, it is our way to sing a hymn, and with your permission, Panec, we will do it now."

"With all my heart," said Václav.

The pastor called for silence, and struck up an old Bohemian hymn, in which all joined, and none more heartily than the children on the wagon, who beat time with their little feet, and sent the words of faith and hope ringing up to heaven in their clear, childish treble,

Should hosts arise against me,
I know no fear at all;
For God is fighting for me,
And will not let me fall.

Václav joined also; and his party, hearing the familiar air and words, contributed their manly bass to swell the tide of sacred song,

> *For He is with me still,*
> *In whom I trust forever;*
> *He will His word fulfil:*
> *Despair shall find me never.*
>
> *This one thing from my God*
> *I crave with longing mind —*
> *Within His blest abode*
> *My resting-place to find.*
>
> *Hear me, O Lord, I pray;*
> *My spirit longs for Thee:*
> *Turn not Thy face away,*
> *But ever dwell with me.*
>
> *Look back upon me, Lord,*
> *Amidst the thickest fight,*
> *Thy gracious help afford,*
> *And change to day my night.*

This was not the last hymn they sang together on their way, and as they neared their destination they heard the same sweet sounds from other bands of pilgrims whom they overtook, or who overtook them.

At length the crowds became so dense that the parties had to separate. The Pihel men, of course, got on more quickly than the others, as they were all mounted.

"If you please, Master Hubert, what are we to do for quarters?" asked Vitus, bringing up his horse abreast of the squire's.

"Take what we can get," returned Hubert. "Never saw I such a multitude — scarce even in Constance."

"I wish we saw our way to a lodging and a place for the horses," pursued Vitus.

"A lodging!" laughed Hubert. "I warrant but very few of all this multitude will sleep under a roof tonight, and we shall not be among them. Some have brought tents, perhaps; but only women and children will care for them. Well for us that we have bread and meat in our haversacks and there are brooks enough to quench our thirst."

Austi they avoided: they knew it was already full to overflowing. They sighted the fortress of Luschnec, but did not approach it; and along their route they saw few houses, or none. At last they came to the entrance of a pass which led to the hill of Tabor, and was, in fact, the only way of approaching it, as its other sides were defended by rocky ravines, through which streams of water were flowing. Here they were met by certain of the inhabitants of the place, if those could be so styled who dwelt in tents upon the hill or in its neighbourhood. They saluted the newcomers as brethren in the Lord, and, regretting that they could show them no better hospitality, offered to find them a place for their bivouac, and to supply them with food.

Hubert thanked these new friends, and said that they had their own provisions, but would be glad to know where they might spend the night without inconveniencing others. Accordingly, they were shown a field on the southern slope of the mountain, just over a steep ravine. Here they picketed their horses, and supped upon the food they had brought, with the addition of some light wine given them by the people of the place. Then they prayed, sang a hymn, and lay down to sleep in their cloaks, the grass beneath them and the stars above their heads.

Sleep was not easily won. Almost throughout the night parties kept arriving and settling near them. Some set up tents, but most were content with the primitive arrangement they had themselves adopted. But although the noise of voices and the trampling of men and horses were of course considerable, above and through all other sounds the whole night long came that of sweet singing. It seemed to come from every part of the hill.

At last Hubert fell asleep, but was awakened by feeling the hot breath of a living creature on his cheek. He started up, and saw a horse, not one of their own, composedly cropping the grass by his side. For fear of accidents, he rose and drove the intruder away. Then he looked around him. No one near him was awake. The sacred dewy silence of the starlit summer night was only broken by the voices of those who sang far away in the distance,

Praise God, from whom all blessings flow.

Too full of solemn gladness to sleep again, he withdrew a little from the rest, and knelt down on the grass. God was very near him in that hour. God was very good; the earth was full of His glory. All things praised Him — the world, the sky, the stars; and now the sons of men were learning to give thanks to Him, and to honour His great name. Everywhere His Word was preached — surely the day was coming, foretold and promised long ago, when the knowledge of His glory should cover the earth as the waters cover the sea, when the kingdoms of this world should become the kingdoms of our Lord and of His Christ, and He should reign forever and ever. Hubert did not consciously connect the promise for the future with the peace of the present; yet is it true that all fair scenes of Nature are charged with a burden and a message for the aching, yearning heart of humanity. "Wait," they whisper softly; "wait and trust. All will be well yet. For, behold I make all things new! *And I am coming.*"

Perhaps the heart of Hubert was the more open to these influences because of another whisper — "a little whisper, silver clear" — which told him there was hope for him of the brightest and fairest joy earth had to give. From where he was he could see in the distance the stately tents of the lord of Hussenec, lit up in the darkness by the glare of torches and watch-fires; but he was not tempted now to envy the heir of the mightiest baron of Bohemia. Can even fruition bring with it anything more bright and glad than the witching hour when Hope first touches the hand of Joy?

To him the time seemed short until the heavens whitened into dawn, and the first drowsy notes of the birds began. Soon the sun shot up; the glory of the morning was around him, and every blade of grass at his feet was quivering with misty sunlit dew. His companions were beginning to stir. Václav leaped first to his feet, eager to lose not a moment of the long, happy, glorious day. A rapid toilet was performed, prayers were said, and a hymn was sung; but no one tasted food, for all intended to communicate.

Early as they were, others were astir before them; going to the great central field or plain, the crown of the hill, they found eager crowds already gathering at the various stations where preachers of note were expected to take their stand. The multitude was far too vast to be addressed by *one*: it broke itself up, though in a quiet, orderly way, into several distinct congregations. Happily, the space was ample; there was room for all. Hubert and his companions were attracted toward a compact, soldierly band, which might, indeed, have been called an army. The men wore no special dress, but they stood in ranks, and all had arms of some kind — swords, pikes, hooks, or hails. Over them waved a banner; all the field was bright with banners and pennons, but this was a strange one, which Hubert had never seen before. It was black, and bore upon it in red the sacred emblem of the Sacramental Cup. As the strangers approached, the whole company were thundering out, in their deep, manly bass, the strains of a martial hymn,

> *Soldiers of God! Arise*
> *And combat for His laws!*
> *Implore His present help,*
> *And trust to Him your cause;*
> *For he who owns the Lord his friend*
> *Must ever conquer in the end.*

When the hymn was finished, a young man came forth out of the ranks, and, throwing his arms around the neck of Hubert, bestowed upon him a hearty embrace. It was Ostrodek, grown to his full height, and altogether much improved in appearance. He embraced Václav also, and greeted Vitus and the other men in friendly fashion.

"Is Kepka here?" he asked eagerly.

Hubert told him where he was, and what he was doing; and then in his turn inquired the meaning of the warlike array.

"My lord trains his following somewhat in the use of arms, and in those habits of regular and orderly movement men must acquire if they are to serve in war," said Ostrodek; and he began to chant, to a rather plaintive yet stirring tune, a verse of the hymn they had been singing,

> *The watchword bear in mind*
> *Which first was given to you;*
> *Mark well your Captain's eye,*
> *Be to your comrades true;*
> *In ordered rank and file stand right —*
> *So heroes conquer in the fight.*

"But look! There is Zisca himself, beside that tree."

Hubert saw a dark, soldierly man with a shade over one eye — more he could not discern at the distance.

"We are now going to hear a sermon," pursued Ostrodek. "Stay with us, Master Hubert, and listen. It will be well worth your while."

Ostrodek had not been wont to pay much heed to the rather monotonous pulpit utterances of Stasek, so Hubert was surprised at his zeal.

"Who is the preacher?" he asked.

"Martin, a priest, whom we call Loqui for his eloquence. He preaches splendid sermons, Master Hubert. He expounds the Apocalypse of St. John; and tells us all about the Battle of Armageddon, and the Seven Last Plagues, and about the Great Red Dragon, and the Woman clothed with the Sun."

In spite of this attractive bill of spiritual fare, Hubert had the bad taste to decline, as he wished to hear Václav's friend, Wenzel.

Ostrodek pitied him for losing his chance of hearing the most eloquent preacher in the field, but proposed that he and the other Pihel men should come back and dine with the people of Zisca.

"You will know where to find us," he said, "by the standard of the Cup. We are the servants of God and of the Cup, Master Hubert."

As everyone was free to do as he pleased, some of the Pihel men remained to hear Martin Loqui; while Hubert, Václav, Vitus, and others wandered through the field in search of Wenzel.

While thus engaged Hubert happened to catch a few words from an old man who was addressing a dense crowd of peasants, all men, for the women and children formed congregations apart. The words arrested him, and he stayed, telling Václav and his companions not to wait for him.

This was what the aged preacher — not a priest, but apparently a peasant like themselves — was saying to the multitude: " '*This same Jesus*, who is taken up from you into heaven, shall so come in like manner as you have seen Him go into heaven.' Do you know this, my brothers? Do you believe it? It is written in the Holy Scriptures, and not in this place alone, but in many places, more than I can tell you. Do you know that a day will come which will begin like this day, with the sun rising in yonder sky, but will not end like any day there has ever been since the making of the world? For it is the Day of the Lord. That day the heavens shall open wide, and He that shall come will come in the clouds of glory, His holy angels with Him. His holy angels! Dearer than angel faces will be seen around Him then. For 'those who sleep in Jesus will God bring with Him!' — I know *one* who will surely come again with Him that day. You all know him. Once more our eyes shall see him, our ears shall hear his voice, our hands shall touch his hands — though wicked men burned him to ashes in that fire at Constance. Shall we be glad of it, my brothers?"

Through the densely packed and breathless crowd there ran a quiver, a thrill of deep emotion. A murmur rose, to be checked instantly by the next words of the speaker.

"But, behold! I show you a mystery. We shall not be glad of it at first. We shall not think of him, we shall not even look at him. Friends, brothers, the desire of whose eyes has gone from you to the

327

grave, before you look upon those dear faces when God brings them back, you will look upon the face of One — that One who died for you; you will kiss His blessed feet, you will touch His blessed hands, which were pierced for you.

"To you who love Him *thus*, I say that you shall see Him, and that soon! How soon I cannot tell. Perhaps today, while we are waiting and looking for Him — perhaps tomorrow. Perhaps not until next year, or a few years hence. He may tarry even until His people are in sore need and trouble, and their foes prevail against them, as says the Scripture, 'Many shall be purified, and made white, and tried.' But surely He comes — He comes! And we who love His appearing shall go in with Him to the Marriage Supper of the Lamb, and rest and rejoice with Him forever."

Much more was said, but for Hubert this was enough. His soul had grasped a new truth. All his life he had been repeating in the Credo, "Who shall come again with glory, to judge the living and the dead." But if he thought at all about it, he thought this "coming again" was something vague and mystical, and very far away. It was a "mystery of the Faith" — one of "the four last things" which should accompany the end of the world. Of how long the world had lasted, of how long it might last yet before that consummation, he had not the least idea. That the Lord Christ might come again *soon* — any day and that His coming would be joy unspeakable to those who loved Him, was a new and wonderful and rapturous thought. It filled his whole heart. It vivified and strengthened that passionate, personal love to Christ — that intense realization of His presence — which had come to him first in Constance.

What if, in another sense than Chlum meant it, "the time was short?" What if, in that world to come, they should be "as the angels of God in heaven?" Still, they would be *together* there; and, in that hour of exaltation, this was enough for Hubert Bohun.

Then old thoughts swept over him. He remembered his dear young brother; he remembered Constance, and the great chancellor, and the great Council. He thought tenderly of Armand, trusting that he too would be ready when the King came. And the chancellor? Was not that just what he was longing and toiling for, though he knew it not himself? It was from the chancellor Hubert had learned, in those old days, half to adore the great Council — to dream of it as Michael the archangel with the dragon beneath his feet. Now, at last, he was comforted concerning the great Council's failure and the great chancellor's broken heart. *This* was what Council and chancellor meant, though the one was not pure and the other not strong enough to inaugurate it — this reign of truth and justice upon earth. It was *the reign of Christ*, and He was coming from heaven to establish it. When He came, would He judge Jean Gerson for his share in the death of His saints?

"Well, if He does," thought Hubert, "if He even slays him for it with the sword that is in His mouth, Jean Gerson will rejoice in dying, because He is there, and because He has won the victory."

Finally, the preacher exhorted his hearers to approach the table of the Lord, and, by partaking of the bread and wine, to "show forth His death *until His coming again.*"

Thus, for the first time, was the *onward* look of that blessed ordinance emphasized for Hubert. Almost in a dream of rapture he mingled with the crowd who knelt reverently "in ranks upon the green grass," while some of the exiled pastors, with prayer and solemn rite, administered to them the "Bread" and the "Cup of Christ."

Heaven seemed so near, and earth so far away, that, when the rite was over, the voice of Václav by his side made him start as one too suddenly awakened.

"Where have you been, Hubert?" he asked. "I have heard two sermons and partaken of the Holy Sacrament. Also I have seen the lord of Hussenec; and you should go to him after dinner. Klaus has come home at last, and he has a letter for you from England. But he can scarce talk of anything save a horrible sight which he saw there — the cruel martyrdom of a great English Hussite — (there they call them Lollards) — a knight and baron named Lord Cobham. You ought to hear him, Hubert."

"Yes, I will go to him. Do you know whom the letter he has for me is from?"

"He says it is from the chief of your name, asking you to go back to England, and he would advance your fortunes there. I answered him, 'My father will not like to see Master Hubert go to England, since he is as a son to him; and, moreover, I think there is one in our house who would like it even less!' "

"*Oh, Václav!*"

"Klaus looked savage; I thought he would have slain me on the spot. But I tell you, Hubert, it was quite different with my lord of Hussenec. He smiled, and was gracious. He has a great respect for Kepka, he said. He wished him and all his house every happiness and prosperity. Brother, the truth is that my lord of Hussenec is just now the greatest man in the kingdom, and I submit he is not sorry that his son is free to seek an alliance with some lordlier house than ours. I, for one, will not contradict the word my father spoke before the Council, when he called himself the least of the barons of Bohemia," said young Václav, with proud humility.

They dined with Zisca's men, and might have dined, if they could, in twenty places at once. Unbounded hospitality and frank brotherly kindness reigned throughout the vast assembly. Those who dwelt on the spot and those who had brought provisions with them shared their stores most generously. Bread and meat, wine and beer, were abundant everywhere, yet was there no single instance of excess. No riotous merriment, no rude behaviour, no quarrelling, stained the record of the day. The great heterogeneous mass, composed of all ranks and classes, not only behaved with sobriety, quietness, and good order, but showed a quite marvellous gentleness and courtesy. Peasants in ragged frocks might have shamed half the courts of Europe in all that constituted genuine good breeding and good manners.

After the noonday meal Hubert said he was going to the quarters of Hussenec. Vitus came forward from among the Pihel men, who were fraternizing delightedly with the followers of Zisca, and asked leave to wait upon him. As they passed along through the happy, festive crowds, seated on the grass or standing about in groups, talking or singing, he drew close to him, and asked, "Master Hubert, does this remind you of anything we read of in the Holy Gospels?"

"Truly, I have not thought," returned Hubert.

"I have, Master. I think it is like that day when the multitude sat down on the green grass by hundreds and by fifties, and the Lord fed them Himself. I think, Master Hubert, He is here today."

"And so think I," returned Hubert. "To me, Mount Tabor has indeed been the Mount of Transfiguration, where I have seen the glory of the Lord."

"There is something better than the glory," pursued Vitus, who knew his Czech Bible well. "It is written that 'when they looked up they saw no man, save Jesus only with themselves.' "

Soon they reached the handsome pavilion of the powerful baron who was then the recognized chief of the Hussites. He received Hubert with a kindness just touched with condescension, which confirmed Václav's view of his sentiments. His son was barely civil at first, but thawed as he talked of England. He gave Hubert his letter, which proved to be from the Earl of Hertford, his father's cousin, and the chief of his name. The family arms, which Hubert also had a right to bear, were emblazoned on the cover — a field azure, with six lioncels (little lions) of gold on a band of silver.

"He bade me tell you also, by word of mouth," said young Hussenec, "what no doubt this letter contains, that if you will come to England he will see well to you, and ensure you an honourable career; seeing you are of his own blood, and that, moreover, he held your father dear."

Then they glided into talk about the state of the country, and the best way of securing toleration and the freedom of worship; and, presently, Hubert took his leave.

Little as earthly distinctions appeared to him just then, he was not sorry to find himself recognized and sought after by his relatives in England. He would not have scorned even a wayside flower, if by laying it at the feet of Zedenka he could have given her a moment's pleasure. How, then, should he scorn an honourable blazonry, a long pedigree, a knightly name and rank among his peers! Still, he never thought to see the shores of fair England. Bohemia was his country now.

The rest of the long, happy summer day was spent in religious and social fellowship, in meetings for prayer and mutual edification, in singing Psalms and hymns. Toward the evening Hubert was joined once more by Ostrodek, and they strolled together through the crowd. Hubert wondered more and more at the change in him — a change wholly for the better. He could not but own that Zisca had done more for him in six months than Chlum and Stasek and himself together in three years. A sharp, strong discipline was just what he needed. He had learned to obey, and that very thoroughly; and now he was advancing to the second lesson, and already beginning to command.

Moreover, gentler influences were at work upon his heart that day. The nameless preacher Hubert happened to hear was but one among many who thought and spoke of the coming of the Lord; supposing Him, as did the Christians of the apostolic age, to be at hand, "even at the door." Martin Loqui preached the same doctrine; though he mingled it with wild and fanciful interpretations of obscure prophecies, which sober-minded people tended to discredit, even as a similar mixture has had in our own day a similar result. In the course of their wanderings Hubert and Ostrodek fell in with a company of children, who were singing with their young glad voices Psalm 121,

To Zion's hill I lift mine eyes,
From thence expecting aid.

With a softer light in his fierce dark eyes, Ostrodek turned to Hubert. "I think Zion's King will come to claim His kingdom soon," he said, "and His faithful soldiers and servants of the Cup will be near Him then."

When the singing was over the children began to disperse. Hubert recognized among them the little ones of Arnoštovic, especially the two golden-haired babes who had been on the wagon. He coaxed them to his side, and they came very willingly, admired his dress and arms, and those of Ostrodek, and soon struck up an intimate friendship with them both. Hubert perched one of them on his broad shoulder, while Ostrodek did a similar kindness for the other, and they walked about with them through the field. It was a day when strong men became as little children in gentleness, trustfulness, and docility, while "thoughts that manhood could scarcely bear" took root in the hearts of children.

Some clouds had come up from the west, and the setting sun was glorifying them with "purple and gold and crimson, like the curtains of God's tabernacle." Over Hubert's shoulder a dimpled hand pointed to the sky, while a little voice whispered, "Is that the glory of the King who is coming out of Zion?"

"No, little one, not yet. That will be greater glory still; so great that we cannot guess what it will be like. But we shall see it. You, at least, will surely see Him come," said Hubert; thinking that even if He tarried far longer than they expected, these little lives, only just begun could hardly end before the promise of His coming was fulfilled.

Now, for long centuries, all these have fallen asleep; and still we wait for His appearing. So long, indeed, His Church has waited that she has almost forgotten that she waits at all. The poet's wail is sounding in our ears, and our sinking hearts are tempted to re-echo it,

> *No one asks his brother more,*
> *"Where is the promise of His coming?" but*
> *"Was John at all, and did he say he saw?*
> *Assure us, ere we ask what he has seen."*

Ever and again, throughout the ages of the Church's history, the hope has sprung up again, the cry has been raised, "Behold, the Bridegroom is coming!" Faithful hearts have heard, and started from their sleep, and stood expecting; while upon their watching, upturned faces there has come a glow and a glory visible to all. Was it from the light they thought they saw? Then the voice died away, and the watchers "slumbered and slept." Slowly, steadily, from year to year, from century to century have the wheels of Time rolled on, with no hand stretched out from within the veil to stop their movement. They roll on still.

Brothers and sisters of that far-away time, can you see, from your place of happy waiting in the light of His presence, how we of the outer sanctuary still wait sadly in the darkness here below? If indeed you can, it must add a strain of intenser human pathos to your "loud voice, saying, 'How long, O Lord, holy and true?'" and to your impassioned prayer, "Come, Lord Jesus, come quickly!"

This at least we know: the King sees, the King hears all. Year after year we cry to Him, and say, "Lord, behold the world which Thou lovest, which Thou didst die to save, *is sick* — sick unto death." And although He abides still in His heaven, not *two days*, but nearly two thousand years, yet we hear the words He speaks to us, *leaning from the golden seat*, "This sickness is not unto death, but for the glory of God."

Meanwhile, each believing soul finds the promise sure for himself, bears emphatic witness for himself that not one good thing has failed of all which the Lord has spoken. He who ever keeps His pledges to the one, will He break them to the many? He who never yet cast out the prayer, or disappointed the hope, of one suppliant, will He scorn the cry and cut off the expectation of His whole believing Church? No; all things in earth and heaven, all voices within and without us, answer *No*. Therefore, after all the centuries, still in love unquenchable, still in trust unshaken, do we

> *Look sunward, and with faces golden*
> *Speak to each other softly of a hope.*

Therefore do we join the grand chorus, chanted consciously by His waiting Church, and all unconsciously by the whole creation, groaning and travailing in pain until now, "Even so, come, Lord Jesus."

XIX

FAITHFUL VITUS

In yon straight path a thousand
May well be stopped by three;
And who will stand, on either hand,
And keep the (gate) with me!

— Lays of Ancient Rome.

A few days afterward Hubert and his companions, on their journey back to Pihel, were drawing near Prague. They halted for their noonday meal — the last before reaching the city — in a broad, open meadow, where the new-mown hay furnished them with luxurious seats. A stream flowed beside them, and behind there was a large, carefully walled garden, where crocuses were cultivated for the production of saffron. The same resting-place was chosen by another band of pilgrims, returning from Tabor to their homes in the city. With them were many women and a few children, and a great deal of friendly talk ensued, with a general sharing of provisions. After the repast they all sung a hymn together.

While they were thus engaged, Hubert and some others observed in the distance the flash of sunlight upon steel, and became gradually aware that an armed company was approaching them. Little alarm was felt at first; the sights and sounds of Tabor had accustomed them to hear the clash of arms, and to see the movement of ordered ranks. These, they thought, might be some of the people belonging to Hussenec, or some of Zisca's men. But as they drew near it became abundantly evident that they were anything but friends. Their dress and arms showed them to be Germans, doubtless some of the mercenaries sent for by King Wenzel expressly for the purpose of coercing his Hussite subjects. The sound of the singing convinced them that the crowd they saw before were a sample of these Bohemian heretics, and they thought it well to begin their campaign by attacking them. The old race-hatred between Czech and German mingled with religious fanaticism in the cries and shouts with which they advanced on the unarmed multitude: "Heretics! Hussites! Bohemians! Die like the dogs you are!"

For an instant the crowd stood still, in sudden, speechless terror, too panic-stricken to run away. Then a few boys, who happened to be near the brook, each caught up a stone, and hurled it at the assailants, by no means without effect. Some of the Germans, who carried great cumbrous weapons, like large cross-bows, halted, and seemed to be preparing them for use.

Hubert glanced at the garden gate, and saw that it was not over well secured. He rushed at it, and burst it open with a great exertion of strength, then shouted in Czech to the bewildered crowd, "In there! In, for your lives!"

He was not too soon. There was a strange, sharp sound, a succession of flashes, a cloud of smoke, and, struck by some mysterious agency, a man and a boy fell down, and lay bleeding on the ground.

"It is the devil! It is the Red Dragon from the bottomless pit!" cried the terrified crowd. No more was needed to drive them, like a flock of frightened sheep, inside the gate.

Only the Pihel men remained outside. "I have heard of this thing," said Hubert. "These fire-weapons — *arquebuses* — are no great matter after all; good swords are better. Vitus, Prokop, Martin, take up the wounded and bring them in there. Václav, you go in at once. Stay, Vitus, give me your pike." As he spoke, he tore out of his haversack a napkin of snowy damask, in which provisions for the way had been wrapped, and tied it to the top of the pike. Then he sprang on his horse, which happily was close at hand.

"I go with you," said Václav, seeing his purpose.

"You do not. Take care of the people in there: speak to them — reassure them."

So saying, he advanced alone toward the enemy, bearing in his hand the flag of truce. Did they know the laws of civilized warfare? Did they mean to observe them?

That was what Václav, Vitus, and the others asked themselves as they bore the wounded into the shelter of the garden. They were not long left in doubt as to the answer. Hubert speedily wheeled his horse about and rode back to the gate, followed by a shower of cross-bow bolts; for some of the band had the old weapon, and some the arquebus, or earliest kind of firearm.

"Will you shut the gate, Master?" cried Vitus, as he neared it.

"No. It would not hold — no better than old firewood. Can you get your horse?"

"Yes, Master; and the Panec, and Prokop."

"Quick, then, for all *those* lives!" pointing to the garden. "Three mounted men can hold the gateway against that rabble. In the name of God!"

There were four who placed themselves in the gateway, side by side, and stood like rocks against the advancing flood. Again Hubert spoke to Václav. "You are too young for this, dear boy. Think of your sister."

"I do think of her. There are boys' sisters as well as men's sweethearts in there, Hubert. Besides, I am Kepka's son."

In the wild fight that followed all else was forgotten. "Ha!" cried Hubert, as he saw their foes throw away the now useless arquebuses, and take to their swords and pikes. "Ha! The wasps have lost their sting!" It was the last word spoken for the space of an hour and more. Sword to sword, hand to hand they fought. The Germans had the immense advantage of overwhelming numbers; but the Bohemians were on horseback; were protected in the rear and partly at the side; and, best of all, were fighting for dear life, and for the lives of the multitude behind them.

At last a hoarse shout of triumph came from a hundred German throats. Václav was unhorsed. A pike-thrust had slain his steed. The boy was on his feet, fighting alone among a dozen; the next moment he was down on the ground. Hubert saw, and struggled madly to get at him. But between them was a dense and seething mass of heads and bodies, arms and legs, all mixed together in one frantic struggle for life. Vitus saw too; and he was nearer to Václav. Springing from his horse, and making for a gigantic German who was standing over the boy with sword upraised to give him the death-blow, he hewed off his hand with one stroke at the wrist. Then he helped Václav up, and in another moment the boy was fighting like a lion, with the remains of his shattered sword.

Across all the tumult Hubert sent a ringing shout: "Well done, faithful Vitus!"

So Master John had called him. He heard, and the light of a sudden smile flashed across his face. But that instant a German, with his broadsword, thrust him through the heart. He fell, without groan or struggle, and with the "self-same smile" "lingering on the dead lip still."

They could not stop to look. Ever faster and more furious grew the fray. Václav leaped upon the horse of Vitus, and with Prokop and Hubert fought on. But the fearful odds were beginning to tell.

Prokop was wounded, and the strokes of all were growing feebler from exhaustion.

Suddenly some boys who had climbed upon the wall, and were trying to help by throwing stones at the Germans, raised a shout. "See! See! A rescue! A rescue! Our friends are coming!"

Hubert looked. A body of men was approaching, and, as he saw presently, over them waved a black flag with a red cup upon it.

"Zisca! Zisca!" he cried aloud, with all the strength left in him. "Zisca! Zisca! The servants of God and of the Cup!"

Others took up the shout. Again and again it arose, echoing and re-echoing from the crowd in the garden, mingled with cries of joy.

"Thank God!"

"God be praised!"

"We are saved now!"

In very different accents did the Germans take up the cry.

"Zisca! Zisca!" rang out from trembling lips. It is true they scarce knew yet who Zisca was, but they saw his name lent new strength to their foes. Already weary and discouraged, they had no mind to be taken in the rear by a fresh enemy, and that no doubt a formidable one. As the newcomers advanced, singing their battle hymn, and swinging their terrible flails, the Germans seemed to melt before them. Right and left, far and wide, they scattered, most of them, however, taking the road to Prague, but without method or order. The Bohemians failed not to send after them derisive shouts and cries.

"Go and take your spoils to those who hired you. Much thanks they will give you for this day's work."

After all, Zisca was not there. The armed band of Hussites was led by one of his friends, a priest named Procopius, of Kamenec, a tall, dark man, in a long black cassock; with a two-handled sword in one hand and the sacramental cup in the other, he looked as formidable an antagonist as any foe need wish to face. He complimented Hubert and his companions most warmly on their courage, and asked Hubert to come with him to Zisca, who would make a captain of him.

Hubert thanked him, but said it was neither his duty nor his wish to fight: he was bound to return at once to his lord, the Knight of Chlum.

"However little you and he may wish to fight," said the Hussite chief, "there are those yonder" — and he pointed to the distant towers of Prague — "who will make you do it. Young man, you will fight one day, and under the standard of Zisca and the Cup. Still, for the present go your way and God be with you!"

PROCOPIUS

Hubert, Václav, and the rest gave thanks to God for their victory, but as they looked on the dead face of "faithful Vitus" they thought it had been dearly bought.

Before they resumed their journey they buried him where he lay, and sang a farewell hymn over his grave.

"He was indeed found faithful," said Václav, with tearful eyes, as he turned away from the spot. "Before this he has told Master John that his word was true."

"I do not think he has seen Master John," returned Hubert. "I think that when death was over he 'looked up and saw no man, save Jesus only.' "

XX

SBOIM

A little more, and how much it is;
A little less, and what worlds away!

— R. Browning

It seemed as if the poem — *an Idyll* it has been called even by unfriendly pens — which was lived out on Mount Tabor in those bright midsummer days was given to strengthen those who were there for the long and bitter trials that were to follow. Immediately afterward a Hussite priest who was bearing the Host in procession through the streets of Prague was struck by a stone and killed. The cup of persecution was already full, and this drop made it overflow. A revolt followed, which, under the able leadership of Zisca, proved a veritable *revolution*. The weak and wicked king on hearing the tidings, fell into a rage which brought on a fit of apoplexy. After lingering for a few weeks he died, and his death was the signal for fresh tumults. The royal garrison in the Hradschin was composed of German mercenaries, and had long insulted and threatened the citizens, who were not slow to retaliate. At last a regular and most obstinate battle was fought in the streets of Prague, and fought, too, to the bitter end. The national and Hussite party, led by Zisca, was victorious everywhere. Finally, a truce was agreed upon guaranteeing to the Hussites all that they really wanted — full liberty of worship. But it was very ill observed. The Papists boasted everywhere that the Emperor was coming presently with all his armies to do them justice, and to exterminate their heretical foes.

During the summer Chlum had removed his family and most of his household from Pihel to Melnik; and there he was rejoined by his daughter, who came back full of interest in the work of Pánna Oneshka, and apparently feeling the attraction of the kind of life that lady had chosen for herself. Amidst many toils and cares, and many fears and anxieties, winter drew on apace.

The Outrage at Prague

The November winds were wailing among the hills, and shaking the few remaining leaves from the trees beside the river, when one evening the family gathered around the blazing logs in a tapestried chamber less bleak and comfortless and more adapted to private converse than the great hall.

The lord of the castle sat in his armchair. His looks were troubled: he seemed lost in anxious thought. Zedenka had evidently been playing and singing; she held in her hand a small stringed instrument called a rota, which she seemed about to give back to her attendant bower maiden. Aninka looked slight and colourless as ever; but her pale features were redeemed from insignificance by the sweetness of her smile and by the steadfast, thoughtful look that came sometimes into her quiet gray eyes.

Hubert was standing near Zedenka, for he had been singing with her.

Václav had gone over to a table fastened against the wall, and was turning over the leaves of a large book which lay upon it by the light of a blazing torch of pinewood which he held in his hand.

"Take care, my son," said his father. "The sparks are falling. You will burn the Bible."

To burn their Bohemian Bible would have been accounted as great a misfortune as to burn the castle down to the ground. Václav blew out his torch, closed the book, and joined the group by the

340

"Take care, my son," said his father.
"The sparks are falling. You will burn the Bible."

fire. "I was looking," he said, "for the place in which it is written, 'Where the tree falleth, there it shall lie.' "

"It is in the Book of Ecclesiastes, the Preacher," said Hubert, whose study was much in the Bible.

"Wherever it is," Chlum observed, with some warmth, "I think it can scarcely mean that I may not say a prayer for the sinful soul of my king, whom I have ever served loyally."

"Indeed, dear Father, that you have," said Zedenka. "To the last you tried to save him from himself."

"I tried — and failed. It has ever been my lot to fail. Still, if my life would have done the work — and it was said to me once, and the words are true, 'God's love is not less than thine!' "

"I think, Sir Knight," said Hubert modestly, "that some things are mysteries of the faith, which we cannot expect to understand."

"So I think; but you who are young expect to understand everything. You have changed so many things that our fathers believed and observed."

"We desire to believe and to observe all that is in the Word of God, and no more," said Václav.

"I know it, dear lad. Still, was it necessary to take away the image of the Virgin out of the chapel, and give so much offence to the Melnik folk, who are not like those of Pihel?"

"Dear Father, is it not idolatry to bow down before an image — or, indeed, to worship any created being? And the Blessed Virgin was created. She is not God."

"So said Master John," Zedenka added. "You remember his words, that 'we ought not to believe in the Mother of God, but ought to believe that she is the most holy Mother of God, more worthy than any saint. And yet there is one Virgin, who is the Bride of Christ, more worthy than the Virgin Mary, and that is the Holy Church, the congregation of all saints, who will finally reign with Christ forever. For the Virgin Mary is a member of the Holy Church, and cannot be of such worthiness.' "

"Yes, Child, I remember Master John's words; and I would the new generation remembered them half as well. It is not now with them what Master John said, but what Martin Loqui, or John the Praemonstrant, or Korianda, or some other new preacher says. Young Frantisek told me when he was here that he would not say an Ave even to save his life. Now, Master John prayed to our Lord as if he was standing in His presence and saw His face, yet did he not forbid these old customs that we learned from our fathers."

At the mention of Frantisek the pale cheek of Aninka flushed hotly. With a bowed head and a beating heart she came forward and spoke, "If it please my lord, Frantisek meant not to blame anyone. He only meant, it is against the Holy Scriptures, and a breach of the Second Commandment."

"*Only?*" repeated Václav. "I never heard any man — even at Tabor — say more than that. Truly, Mistress Aninka, a soft hand can deal a shrewd blow."

"I ask my lord's forgiveness if I have spoken anything wrong," said Aninka meekly.

342

"No, my girl, you have not spoken wrong," returned Chlum kindly. "Always speak out bravely for your betrothed; and I hope your lady, when she is in the same case, will do the same," he added, with a look at Zedenka which made her cheeks as red as those of her handmaiden. "Yet I think the Church had wise and holy men in her before you and I, and your Frantisek, were born."

"Surely, Father," said Václav. "But Frantisek and the rest of us are only keeping the charge Master John gave us himself when he said, 'Therefore, faithful Christian, seek the truth, hearken to the truth, learn the truth, hold the truth, defend the truth, even unto death.'"

"It is likely it will be unto death," Chlum answered sadly, "if Emperor Sigismund comes upon us with his army."

"It may be, Father," said Zedenka softly, "that another King may come first." For she had drunk in with all her ardent soul the teachings of Tabor about the approaching coming of the Lord.

"It may be," said Chlum reverently, "for with Him all things are possible. Yet I doubt the end is so near as you young folk seem to think. And as to seeing Master John again, which you talk to me of, I am content to say, like David, 'I shall go to him, but he shall not return to me.'"

There was a silence, which Václav broke at last with a question: "Will you tell us, Father, what you said in the Council of the Barons about acknowledging Sigismund as King of Bohemia in place of King Wenzel?"

"You know it well enough, Václav. I said what I ever say. I will have no part in the setting up of any other king, be it my old friend Hussenec, or anyone else; for the crown should come to Sigismund, and his it is. But I will never raise my hand in service, nor bow my knee in homage, before Sigismund the Word-breaker, who gave John Huss up to his enemies. Children," he went on, after a pause, "you talk of deep teaching, and new lights upon the Word of God. You think you know some things which God has not revealed to me — and I do not doubt it. But, for my part, I had rather be sure I forgave Sigismund with all my heart than interpret the whole Apocalypse of St. John."

"But, Father," said Zedenka, "you forgave him long ago."

"Yes, in Constance, in the year of the Right Hand of the Most High. I had that, my children, though I had not your Mount Tabor, and the rest of it; and I am content. What was given me then I keep, by the grace of God, only not as being perfect, nor as having attained."

"Sir Knight, there is a German peddler in the hall, who desires to speak with you," said Karel, coming in.

"An ill night for him to have travelled, poor man. Bid the men see to him and give him meat and drink in plenty."

"He has had all, Sir Knight. He came an hour ago."

"Well, then, let him show his pack to the lads and lasses. That is what he wants, I suppose; or else a safe-conduct to pass into Germany."

"No, Sir Knight. He says he has some tidings for your private ear. He was here, or rather, I would say, at Pihel, long ago, before I came."

"Ah!" cried Václav, "perhaps it is Hans Kaufman. Don't you remember Hans Kaufman, Father?"

"Oh yes, I remember him," said Chlum.

Zedenka added, "Truly, I remember him, for I cured him of the hurts our peasants gave him for speaking ill of Master John."

"Yes; and before he left us he sang another tune," said Václav. "I will go to him."

He returned presently with the peddler, who faltered out a few grateful words about the kindness he received four years ago, and then began: "Sir Knight, I have been at Kuttenberg of late, and I have brought some ornaments of silver from there which it may please you and the Pánna to look at."

"By-and-by," said Chlum. "I guess from your face that you have something more important for us than silver from the mine. If you have tidings or messages, speak on."

The peddler looked cautiously around him. "There are none within earshot save your own, Sir Knight?" he spoke in a low voice, and drawing near him. "I could not speak out in the hall, as I knew not who might be about, and so many of these people are strange to me. I thought I saw a shaven crown, and such are never to be trusted."

"My chaplain, Master Stasek, may be well trusted. But what have you to say to me?"

"Sir Knight, have you heard how they are keeping the truce in the parts about Kuttenberg?"

"I know how they are keeping it elsewhere — to my sorrow."

"So do we all," said Václav. "The cries of our brothers who are wrongfully imprisoned, and starved, and tortured, ring in our ears day and night."

"Sir Baron, your own vassals are being thus treated by their Papist neighbours."

"In God's name, Man," said Chlum, with a rising colour in his cheek and a gathering frown upon his brow, "speak out and tell us all!"

"Sir Knight, the men of your estate near Kuttenberg, which is called Janovic, are sore harassed and oppressed by their neighbours. The lord of Rosenbek has seized some of them and thrown them into his dungeons for asking the Communion of the Cup. But worst of all are the miners of Kuttenberg, Saxons like myself. I am ashamed of them. Every Hussite they can lay their hands on has a short shrift, and is flung into the mines. 'Tis said that two or three of your men, Sir Knight, have had such measure dealt out to them."

"*Good God!*" cried Chlum; and great must have been the horror that wrung the sacred name from those reverent lips.

"How did you hear of it?" asked Hubert of the peddler, in the forlorn hope of finding that the story had been exaggerated.

"From the lips of a man belonging to the village, whom I met at Kolin. He was called Petr — Petr the smith. He says your steward, Kralik, has abandoned the Communion of the Cup out of fear; and that your peasants know not where to turn, or whom to trust. Men think nothing of the truce there — little enough of it anywhere — excepting in those places where the Hussites have power to take care of themselves, or the barons are on their side." The peddler went on to give instances of the violation of the truce, some of which his hearers had heard before; others were new to them. When he had told all he knew, he was thanked, and dismissed for the night to the comfortable quarters provided for him in the castle. Aninka went out also, and Chlum, Zedenka, Hubert, and Václav stood in silence, and looked one another in the face.

At last Chlum said slowly, and as if to himself, "I must go to my people, who are as sheep having no shepherd."

Zedenka and Václav looked at each other in dismay, and Hubert said, "Pardon me, Sir Knight, but that is impossible. You are bound here by what is stronger than fetters of brass and iron — the command of your sovereign, the queen."

It was too true; and Chlum was forced to acknowledge it. He bowed his head sorrowfully and was silent.

Suddenly Václav cried out, stamping his foot with eagerness. "I have it! I have it! Father and Knight, this is what I will do. I will take that peddler fellow's clothing and his pack, so will no man know me, though I go through the length and breadth of the land. I will go to Kuttenberg, and find out the truth and the whole truth, for I wager a kop of new groschen against a stirrup-cup of ale things are not as bad as he says. Petr the smith may be a liar. The Master of the Mint dwells at the Welsh Castle hard by; and we know what a good Hussite he is. So, of course, are his people, and he would be the last man to leave them unprotected."

"Your plan is excellent, my son — but not for you. One of our men can go."

"No, Father — with your good leave. We have not one here who could gather our people around him, and counsel them, and tell them what to do. Vitus perhaps might have done it, but there is no one now."

"Except yourself," said Chlum, with a sorrowful smile. "Do you think you could do it, my son?"

"Sir Knight," said Hubert, stepping forward, "hear me a moment, of your grace. I also think that Václav's plan is excellent. But seeing I am older than he, and better acquainted with the German tongue, it is clear that I, and not he, should be the man to go."

Václav cried out; from Zedenka's lips also came something between a gasp and a cry. But it was instantly suppressed, and only one had heard it. Chlum spoke, and not without emotion.

"I do not spare one of my sons to peril the other."

"The peril is slight," said Hubert. "I can easily assume the manners of a foreigner — being one, in fact. I am not known in those parts at all, and, if questioned or suspected, can easily make myself out a stranger in a strange land, with no part in its quarrels and contentions. Sir Knight, will you give me — not a letter, for that might be dangerous — but a message and a token for your people?"

"Let me think of it," said Chlum, raising his hand to his head. "Tomorrow . . ."

"Tomorrow I should set out. It would be well, I think, tonight to arrange matters with Hans. Do I have your permission to speak with him, and to find out upon what terms he will be willing either to lend or sell me his merchandise?"

"You do press me hard, Hubert. Well, I cannot say no to you. Speak to Hans if you will."

Later that night Hubert sat in the library or writing-room, writing a letter to his brother Armand, in France. This letter he intended to leave in the care of Václav, who would, he knew, find means of forwarding it (if possible) to its destination, in case he never returned from the proposed expedition. It was full of faith and courage — only one sentence showed a touch of sorrowful feeling: "Commend me unto the Lady Jocelyne, who is, I hope, by this time a sister unto me. You are happier than I, Armand, in that you know yourself loved. True, indeed, I have hope, but I have no certainty."

He folded his letter, tied it carefully with silk, and sealed it with many seals. Then he put it for the present inside his doublet, and, taking in his hand the little oil lamp which had given him light, he went toward his sleeping-apartment.

On the way, much to his surprise, he encountered the Pánna, who was coming forth from the chapel, a large book in one hand, and a little lamp like his own in the other. She, too, was surprised, and the book fell from her hand.

Hubert picked it up and gave it back to her, noticing as he did so the extreme paleness of her face. The thought crossed his mind that some of the Melnik men, angry at the removal of the image of the Virgin, had committed some outrage in the chapel, which she might look upon as a menace of other violence to follow. "Is anything wrong, Pánna?" he asked in a tone of concern.

Instead of answering, she said hurriedly, "Master Hubert, this thought of yours is too rash. I have spoken to my father."

"Your father, Pánna, is one of God's truest servants upon earth — so true that he bade his dearest friend go and die for Him. How, then, should he withhold a servant of his own, even if it be one whom he had been good enough to call — *a son*?" asked Hubert, infinitely gratified by her solicitude.

"It is easy for you who are strong — who can go out to do and dare."

"Pánna, what makes us strong is the thought of those who stay at home, and think of us, and pray for us. Will you think of me and pray for me when I go away tomorrow?"

"If — if — so it must be. We will all pray for you, Master Hubert."

"Not as all pray for all, but as *one* prays for *one*, Pánna? You know my meaning, and my heart."

"This is no time for words like these."

"I know it, Pánna, and I crave your pardon. I am willing — no, I am proud and glad — to give all, and to ask for nothing in return. Stay — one thing I ask to take with me through my journeying — through my perils — and to make me strong to face them all, and to come home safe again. It is only a word. If you think a little kindly of your servitor, all unworthy though he is, say to him tomorrow, before he goes, your sweet Bohemian farewell — *SBoim* — go with God."

Next morning a tall young man, bearing on his shoulders a peddler's pack, walked forth from the gate of Melnik. By his side walked the Panec Václav, who intended to bear him company for a stage or two. Many a hearty loving word of farewell sounded in his ears, and would linger long in his memory; but dearest of all was that one Bohemian word, breathed softly in a gentle voice — "*SBoim*."

XXI

THE MINERS OF KUTTENBERG

Denn fühllos wie das Eisen war
Das Herz in ihren Brust.

— Schiller

Not far from the town of Kuttenberg, in Eastern Bohemia, there stood in those days, by the wayside, a little country inn called *The Silver Pickaxe*. It was now the last day of February; but Winter as yet showed no sign of abdicating her throne. The snow was falling thickly; not the door only but the unglazed windows also, were closely shut and barred to exclude it. Within, a great fire of logs was blazing on the hearth, and on the settle near it a small, spare, insignificant-looking man, with dark Czech features, was lounging at his ease, and sipping a tankard of weak wine. At a press or dresser near the wall two women were standing, busily engaged in polishing the pewter vessels upon it until they shone like silver in the firelight. One of the women, though not really old, was wrinkled and gray-haired. Tall, and stout in proportion, she scoured her pewter with an air of energy and determination, as if she felt it meant to resist her efforts to the utmost, but intended to stand no opposition from it or from anything else. The rough, red-haired girl beside her, evidently a servant, imitated, at a humble distance, the activity of her mistress. On some straw in a corner a boy was asleep, with his head swathed, and a rug thrown over him. These constituted the human occupants of the great room, which formed the whole lower storey of the wooden house; but a little flock of geese had also found shelter there from the inclemency of the weather.

A gust of wind blew the door open, letting in a shower of snow upon the sanded floor. The good man of the house shivered, drew his cloak about him, and said briefly, "Wife, shut the door."

"Get up and shut it yourself, lazybones," was the polite reply. "I am busy, and you are doing nothing. The usual way."

The man looked from his wife to the open door, and from the open door to his wife again. Evidently it was not "the usual way" for him to dispute her orders, nor yet to be over hasty in obeying them. While he hesitated, the girl slipped past her mistress, and quietly performed the service. "Shall I put the bolt in, Mistress?" she asked.

"That you may. Such a day as this there is none likely to come near us."

"Easy to rate me for doing nothing, and to call me out of my name," grumbled the master of the house. "What can be done in a snowstorm, and without light enough for a man to see his hand before him?"

"A man who was a man would chop firewood, or mend the donkey's harness, or cobble his old shoes; anything rather than sit by the fireside the whole blessed day, drinking himself drunk."

"Drunk! Now, Mistress, that is too bad! You know that never once could that have been said of me in the last six months. Nor would it then, except for those devils of miners."

"Yes, in a general way you have kept sober, that I will say for you. No great credit to you, however." She paused a moment in her work, turned around to face her husband, and glanced significantly at a stout serviceable broom, which hung against the wall.

The little man cowered visibly, and through his dark features there came a tinge of red. "At least," he muttered uneasily, "no man could get drunk on this hog-wash."

"Yes, I suppose you would like it well to keep the key of the chest where the strong waters are. Then, the next time the miners came to us, there would be murder done in the house."

"God knows, I wish the miners had never crossed our threshold," said the man earnestly. Probably he thought that for once he was saying something with which his wife would cordially agree.

He was mistaken. "A fine word for a man to say who has heavy dues to pay to the lord of the soil, and then to live himself, with a wife, a maid, and a crippled son! Who else can afford to pay us, during these bad times, I would like to know? Good groschen from the Mint are not spoiled by coming to us through German hands."

"German hands? Yes, and German hands stained red with good Bohemian blood."

"That is none of our business," said the woman, turning back to her work, and polishing a pewter basin with desperate energy, as if the bloodstains were upon it, and she could rub them out. "This you can do, at least," she resumed after a minute; "take that poor child in your arms, and carry him up to his bed."

"Why disturb him? He is fast asleep."

"Always excuses when one asks you to do something. You need not awaken him. He will sleep sound enough now for hours."

"Thanks to your dose of poppy-juice. Heaven grant you have not poisoned the child!"

"Don't be a fool!" was the courteous retort. "Was I to hear him crying all day with the pain of his tooth? If you were a man, you would set him tomorrow on the donkey, and bring him to the town, for the barber to pull it out."

"He would cry louder for that," said her husband, truly enough. "Hark! Is that a knock at the door?"

"No, it is the wind. Go on with your work, Maria. What is the matter?"

"Mistress, it is a knock. There's another!" Maria laid down the flagon she was burnishing, and hurried to the door.

She admitted a peddler with his pack, both well covered with snow.

"*Gott grüss euch!*" he said in German as he entered.

The housewife answered him in the same language, which she spoke fairly well, bidding him welcome, and asking him to come near the fire. Then, addressing her husband in rapid Czech, she bade him assist the stranger to unloose his pack, and to take off his dripping cloak.

"I speak Czech also," said the packman, "although I am a foreigner. Pardon me for bringing all this snow and mud into your comfortable room," and he looked with evident satisfaction at the blazing fire, the neatly-sanded floor, the dresser with its bright array of newly-polished vessels.

Propitiated by the compliment, the landlady bustled about to prepare a meal and a bed for the stranger, assisted by her handmaid. Meanwhile the landlord performed his share of the duties of hospitality as he understood them, by heaping fresh logs on the fire, and inviting the guest to dry himself and his garments. He also thought it fell within his province to converse with him; but the stranger, though courteous and affable, was somewhat reserved; indeed, a stranger who showed himself otherwise would have been, in those days, a very imprudent person.

There was one subject, however, at once safe and interesting — the contents of his pack. He professed himself willing to exhibit them, but Melicia, as the housewife was called, interposed her veto.

"Not until you have eaten and drunk," she said. "Do you drink beer or wine, Master Chapman?"

At this delay Maria, who was setting a board on trestles for the stranger's meal, heaved an audible sigh, for she was longing to choose a breast-knot for herself and a pair of buckles for her lover; while Matej, the landlord, observed sententiously, "What is put off never comes to pass."

For once he was in the right. While the peddler was washing down his meal of smoked goose and rye bread with a draught of much better wine than Melicia allowed her lord and master, some person or persons began to thunder for admittance at the door. The snow had prevented those within from hearing the approaching footsteps.

Maria opened it not a moment too soon, for the newcomers would have broken it in with scant compunction. Large as was the room, it seemed to be filled instantly. Fierce-looking men, in rough white coats and hosen, and with pickaxes slung from their leather girdles, passed in, leading or dragging with them a little group of peasants, strongly bound with ropes.

Then all was bustle and confusion. The women hurried to and fro, filling every cup or tankard they could lay hands upon with beer or wine, and serving their guests as quickly as they could, from fear, if not from goodwill.

The sleeping boy in the corner, awakened by the noise, began to scream, whereupon his father took him in his arms, and managed, though with much difficulty, to drag or carry him up the ladder to the loft.

The chapman — that is to say, Hubert Bohun — withdrew to the corner thus left empty, and, standing unnoticed in the shadow, surveyed the group of captives with a sad and pitying eye. This, then, was what he had heard. The Saxon miners of Kuttenberg, fierce and savage men, accustomed to wage war with the sternest forces of Nature, and hardened in the contest, ranged the surrounding country, making captive every Hussite they could lay hands on. What spoils were they bringing in this snowy wintry day?

Five persons, all peasants, composed the little band. There was an old man with silver hair, two young men, and a boy and a girl of about fourteen or fifteen. The two last were sobbing bitterly, the girl with her head on the boy's shoulder; the younger men looked sullen and angry, the old man resigned and calm.

Meanwhile the miners were quarrelling for places near the fire, and seating themselves as best they could on the settle, or on benches which Maria brought for them. They complained loudly, in German, of their ill-luck in only securing so poor a prey after a holiday spent in the chase.

"Not one of them worth more than twenty groschen," they said to one another. "And it is doubtful if the Town Council will pay us more than half-price for the girl and the boy."

Presently Hubert saw Maria fill a cup with wine, and, watching her opportunity, give it, when no one was looking, to the weeping girl; but the child's bound hands could not take it, and Maria could not wait to hold it to her lips — already half a dozen rude voices were calling her. He came forward, took the cup, and held it until the poor child's thirst was satisfied; then he gave what was left in the same way to her brother. Without any interference from the miners — who seemed to care little what was done with their captives so that they did not escape — he refilled the cup again and again until they had all had enough.

One of the younger men said to him in Czech, "Master, you seem to have a compassionate heart. Can you speak German?"

"Yes."

"Then please, Master, will you tell these men that I and my companion here are not Hussites at all, but good Catholics? We have never taken the Cup, nor done any other thing which the Church forbids. We detest heresy and heretics. But these white devils cannot understand a word of good Bohemian; or if they do, they will not listen to it. The reward the Town Council (God's curse on it!) gives them for every Hussite brought in has turned them into sheer highway robbers and murderers."

"What do they mean to do with you?"

"They will bring us first into the city, to the Town Hall, that they may get their ducats. That is all they care about. Then — God help us — they will drag us to the horrible pits they have dug in the bowels of the earth. Happy are those the fall makes an end of at once! Master, if you have any bowels of compassion, if you wish God to show you mercy in your own hour of need, speak a word for us now. Say we are no Hussites."

"I will do what I can," said Hubert sadly. "And you, Father," he added, turning to the old man, "do you also suffer through a mistake?"

"Not so," was the calm reply. "I learned to know my Lord Jesus through the preaching of Master John Huss when he abode at the Welsh Castle, and therefore I am called a Hussite. Those are my grandchildren," he looking toward the girl and boy, "and I will take them with me to God."

" 'For if we suffer we shall also reign with Him,' " said Hubert, much moved; his heart went out to this brother in the faith. More really worthy of pity, it is true, were the two unhappy "martyrs by the pang without the palm," but with far less power to touch the nerve of sympathy, and make it quiver with passionate pain. "Can I do something for you, Father?" he asked in a broken voice.

"Not much, though I thank your good will. I and mine need little more now. Yet there is one thing, if you will. They have led us a long way from our home, and we would fain rest our weary limbs before they take us farther. The children are very tired."

"I will speak to the mistress of the house," said Hubert.

This was more easily said than done. However, at last he laid hold of the busy woman, and, by offering his help in broaching a barrel of ale, gained her ear for an instant.

"Oh yes — take them to that straw where the boy was lying. I'll make it all right with the miners, who care nothing so long as they are safe. Please, Master Chapman, have you seen my man anywhere?"

"No, Mistress, not since he went upstairs with the boy."

"And stayed there, most likely. One might as well have a broom-head for a husband and the master of a house! Will you do the act of a Christian, Master Peddler, and fetch him down? Heaven knows, it is not for the work he does, but — think of it — two lone women to wait on all those ruffianly fire-eaters. It is neither safe nor respectable."

"I will do the errand for you, Mistress," said Hubert.

First, however, he brought his new friends to the place which had been indicated to him. There was plenty of straw, and he shook it out to allow them to sit or lie at their ease, also helping them to remove a few soaking outer garments. Melicia was as good as her word. She told the miners that the peddler was a German like themselves, and no doubt a very good Catholic, but these people who wandered about the world had sometimes soft hearts — most likely he pitied the girl and boy, who were not much more than children after all.

"Perhaps, Master Miners, when you have rested and refreshed yourselves you may care to see the contents of his pack by way of diversion?"

Meanwhile Hubert disappeared up the narrow ladder which served for a staircase. It took him but a few seconds to ascend it, yet the thoughts that flocked through his busy brain might have filled a volume. There was one prevailing cry of passionate prayer: "O God, help me to save these Thy servants!" But how was it to be done? *How*? He wore a small sharp poniard concealed beneath his vest, but what could one weapon, in one hand, avail against so many?

Supposing he first cut the captives' bonds? Still, only the two young men would be able to do anything. Of course the people of the house were not likely to help him; they would probably (although not certainly) side with the miners. Again, should he cut the ropes, bid the captives run for their lives, and standing himself last at the door, delay the miners until their prey was beyond pursuit? No. It could *not* be done! He abandoned the idea — not because for himself it meant certain death, but because, setting all other difficulties aside, he would be pushed and trampled down far too quickly. Once more, could he bribe the miners with the contents of his pack to let the captives go? But then, what was to hinder them seizing the goods by force and laughing him to scorn, as they surely would under the circumstances? Or could he lure them with promises? No. They would not believe him.

By this time he was standing in the wooden upper chamber where the crippled boy lay, again fast asleep, and looking unnaturally flushed and heavy. His father was kneeling beside him, staring at him with a face of helpless anxiety.

Hubert gave him his wife's message, begging him to come down and help her to serve their customers.

Matej rose slowly to his feet. "I am troubled about the boy," he said. "The good wife, to take away his pain, has dosed him with that strong decoction of poppies."

"He will sleep it off," said Hubert, his head full of other thoughts. "Come down, man, and help your wife. In truth, it is your duty."

"Melicia is well able to help herself, and half the world besides," returned Matej. "Everything she does has twice the strength in it of other folk's doings. Saints in heaven! When she gets a stick in her hand it is something to see or to *feel*! Even when she undertakes the preparing of herbs, in the case of sickness, such as poppies and such . . ." he glanced at a large jar, three-quarters full, which stood on a chest by the bed.

Hubert's eyes followed his; and the same instant a new thought, a new hope, sent the vibration of a sudden thrill through his soul and body. His plan was made in a moment.

"Listen, Friend," he said, laying his hand on the arm of Matej. "If I make friends with the miners, and treat them to strong drink in plenty, the chances are they will buy half my pack, and pay well for it too, for I know they are well paid themselves, in the same good silver they dig out of the mine. Do you have any strong waters in the house?"

"My wife has — a little. She keeps the key."

354

"Get it from her, man. Whisper to her in Czech. Tell her why I want it."

"No use, no use," said Matej helplessly. "She would never give it to *me*. Speak to her yourself."

"Very well, then," returned Hubert, hastily catching up the jar of poppy-juice.

"What will you do with that?"

"I will tell your wife. I will explain things to her. You go to your guests, and keep them in as good humour as you can, and soon I will reward you with a drink such as you have never tasted yet."

Poor soul, to be bribed with such a reward! So low can our nature sink; and yet, thank God! The heights it can reach, through His grace, are still more wonderful. The old man who sat a few yards off calmly awaiting martyrdom, and in the meantime holding communion with his God and consoling his fellow-sufferers, was, like Matej, only a Bohemian peasant, who could neither read nor write.

Under the stress of emotion the mind acts with inconceivable rapidity. Almost before Hubert's descending feet touched the sanded floor all the details of his plan were fixed clearly in his mind. It was easier now to secure the ear of Melicia, and to speak to her apart as she set the board for the substantial supper her guests had ordered. Hubert communicated to her the hopes he pretended to entertain, and contrived to hint that if he did a good business "the house" should profit by it. But it would be necessary to open the hearts and purses of the miners. The Saxons liked strong drink. So did the English, and he was himself half an Englishman. Moreover, he had been bred in Paris, and he had learned there the secret of compounding a certain drink, called Hippocras, most rare and delicious, which would — but here Hubert's imagination failed him, and he was inclined to conclude with one of the proverbs of Solomon — which would "make the lips of them which were asleep to speak." The necessary ingredients were strong waters and certain spices, which however, he carried in his pack. He had, in fact, a little pepper, ginger, and saffron.

At the mention of strong waters Melicia hesitated.

"You will make the miners mad, and they will be for killing us all," she said.

"No fear, Mistress. I shall put in plenty of fair water. But trust me for making your house famous through the country. If you will, I will tell you afterward how to compound it."

The end was that Hubert got what he wanted — a good supply of strong waters, and the services of Maria to wait upon him.

The miners were not indisposed to fraternize with their supposed countryman. They asked him to join them at supper. Hubert said he had supped already, but in return for their civility they must drink with him afterward.

Then, while the miners supped great mysteries went forward over the fire. Strong waters and honey were contributed by the house, and Hubert added what he styled grandly "rare spices." But in place of fair water he contrived surreptitiously to empty into the pan the whole contents of the great jar of poppy juice. The mixture was just ready when the miners had finished the substantial part of their repast. It was received with acclamation. And certainly on a snowy afternoon, when the thermometer, had such a thing been known, would have stood somewhere near zero degrees Fahrenheit, there was much to be said in its favour. Hot, at once with the heat of fire and the pungency of spice, sweet, and above all things, strong, it tasted of everything the miners had ever known or liked. Had a Scotchman been among them, he would certainly have declared, in praise of it, that "it bites in the mou'!"

Hubert intended to administer his potion to the people of the inn, as well as to the miners, lest they should interfere with his plans. But it was not easy to do it, save to Maria. Melicia was habitually temperate; and poor Matej was just going to enjoy a cup of the fragrant mixture, when his spouse snatched it almost from his very lips, saying, "Drink when your guests are gone, fool! Go now, and get some logs for the fire, else we shall be in darkness presently."

The miners talked and jested, and drank success to themselves and their friends, and confusion to their foes. One of them proposed the health of the Donkey of Kuttenberg, adding the wish that his ears might forever remain untouched. Hubert, as a stranger, asked for an explanation, and a miner told him, in reply, that the excavations for the silver mines underground were in the form of a donkey, and that, whenever any unfortunate explorer should happen to touch the ears, the ground would fall in and the whole place come to ruin! "The — whole — place — come — to — ruin," repeated his informant, nodding drowsily at every word.

His drowsiness seemed infectious. Hubert, with secret exultation, watched the band, as the poppy juice, aided by the potent spirit, the heat, and the spices, took effect upon them one by one. Some yielded fairly to the spell, and stretched themselves on the ground; others slumbered as they sat, in various attitudes, more or less uncomfortable.

Maria slept as soundly as anyone: and, what was more to the purpose, the modest portion she had tasted, "just to see what it was like," took effect on Melicia, the rather because of her habitual temperance; having allowed herself to sit down in a corner for a moment's rest, she was neither seen nor heard anymore. Hubert did not think much of Matej one way or the other, but supposed he was asleep also.

So, at last, the moment for action had come! Hubert sent up a strong, brief, silent cry to God for help. Then he took off his shoes, and stepped noiselessly through the sleeping miners to the corner where the captives lay. The girl and boy were fast asleep, and the old man's eyes were closed, though his lips were moving as if in prayer. The two younger men, however, were awake, and watching every movement with anxious and wondering eyes.

"Now — now or never!" whispered Hubert to them in Czech, as he drew out his poniard. "There's a chance for your lives. See! Father, I begin with you," and having gently touched the old man to arouse his attention, he severed the cords that bound his hands.

"Now rouse your grandchildren without noise. For their lives and yours, not a word! The miners are all asleep. If God be with us, we can go forth unhindered."

The girl awoke crying, but her brother, who understood the situation, put his hand promptly on her mouth.

"Now go, one by one," whispered Hubert again. "Keep close by the wall, in the shadow."

Not a sound was heard, save the heavy breathing of the sleeping miners. Hubert led the way, then came the two young men, then the children, lastly the old man. The steps of all were slow, noiseless, cat-like. As their enemies had crowded around the hearth, they took care to keep close by the sides of the room.

They had well turned the corner — they had come within a few paces of the door, which had not been locked since the entrance of the miners. Three steps more — and then freedom and safety!

Those three steps were never taken. Suddenly the door itself burst in with a loud noise, and a chorus of rough voices shouted, "Are you all here dead or asleep?"

The flickering light of the fire showed the white garments of miners — more miners, and ever more — who crowded in, nearly trampling on their sleeping comrades. *The Silver Pickaxe* was a common place of rendezvous for these fierce and formidable men.

If ever a living man felt the bitterness of death, Hubert felt it then. He knew in one moment that all was lost. Some of the newcomers stood between the fugitives and the open door, others were already rousing their comrades with kicks, shuts, and blows.

One of the young Bohemians incautiously made a step forward, and the light of the flame fell on him, showing a piece of knotted cord still hanging from his left arm. That was enough. There was a shout, a spring, a simultaneous rush upon the little band. Half a dozen hands at once seized each of them, including Hubert. The two young men struggled desperately with their new captors; but Hubert called on them to stop. Resistance was useless, and worse.

Then a strange thing happened. A stalwart miner had laid rough hands on the shrinking girl, and was going to bind her. She gave a piteous cry, and instantly someone wrenched her from his grasp, and dealt him a shrewd thrust with a knife in his right arm. It was Matej. He had seen much further into the business than Hubert suspected; he wished well to his countrymen, and their recapture nearly broke all the heart his idle, self-indulgent life had left in him. Besides, the girl bore a likeness to a child of his own, whom he had laid last year in the churchyard, and it filled the cup of his indignation to see her roughly used. He was beyond himself in more ways than one. Melicia, awakened by this time, was horror-stricken at the sight of her husband being laid hold upon by two or three furious miners. But neither her cries and protestations, nor even the blows of her strong right arm, availed anything now. Matej at last, as well as the others, was overpowered and bound; but he gave his captors more trouble than all the rest together. In fact, neither the old man, nor the children, nor Hubert, had resisted at all.

There seemed some likelihood, however, of a free fight among the miners themselves, such of the first comers as were by this time sufficiently awake claiming the captives as their own, and the others stoutly denying the claim. While they exchanged hard words and harder blows, Hubert, in his desperation, resolved upon one last effort for his own life and that of his companions. He succeeded in gaining the ear of a miner less excited than the others. Knowing their greed, he bade high, revealing the fact that he was not what he seemed, but of noble birth, and the squire of a baron who could, and would, reward his preservers handsomely.

But all the consolation he received was an exhortation to stick well to his story before the magistrates, as that would ensure his captors the larger recompense, while they, by way of thanks, would give him the best chance they could of a speedy end when they got to the mine. But as for sparing his life, or that of any of the accursed brood! what did he take them for? They were Christians, and Catholics, and they wanted to "make their souls," and to earn a place in Paradise. Moreover, they had taken a solemn vow to the Blessed Virgin never to let a Hussite leave their hands alive. If they were so wicked as to break it, and to bring the guilt of perjury upon their souls, Our Lady would know how to punish them.

So all Hubert's arrows fell idle and useless from the impenetrable shield forged of that strong mixed metal, greed and fanaticism combined. Both together are far harder than either by itself. Many a heart, not destitute of human softness, have they hardened so that neither groans nor cries, neither prayers nor tears, could avail to pierce it. Sorrowfully he recognized the fact that all was over now. From now on they had not to struggle, but to suffer. Not conflict was before them, but martyrdom. He bowed his head in speechless agony. No prayer came from his lips — no prayer, in words, from his bleeding heart. Yet the God of his spirit, the Life of his life, was not far from him even then. The secret things of darkness are known to Him.

When, presently, the old man said meekly, "The will of the Lord be done!" Hubert Bohun was able to respond "Amen!"

XXII

THE WAY OF THE CROSS

It is the sting
Of death to leave that vainly precious thing
In this cold world. What would it be if thou,
With thy fond eyes, wert gazing on me now?
Too keen a pang! Farewell! And yet once more
Farewell! the passion of long years I pour
Into that word: thou hear'st not, but the woe
And fervour of its tones may one day flow
To thy heart's holy place. There let them dwell —
We shall o'ersweep the grave to meet. Farewell!

In the midst of the maddest whirlpool that ever lashed the seething waters into foam there is a spot of absolute calm. It is often thus in the whirlpools of life. In what seems to outsiders the very crisis of the agony there is sometimes, for the sufferers, no agony at all. We stand and see the sod fall on the coffin that holds all that is dearest to us, and the crowd around is weeping for our sorrow — but *our* eyes are dry. We have suffered — we *shall* suffer through long years — but just then we do not suffer at all. We can hear and see, we can think hazily of irrelevant trifles — only we cannot feel. God has sent upon the nerves of feeling a numbness merciful indeed, since but for such respites the spirits would fail before Him, and the souls which He has made.

Such a numbness fell upon Hubert when, after the confusion and surprise of the recapture, he found himself walking in the snow, under the escort of the victorious newly-arrived miners, who left their comrades behind, to resume if they pleased their interrupted slumbers. Hubert was bound to the unfortunate innkeeper; before him walked the two young men, and behind him the old man with his grandchildren.

It was evening now, a little after the early winter sunset. The storm had passed, the clouds had rolled eastward, the wind had dropped to a whisper, scarcely stirring the snow-laden branches of the leafless trees by the wayside. A faint light still lingered in the west, while near the horizon, pale and queen-like, the moon held unchallenged empire of the sky. The new-fallen, trackless snow which covered the wide plain seemed pure and spotless enough even for her dominion, and she touched and glorified it with the silver sceptre of her rays.

Hubert saw the moonlight and the snow, and was vaguely conscious of the brightness of the one and the chill of the other, after the heated atmosphere of the inn. Then he noticed that the fur cloak which the weeping, protesting Melicia had thrown over her unfortunate husband had fallen loose and was slipping off. Although his hands were bound, he contrived, with the help of his teeth, to pull it up and fasten it for him. This appeared to arouse the poor man, who until now had seemed as one dazed, and he broke suddenly into sobs, mingled with complaints and protestations. It was the burden of his lamentation that the miners would not listen to Melicia, who could have explained everything, and proved to their satisfaction that he was no Hussite.

But one of the young men who was walking in front of them turned around to him and said, "Still, you know, you struck that fellow with the knife."

"I was mad — the saints know I was mad," wailed poor Matej in his sore distress. "It was when he touched the girl, who is like my Ofka. See that church spire! Ofka lies buried there, and I had my place chosen beside her, and the fees paid to the priest. And now, God help me! I shall not be buried like a Christian at all, but flung into a hole like a dog."

There was another burst of tears, then he said, suddenly turning to Hubert, "Do you think, Master Packman, will they let us have a priest?"

"I think not," answered Hubert. "But what does it matter? The Lord Christ Himself will be our priest."

"It may matter nothing at all to you, Master Chapman, who, for all I know, may have lived like a saint. But I am a sinful man — the Lord forgive me this day! I have been drunken, idle, lazy. I neglected Mass and confession, I paid the priest his tithe in mildewed corn . . ." And so he went on through a long catalogue of sins, real and imaginary.

Hubert, who felt nothing for himself, felt a movement of pity for his companion. When life begins to return to a frozen arm, the first thrill is at the finger-tips. He turned to him kindly. "Your sins, likely, are many," he said. "So in truth are mine. But God is good. He says to us in the Holy Scriptures, 'Though your sins be as scarlet, they shall be as white as snow' — as this snow beneath our feet, Matej."

"But we must confess — do penance — get forgiven by the priest."

"Yes, we must confess to God, and be forgiven by the Priest, who is our Lord Jesus Christ."

"But how can I? Here in the snow, with my hands bound, neither priest nor church within call?" This came out brokenly, intermixed with sobs.

"Listen, Matej," Hubert said gently. "Your Priest and mine, the Lord Jesus, is within call. He is nearer to you than we are to each other, though they have bound us together. He is *here*. His heart will meet yours, if you will only ask Him to forgive you, and to take away your sins. He died for you, Matej."

"Died for *me*?"

"On the cross. Do you not know it?"

"Oh yes — the cross. Do you have a cross?" he moaned, his bewildered mind groping helplessly among signs and shadows.

"You do not need one to look at — it is enough to think of it. Think of Him who died there — died there for you, Matej, because He loves you. You loved your child so as to risk your life for another, who was but like her in your eyes. So — but so much more that I cannot tell it — the Lord Christ loves you. Tell Him you are sorry for your sins; ask Him from your heart to forgive you — and He will."

"I'll try," said poor Matej. He began to hurry over Aves and Paternosters, but Hubert stopped him.

"Ask Him in your own words, Friend," he said, "as you would have wished your child to ask your forgiveness if perhaps she had angered you in something."

There was a long silence; then suddenly the lamentations broke out afresh. "There's the boy! Who's to see to him, and to carry him about? The mother has no patience with his helpless ways, and his crying for this and that when she is busy. As for the house and land, they will get on well enough. Melicia will manage all that, and twice as well as I. Yes, a brave woman she is — a brave woman; and a proud lad was I when she married me — she that could have had the pick and choice of three villages around. Eighteen years ago come Michaelmas — eighteen years! We have had words now and then, like other Christians — and my fault too, and the fault of the wine

362

cup, that I could not keep from my lips. But loyal and true we were ever, and loved one another as man and wife should. And now I shall never see her face again, God pity me!"

The tide of life swept back now, to the frozen heart of Hubert, with a fierce passion of pain, the maddening pain of envy. How he envied the poor, weak, half-besotted creature by his side! Those eighteen years of his past, what a priceless treasure they looked to Hubert! Eighteen years! This man, so poor in all else, at least was rich in life; *he had lived. He* was not going out of the world — God's world that, after all, looked so fair and was so full of sweetness — without tasting the best it had to give. *He* did not leave behind him lips he loved, yet on which he had never pressed a kiss — a heart that knew his own, and yet had never answered him. In that bitter hour Hubert's fate would have seemed a thousand times more tolerable if he could have been but as Frantisek, the betrothed of Aninka. To lose is terrible; never to have had is infinitely worse and sadder.

Should *he* be wept and mourned for, as Frantisek, in like case, would so surely be? In spite of all, his inmost heart whispered the assurance — was it comfort, or was it new pain? — that he *would.* That would be a sorrowful day when the news of this night's work came to Melnik. If, indeed, it ever came; — but he hoped it would, since long uncertainty and vain watching are harder to be borne than the knowledge of the truth.

A vision came to him of Zedenka moving among her handmaidens sad and pale, with silent lips and aching heart, looking as she used to look after her mother's death. He knew well what she would do. She would minister to her father while he lived, then she would go to Prague, dwell in Pánna Oneshka's house, have *béguines* with her there, and do works of charity and mercy. She would never marry, that he knew full well.

Perhaps the tide of persecution might rise higher still, and sweep away the peaceful habitations of Pánna Oneshka and the other ladies who had gathered around the Church of Bethlehem. It was but too likely. God only knew the perils, the sufferings, that awaited those who held His truth in Bohemia. Was not death rather to be chosen for them than life amidst these? Were it not well — very well — for both of them if Zedenka were now by his side, and he could take her with him to God, out of all earth's snares and perils, as the old man behind him was taking those he loved?

No, no! Not *thus*! Not by *this* path of terror and of anguish. When he thought, for her, of the horrible pit, he shuddered as he had not shuddered for himself. What would it all be like? he wondered. To fall — fall — fall into darkness; then to meet a shock and agony; then, perhaps, to know no more — and that would be well. *Perhaps*? Only perhaps, for a lingering death might follow, of hunger and misery and the anguish of broken limbs, there in the dark. None to know, none to pity; no ear to catch the last faint words, the dying moan. No, no! In the midst of all his pain he thanked God in his heart that Zedenka was not with him now.

"Eighteen years" Matej had said. More than eighteen years ago his mother died, and he was sent, still almost a babe, to the monastery at Rouen. Before another eighteen years, what might not come and go? There was one thing, he thought, almost sure to take place — that *coming of the Lord*, of which he heard at Tabor, which he looked for ever since.

Why need the wheels of His chariot tarry even so long as that? The Lord might come at any time; yes, even this very night. What was there to hinder? Hubert knew not anything. He looked up from the snow-clad earth to the trackless sky, where the moon was walking in brightness, and on his lips there trembled the passionate prayer, "Oh that Thou wouldest rend the heavens and come down! O King of Glory, our King for whom we wait, appear for us — help us — save us — we are Thine!"

But the awful silence of the heavens and the earth, which the sobs and wailings of a hundred generations have failed to break, was not to be broken now by the feeble cry of Hubert Bohun.

The silence fell upon him, closed around him like a pall, sank into his heart like lead. For the first time since the days in Constance before he "knew the Lord," it seemed as if his prayer had failed to pierce the vault of blue, had never reached the Throne of the Most High. There came over him, first a cloud of doubt, then a horror of great darkness. What if he and the rest were but throwing their lives away? What if it did not matter who was in the right — or whether there was any right at all?

He could not think this, really, for a moment. He could not, and did not, doubt in his inmost heart that John Huss and those who followed him had the truth. Still, this conviction did not help him just then. He might know there was light, but he could not see it. Rather was he as one who groped in thick darkness, stretching out his hand to the hand of a friend, which yet, with all his groping, he could not find.

Then he seemed already to be falling into the dark, deep pit — falling, falling — clutching vainly at the sides, and falling still,

Through nothing to no place.

Terror swept over him. Was God not there at all? Could not the voice of his agony come before Him? "O God!" he cried, and unconsciously he cried aloud, "O God! Why hast Thou forsaken me?"

He did not hear the voice of Matej, who turned to him and said, "Poor lad, don't you lose heart after comforting me;" nor yet the whisper of the old man, as he bent forward toward him, "Hope in God, for you shall yet praise Him."

What he heard was the echo of his own words; what he realized with a sudden shock was that another had uttered them before, *"Why hast Thou forsaken me?"*

Suddenly, before his eyes the cross rose up, with the form of Him that hung upon it. *That* was agony, worse than the worst, to which every step he took in the soft, pure snow was bringing him nearer. But it was much more than agony. Could it be that He — even He — felt Himself forsaken? It must have been, else why did He send up that broken-hearted cry through the darkened heavens? He has passed through all Himself, He knows all, thought Hubert. He has borne it for me, and oh, mystery of mysteries! He bears it now with me. *He is here.*

So Christ came to him that night. It was not the victorious Christ, who rent the heavens and came down in answer to his cry; it was the suffering Christ,

The manifest in secrecy,
Yet of his own soul partaker,

who came to share his anguish, and, so sharing, transformed it into something brighter than glory, better than joy. Like another martyr on his way to death, to whom thus suddenly and wondrously Christ revealed Himself, he cried aloud in the gladness of his heart — "He has come! He has come!"

A great longing swept over him to tell Zedenka of it all. If she and the others could know how Christ had come to him, they would be able to bear it; they would even learn in time to be glad for him. More than that, could He not come to them, to her — just as really as He had done to him? He knew the need and the pain would be as great, or greater. And He remembered, not only the hurt of bleeding hands and feet, but the fall of teardrops over graves.

Hubert knew it would comfort Zedenka to think that he died a martyr. Christ was giving him this great honour. He had chosen him to die for Him, as Master John died for Him in Constance. It was glory beyond any earth could give. Never now might he win the golden spurs of knighthood. What of that, when God was setting upon his head a crown of pure gold? That crown Christ would give him — oh, did he dare to think it? Then he thought no more of the glory and the crown; he thought only of His pierced hand, only of the joy of seeing His face.

"Perhaps in two hours, perhaps in less," he said to himself. "Surely before the moon now climbing the sky has dropped again to the horizon." That joy contained and consummated all the rest. His heart grew still and quiet in the intensity of his rapture, as it had done before in the numbness of his grief. After the earthquake, the fire, and the storm, had come the still, small voice, and God was there.

"Master Packman," said Matej, "I have been praying as you told me, and I think the good God has heard me. Somehow I feel comforted. And I'm sure Melicia will carry on the business better than I."

"Look, Master," said one of the young men, turning around to him, "there is the town — we shall soon be in it. You have a good German tongue in your head. Please speak for us like a man, and let it be known we are no Hussites."

Hubert's own joy touched his heart with compassion for those unwilling victims, who knew not the joy, though they shared the suffering.

"I will do all I can," he said, "although I have little hope of the result."

Thus they came to Kuttenberg. It was not much more than eight o'clock, though the winter night had fallen long ago. The city gate opened readily to the miners, whose errand was well known, and they marched their captives through long narrow streets to the market place, a triangular space on the slope of a hill. There stands now in the midst of it a rude and ancient statue, said to represent St. John Nepomuck, the patron saint of Bohemia; but antiquarians tell us that, like other statues of the kind, it was originally dedicated, not to the legendary martyr of the Moldau, but to the historic martyr of Constance.

Across the spot now occupied thus, Hubert and his companions were driven, like sheep appointed to the slaughter, toward a building which Hubert supposed to be the Town Hall. After some knocking, and a good deal of wrangling, both among themselves and with those that kept the door, some of the miners were allowed to enter, and to bring their captives with them. They found themselves in a spacious hall, hung with tapestry, and lit with torches. At a table near the upper end two or three men in long robes, with pens, parchment, and inkhorns were sitting. Here they were kept waiting for what seemed a considerable time but at last a side-door opened, and there entered, first a servant bearing some sort of mace or staff of office, then an imposing personage in a furred robe and golden chain. He looked in very ill-humour; he had probably been called from his "rear supper," if not actually out of his bed: for in those days men kept early hours. The miners came forward, told their tale in rapid German, and exhibited their captives. Then Hubert, the only one among them, except Matej, who knew the language, asked permission to speak for them all.

"Make it short, then," said the magistrate, if magistrate he were. "The hour is late, and you Bohemians lie like Egyptians."

"Good Master," began Hubert, "you appear to forget the Truce of God, made and sworn to in Prague, wherein it was enacted that no man throughout the land should be troubled on account of religion."

"It is a far cry from Prague to Kuttenberg," said one of the scribes at the table, with a scornful laugh.

But the judge or magistrate silenced him with a look, and said to Hubert, "If you have not heard before this that the truce is torn to fragments, hear it now. Man forbids no longer what God commands — the destruction of His enemies. If you have no more to say than that, better say your prayers instead."

"I have more to say, Master Councillor — or whatever may be the title of your office. There are seven of us here tonight, and of those seven at least three have never received the Communion of the Cup, and are no Hussites. If people may be torn thus from their homes, and condemned and executed without a hearing, no man's life in the whole country will be worth a silver groschen."

This pleading availed so far that a few hasty questions were asked of Matej and the young men, Hubert acting as interpreter. But the miners, determined not to lose their reward, swore that the two young men had been taken at a meeting of Hussites; and the fact that Matej had struck one of them with a knife told fatally against him. They were all condemned.

Then Hubert said, "Masters, you owe it to us, whose voices so soon may be silent forever, to hear us yet once more. We will not keep you long. As for me, though I wear this dress, I am by birth noble, by calling a squire. I serve the knight and baron Ján z Chlum, lord of Pihel and other places, and at present castellan of Melnik. Still, I have put my life to hazard, and I do not complain of the result. I die willingly for my faith and my God. All I ask is, that you will report truly to my lord at Melnik that which has been done with me."

His judge heard his story, without for a moment believing it. "Is that all you have to say, Master Squire or Chapman?" he asked scornfully; and one of the scribes added, "We will send you to seek your silver spurs at the bottom of the mine they were dug from."

"God's will be done," said Hubert. "But," he added, addressing himself to the judge, "I beseech you to look upon the case of this old man and these children. It may be you have an aged father still left to you, and it would go hard with you to have his gray hairs brought down to the grave with blood. Children, perhaps, you have too, whom you love; I pray you for their dear sakes to have compassion upon these, who are weak and helpless, and guilty of no crime."

But here he was cut short. "We cannot sit here all night," said the impatient magistrate. "Master Notary" — he turned to the man on his left hand — "pay the miners their money and let them go. A ducat each for the men, and a half-ducat for the boy and the girl. Six in all."

Some altercation ensued, the miners claiming more for Hubert. Heavy silver pieces were counted out; and the notary put on his great horn-spectacles, and made certain entries in a book before him. Pausing for a moment, he looked up and asked his fellow, "Can you tell me, please, what day of the month it is? I have forgotten."

"The twenty-ninth day of February, this being Leap Year," was the answer.

Hubert at the moment was trying to comfort Matej, who had broken again into bitter weeping. But the words "Leap Year" struck upon his ear, and brought back to him suddenly the recollection of the Jewish doctor and his prophecy. The very night, thought Hubert, that he told me the moon was to be darkened. Now I suppose I shall not know if he was right. Before the hour comes I shall be beyond sun, or moon, or star.

He turned to go along with his companions, but the old man leant over and said a few words to him in Bohemian. He turned back again, and spoke once more to his judges. "My friend here," he said, "bids me tell you, on behalf of himself and his grandchildren, I also agreeing, that we forgive you, who have adjudged us unto death, and these men who have wrongfully taken, and are now about to slay us — and we pray God to forgive them and you."

The prayer was not heeded at the moment, but it may have afterward recurred to the memories of some who heard it.

Another minute, and they passed out of the lighted hall, and began their march to the place of execution. The streets through which they went were for the most part silent and empty. Such a procession was evidently too common to attract notice. But here and there a burgher, returning late to his home, stopped to look at them with pity or with curiosity, or to exchange a word or two with the miners. One spoke thus to a man who walked at Hubert's right hand.

"How did you make out, Max?"

"Ill enough, friend. A sorry lot; only six ducats for the whole. My share of that won't do to marry on."

There were some other words, followed by a laugh, but Hubert did not heed them — indeed, he scarcely heard them.

Presently they went out by another gate, and turned into the desolate snow-white road which stretched onward from the town to the hill of the fatal mine.

XXIII

THE DARKENED MOON

It is an honest ghost, that let me tell you.
— Shakespeare

The sad procession moved along in silence. The miners were sullen, disappointed, and tired. They had no thought of mercy, for their hearts were as hard as the iron in their axes. Yet they had little desire to exult over their prey. The victims, in their various ways, seemed more or less reconciled to their fate; indeed, the weaker among them were by this time scarcely conscious of anything save fatigue. At length the old man's weary feet began to stumble; some of the miners would have urged him on with blows and curses, but Max, who seemed rather more compassionate than the rest, gave him for a staff a club he was carrying, and cut the cords that bound his hands to enable him to use it.

The road soon began to ascend, and here and there clusters of miners' huts, looking black in the moonlight, dotted the white landscape. In most of these sleep and silence reigned. Not in all, however. Sometimes the inmates were on the watch; wild, half-clothed figures rushed out at the approach of the party and greeted the miners with shouts, and the unfortunate captives with abuse and curses, which, happily, being in German, were understood by none of them save Hubert and Matej. Some of these people had torches in their hands, and offered them to the miners; but they refused them, saying, "It will be as light as day on the hill."

The road continued to ascend. Soon the ground grew rugged and uneven; there was everywhere a confusion of low, irregular mounds and hillocks, formed by the excavations from the mines, which cast dark, broken shadows on the snowy ground.

The miner on Hubert's left hand touched his arm, and pointed to a hill which rose above the rest and bore upon its slope a cluster of dark fir-trees.

"Do you see that mount, my friend?" he said, laughing. "You shall climb presently to the top, but we will save you the trouble of coming down again. There is your journey's end. Beyond that clump of firs you see a straight line, a break, and a dark spot. *The pit's mouth is there*. In another hour you will be at the bottom."

"We all know that," said Max to his comrade. "Hold your tongue, and let the lad make his peace with God — if he can."

"I have peace with God, through our Lord Jesus Christ," Hubert said calmly. Even his strong young limbs were growing weary now. But what did it matter? Weariness would soon be passed forever. All that long night One seemed to walk beside him, whose presence filled every recess of his soul, touched every nerve of his being. He did not understand it — he did not try. Everything seemed mysterious to him, and yet nothing seemed perplexing. Latterly he did not think much, he did not even pray consciously or in words. He only felt that Christ was with him now, and that soon he would be with Christ forever.

The longing came back to him to tell Zedenka of the joy that Christ was giving him. Might not this, after all, be possible? He spoke to Max.

"I heard you say to someone in the town, 'That won't do to marry on.' Do you want to marry, then?"

"Yes, truly. I am hand-fasted to a girl in Cazlau, and as fine a girl as there is in all the country. But what is that to you, Hussite?"

"This much: You can tell what I feel for the one I love. Will you bear her a token, please? My lord, the Knight of Chlum, of whom I spoke to the magistrate in the town, will reward you well."

"We shall see. What will you give me as a token?"

"Beneath my vest, and next to my heart, is a small packet. It is nothing more than a bit of lace — a lady's ruffle — wrapped in paper and bound with silk. Lest any should call you in question about the paper, I will tell you that it contains but two words, which are in Latin, and mean simply 'Go quickly.' "

"Is it a charm?"

"No; only the writing of a man I love."

"Your friends may have it, then, as soon as the foul fiends at the bottom of the pit."

"But you must search for it, and take it yourself, since my hands are bound. Bring it to the Knight of Chlum, who is called Kepka, and say to him and his that I die not in peace only, but with joy unspeakable and full of glory."

Max paused a moment and looked at him with a passing thrill of wonder. Then he put out his hand, and began to search for the token.

"A plague on the thing!" he muttered. "I can't get at it! I can't *see*! What's the matter with the moon?"

They had now begun the ascent of the fatal hill. It was long and steep, and victims and executioners paused to breathe.

The same exclamation, "What's the matter with the moon?" came at almost the same time from several lips. Hubert looked up, as did the others. At the edge of the planet was a strange, dark shadow, slowly creeping inward. Solito was right after all, thought Hubert. The moon is growing dark with the shadow of the earth. But what does it matter to me? I shall be beyond the shadows before yet they have passed from the sky.

The whole band stood in silence, watching. Max forgot his search for the token — his hands dropped idly by his side. As the dread shadow deepened, exclamations of surprise and awe passed from lip to lip. All things around them began to take a weird, unearthly hue. Each man, as he looked in his neighbour's face, thought its pallid hue showed a terror greater than his own. The white of the snow looked ghastly in the glimmering light, which was not light nor shade, not day nor night.

Matej and the two young Bohemians began to pray aloud. "Stop your noise, you heretics!" cried a miner roughly. " 'Tis you who are bringing these portents on the land."

"Ill ever comes of them," said another. "Last year there was a darkening of the moon like this, and a month and a day after it the foul fiends at the bottom of the mine sent out the fire-damp, and forty brave miners met their fate."

"I had rather be choked with the fire-damp than poisoned by the plague," observed a third. "And I have heard my grandfather say that such signs in the heavens always come before the plague."

"A plague upon your plagues!" shouted a fourth. "Come on — let's finish our work!"

"There's sense in that," assented others. "If anything can keep us from harm, it is taking the part of God and our Lady, and doing justice upon these heretics."

"Let's say an Ave first — it would be safer," suggested Max, with a little hesitation.

But the others called him a coward, and bade him say his prayers when his work was done. The taunt made him furious, but his anger was little heeded. A few tried laughter and ribald jests, but they died away into silence as the darkness deepened still. In spite of themselves the miners were terrified, and their terror took the form of cruelty. They wanted to rush upon something and destroy it, and their helpless captives were ready to their hand. Perhaps the human sacrifice they were about to offer would appease Heaven and insure their safety. With a sudden, tumultuous impulse they resumed their march to the mouth of the pit, dragging the captives with them.

Hubert contrived to whisper to his companions a few consoling words. The old man said, "It is the shadow of our Father's hand, so it can only mean good for His children."

"But, Grandfather," asked the boy, "is it not wonderful that these wicked men do not see God is frowning upon their cruelty?"

They saw plainly that God was frowning upon *something*; but they thought it was upon the heresy of their victims. So their blind, bewildered souls vibrated aimlessly between rage and terror. Their feet "stumbled on the dark mountains," and they "looked for light, and beheld darkness and the shadow of death."

This was true in figure, true also in fact. Two or three times they nearly missed, in their confusion, the path to the pit, a path so familiar that they could tread it almost as well by night as by day. At last, however, the goal was won.

A great flat mound of excavated clay stood almost at the brink of the mine. This they ascended, and saw before them the awful chasm, a spot of dense Egyptian blackness in the dim, lurid light. The dark copper-red of the eclipse had now covered all the moon except a tiny glimmering crescent. But the stars shone brightly out, showing the narrow streak of blue-white snow between their feet and the abyss.

Suddenly, from the very edge of the pit, a tall white column shot up into the darkness. It trembled a little, then stood motionless, a pillar of ice against the black of the abyss. Then a wild cry rang out into the awful stillness of the upper air. "The Day of Judgment! The Day of the Lord!" shrieked a strange, unearthly voice. "The great and terrible Day of the Lord! The sun shall be turned into darkness, and the moon into blood, before that great and terrible Day of the Lord!" The voice sank, the cry died away into a wailing moan. But it rose again in yet wilder, more thrilling tones, half a scream of terror, half a shriek of agony. "Say to the mountains, 'Fall on you,' say to the rocks, 'Hide you from the face of Him who sits on the throne, and from the wrath of the Lamb.' For the great day of His wrath is come, and who shall be able to stand? For you have shed the blood of prophets and of saints, and of all that were slain on the earth. Therefore shall you drink of the wine of the wrath of God, which is poured without mixture into the cup of His indignation, and the smoke of your torment shall ascend up forever and ever from the pit — from the pit — from the bottomless pit."

The miners, already unnerved by the eclipse, were seized with uncontrollable terror. First they stood stupefied, then they trembled, wavered, broke their ranks in confusion.

"The Day of Judgment!" shrieked some.

"A witch!"

"A warlock!"

"A foul fiend!"

"An angel of God!" cried others.

Whatever the thing might be — fiend or angel, or messenger of doom — they had no will to stand and face it. They turned their backs, and in another moment would have been in full career down the hill.

But Max held his ground, and stayed the rest. "Hear me, comrades!" he cried. "This is no fiend nor angel, but a mortal woman. See, I will lay hands on her! Am I a coward *now*?"

He sprang forward, and clasped the thing in his strong, sinewy arms. For an instant the strange light showed the *two* white figures wrestling together on the brink of the abyss. Then, with a cry of horror "that echoed to the tingling stars," one figure disappeared, and was lost to sight forever.

The white pillar stood unmoved, and out of it came a voice that said, or shrieked, "So perish all Thine enemies, O God! Let them go down quick into the pit! The pit! The bottomless pit!"

No earthly power could have stopped the miners then. They dashed down the hill at headlong speed, as if all the spirits — demons, gnomes, or kobolds, with which their superstition peopled the depths of the mine — were at their heels in avenging fury. The unreasoning panic infected even the captives. Matej would have joined the flight had not Hubert, to whom he was bound, held him back by force. The two young men ran with the rest, but one of them stumbled over a heap of rubbish, and dragged his companion with him to the ground. Only the old man and his grandchildren did not stir from the spot where they stood. Meanwhile, the white pillar vanished silently — like a dream.

It was strange that Hubert's first thought, when he could think at all, was one of pity for the poor girl at Cazlau, who would wait and watch in vain for the coming of her betrothed. That one touch of nature had made kin of the intending murderer and the intended victim. Should his queen, his beloved, watch and wait for him so at Melnik? *No*, thought he, God is giving back our lives to us. I shall live — for her.

Immediately thought became action. He went to the side of the old man. "Father," he said, "look up! God has delivered us out of the hands of our enemies."

The old man looked up, bewildered and incredulous. "We are ready to die for our faith," he said.

"I know it, Father. But God bids you, instead, to live for it."

"To depart and to be with Christ is far better."

"But 'to abide in the flesh is more needful' — at least for these children. Father, think of *them*, and help me to save us all."

Hubert turned to the boy and girl. The boy had his arms around his sister, who seemed to be half insensible. But Hubert's voice aroused her, and she set up a piteous cry, "*Don't* let them throw us into that pit, Grandfather!"

"Father," said Hubert, "you must cut our bonds. Quick, for this darkness, like the pillar of cloud you know of, is terror to our foes and safety to us."

"There is no knife."

"There is. They have taken my side knives, and my poniard I left at the inn; but put your hand in my left boot, and you will find a small clasp knife which I always carry there. You men, be brave now, and you shall see your homes once more. Matej, remember Melicia and the boy."

The old man roused his failing energies, got at the knife, and cut the bonds of Hubert, who then quickly freed the rest. The first use Matej made of his liberty was to take off the fur cloak his wife had given him, and to wrap it around the shivering form of the bewildered girl, who was just beginning to understand that she was not, after all, to be thrown into the pit.

"Where do your homes lie?" asked Hubert of the two young men.

"Straight across there, Master, as the crow flies," cried one of them, pointing toward Kolin. "But for this awful darkness we could see our church spire from this hill."

"Bless God for the darkness, and guide us through it to there if you can. That will be much safer than venturing back to the inn. See already the eclipse is passing, and the light will redouble our danger. How far is it?"

"Not two leagues. Kuttenberg was far out of our way; though they needed to drag us there to get their reward, and much good it has done them. Do you think, Master, that the spirit of the mine will do us a mischief? I saw it vanish away just now, behind yonder fir-grove."

"My masters," said Matej suddenly, "don't mock at me if I tell you a thing which I heard in the town one of the last days I went there to do my business. There was a merchant of wool, named Schubart, a German, but he and his son were determined Hussites. After much ado, one way or another, to make them good Roman Catholics, they were given over to the miners and thrown into the mine. The poor wife and mother has been crazed ever since, and it was told me that she had escaped from her kinsfolk. Where would she be more likely to go than to the spot she must be thinking of day and night? God help her!"

But the two young men fell on him angrily for the suggestion and even the gentle old man was ill-pleased with it.

"It was the finger of God," he said. "That is all we can tell. His ways are past finding out."

Matej, accustomed to be told he was stupid and a blunderer, felt ashamed of his conjecture and held his peace.

Hubert hastened their departure, pointing to the moon, from which the friendly darkness was now fast disappearing. Hope and courage lent strength even to weak and weary limbs. They all descended the hill at a quick pace, and in the silence and solitude of the night began their march across the plain.

Few words were spoken as they walked along. Once, however, Hubert said to the young men, "Friends, what is your calling?"

"We dig the coal out of the bowels of the earth, as the miners do the silver."

"What for?" asked Hubert, who was used only to fires of wood.

"Mostly for the miners. They want furnaces for smelting their ore, and for many things besides."

"Then without your coal they could not use their silver? You say you are not Hussites. Very well; but you are Bohemians. And I suppose you do not want treatment such as you had tonight?"

The answer was decided and energetic.

"Then, my friends, you have the cure in your own hands. No more coal for the Saxons — until such time as the Saxons learn the lesson — no more Hussites for the mines."

The young men shook their heads. "We are not strong enough," they said.

"Here, friends," interposed Matej, "is a road branching off to the left, by yonder farmstead, that leads straight to *The Silver Pickaxe*!

Come with me, and break your fast before you go farther. I know Melicia will not think the best flask in the cellar too good for us tonight."

The young men, very naturally, declined this hospitable proposal, on account of the danger of recapture in a place so constantly frequented by the miners. For the same reason it was thought safer for the old man and his grandchildren to return at once under their escort to their own home.

Hubert, however, said that he would go back with Matej to the inn; partly in the hope of recovering his pack, but more that he might try and persuade the innkeeper to leave the place, at least for the present. He feared that Matej had not the slightest idea of the danger he had incurred by his share in the night's work, and that the best way to secure his safety would be to awaken the apprehensions of his more quick-witted and energetic spouse. She ought to know that the miner he had wounded, and his friends, would be certain to seek revenge.

Hubert's parting with the old man and the children was affectionate. As in the old Scripture times, they embraced and kissed one another, and wept on one another's necks. They did not expect to meet again in this world, but looked forward confidently to a joyful reunion, "in the presence of the King."

In the dim gray dawn of the winter morning there was heard once more a knocking at the door of *The Silver Pickaxe*.

Maria opened it cautiously a little way. "Who are you?" she asked, peering through the uncertain light. "If you will come in, step softly, for my poor mistress is nearly out of her senses with trouble, and has not slept the whole night long — at least, unless she is dozing now. Holy saints! It is the master, or the master's ghost!"

Her cry brought Melicia to the door, with disordered dress, uncovered head, and gray hair streaming in the morning wind. Another moment, and the little innkeeper was completely lost to sight in the encircling arms of his stalwart spouse.

"Good wife," said Matej, as soon as he could speak, "let us thank God. He has delivered us from our enemies, by reason of the moon, and of a ghost, and of this brave chapman here, who kept his wits about him and knew always the next thing to do. At least," he added, "the rest all say it was a spirit or an angel that appeared to us; and why should I set myself up as knowing better than they?"

Then Melicia extended to Hubert a welcome which for warmth left nothing to be desired. In fact, he barely escaped an embrace.

The travellers were soon seated, the fire was kindled, and the best the house contained in the way of food and drink was set before them. As his strong tension of soul and nerve began gradually to relax, Hubert could not help observing, with some amusement, the transformation Melicia had undergone. The vigorous, capable woman, rough and coarse, but true of heart, was absolutely ready to bow down and worship the weak creature whom until now she had ruled with a rod of iron. Was he not her "man," the father of her children, given back to her, by a miracle, from the dead? No more, he had done something: he had fought with the miners, wounded one of them, been made a prisoner, been nearly put to death. He was a hero, if not a martyr — a true Bohemian, who stood up for his country against the Germans. He was a person to be respected, venerated, to sit unchallenged in the armchair, and to drink the best of wine, or strong waters even, if he liked them. Would he have some now — he and the master chapman also — to keep out the cold?

"No, wife," said Matej, "give me good honest beer. I vowed at the pit's mouth, when Master Packman cut my bonds, that if I got home safe I would stick to that, and not too much of it either, so as to mind you, and the boy, and the business, and live as a Christian man ought to do."

XXIV

AT LEITMERITZ AGAIN

They will not cease, they will not hush, those voices of the wave,
Forever, ever murmuring above the martyrs' grave.
'Tis heard at morn, 'tis heard at eve, the same low, wailing song,
In murmur low, in cadence loud — "How long, O Lord, how long?"

It was on the morning of March 1, 1420, that Hubert sat in the little wayside inn a rescued man, and with all his heart gave God thanks for his deliverance from the miners of Kuttenberg. That very day was published the Bull of Martin V which proclaimed the crusade against Bohemia. The pope called upon all Christendom to fly to arms, and crush the impious nation, "as rebels against the Roman Church and as heretics." Every boon claimed by Papal prerogative in this world or the next was offered in guerdon to all who should obey the summons. The pope, as he said, "by the mercy of Almighty God and the authority of the holy apostles St. Peter and St. Paul, as well as by the power of binding and losing bestowed by God upon himself, grants to those who shall enter upon the crusade, or to such even as should die upon the road, plenary pardon of their sins, if repented of and confessed and in the retribution of the just, eternal salvation. Such as could not go in person, but contributed to the cause by sending others, and equipping them according to their ability, should have full remission of their sins. Even such as had laid violent hands upon the clergy, or had been guilty of arson or sacrilege, might hope to fight their way into heaven by warring against the followers of Wycliffe and Huss."

This invitation to all the valour and chivalry, *and also to all the ruffianism and crime*, of the civilized world, to pour itself in a devastating torrent upon heretical Bohemia had long been expected, and was therefore promptly obeyed. The invading hosts streamed into the country from the north, and Leitmeritz and the surrounding districts were among the first to suffer. The Emperor Sigismund, who, at the head of the crusading host, was asserting his claim to the crown of Bohemia, took up his headquarters in the neighbourhood, and numerous acts of oppression and violence signalized his presence. Everywhere the Papists were exultant, the Hussites cowed and panic-stricken.

Meanwhile Hubert Bohun, still in his lowly disguise, travelled slowly westward. He had been detained in Eastern Bohemia some time after his adventure with the miners, so many sorrowful hearts did he find to comfort, so many perplexed minds to enlighten, so many faltering wills to strengthen, as he passed along. Now his way led him through Prague, where the aged friend of Chlum and of his house, Pánna Oneshka, lay on her deathbed. He waited to see the end, and to receive her last messages for her favourite pupil and adopted child, Zedenka.

"I have willed to her this house, with all its furniture," she said. "Though I doubt if my testament will be worth any more than the parchment it is written on. We have fallen on evil days, Master Hubert, and there is now among us no prophet Jeremiah to tell us that men shall yet subscribe evidences, and seal them, and take witnesses in this God-forsaken country. But as for me, I go in peace, being gathered unto my fathers, according to my desire. I love them, and belong to them, and have been but a stranger in the earth since they left me. I pray God to preserve His own believing remnant in this present evil world: and I place all my hope in the merits of His cross and passion; even as my father taught me, whom I shall soon see again in His presence."

As soon as the funeral was over Hubert set out for Melnik. But he found, on reaching it, that Chlum had resigned his charge, and returned with his family to Pihel. He had, therefore, no option but to continue his journey, and set his face toward Leitmeritz. It was now the joyous month of May, but the joy of the springtime was not in his heart. Rather, it seemed to him as though the earth and sky foreboded the evils that were coming on the land. Even the field-flowers looked as if they knew their destiny — to be trodden down by hostile feet, drenched with blood, or scorched with martyr-fires.

Still, no one thought of molesting the German packman on his journey. Late one evening he drew near the gate of Leitmeritz. He thought it too late to go on that night to Pihel; and, moreover, he wished to assume his proper dress before appearing there. He knew Frantisek would rejoice to welcome him, and he hoped to hear news of all his friends from him.

He found the gate still open, and a troop of pikemen marching in; crusaders, he thought, as he looked at them with a mixture of

380

curiosity, repulsion, and fear. There was no attempt at uniform; their clothing was of the most motley description — some were even ragged, but they were all armed to the teeth, and their looks were fierce and truculent. A disorderly crowd followed them, among whom Hubert entered unnoticed. None of the townsfolk were in the street; the houses were for the most part shut and barred, though here and there lights showed faintly behind the lattices. Hubert went at once to the house where Frantisek lodged, and knocked.

After an interval Frantisek appeared, torch in hand, and, opening the door a little way, asked his business. Hubert would have stepped inside to let him see his face in the torchlight, but Frantisek forbade him with a peremptory gesture. "Your name and your business first," he said.

"My name is Hubert Bohun, my business to ask a night's lodging of a good friend."

"Master Hubert! Dear Master Hubert! God save you, Sir! Welcome, welcome, a thousand times, in His name! Come in, Master Hubert!"

He drew him in, shut and barred the door behind him, then called aloud, "Aninka, dear heart, come here!" The call was promptly answered by the former bower maiden, now wearing the honours of the matron gown and coif, and with the housewife's keys hanging from her girdle. Glad and proud was the welcome she bestowed upon "Good Master Hubert."

"Now there will be great joy at Pihel," she said, "and the roses will come again to the cheek of my dear lady." Hubert thought they had come in a marvellous way to her own. Very rapidly had the pale, meek, almost too spiritless bower maiden blossomed out into the happy, busy, important wife.

Wife and husband vied with each other in the pleasant cares and duties of hospitality. They led Hubert into a comfortable, well-furnished room, relieved him of his pack and his outer garments, and gave him "fair water" for his face and hands in a pewter basin which might have been burnished by Melicia. The best they had in the shape of meat and drink was promptly set before him, and they both waited upon him assiduously, as did also an aged woman, who seemed to be at once their servant and their friend. Aninka named her to him as Alsbeta, her nurse, who had come to live with them.

Hubert heartily congratulated his friends. "I had not heard of your marriage," he said.

"It is one of the good deeds of noble Kepka, whom God reward," said Frantisek. "When he was returning from Melnik to Pihel, he lodged three nights here in the town. So well did he manage matters with Master Peichler, that he gave his consent that what was promised so long should come to pass. For fear he should change his mind, Kepka had it carried through there and then, giving as his reason that Aninka's mistress, the Pánna, wished to be present at her wedding." Frantisek paused, looked around, saw that Aninka was not at the moment in the room, and continued hurriedly in a lower voice: "Master Peichler never would have yielded, only that he was loath to lose the handsome dower Kepka has given to my Aninka. For he hates me in his heart. Master Hubert, I wonder sometimes if that which was done was well done."

"*Well* done!" echoed Hubert amazed. "In this sorrowful world is there anything so well done as the joining of hands when hearts are joined already?"

"St. Paul thought not that, and the times he lived in were no worse than ours. Master Peichler is burgomaster again this year; he was ever bitter against the Truth, and now he would sell his very soul to please the Emperor and the crusaders."

"Yet," said Hubert, "if anything could restrain him, it would be the knowledge that his only daughter is the wife of a Hussite."

Frantisek shook his head; and at that moment Aninka re-entered, busy and smiling. She carried in, and set proudly before Hubert, a savoury dish of her own preparation, eggs "in the poach," not as we know them, in unadorned simplicity, but smothered in an elaborate sauce, made of milk, honey, saffron, and ginger.

Hubert, while beginning to do justice to this remarkable compound, asked Frantisek if he knew why Kepka had resigned his charge at Melnik, and returned to Pihel.

"I think, Master Hubert, you can guess that yourself."

"Perhaps I can, but I want to hear what you, who have spoken with him, have to tell."

"He had the keys from the queen, as you know, Master Hubert; but to whom should he give them up? To the Emperor and the crusaders, or to Zisca and the League?"

"Not, surely to the first. That were to give the key of the victim's chamber into the hands of the assassins. Nor yet to the second, without leave of the queen, which leave she dare not give. It were a breach of faith and fealty so to do. I fear, verily, my dear lord has been in a sore strait," said Hubert.

"There is always a right course, and he has found it," Frantisek answered. "He has given back the keys to the royal hand he had them from — a kind hand, Master Hubert, which would protect us if it could, but is forced instead to clasp the bloodstained hands of our foes. And now he has gone home to Pihel, to do what he can for the safety of the people on his lands, and of the whole district. I own it seems strange to me how even yet he cannot see that Sigismund the Word-breaker has lost all right to the crown of Bohemia. He will not forswear his allegiance to him, though he cannot help him to plunge a dagger into the breast of his country. I sometimes think, between all these things, the heart of Kepka will be broken."

"God forbid!" said Hubert.

"I thought," pursued Frantisek, "that the cruel martyrdom of the heroic Paul Krasa, and of Nicholas of Bethlehem, would have opened his eyes."

"Opened his eyes, dear heart!" exclaimed Aninka, in mild expostulation. "As though they were shut! Depend upon it, my lord knows more than you or I. Likely he hopes God will change the Emperor's heart. Perhaps He may, and use the faith and patience of His martyred servants to do it."

"No, it is worse he grows every day, and more cruel," returned Frantisek. "That first sin of his, when he gave up Master John, seemed like the turning of his back upon the light. Indeed, in all ways it was his ruin. What Kepka says of him is this: 'By that deed he at once armed Bohemia against him, and took from Bohemia the one man who could have controlled, and guided, and kept her in the paths of peace.' But there are others that say far worse things of Sigismund the Word-breaker. They say he is the rider upon the Red Horse spoken of in the Apocalypse, unto whom it is given to take peace from the earth, and that men should kill one another. There are even some who think he is the great Red Dragon."

Meanwhile a whispered colloquy between Aninka and Alsbeta was going on at the door, and Hubert caught the mention of "fair linen sheets laid in lavender."

Persons in the position of Frantisek and Aninka would not have a guest-chamber; and Hubert could not permit them to resign to him their chamber, as he was pretty certain they meant to do. He therefore announced his determination to sleep nowhere but on the settle in the living-room, wrapped in his cloak.

But this his kind hosts would by no means allow. Aninka's remonstrances were particularly eloquent. Hubert thought he had scarcely heard her utter so many words at one time during the years they dwelt together at Pihel.

At last he said, "Then this is what I will do, Mistress Aninka. *The Golden Goose*, where Kepka lodges when he is here, is but a few paces off, and the widow who keeps it is a worthy woman. I shall find a bed there, and come back to you in the morning, to break my fast on some of your good cheer before I set out for Pihel. I suppose, Frantisek, you can help me to some raiment from the shop! I care not to show myself at Pihel in this gear."

"Yet I would counsel you, Master Hubert, not to change your dress until you are safe within the castle-gate. Better so, these ill times, with the crusaders ranging the country. Well, Master, if you *will* go to *The Golden Goose*, I shall have the honour of attending you."

Aninka, who evidently thought her husband was yielding the point far too soon and easily, raised an eager protest but Frantisek failed to sustain her adequately; he said little, and that little with a touch of constraint. His lack of insistence was one of those things scarcely noticed at the time which recur to memory afterward.

Hubert bade him a cordial good night at the door of the hostelry, promising to come to him early in the morning. At first he saw little prospect of a comfortable night, for the inn seemed to be overflowing with armed men bearing white crosses on their shoulders — the crusader's badge — and eating, drinking, quarrelling, or sleeping all over the place. But the hostess, on learning who he was, beckoned him aside and whispered: "Master, the little room in the roof has been engaged by a physician, a very civil gentleman, and well spoken, although, poor soul, he will eat nothing but bread and wine, and refuses to touch my pork sausages, which are fit for the king's table. I make no doubt he will let you sleep with him."

"I shall be much obliged to him," said Hubert, such an arrangement being quite in accordance with the feelings of his age, however repugnant to ours.

He ascended to the lofty altitude proposed to him, and knocked at the door. The physician, who had not yet retired to rest, bade him come in. Great was his surprise to see before him his old acquaintance Solito!

Mutual explanations followed. Hubert told his reasons for assuming his present lowly disguise; and learned in return that the Jew had just obtained the post of physician to His Highness the Emperor, through the recommendation of his former patroness, Queen Barbe. It was evident that the appointment gratified at once his ambition and his love of gain. Yet his pleasure seemed greatly chastened by what he saw of the state of the country, and what he feared he should be obliged to see in his attendance on the Emperor during his campaign. Hubert responded further to his confidences by telling him how well the moon had kept her appointment on Leap Year night, and what good service she had rendered thereby to him and to his companions.

There was all the time an undercurrent of perplexity in his mind. No Christian in his age, and of his rank, or even a much lower one, would have liked to share the couch of a Jew, were he ever so respectable a personage. Yet by refusing Hubert would probably give mortal offence. He decided at last to sacrifice his feelings, rather than wound those of one whom he desired earnestly to win for the faith of Christ.

A sound sleep in an excellent bed rewarded his sacrifice. He woke refreshed, to see the sunshine streaming in through the little eye-shaped window in the attic. When he came down he found a party of soldiers, not only up already, but apparently returned from some expedition, for they were divesting themselves of their weapons and clamouring for food. The hostess, with a hushed and troubled face, was cooking something over the fire, while her handmaids were setting tables.

"Will it please you to break your fast, Master?" she asked Hubert; and as she looked at him he saw that her eyes were red with weeping.

"No, good woman. I have promised to break bread with Frantisek."

An expressive look and gesture brought him to her side, and she whispered, "You will not break bread with Frantisek this morning, God help him! Last night, when we were all asleep, the burgomaster sent out the town-guard and the soldiers, and twenty-four good Hussites were arrested in their beds, Frantisek being one of them. He has thrown them into the dungeon by St. Michael's Gate. The whole town is in consternation."

An hour later the physician leisurely descended the narrow stairs, musing the while upon many things. He thought of the difficulty of making his way to the Emperor's headquarters, of the probable amount of his reckoning, of the strange apparition of Master Hubert Bohun dressed as a packman. Between and beneath these commonplace thoughts the philosophical speculations of his master, Averrhoës, were floating vaguely through his mind: "how at death the universal will be joined to the universe, and the particular will return to the part." His thoughts were not as the thoughts of the men of his age, of Chlum, of Hubert, and the rest; in some ways they were more like the thoughts of our generation, though again in others curiously unlike. Happily, there are things in which all generations meet.

At the foot of the stairs Dr. Nathan encountered his roommate, who had just hurried in with a pale, agitated face.

"Good master physician," he said, "will you come with me, for God's sake, and bestow your skill on a poor distracted girl, who is falling from one swoon into another? The women about her think she will die. I say 'for God's sake,' and I mean it; nevertheless, we will duly recompense your pains."

"I go. Let me first go to my room, however, to fetch my lancets. That imp of a boy of mine, whom I brought with me from Prague, went out yesterday to see the soldiers, and has not returned."

"Never mind your lancets. If needed, you can send for them."

"Very well; but a physician cannot get himself believed in unless he terrifies the vulgar."

"There is too much terror here already. The poor young creature, a bride of a month's standing, had her husband torn last night from her side by armed men, and flung into a dungeon, which it is likely he will only leave to die."

"Heaven help her! What had he done?"

"Only received the Communion of the Cup, and learned and loved the Word of God."

"Ah, the madness of you Christians! When will you cease to slay one another in the name of your Christ? I go with you, Master Hubert."

The room which had so nearly been Hubert's own was crowded now with agitated women, and the hot, stifling air was poisoned with the odour of burnt feathers, and of other still more nauseous and equally ineffectual remedies. However, when Hubert and the physician entered the patient had recovered consciousness, and was sitting up in bed, wringing her hands, and wailing and moaning pitifully, the women joining in her lamentations.

Solito put them all aside, and made his way to the bed. He laid his hand upon poor Aninka's burning forehead, looked into her dry, tearless eyes, felt her pulse. "Has she a mother among you?" he asked.

Alsbeta came forward. "Master Physician," she said, "I am her nurse and servitor. Her mother is dead long ago, poor lamb! And her father, the burgomaster, is he who has wrought all this ill."

"What? Her father is the burgomaster? Then, instead of lying there, weeping and wailing, she should rise up, don her fairest smock and kirtle, and braid her hair, and go and beg for her husband's life on her bended knees."

They did not think she heard or heeded, but they were mistaken. The paroxysm of what we should now call hysterical crying ceased suddenly, and the large wild eyes, full of anguish, were fixed on the physician's face. He was a man of tact, and saw his advantage at once.

"Come here, Master Hubert," he said. "Tell her, instead of making idle moan, to go and do something for her husband's deliverance." Then he turned to the patient: "Come, my mistress," he said, "be a brave woman, and it is likely you will save your husband. Go to your father, and soften his heart with your prayers and your tears. I think he loves you in spite of all. Many a father have I seen who cared little for his sons, never one yet who did not love his daughter."

Aninka with a great effort stifled the cry that was just beginning again, and murmured, "He used to — long ago."

"At least he will listen to you. You will get his leave to go and see your husband in his prison, and then you will beg of him, by the love he bears you, to do whatever is required of him, and to make his peace with the Church."

Aninka fixed her large eyes on his face again, and with labouring breath faltered just two words: "I — *cannot*."

"No, but you can. Strength will be given you for the task. Rise — make the effort!"

Aninka struggled evidently to frame a connected sentence — lost it — found it again — managed at last to say, with great effort, "Strength will be given me — *not* to bid him deny . . ." There her voice failed.

At such words as these from the lips of this poor, weak, agonized creature, Dr. Nathan Solito stood amazed.

"In the name of God," he said to Hubert, rather than to her, "what does this fanaticism mean? Will the bride send the bridegroom to his death — though her own heart breaks — for the sake of this John Huss, whom, likely, neither he nor she has ever seen?"

Before Hubert found an answer there came from the pale lips of Aninka a passionate, "No! Not for Master John — for the Lord Christ — 'whom, having not seen, we love.' "

The physician turned his face away, and was silent. After a pause he said to Hubert, "I have marvelled often at the strength of the strong; I see now a greater marvel — the strength of the *weak*. But no skill of mine can avail here. Try and rouse her to action. Persuade her to get up, and to take food. Let her go to her father and try to melt his heart with all the eloquence she can use. Probably she will not save her husband — you Christians are so hard and pitiless — but she may save her own life, or her reason."

So saying, he withdrew leaving Hubert, Alsbeta, and the others to follow his directions if they could.

Some hours afterward a veiled and muffled figure, leaning on Hubert and followed by Alsbeta, trod with weak and trembling footsteps the short distance between the lodging of Frantisek and the house of the burgomaster. But it was in vain that Aninka braced herself to make the effort. Her father refused to see her.

Hubert wrote a brief note to Chlum, and despatched it by a trusty messenger, whom Alsbeta found for him. He knew his lord — *and others also* — would be glad to hear of his safety, and he wished to inform them of the reason of his detention in Leitmeritz. He felt he could not now abandon Aninka, who, in her distress, clung to him as a tower of strength.

Two days passed away. On the third the town was in commotion. A rumour that the prisoners were to be taken out of their dungeons, judged and sentenced, was passing from lip to lip. Hubert came to Aninka, whom Alsbeta had been tending and feeding almost like an infant.

"Be strong today," he said to her, "and you will see his face again. Perhaps also you may be able to speak to — to the burgomaster." He could not bring himself to say — "to your father."

"I am strong," said Aninka. She looked as though a breath might kill her, but her cheeks were burning and her eyes full of light.

Alsbeta waited on her tenderly, and dressed her with special care. When at last she was ready to go out she paused a moment, as if in thought, then took up a large pair of shears that lay on the table, and fastened them to her girdle.

Hubert felt alarmed. Had she some hidden purpose of injuring herself? He did not suspect her of a design to injure anyone else.

"What are those for?" he asked, pointing to the shears.

"Oh, I do not know." But presently she added, "You would have been ill off at the mine without your clasp knife, or something of the kind."

Hubert remembered that he had tried to while away one of the interminable hours of the last two days by recounting his adventure with the miners. Had she any hope that a rescue might be attempted? *He* saw none, no possibility even; but he did not care to say so.

The town hall was very full. A strong body of crusaders with swords and pikes surrounded the dais where the judges sat: the burgomaster in his robes of office, and, for form's sake, a few of the town council, with him. The town-guard led in the prisoners, a forlorn and miserable group, pale, dishevelled, and unshorn. Ever since their arrest they had been kept without food, in the death-like chill and damp of a subterranean dungeon. They looked half dead already, and some of them were scarcely able to stand.

Their process was a very short one. They were simply asked if they would renounce the Communion of the Cup, and approve the acts of the Council of Constance.

From those pale and haggard lips one word — and one word only, came in answer. It was a simultaneous "No!"

Then, as if he dreaded an instant's delay, the burgomaster pronounced hurriedly on them all the sentence of death.

But in what form? "*Not the fire*," prayed Hubert in his heart. "O God of mercy, let it not be the fire!" His prayer was heard. Christ bade these His servants come to Him on the water. Their sentence bore that they were to be bound hand and foot, thrown into the Elbe, and drowned.

A breathless silence followed the words of doom. In that awful pause Aninka slipped from her seat between Hubert and Alsbeta, and swiftly, noiselessly, glided through the throng. By a common impulse everyone gave way to her. Even the crusaders opened their ranks to let her pass, and more than one put out a hand to help her. At last she reached the seat of judgment, and, falling at the feet of her father, called on him, with clasped hands and streaming eyes, "Father, have mercy! In God's name have mercy! If you have ever loved me, your only child — if you have ever loved my mother, who is dead — have mercy! Spare my husband's life!"

It may be that Peichler, though brutal and merciless, was not quite a monster. It may be his heart relented at that cry. But the soldiers and half the town were looking on. He dared not yield *now*. If he spared one Hussite, he must spare them all — make the Emperor his enemy, and become the laughing-stock of the crusaders.

"Rise up," he said to his daughter, "you know not what you ask. Dry your tears; I will find you a better husband."

Aninka obeyed. She rose up and stood before him with tearless eyes, strangely calm, strangely proud, in her uttermost agony.

"Father," she said, "you shall never give me in marriage again."

Then she turned away and was lost to sight in the crowd that followed the victims to their doom.

Hubert and Alsbeta followed also, down the long street, through the gate, to the banks of the river. Standing on the brink of it, surrounded by armed men, a company of broken-hearted wives and children were bidding those they loved a last farewell. The martyrs exhorted their friends to continue steadfast in the faith, prayed for their enemies, and commended their souls to God. But the executioners soon thought the scene had lasted long enough. They tore their victims from the clinging arms that would have held them fast, bound them hand and foot, and hurried them into a large boat. The bank of the river, for a considerable distance, was lined with soldiers, who drove back the crowd with their pikes. Amidst the wailing, sobbing throng Hubert lost sight for a moment of Aninka and her nurse. Presently he saw them again, to his surprise, *within* the line of soldiers. How they contrived to remain there, while all the rest were driven back, he never knew.

Meanwhile the boat glided on into the midst of the broad, bright river, and stood there still, a dark blot upon its sunlit bosom. One by one the victims were dropped over the side — silently, save for the dull plash that scarcely reached the shore. But when it came to the turn of Frantisek, a great cry broke the stillness, and rang through the air. It was from the lips of Alsbeta. Aninka had left her side, and with one quick movement thrown herself into the river. The nurse gazed after her with straining eyes and outstretched arms. She disappeared, she rose again, she floated. The waters, less pitiless than man, bore her kindly toward the bound and helpless form of her husband. They saw — they recognized each other — Aninka's arms were stretched out toward him.

Then the soldiers forced Alsbeta from the spot, and she knew no more.

XXV

FOR THIS

Better thou and I were lying hidden from the heart's disgrace,
Rolled in one another's arms, and silent in a long embrace.
— Lord Tennyson

Next day a party on horseback approached Leitmeritz by the road beside the river. Their leader was young Václav, the Panec of Pihel; and beside him, on Rabstein, rode a lady, in a close-fitting robe of white, the colour of mourning. Lucaz, the new squire, and Karel, the page, rode behind them; the rest were attendants of lower rank.

They paused, observing with curiosity a crowd by the river, apparently gathered around some object which they could not see. Some of the crowd were uttering cries and lamentations. Karel spurred his horse forward. "Shall I go and see what it is, Panec?" he asked Václav.

"Do so," answered Václav.

But as Karel turned to go someone came toward them from the crowd.

As soon as the approaching figure became distinctly visible, the whole party set up a unanimous shout of joy; and with a common impulse everyone, except Zedenka, sprang to the ground, and advanced to meet "Master Hubert."

"Welcome! Welcome!" was the universal cry.

But Hubert's face was grave and sad as he grasped the outstretched hand of Václav.

"Come to Zedenka," said Václav briefly, leading him to where she sat.

How Hubert had dreamed of this moment! How, through all his perils, he had longed for it, yearned for it as the traveller in Sahara yearns for the water-brooks! Now at last it had come, and it was quite other than he dreamed! His lips pressed the hand of Zedenka, his eyes looked into her eyes, yet he thought the while, not of love, but of *death*.

"Pánna," he said sadly, "it is over."

Zedenka bowed her head. "I knew it," she answered. "Dear, good Frantisek! He is, then, a martyr of God?"

"Yes, he has glorified God."

"In the fire?" said Václav.

"No; God called him home by an easier path," said Hubert, pointing to the sunlit waters of the Elbe. "As you said in Constance, 'Water does not hurt like fire.' "

"Then bring me to poor broken-hearted Aninka," said Zedenka. "I have come to comfort her, and to take her back with me to Pihel. From now on she shall be my sister."

"Pánna, she is comforted."

"Thank God! But then, great anguish stuns at first. It is the after-days that are terrible."

"For her," said Hubert, "there will be no terrible after-days."

Something in his voice struck both Zedenka and Václav with a kind of surprise. "From your words," said Václav, "one might almost think they had slain her too. As for the crusaders, there is nothing too bad for *them*. But her father — her own father! Speak, Hubert, in God's name! What has befallen the poor girl?"

"The best thing that could befall her. She and Frantisek are together."

"I shall slay Peichler with this hand as a monster!" cried Václav. "To murder his own child!"

"Spare your wrath, Václav. Peichler has enough to answer for, but not that. Mistress Aninka followed Frantisek into the water."

"Then she meant to die with him?" said Václav.

"I think, rather, she meant to save him," Hubert answered. "She had with her the means of severing his bonds. And, indeed, she had freed his hands."

"She meant life or death — with him," said Zedenka softly.

"She has found it," Hubert continued. "We knew no more until today. All yesterday the soldiers lined the banks, lest any of the martyrs, though bound hand and foot, might struggle to the shore, and be rescued. But today we are allowed to seek for our dead and to bury them. Pánna, are you brave enough to see what the river has just given back to us?"

"Aninka is dear to me in death as in life," said Zedenka.

Hubert drew near and helped her to dismount.

Rabstein whinnied, and thrust toward him his beautiful head, expecting a caress, and Hubert patted his neck before he turned to lead the way to the group beside the river. Václav followed, with all the rest, except two or three who remained in charge of the horses.

The crowd divided to let them pass. There in the midst, on the green grass starred with flowers, the sleepers lay. Loving, reverent hands had smoothed the damp, dishevelled hair, covered the disfigured faces with a snow-white kerchief, arranged and straightened the disordered clothing. But there was one thing no human hand could do. The clasp of the dead hand defied the utmost strength of the living to unloose it. Those two lay locked in one another's arms, as if defying earth and hell to divide them now.

Zedenka stood gazing on the dead, but chiefly on the gentle girl she had loved so well. Her cheek and lips were white as marble, but she neither spoke nor wept. Those around her stood in silence also. At last she knelt down on the grass, and touched reverently with her lips the cold and rigid hand of Frantisek, "For he is a martyr of God," she said. Then, brave in her great love, she uncovered the face of Aninka, and kissed her lip to lip. But at the sight and touch her "tears broke forth at last like rain." For some minutes she sobbed without restraint. Then she rose up slowly, still weeping, and said, stretching out her hand, "*Hubert*, take me away."

Hubert took her hand in silence and led her out of the throng. Then he said, "Pánna, be comforted; it is well with them."

"It is well," she sobbed. "Nothing can divide them now."

That evening devout men carried Frantisek and Aninka to their burial, and with tears and lamentations laid them "in one grave." Among those who came to see the funeral was the Jewish doctor.

"I respect your martyrs, though I do not understand them," he said to Hubert. "I own it is not John Huss who has made these; it is more like that which made John Huss. What that may be, I know not. But farewell, Master Hubert, for I am going to the Emperor. Some of these crusaders will give me safe escort to his headquarters."

Zedenka meanwhile was standing by the grave and trying to console the broken-hearted Alsbeta. "Come with me to Pihel, Mother," she said. "We will mourn together for your child. She was very dear to me."

Hubert drew near, and asked Zedenka to allow him to lead her from the sad spot.

She gave him her hand simply and trustfully, as she had done a while ago by the river-side.

They went on a few paces in silence, then Zedenka said, as if to herself, "Thank God! They have had — they *have* — forever."

"Can you thank God, Pánna, that they loved, that they wedded, for this?"

She turned, and flashed an expressive look on him through her tears.

"Yes," she answered, "they are thanking Him together now."

At the words Hubert's strong heart quivered through and through. The answer, which was also a question, sprang unawares from his mouth.

"Pánna, could you give what Aninka gave to Frantisek — to me — for this?"

She trembled, but did not speak.

"Will you?" His hand closed on her hand, his eyes looked into her eyes, and this time love, not death, was in them.

"You know my heart has lain at your feet these long years. You know, too, that death — that martyrdom — may be our next day's task and calling. Will you, then, take, and give, though it may be for this?"

"I take and I give," said Zedenka softly, "*for this*, and for heaven beyond."

XXVI

A LITTLE SHOE

Oh, weep not o'er thy children's tomb,
O Rachel, weep not so!
The bud is crept by martyrdom,
The flower in heaven will blow.

— Heber

Are we oppressed upon our mountain sod!
Then must men arm, and women call on God.

May melted into June, June burned and brightened into July. Kepka and his household still dwelt at Pihel, although Václav had entreated, almost with tears, to be allowed to join the host of Zisca and the League. Chlum could not yet persuade himself that he or his ought to take up arms against Sigismund. The faithless, dishonoured man was still in his eyes the lawful sovereign; perhaps he was even, under all the circumstances, the best sovereign that could just then be found for Bohemia. Moreover, the excesses of some of the popular party, and especially the destruction of certain monasteries, alarmed and perplexed a mind essentially loyal and reverent, also, perhaps, somewhat slow in its processes.

By this time the division, sure to supervene in all great parties, between the moderate and the more advanced, was showing itself distinctly among the Hussites. Those who contented themselves with demanding the communion in both kinds, and the free preaching of the Word of God, and maintaining the supremacy of the Holy Scriptures as the rule of faith, were styled Utraquists, or Calixtines. Those who went further, and rejected all, or nearly all, the distinctive tenets of Romanism, were beginning, on the other hand, to be called Taborites.

Chlum's acquaintances called him a Calixtine, while it was pretty well known that the sympathies of his family were with the Taborites.

None the less, but all the more probably, did his heart ache over the tidings of rapine, violence, and cruelty which reached him every day from the districts ravaged by the crusading army. His soul was torn asunder by conflicting claims and duties. Often, indeed, did the aspiration breathed in every time of sorrow or perplexity fall sadly from his lips: "Oh for Master John!" "We do not see our tokens; there is no prophet anymore," he would sometimes add mournfully.

Still, perplexity need not involve idleness, and did not in this case. Chlum found enough to do in keeping peace in his own neighbourhood, and protecting his own vassals from the outrages of the crusaders. He could not, indeed, prevent the tragedy of which Frantisek and Aninka were the victims, but other acts of violence he was able to prevent. There was something else he could do. Pihel soon became known as a refuge for the distressed; and before long it was crowded with those left homeless by the ravages of the crusaders, or fleeing from them for their lives.

Hubert and Zedenka were betrothed formally, though without the festivities usual on such occasions. They joined their hands together as those might do who stood beside a grave. Yet love and faith will find out the path to joy even in the midst of sorrow. Zedenka confessed to Hubert that she "had not liked him ill" since the days when they rode together to Prague, "nearly five years ago." And Hubert said, "I think I loved you, though I knew it not myself, from the first hour I saw your face." Both agreed that "Love once begun can never end" — in the words of the soldier-poet, penned two hundred years after their day, and quite as many before ours.

The sixth of July was observed, as usual, with solemn religious services. Chlum further signalized it by an act of mercy. Seeking in the fields the solitude so hard in those days to find within doors, he came upon a gray friar, sitting under a hedge, sick and weak. He was one of the many left homeless by the pillage or destruction of the monasteries, in which, strange to say, the crusaders, who ought to have protected them, bore their full share. He had been trying to reach Leitmeritz, hoping to find refuge there, but, through fatigue and illness, had fainted by the way. Chlum assisted him to rise, and supported his tottering footsteps until they were near enough to the castle to procure other aid. The monk proved to be in fever, and had to be nursed and tended by Zedenka and her women: nor was he the only sick person in the castle, some of the fugitives being actually ill when they arrived, others bringing with them the seeds of the maladies engendered by want and exposure to the elements.

Next morning at the usual hour, that is to say about ten o'clock, all the inmates of Pihel, except the sick and their attendants, were seated at dinner in the great hall, the tables being so arranged as to accommodate the largest possible number. Chlum sat in his place at the head of the principal table; but he looked pale, and did not eat. Zedenka, who sat next him, watched him with some anxiety. The meal was more than half over, when they heard the sound of horse-hoofs outside. The arrival of a single horseman meant tidings, and a murmur of expectation ran through the company, as the porter rose from his seat at the lower end of the board and took from his girdle the great keys of the castle-gate.

Presently, with strong, rapid steps, as one upon an errand of life or death, Ostrodek strode in. Bareheaded, dusty, and travel-soiled, he stood before them all, his raven hair streaming over his shoulders, his black eyes wild with wrathful fire, an angry flush on his dark cheek. He saluted no one, not even Kepka, who for a moment was silent from surprise, then said gently, in words used before by another, "Welcome, Ostrodek."

Ostrodek took something from beneath his vest, and flung it on the table before him. "Noble Kepka, Knight and Baron, look there! You men, who have the hearts of men in your bosoms, look there! You women, who send men out to battle, look there!"

Chlum took up the thing and looked at it, bewildered and uncomprehending. It was a very innocent, very homely thing — only a little, half-worn wooden shoe, such as peasant children used, when they had shoes at all. The child who wore this might have been seven years old. While all wondered what it meant, Václav filled a cup of wine, stood up, and offered it to Ostrodek.

Though his lips were parched and dry, he put it by untasted, "I will not drink," he said, "until I have told my tale. Then, if you are the men I take you for, you will drink with me in another cup."

The word had a spell in it. "The Cup! The Cup!" shouted several at once. "Yes! Yes! Yes! We all take the Cup."

"You take the cup of wine," said Ostrodek, with a fierce blaze in his wild eyes. "But today I bid you drink with me in another cup — the cup of the wine of the wrath of God — the cup of *blood*! For it is not with men we have to do, but with fiends. The crusaders are the armies of Apollyon, the locusts of the Apocalypse, sprung from the bottomless pit. Is it a time for you to sit at home at ease, to eat and drink, to marry and be given in marriage, when in Bohemia they are making their burnt sacrifice of babes like him who wore that shoe?"

"What! They have been burning villages again, with the people in them?" cried Václav.

"That would be bad enough, but that has been done before. Heathen, Paynim, Infidels, Turks, and Tartars have wrought such things on the earth. But it was reserved for the soldiers of the cross to build piles and to kindle faggots for the burning alive of seven-year-old babes."

Chlum turned to Ostrodek, and spoke in a tone of authority.

"In God's name, calm yourself, my son! Tell your tale clearly, so that we may understand it. What is that which has been done?"

Ostrodek made an evident effort to control himself, and to find coherent language. Twice over he began, but faltered — stopped, as if the words choked him. Some who watched him began to fear that the horrors he had witnessed had disordered his mind. But at last his eye fell on Hubert.

"Master Hubert," he said, "do you remember, last year at Tabor, the pretty babes you and I caressed and played with, and carried on our shoulders about the field?"

"Yes," returned Hubert, wondering. "Pastor Wenzel brought them to Tabor from his village — Arnoštovic."

"Pastor Wenzel!" cried Václav. "I trust in God no harm has come to him!"

"Do you think it hard for him to die, as Master John died in Constance?"

Cries of grief and horror sprang from every mouth.

"Alas! Alas!" said Václav, bowing his head, "That holy man of God! It was he who first gave me the Cup of Christ."

"A holy man, a saint indeed!" said Chlum's quiet voice. "He was ever modest, calm, and prudent. He ran to no extremes, changed no custom of our fathers. He only preached the Word of God, and gave the faithful the Cup of Christ."

"At the cost of his life," said Ostrodek.

"How was it? How was it? Tell us!" asked a dozen confused voices at once.

Hubert's, following the rest, fell with the greater distinctness in the ear of Ostrodek. "How did *you* come to know of it?" he asked.

To him Ostrodek seemed to direct his reply: "My lord, Zisca — who has made me his aide-de-camp — sent me out from the Vitkov hill of Prague, where he has his headquarters, on a special errand. No matter about that now, save that it was both secret and perilous, and that it led me through a district occupied by the crusaders — almost, I may say, through their very host. I disguised myself, however, and all went well; they being, I believe, like the hosts of Samaria, blinded of God. I was on my way back, glad enough of my success. Coming from Milic to Prague, I passed through Bystetic, where the Duke of Austria was with his crusaders. That was yesterday morning. I saw the crusaders bringing faggots and preparing a great pile, and such of the people of the place as they had not driven away or frightened out of their senses standing around, looking on. I asked what it all meant, and was told that Pastor Wenzel of Arnoštovic and his vicar were to be burned there, for holding the Communion of the Cup. I was told, too, how they had been abused, insulted, threatened, but all in vain. They were firm in their faith. That, indeed, I expected — but not the rest — oh! Not the rest! I need not tell you I stayed to see all."

"Oh, how could you?" cried Karel.

"Karel, I am no child. Though, if I *were* a child like some, I might shame the mightiest. After long waiting, they led the prisoners out. First came Pastor Wenzel, his face covered with blood, for one of the crusaders — a *knight* (God save the mark!) had struck him with his iron glove. His vicar followed. Then came four old men, peasants, brave and quiet, looking as if they were only going out to their day's work in the fields. Then a little lad about the size of Karel when we came here first, and the two fair-haired babes we met at Tabor. I saw them run up to the pastor, and take each one of his hands. When all stood near the pile, the crusaders bade them abjure the doctrine of the Cup, and live. The pastor answered for them all. 'Far be it from us! We would sooner die, not one, but a hundred deaths, than abjure so plain a doctrine of the Gospel.' And they all said they would die with him."

Ostrodek paused. Not a sound was heard from anyone. Chlum sat motionless, his head buried in his hands. Karel and some of the women were weeping, but in silence.

He resumed. "I stood as near the pile as I stand now to you, Kepka — it was then I got that token. I saw the faggots kindled — I saw the flames rise up — I would have seen the end, only for the children . . ." His head sank down, his voice faltered, stopped.

"For the children's cry?" suggested someone.

"For the children's *singing*!" said Ostrodek, raising his head again. "Pastor Wenzel put his arms around them, and held them to his breast. Then, as the flames rose up, they sang aloud a hymn of praise to God. That childish singing was the last sound I heard as I turned away. I hear it now — I shall hear it until I die."

Almost everyone at the table was weeping now. Ostrodek looked down the long lines, and said, "To you women who weep I have nothing to say; but to you men, this — if for such deeds you sit here and weep womanish tears, then are you men no more at all. Men? No, nor women like those who in our beleaguered Prague tend the sick and wounded, or stand on the ramparts beside their sons and husbands. Men? No, nor children like those who sang their hymns of praise in the fire. You will be like the dumb creatures of God, the beasts of the field, to whom He has denied the understanding to combine against their oppressors. You will deserve to see your own children burned at the stake before your eyes, and your own wives and daughters — Woe, woe is me that I have not the tongue of the learned! My words are at my sword's point, and I suggest they will be graven deep with that! Hubert, you are eloquent; speak for me! Václav, you loved me once; speak for me! No, you are a *man* now; speak for yourself. Claim your right to take a share in the war of vengeance, of freedom, of God!"

Václav rose up, left his place, came to where his father sat, and knelt down before him.

"Father," he begged, "bless your son for this war, for it is the war of God."

Chlum withdrew his hands, revealing a pale and troubled face; but he did not speak.

"The noble Kepka will lead you himself!" cried Ostrodek. "The sword that fought so well against the Turk and the Italian will spring once more from its scabbard in a nobler, holier cause."

"I think," said Chlum, and he spoke feebly and with effort — "I think another hand must wield it now. Rise up, Václav. Hubert, still at least for this day my good squire, go to the oak chest in the wardrobe — here is the key. Fetch from there my suit of Venetian armour."

When he was gone, Zedenka touched her father's arm, and whispered something in his ear. He answered aloud, "I shall be when this thing is done."

Hubert soon reappeared, carrying a very beautiful coat of mail of Venetian workmanship, made of minute steel scales or splints, so exquisitely fitted as to be flexible as a glove, and at the same time wholly invulnerable. No mirror could have been brighter, part of Hubert's duty as squire being to keep it, and other armour belonging to his lord, in perfect order.

"My son," said Chlum to Václav, "I give you this to wear in the war of freedom. Be a true servant of God and of the Cup."

"Knight and Father, will you not wear it yourself?"

"Not now, my son; I send you in my place."

"Sir Knight," asked Hubert, "shall I put on the coat?"

"Not so; no hand but mine shall arm my son for this conflict. I believe Zedenka will do the same service for you, Hubert. As for you, my children," he added, standing up and addressing those who sat below the salt — "as for you who hold service under me or live upon my lands, I leave you free this day to follow the Panec and Master Hubert if you will, and to fight under the banner of the Cup for your faith and your country. If you return in safety and honour, I will bid you welcome, and give you back your places or your lands; if you fall, no mother, sister, wife, nor child of yours shall lack a friend while Kepka lives. Or," he added, apparently correcting himself — "or the Panec being lord here in my stead will do all I would have done."

Every man present sprang to his feet with a shout that made the old hall ring again. "For God and the Cup!" they cried. "We will die for God and the Cup!"

While they were still shouting, Chlum passed slowly out into another room.

Zedenka followed him, but presently returned with an agitated face, and said to Hubert, "My father is ill. I do not doubt he has caught the fever from that friar. But he will have nothing changed or delayed on his account. It is his will that you and Václav and the rest — save only a few of the older men, and Karel, who is too young — prepare at once to march with Ostrodek to Prague and to join the army of Zisca."

XXVII

THE DAY OF BATTLE

His oaken spear
Was true to that knight forlorn,
When the hosts of a thousand, were scattered like deer
At the blast of the hunter's horn —
When he strode on the wreck of each well-fought field,
With the (raven) haired chiefs of his native land,
His lance was not shivered on helmet or shield,
And the sword that seemed fit for archangel to wield
Was light in his terrible hand.

— T. Campbell

Chlum's strong will sustained his fainting frame until he had clothed Václav in the beautiful coat of Venetian mail, had clasped the girdle around his waist, and given into his hands the good Damascus blade. "For vengeance, do not strike one blow," he said. "For faith, for freedom, and for God, strike until you have conquered, or fallen upon the field."

The mail hung loosely around the slender form of the tall stripling of seventeen, in spite of the thickly-padded jerkin that he wore beneath it; but his young heart was as brave and strong as that of any man in all Bohemia.

Hubert's suit of plate armour, the one given him when he came to Pihel, though less rare and costly than Václav's, was still very valuable. It had been always precious in his eyes as the first gift of Kepka, and now it was made a treasure beyond price by the touch of the small hands that clasped strap and buckle so deftly and so carefully, each in its place.

"*For this*, dear heart," he said to her, recalling the words with which they pledged troth by the grave of Frantisek and Aninka.

"Yes, for this," she answered steadfastly. "For doing or for suffering the will of God. For life and death, and for the long forever." Then came the parting kiss, which lingered yet on the lips of the young soldier of God as he rode away.

It was a gallant band which rode forth from the gates of Pihel to join the Army of the Cup. Besides the soldierly retainers of Kepka, nearly all the fugitives, not ill or disabled, swelled the ranks. As they passed through the village their host was augmented by a crowd of peasants, armed with their formidable flails or with clubs and reaping-hooks, and full of zeal for the cause. Almost every hamlet through which their way led them added a similar contingent.

All the land, as they passed along, was full of the sounds and sights of war. Tidings reached them on their way of a great victory at Tabor; they heard with wondering joy how the knightly hosts that beset "the Mount of God" had fallen beneath the iron flails of undisciplined peasants.

The coal-diggers, it was said, had risen also against their oppressors, and, armed with their axes, had stormed a strong fortress in the Kuttenberg district. Hubert, hearing this, smiled inwardly, remembering his companions in misfortune at the mine. But other tidings came to them also, thick and fast as leaves in autumn. The crusading hosts were drenching the land with blood and scarring it with fire. The worst and most appalling atrocities shall be here unnamed, as they ought to be. Enough to say that the horrors of the death of fire were no longer reserved for "professed, impenitent heretics" like Pastor Wenzel and his companions. It was the common fate of all their prisoners, Hussite and Roman Catholic alike. To beg for mercy in the *Bohemian* tongue was quite enough to consign the suppliant to the flames. The war was fast becoming a war of race as much as a war of religion.

At last the Pihel men drew near to Prague. As they rode over against the Monastery of the Holy Cross and the Church of St. Valentine, they saw above them on the heights the vast camp of the Emperor and the crusaders. Nor were they themselves unseen. Stones and darts were thrown at them, and a motley crowd of crusaders and camp followers loitering on the nearest hill mocked them with shouts and cries of, "Huss! Huss! Heretics! Heretics!" and imitated the cackling of geese and the barking of dogs.

Still, no serious attack was made upon them. Guided skilfully by Ostrodek, they passed with safety, under the very eyes of the crusaders, to the Vitkov or Gallows Hill, on the east side of the city, over which was floating the black flag with the red cup upon it, the Standard of Zisca.

At that time it might almost have been said of Prague that it was at once besieging and besieged. For the whole city was in the hands of the Hussites — indeed, nearly the whole city except the Neustadt *was* Hussite; only the strong fortress of the Vyssehrad, under its governor, Czenko, held out for the Emperor. While the citizens, under Zisca, were endeavouring to reduce the Vyssehrad, the vast host of the crusaders had gathered its scattered masses, welded its huge, unwieldy bulk into something like unity and was rolling onward, an overwhelming, devastating flood, to take upon the heretical city such vengeance as should never be forgotten so long as the world lasted.

The inhabitants very well knew what mercy they had to expect if the crusaders entered their gates. Every man able to bear arms either joined the skirmishing parties that went forth continually from the town, or stood upon the ramparts. Women carried off the wounded at the peril of their lives, and sometimes even mingled in the fray, or hurled stones from the wall upon the enemy. Boys acted as scouts and messengers, or caught stray horses in the field and brought them to their friends. Aged folks and little children, who could do nothing else, flocked to the churches, and spent their days in impassioned prayer to the God of battles.

The first thing the Pihel men did when they reached the Vitkov was to lay aside their armour and their weapons, to take pickaxe, spade and shovel, and to dig, dig, dig, as if their very lives depended upon it. So they probably did; and the lives of the helpless thousands beneath them in Prague. For Zisca, in hot haste, was fortifying the hill, having discerned with the eye of genius that it was the true key to the city. That safe, all might be safe. That taken, Prague would lie at the mercy of the savage horde who knew not what mercy meant.

Those Pihel men who lived to look back on that wild time scarce knew how they spent the days, digging the trench, carrying earth, piling stones. They only knew that they worked on madly, stopping hardly at all for sleep, hardly long enough to eat the food women brought them from the town in baskets, or to drain the wine-cups they held to their lips. Hubert, Václav, and Lucaz Leffle set an example of untiring industry to the rest. Ostrodek was otherwise occupied, being in immediate personal attendance on Zisca.

Their toil, happily almost ended, was broken rudely in upon by the sound of trumpets and the call to arms. Spades and shovels were dropped, and swords and pikes grasped in an instant; while Hubert, Václav, and the others who had defensive armour threw it hastily on, and got their comrades to buckle it for them.

404

Not a moment too soon. The flower of the crusading chivalry, eight thousand strong, led by the Duke of Misnia, were spurring onward to storm the Vitkov Hill. In the desperate fight that followed, sword to sword and hand to hand, each man only saw his own antagonist, only knew how his own sword rose and fell, which strokes he parried and which he returned, how that man at his side sunk beneath the horse-hoofs, and that other plunged his sword into the breast of his foe. Yet each man knew he was fighting not for his own life alone, but for the lives of tens of thousands. Nor could he have fought better had he also known that the attack on the Vitkov was a preconcerted part of a grand assault upon the whole city, and that this was, for Prague, "the day of decision."

At an early hour of that terrible day Hubert was near Zisca, who stood leaning on his great two-handed sword, and surveying the field with his single eye of fire.

He pointed to a small, roughly-constructed wooden tower or shed, with an overhanging roof and a little balcony, and said briefly, "Englishman, keep that as long as you can." Accordingly Hubert, Václav, and some of their men threw themselves into it just in time to receive the shock of the advancing foe. A few peasants armed with pikes were already there, and three women, who had come to them with provisions. These fought as bravely as the rest, hurling stones at the enemy, either with their hands or from a rude but effective machine which projected from the balcony.

Hour after hour they fought on — bravely, desperately, amidst showers of stones and darts, bolts from many a cross-bow, and bullets from many an arquebus. Charge after charge of horsemen shook the frail fort to its foundations, yet could not daunt the steadfast hearts that held it still "for God and the Cup."

But this could not last forever; a pause and stir among the crusaders announced a new mode of attack. With a great shout they dragged forward a cumbrous mangonel, or cannon, and planted it near the wall — which, indeed, was already tottering. Even the bravest knew that hope was over now. Some spoke of surrender. While the words were yet on their lips, the iron throat of the mangonel gave forth its thunder, and a breach yawned in the wall beneath them. But one of the women cried aloud, "Christian believers ought not to give ground to Antichrist," and taking up a stone hurled it at the first crusader who tried the breach. She soon fell, covered with wounds. Hubert meanwhile saw just a chance of preserving the lives of the rest. He formed them rapidly into a solid square, with the two surviving women in the midst, and bade them fight their way through the enemy.

These, content with what they had gained, and no doubt fearing the desperation of the Hussites, gave way before them, and they reached their comrades in safety — a sorely diminished band, who had won no victory, and yet had rendered inestimable service to the cause, by detaining a multitude of crusaders at an insignificant point during the crisis of the battle.

Their friends, who thought them dead, received them with shouts of joy. Together they hurried to the relief of Zisca, who was personally hard pressed by the foe. For one perilous moment he even lost his footing, and the hoofs of the crusaders might easily have crushed out the strongest hope of the Hussites. But a score of dauntless "brothers" rushed to his help, and succeeded in placing him in safety. Just then they became aware, amidst all the noise and turmoil, of strange sounds from the city beneath them. Every bell in Prague was ringing its loudest but yet hoarser and more deafening was the clamour that rose from ten times ten thousand throats.

Such shouts as rent the heavens that day were surely never heard before, nor would be again until the Day of Judgment. Crusader and Hussite alike suspended their desperate conflict to listen and to look. From the height in Vitkov they beheld a strange procession issuing forth from the gate of Prague. A priest went first bearing the Host, fifty archers followed him, lastly came a crowd of peasants armed with hooks and flails. As they marched they sang — to an air plaintive in itself, yet, like "the Dorian mood of flutes and soft recorders," all the more mighty to stir the pulses of fighting-men — the song of Zisca and the Cup,

Soldiers of God, arise,
And combat for His laws!
Implore His present help,
Maintain His holy cause!
For he who owns the Lord his Friend
Must ever conquer in the end.

The Lord commands His own
To have no fear of death;
The worst of mortal foes
Can take but mortal breath.
Be strong, then, soldiers, in His might
Go forth, and combat for the right!

406

Christ shall repay your loss
A hundred fold and more;
Who gives his life for Him
Shall have, when death is o'er,
A glorious, blessed life on high,
In everlasting victory.

Therefore, who bends the bow,
Who wields the knightly brand,
Who swings the deadly flail,
Arise, at God's command,
And, thinking on His promised grace,
Let each man combat in his place!

Dread not the foeman's might,
Nor fear his vast array;
Lift up your hearts to God,
And fight for Him this day;
No foot-breadth to the foeman yield,
But die, or conquer on the field.

It was the hour of the Lord's deliverance. As the procession moved toward them and the solemn strain sounded in their ears, a wild uncontrollable panic seized upon the crusaders. They thought the whole city, mad with fury, was pouring out upon them in the wake of this strange vanguard. Watching from their height, the defenders of Vitkov saw that their foemen in the plain were wavering — beginning to flee. They raised a deafening shout of triumph, and with strength renewed by hope and joy rushed once more on their assailants. They drove them out of the entrenchments, slaying many, and hurling more over the rocks into the valley beneath.

Before sunset the battle was won. The brave defenders of the Vitkov — from now on and forever to be called the Ziscaberg, the Mountain of Zisca — marched back to the town in triumph, to congratulate their friends, and to be congratulated by them. It is needless to say that all were not there. In the words of a greater soldier and general even than Zisca, "There is nothing sadder in the world than a victory, except a defeat."

Those, however, whose names we know, and who had been on the Vitkov were all there. Some of the Pihel men had fallen, but Hubert could only be thankful that the loss was not greater, and especially that Václav was safe. Lucaz was wounded, but not seriously.

He himself, notwithstanding his desperate valour, had escaped with no worse harm than a slight cut in the left leg, through the joint of his armour, between the "cuisse" and the "greave."

He was still lingering with his friends in the Grosser Ring, hearing the details of the battle from some who had fought in the plain, when a lad in a smart jerkin forced his way through the group and caught him by the arm. "Master Hubert Bohun!" he cried, breathless. "At last! I have been seeking you everywhere. I have a message for you."

"Who are you? I have never seen you before to my knowledge," said Hubert, looking at him. He spoke German, but his face showed him unmistakably a Jew.

"But I have seen you at Leitmeritz. At the funeral, when they buried those the Elbe gave back. I am the assistant and the pupil of the great Doctor Nathan Solito, physician-in-ordinary to his Highness the Emperor," the urchin continued grandly.

"Then what business do you have here?" cried Prokop, who was standing near. "Go back to your master, and tell him he serves a word-breaker and a murderer."

"Yes, go — lest we throw you over the wall," added another.

"I will go back to my master when I have done my master's errand. Master Hubert Bohun, he bids me tell you that your friend Ostrodek — whom he saw at Pihel — and ten other prisoners with him, are to be burned tonight in one great fire by the crusaders, by way of consoling themselves for their fright and discomfitures."

Exclamations of rage and horror came from all the group. Ostrodek, not having been with them on the Vitkov, had not been missed until now. If they had time to think of him at all, they concluded Zisca had sent him somewhere, as indeed he had, and the errand had proved the occasion of his capture. There was no reason to doubt the horrible fate intended for him and his companions. The crusaders were not likely to show more mercy to their prisoners after their defeat than before it.

There was only one improbable feature in the story. "Ostrodek would never let himself be taken alive," said Václav.

"His sword arm was broken," returned the youth briefly.

Hubert, who had been sitting on the ledge of a shop window, stood up and said, "There is but one thing to do. I, at least, shall not break bread until I save Ostrodek, or die in the attempt."

"I also," said Václav, laying his hand on his sword.

But others, more prudent, would have held them back. "Take care," they said. "It may all be a snare. How do we know that this urchin's tale is true? He may be bribed by the crusaders. It may be a trick to lead us out of the city, that we may be taken ourselves and burnt like the rest."

They spoke in Czech, but the Jewish boy who had been bred in Prague, understood them perfectly. He came close to Hubert and said, "My master gave me a token for you, Master Hubert, to show that I speak the truth."

"What is it?" asked Hubert eagerly.

"This. He swears to you that this thing is true, by the faithful witness in heaven, who kept her tryst so well on the night of Leap Year Day."

"*Good*. But can you lead us rightly to the place, Boy?"

"That I can, and will, I stake my life upon it. That is to say, if these gentlemen do not prefer first throwing me over the wall."

"No! If we save our friends we will reward you instead."

"Yes," cried Václav. "Lead us on, Boy. We must save Ostrodek."

"You say you will not break bread until it is done," said a citizen, standing by. "I pray of you break bread first, that you may do it. Else you will faint by the way."

There was reason in this. Hubert and Václav, and the eager band who volunteered to join them, consented reluctantly to a brief delay, just sufficient to swallow the food and wine which the citizens brought out to them from their houses.

Thus, instead of rest for the weary Pihel men and their friends, there was still a rally and skirmish that night.

Such rescue parties as theirs were not uncommon, and, what is strange, they seem often to have been successful. This may have been owing to the great extent of country over which the vast, unwieldy, crusading host had spread itself; to the lack of communication between its many divisions and subdivisions; and to the want of proper outposts, and other military precautions. The night succeeding the battle afforded an exceptionally favourable opportunity for such an expedition, on account of the confusion and disorder which pervaded the panic-stricken host.

XXVIII

GOLDEN SPURS

By the sword and by the spear,
By the hand that knows no fear,
Warrior, nobly shalt thou fall!"

The sun was rising over Prague when a band of horsemen entered the Altstadt, and wound its way slowly to the Grosser Ring. Even at that early hour many of the citizens were already in the streets, and greeted the horsemen with shouts of joy and triumph. For they brought back with them, safe and whole, ten of their friends, whom they had rescued from the doom of fire. They had mounted them on some of their own horses, while on another they set their two prisoners, bound together ignominiously. One was a monk, caught near the pile in the very act of arranging the faggots, and exciting the crusaders to their cruel work: it is to be feared he was likely to receive no gentle treatment in Prague. The other was neither priest, nor monk, nor soldier, but a man of peaceful calling; the Bohemians could not very well explain how they came to take him, unless it was because he seemed to drop into their very hands.

Why they went at a foot-pace, why the triumph of their bearing was shaded with sadness, soon became apparent to the onlookers. In their midst was a litter constructed of lances and borne by four and in the litter lay a wounded, perhaps a dying man. Ostrodek's right arm was broken before his capture, as the Jew had said; and moreover, in the moment of rescue, a crusader, before he fled, gave him a spear-thrust in the side. Hubert, who rode sadly beside him, thought, perhaps hoped, that he was unconscious.

Some of the party asked where they should bring him.

"To the house of Wenzel the cupmaker," said Hubert briefly.

However, as they reached the threshold the wounded man spoke, saying feebly, "Stop!"

"Dear lad, what do you want?" asked Hubert.

"I have always loved the free air. Let me die in it. Lay me down *here*, in the spot where I first saw the face of Kepka."

The faintest whisper of the dying is stronger than the mandate of the crowned king. They laid him down, having hastily thrown some of their upper garments on the ground beneath him, as a kind of couch. Someone came out of the house with a cup of wine, which was borne to his lips.

Meanwhile a brief colloquy between one of the prisoners and those who guarded him resulted in his being unbound, and allowed to dismount from the horse. He came forward with the words, "I am a physician; can I be of any use here?"

Hubert, absorbed with Ostrodek, had not looked at him before. As soon as he did so, he started, and exclaimed in a tone of surprise, "Dr. Nathan Solito! And a prisoner!"

"No unwilling one," the Jew whispered.

"Nor unwelcome to us," returned Hubert. "It is to you we owe the information which has led to this rescue, and we thank you for it heartily."

Before he ended the Jew was kneeling down by Ostrodek and examining the wound in his side. He looked up with a grave face. "Bring me a linen kerchief or two," he said.

"No use," whispered Ostrodek. "I am dying."

The physician did not contradict him. "I will not hurt you," he said gently. "I will but try to stanch the blood a little — for the present."

"The spear went deep," murmured Ostrodek. The one hand he could use groped feebly among the blood-stained garments the physician had displaced. It found what he sought, the glove of Páni Sophia. He held it out to Hubert. "Give that to Kepka with my duty," he said. "My heart's blood is on it." Then a smile flitted across his face. "I knew they would not burn me," he said. "Master John's death was not for such as I."

"No less are you a martyr of God," said Hubert.

"A martyr! Think of His letting me die for Him, when I could not live — as He wished!"

"Dear Ostrodek, can you trust Him now? Do you have faith in Him?"

"Not faith such as good men have. Not faith to forgive and love — like Christ. Only faith to know that He forgives . . ." Here his voice failed, and Hubert and the others feared he was passing from them. But the Jew had somewhat stanched the bleeding of the wound, wine was given him again, and he revived. He looked around him

411

on the group, now augmented by several knights and citizens, and by some of Wenzel's household.

"I would see my lord once more," he said.

A willing messenger speeded off to the quarters of the Hussite general: already one had gone to summon a priest.

Presently the crowd divided of its own accord. One approached the couch of Ostrodek to whom all other men gave place by instinct. The hero of the Hussites was a muscular, broad-shouldered man of middle height. His large, round, closely-shaven head, his dark countenance and long moustache, the straight line down his forehead, called "the warrior's line," and the fire that gleamed in the solitary orb fate had left him — all gave the impress of power, tremendous but terrible. Yet his voice was gentle as a woman's as he said, "Speak, Ostrodek; what can Zisca do for the bravest soldier he ever led to victory?"

"My lord, hear me. Once you promised me a boon."

"Speak on," said Zisca.

"God has given you a great victory. All Prague was your battlefield, and this — whereon I lie — is the soil of Prague. By the rules of chivalry, a conqueror on the field can confer knighthood."

Perhaps Zisca was not unwilling to exercise a prerogative that would stamp his position in the eyes of his followers with a lustrous and shining zeal. "I remember well," he said, "that you did desire the name and the honour of noble knighthood. You shall have your desire, and well have you earned it, brave Ostrodek. Would God it had not come too late! Let someone give me a sword," he added, for he had come forth unarmed.

Hubert stood up from his place beside the dying, and offered his own. Yet as he did so he looked at Ostrodek somewhat sadly. "Dear Brother," he pleaded, "think rather where and to whom you are going now."

Ostrodek looked at him and smiled. "You will know my meaning soon," he whispered. Then he raised his hand and spoke to Zisca. "Stay, my lord. It was indeed my desire to cover my stained name with the glory of knighthood, that it might shine forth once more in the eyes of men, and Zul of Ostrodek lift his head unshamed among his peers. That is over now. Zul of Ostrodek is going where his name shall not once be heard, since when he is called Christ shall answer for him. So, if you will grant me a last boon, give the accolade instead to Master Hubert Bohun, the squire of Kepka, who has done many valiant deeds, even before this rescue of ours."

412

"It shall be done, Ostrodek," said Zisca, not unmoved. "Bohun well deserves the honour for his own sake, not to speak of yours."

"Then, I pray you, do it *now*. I grow faint again."

"Kneel down, Master Hubert Bohun."

Hubert obeyed. Zisca struck him gently on the shoulder with his own sword, saying, "Rise up, Sir Hubert Bohun." Hubert rose to his feet a knight.

"The golden spurs," whispered Ostrodek, who was watching all with eager eyes.

A knight among the bystanders made his squire unfasten his own spurs, and tendered them to Zisca. Then, as the custom and manner was, the general with his own hands buckled them on the heels of Hubert. When this was done, those around set up a ringing cheer.

"*Hush!*" said the voice of power that all men were wont to obey. "We stand in the presence of death."

Once more Hubert knelt down beside Ostrodek. The dim eyes, the labouring breath, and that strange look we never can mistake, all told that the end was near.

"Dear Brother," he whispered, "think on the Lord Christ."

"Dear Ostrodek, remember you are dying for Him," said Václav, who was beside him also.

Ostrodek gathered up his remaining strength to say, "I remember only — He died for me."

There was a pause. The tide of life ebbed slowly — slowly — until it touched the tideless ocean of eternity.

When the end came Ostrodek smiled, and lifted up his hand, as one who beckons the unseen. "I hear the children singing," he murmured.

"It is over," said Hubert reverently. He stooped down to close his eyes, but made room for Václav. "You do it," he said. "The son of Kepka, to whom he owed all, has the best right."

"Yet once more," said Václav, as he did the office of the next of kin — "yet once more my mother has welcomed him home."

"May he rest in peace!" spoke Zisca, as he turned away. "No braver man than Zul of Ostrodek will ever fight under the banner of the Cup."

Then his eye fell on the unfortunate monk, and "the form of his countenance was changed" in an instant. "Take that rascal away, and throw him into the deepest dungeon of the Council House!" he thundered. Men whispered darkly of a cruel wrong done long ago to a gentle girl who called Zisca brother, which steeled his heart against priest and monk as much even as the tragedy of Constance.

XXIX

THE DAY OF VICTORY

Our God hath crushed the tyrant, our God hath raised the slave,
And mocked the wisdom of the wise, and the valour of the brave.
— Lord Macaulay

Over the soldier's grave in which Ostrodek was laid was heard the sound, not of weeping and lamentation, but of joy and triumph. This was well; he would have had it so if he could have chosen. The city, suddenly delivered from overwhelming fear and danger, went literally mad with joy. The churches could scarce contain the multitudes that crowded into them, and made their walls resound all day long with the glorious strains of the *Te Deum Laudamus*. From morning until night the streets were filled with the long processions of men and women and little children, singing Psalms and hymns of praise to Him who saved them from the hands of the enemy.

With shouting and with laughing,
And noise of weeping loud,

friend embraced friend, brother wrung the hand of brother. Fathers took their children in their arms, and, with the rare tears of manhood, gave thanks to God that these tender little ones were not to be thrown into the flames before their eyes. Peals of triumph sounded from every bell in the great city. The rich feasted the poor, the poor blessed the rich. Feuds and differences were forgotten: in this great joy all became as brothers.

The Pihel men and the friends of the other rescued prisoners filled the cap of young Solomon the Jew with good silver groschen, and Zisca's own hand flung upon the top a broad piece of gold. Hubert asked the physician what they could do for him — should they send him back again with a safe escort to the Emperor?

414

Dr. Nathan Solito shook his head. "You would not have taken me if I had not willed to be taken," he said. "The truth is, Master Hubert — no, I crave your pardon, Sir Hubert — the things I have seen in yonder camp are such as it is not good for a man to see. Good consciences are not to be bought again with gold, if once they are lost or disordered — even supposing the gold to be forthcoming, the which I am disposed to doubt," the Jew added thoughtfully. "So I return to my own people, who are here in this city, and shall abide with them for a season."

"We owe to you the rescue of our friends," said Hubert. "I would we could show you we are grateful."

"It was well for the other ten," returned the Jew, "that I recognized Ostrodek, having known him at Pihel. Poor lad! It was hard he should have been the only victim, after all."

"No," said Hubert, "it is well with him."

The Jew turned away, then turned back again, and spoke in low, hurried tones, as if ashamed of himself.

"Sir Knight, I will confess one thing to you," he said. "The Name that was on his lips in dying is like no other name on earth."

"True," said Hubert, eagerly. "It is the one name at which every knee shall bow. Good friend, will you not be won for Him also?"

"No, Sir Hubert, I abide with my own people, as, I think, every man ought to do. That is clear to me, though much else is dark."

Hubert smiled. "What if I say to you what you said once to me — the darkness is on earth, at your own feet; in the heavens above you there is light? But at least I will pray for your conversion."

"To your Christ? I pray you, good Sir Hubert, do not do any such thing."

"Why, in Heaven's name? If it does you no good, at least in your own showing it can do you no harm, He being, as you blasphemously suppose, only a dead man?"

"I am not so sure," said the Jew, as though the words escaped him unawares. "It looks as if for that poor girl at Leitmeritz, for those twenty-four who died there, and for Ostrodek, He *lives*."

"Of whom it is witnessed that He lives," said Hubert.

"Well, there are mysteries," the Jew allowed. "Farewell, Sir Hubert, and the God of our fathers bless you!"

Three days afterward, the festivities of the rejoicing city culminated in a grand illumination, which flushed the midnight sky with a redder light than that of day. But the citizens had not contrived or compassed it. They stood upon their ramparts awe-struck and spell-bound, and watched the raging of the flames. The Imperial camp was on fire.

None knew then, or ever, how or by whom the brand had been flung that kindled the vast conflagration. But it was no marvel if the whisper passed from lip to lip — "*This is the finger of God.*"

Men remembered the days of old. They recalled the smitten thousands of Sennacherib. They thought of

> *The storm that slumbered until the host*
> *Of blood-stained Pharaoh left his trembling coast,*
> *Then bade the deep in wild commotion flow,*
> *And heaved an ocean on his march below.*

Meet and right it was that He whose waves and billows worked His will upon the oppressors of Israel should call now upon His servant Fire, the strong and terrible. Meet and right it was that the Angel of the element they had used for their fiendish cruelties — delivering up to it young men and maidens, old men and children — should arise in avenging fury and pursue them with the terrors of His curse. As the stars in their courses fought against Sisera — as in later ages the stormy wind fulfilled the purpose of God upon the hosts of Spain — as, later yet, He sent forth His ice like morsels, and in Russia the millions of Napoleon could not stand before His frost — so in Bohemia Sigismund and the crusaders of Rome suffered, according to His righteous judgment, the vengeance of the fire.

One sad blot, and one only, tarnished the glory and the joy of the Bohemian triumph. Hubert, Václav, and others with them, stood for hours guarding the door of the Council House, where the Imperialist prisoners were kept. But in vain: the lowest of the population of the great city and the fiercest and wildest of Zisca's Taborites forced open the door, and dragged out sixteen trembling, terrified captives. These they led forth to a high place outside the walls, and burned them in one great fire in the sight of their brother crusaders who had inflicted the same fate on so many Bohemians. Only one escaped, the monk who had been taken at the rescue of Ostrodek, and who promised from now on to administer the sacrament in both kinds. "Burning for burning, wound for wound, stripe for stripe." It was very natural, and very human. Still, we look across the gulf of nearly five hundred years, and wish — oh, how earnestly — that it had not been.

Hubert's deep regret at this affair was driven partially out of his thoughts by a great pleasure. The next day Karel Sandresky rode into Prague, immensely proud of having been allowed to undertake the journey, in spite of its risks, which were very imperfectly known at Pihel, or he would never have obtained the permission. He brought the welcome tidings that Chlum was out of danger: moreover, the Pánna bade him greet her brother in her name, and sent "a token" to Master Hubert, desiring to hear of his health and welfare. Sir Hubert, for answer, took off his golden spurs, and bade Karel lay them in his name at the feet of the Pánna. He added that he hoped shortly to return to Pihel, as the campaign, to all appearance, was near its end.

In this, as well as in many other ways, his expectations were fulfilled. After the defeat of Sigismund and the first crusade, the land had rest for a little while. There was a breathing-space — though it was a short and fitful one, broken by contentions and alarms.

Still, even in brief intervals of sunshine the birds sing, the flowers raise their drooping heads, the heavens smile, and the earth is glad. During those days of peace in the midst of trouble, Pihel was the scene of wedding festivities. They were much more grave and quiet than was at all usual in those boisterous days, yet they were bright with sober joy, and with steadfast faith and hope. Zedenka rewarded the long and patient waiting of Hubert; and Chlum bestowed his castle of Svatkov upon the bride and bridegroom.

Days of warfare came again, all too soon. When Hubert had to go forth once more to fight under Zisca beneath the standard of the Cup, he left his young wife at Pihel with her father. Václav was his well-beloved brother-in-arms, who went out and came in with him, and stood gallantly by his side in many a well-fought field.

So passed the days and years, with their fears and hopes, their joys and sorrows. But the hopes prevailed over the fears, the joys were more than the sorrows. Often did Zedenka think — with a tender, loving remembrance that had no pain it — of the words of her dear, dead mother: "I can wish you no better lot for this world than just such a life as mine."

XXX

THY POOR SERVANT, GERSON

The shadow has passed from his heart and brow,
And a deep calm filled his breast,
For the peace of God was his portion now,
And his weary soul found rest.

Nine years have passed away, and once more there is peace for a
little while in storm-tossed, battle-stained Bohemia. The third and
last crusade has been hurled back, like the others, from the trampled
land, by the courage and devotion of her sons. All men are talking
now of a great Council to be held at Basle, where the question of
the Cup may be fairly and peaceably settled. The representatives of
Bohemia are to appear there, not in safety only, but with honour; a
splendid, warlike band, contrasting strangely in their pomp and pride
with the one poor priest who stood alone and fettered before his
judges in Constance.

Sir Hubert Bohun used this interval of peace to put in execution
a long-cherished design. One of his strongest characteristics was a
singular tenacity of affection. In distant France there were two whom
he had never ceased to love, and whose faces he longed to see once
again before he died. So he set out from his Bohemian home, with a
few well-armed retainers, and journeyed eastward, through Germany,
and across the Rhine. His quest was for the knight and soldier, Armand
de Clairville, and for the great doctor, Jean Gerson, at one time
Chancellor of Paris — if, indeed, they still lived.

He found Armand first. Their meeting was a very happy one;
but its story must remain untold, not because there is little to tell,
but because there is, or might be, so much. For the white banner of
"the Maid" was floating over the fair fields of France, and it was
followed to victory by no more devoted adherent than the Knight of
Clairville. Armand believed in "the Maid" almost as passionately
as Hubert at Constance had learned to believe in John Huss, though
for different reasons and in a different way. When, full of enthusiasm,
he told Hubert of her visions, Hubert felt no difficulty in believing

them all, provided only they were not contrary to Holy Scripture. He recognized with joy and thankfulness that his brother was a true knight, brave and loyal, only anxious to find out the path of duty and to follow it, at any cost to himself. Nor did Jocelyne — now the mother of three blooming boys and a sweet baby girl — seek to dissuade him.

But as Hubert could not espouse the cause of "the Maid" and the quarrel of France, however righteous he might think it, he left his brother to march to the relief of Orleans, and journeyed southward to Lyons. For there, as he had been told, the Great Doctor Gerson still lived, though in retirement, with his brother, the Prior of the Celestine Monastery.

Hubert rode into Lyons on a bright afternoon in July, 1429, and repaired at once to the house of the Celestines. The prior received him very courteously, and told him that his brother lodged in a cell of the cloisters belonging to the neighbouring Church of St. Paul, and would probably at that hour be found in the church itself.

Hubert left his servants and his horses at the nearest inn, and then went to the church. There was no service going on, but he heard voices proceeding from one of the side chapels, and followed the sound. He found the chapel filled, even crowded, with children of all ages, from boys and girls of fourteen and fifteen to lisping babes of four or five. All were speaking together, repeating something aloud in French. Then the sound died away, and there was a moment's silence, broken by a single voice, the clear, sweet treble of a little girl, which fell distinctly on his ear: "Suffer the little children to come unto Me, and forbid them not, for of such is the kingdom of heaven."

There, in the midst, sat the man he sought, the Chancellor of France, the great Doctor of the Sorbonne, the light and soul of the Council of Constance. The tiny golden-haired maiden who had just been saying her lesson sat on his knee, his hand resting on her head. The others stood around him, some in attitudes of childish inattention, but by far the greater number looking, and listening eagerly with serious, wondering eyes fixed on their teacher's face. A few little hands were stretched out, touching his person or his dress with reverent, caressing gestures. But how worn and weary was the face, how white and thin the hair! Sixty-eight years such as he had seen might well have counted for the eighty whose strength is labour and sorrow. Yet the look was gentler than in days of old; and if the lines of pain were deeper than ever, there was far less of strain and perplexity, far less of the asking of unanswered questions, and the violent repression of natural instincts.

419

While Hubert stood in the shadow, as yet unseen, Gerson spoke to the children in simple words of the love of that dear Saviour who invited them to come to Him.

"And now," he concluded, "dear little ones, our lesson is over. Go to your homes in peace; but, before you depart, kneel down and say your prayer for me."

One and all the children knelt, and with eyes and hands raised up to heaven repeated the simple words he had taught them — "My God, my Creator, have pity on Thy poor servant, Gerson."

It was well for Hubert that when they rose they still lingered lovingly for a farewell word or a look — for it went hard with him to keep back his tears. When at last all were gone, Gerson also rose to go, but so slowly, so feebly, that Hubert feared he would fall. He came forward, and, bowing reverently, offered the support of his arm. Any stranger might have done as much, and as from a stranger the old man accepted the courtesy.

They paced slowly together through the dim, shadowy church, out into the sunny cloister. Until then Gerson, who was leaning heavily on his companion, had not spoken, nor did Hubert break the silence. At last Hubert said, "You are doing a Christ-like work here, my lord."

"I am trying to bring the little ones to Christ," he answered.

"In whom alone we find rest unto our souls," returned Hubert.

"You speak as though you knew something of the spiritual life, Sir Knight," said Gerson, looking at him with awakened interest. "But, pardon me, I have not the honour of your acquaintance. You are, I presume, a stranger here?"

"I trust that is true of me in a twofold sense," returned Hubert, smiling. "My lord in the old days used to love those words, 'A stranger here,' applying them to himself, as the interpretation of his own name — Gerson — 'Gershom.' I too, Knight and layman though I am, can now also take up the prayer, 'I am a stranger upon the earth; hide not Thy commandments from me.' "

Gerson started, and his look showed a momentary surprise.

"From where did you learn so much of me, Sir Knight?" he asked. "But," he added, "knowing so much, I marvel that you do not also know that no one now calls me lord or master. I am done with earthly dignities. This is my cell. Come in with me, I pray of you; I would gladly talk with you further."

"I shall weary you, Father."

"No man can weary me who speaks to me of our blessed Lord, and of the divine life which we have in Him."

So Hubert entered a narrow cell, furnished in every respect like that of a monk, with a humble pallet, two or three wooden stools, a table, and a crucifix. Gerson bade his visitor be seated, and sank wearily upon a seat himself. But his joy in finding one who could sympathize with his spiritual aspirations overcame his sense of bodily fatigue.

"Although your dress proclaims you a knight and soldier, you speak like one whom God has called to the life of contemplation," he said.

"Perhaps, in some small degree," said Hubert.

"Well, *even among those who are thus called there are degrees. Some are fearful and anxious, looking upon God as a most severe Judge and austere Master. These do not so much desire eternal rewards as they wish to escape eternal punishment, which even the perfect may cautiously fear.*"[29]

At these words Hubert raised his eyes frankly and joyfully to the sad face of Gerson. He, at least, had no such fear for himself. He knew in whom he had believed, and was persuaded that He was able to keep that which he had committed to Him. But he did not speak, and Gerson went on,

"*These are but the beginners; a second class there are, who advance further. These are called hirelings, seeking a recompense from God for their services, as from a most liberal king, or as from the Father of mercies and God of all consolation. These say with the prodigal, 'Father, I have sinned against heaven and before Thee; make me as one of Thy hired servants.' These rightly behave as sons, but as sons who are conscious of having sinned.*"

He paused, and Hubert spoke now. "The son, when he once saw the father's face, could not say, 'Make me as one of your hired servants.' He only could take the kiss of peace, the robe, the ring, and the shoes."

Gerson's dim eye brightened. Had he found indeed in this stranger knight one with whom was the secret of the LORD, and to whom He had shown His covenant? Such were not found too often, even in cloisters.

"*And having these,*" he went on, with evident delight in the sympathy of the listener — "having these he would be among the perfect. *For there are a third class, fewer in number, who do not serve God after the manner of hirelings. Forgetful of service and reward, and even of paternal authority, they with more than filial mind consort*

---

[29] The passages in *italics* are taken from the writings of Gerson.

with God as a friend with a friend; no, they are knit with Him in a sweeter intimacy still, as a bride with a bridegroom: and their words are, 'I to my Beloved, and His turning is toward me:' 'Whom have I in heaven but Thee? And there is none upon earth that I desire beside Thee.' 'My flesh and my heart faileth, but God is the strength of my heart, and my portion forever!' "

As he said this, with eyes upraised to heaven and voice that trembled with the utterance of what was deepest in his own heart, Hubert could no longer restrain his emotion.

Gerson perceived it, and regarded him with momentarily increasing interest.

"Your voice and your look touch me strangely," he said. "I seem to have known you long ago. Are you, perhaps, some noble person who was known to me in the world, in the days of my prosperity, and who now desires to seek satisfaction, as I have done, in the life of contemplation?"

"I was known to you, Father, not as a noble person, but as a poor, obscure youth, whom long ago you saved and befriended."

"Whom *I* saved?" repeated Gerson, not yet comprehending, though with the dawn of a new light in his dim, weary eyes.

"Whose debt you paid for him in the Sorbonne. Oh, Father, my benefactor, do you not remember Hubert Bohun?"

"Hubert, whom I loved — Hubert! My son Hubert!" The old man's voice failed, and he covered his face with his hands.

Hubert feared he had made himself known too suddenly. But to the old great emotions come softly, like footsteps on moss.

Presently he stretched out his hand to Hubert, who raised it reverently to his lips. "For this hour," he said, "I have journeyed here from the land of my adoption. I longed sore to see my father's face again."

"I did not think to be so loved by any man," said Gerson in a trembling voice. "Hubert, I have never ceased to pray for you; never, since those old days in Constance — those bitter days, that have left such sad memories behind them." He added, as if speaking to himself, "*Who can say, 'I am innocent and pure?' Who will not fear the judgments of the terrible God?*' "

"Those have no cause for fear," returned Hubert gently, "who have had the kiss of peace, the ring, and the white robe."

"The *best* robe," Gerson corrected him. "The *white* robe had another meaning. It is the raiment of the blessed martyrs."

At that word Hubert looked at him — earnestly, inquiringly. It was a look full of gentleness, of love; and yet one which sought to read the inmost secrets of his heart.

It was met unflinchingly, and answered fairly and frankly.

"*That man,*" said Jean Gerson,"*who is put to death in hatred of justice and of truth, which he honours and defends, is worthy in the sight of God of the name of martyr, whatever be the judgment of man.*"[30]

It was enough. Hubert's heart was satisfied; the two he venerated were one at last. Jean Gerson, by these words, canonized John Huss.

A silence fell between them, but it was a silence full of peace. Gerson broke it by asking Hubert for the story of his life since their parting in Constance fourteen years before.

Hubert sketched it for him briefly, saying as little as he could of those Bohemian wars in which he had borne so distinguished a part. He had no doubt that Gerson had already heard very unjust and exaggerated reports of the violence and cruelty of the Hussites; and he feared he would attribute them, with every other evil from which the country suffered, to heresy and heretics. It was not worth while, even if there had been time and opportunity, to try to show him the truth — that the Hussites had been absolutely forced to fight in defence of their lives.

But Gerson passed over these things in silence, with a gentle forbearance that astonished Hubert. It seemed as if he did not care to blame or to condemn even manifest heretics. He made up for this silence, however, by questioning Hubert on more personal matters with evident interest.

"A man who remains in the world does well to marry," he said. "Are you married?"

"Yes, Father. That good knight Jean de Chlum, whom you saw in Constance, gave me the greatest treasure man ever had in his only daughter, Zedenka."

"I remember the Knight of Chlum. Does he yet live?"

"Alas, no! It is now five years since that true knight and loyal friend rejoined those he loved best in the presence of his Lord. I think that, in the after-years, men will name him with the son of Saul in the Holy Scriptures as the type and mirror of the faithful friend."

"Likely, little children smile around you, to console your lady for her loss?"

"True, Father. We have two noble boys and one sweet little maid."

---

[30] There can be little doubt that Gerson, in using these remarkable words, meant to allude to the martyr of Constance.

"Tell me of them — their names, their ages? I would like to remember them in my prayers."

"Johan, Ján, or Jean, as we say in French — the namesake at once of the martyr of Constance and of the Knight of Chlum — is eight years old. Two years later his brother came to us, and he bears a name I shall love and honour all my life, and beyond it — *Charlier Gerson*."

Gerson was deeply touched. To aged eyes tears come readily, and he could not restrain his at this proof of the undying affection of his "son Hubert."

When he could speak, he said with a quivering lip, "It is a strange-sounding name, Charlier Gerson Bohun."

"English blood, Bohemian birth, and a French name," said Hubert. "Even so, in the kingdom, east and west, north and south, shall meet together. But, Father, you are weary. I must leave you now to seek the rest that I see you sorely need."

"Come again tomorrow, in the morning. I have much, very much, to hear from you and to tell you, my son Hubert. My brother, the prior, will lodge you and your people in the monastery. Say to him that you are an old friend — no rather, a son of mine."

"At what hour in the morning shall I wait on you, Father?"

"As early as you will. Too early you cannot come. I sleep but little now."

"That is not well, Father."

"It is very well," Gerson answered, smiling. "In those lonely hours *I converse with Wisdom. She visits me early in the morning, and if I am sad she comforts me*! Here is some of the fruit of my solitary hours."

He took up a manuscript which lay on the table, and showed it to Hubert. It was a commentary on the *Song of Songs, which is Solomon's*.

"Only yesterday I finished it," he said. "Now I am resting, as a man may rest whose work is done."

"And who waits for his reward," said Hubert.

"I am *little anxious now*," said Gerson, "*whether concerning joy, or pain, or reward. I have no hard or uneasy thoughts of God, as a judge who rewards or takes vengeance. What I think of Him is that He is all desirable, sweet, and mild, and most worthy of being loved, even though He should kill me*. And so I think that I — even I — may say, '*My Beloved to me, and I to Him*.' Yes, dear Hubert, it is best that you should go now. Farewell until the morning. As this book has it," he added, glancing at his manuscript with a smile, "*Until the day break, and the shadows flee away*."

424

Early in the morning Hubert came again. He came alone, and knocked softly at the door of the cell, as the prior, who knew his brother's habits, had instructed him to do. There was no answer, so he waited a while, pacing up and down the cloister.

I have come too early after all, he thought.

After an interval he knocked again. Still no answer. He was very weary last night; it is well that he should rest, thought Hubert. I will wait until the bells of St. Paul's begin to ring for matins."

In due time the sweet-toned bells began their early chime. Then he knocked once more. As he stood at the door, waiting patiently for the answer that did not come, a monk approached him through the cloister.

"What is the matter, Sir Knight?" he inquired, after courteous greeting.

"The chancellor has not yet arisen," said Hubert. "I do not wish to disturb him."

"Not yet arisen!" said the monk. "That is unusual. I ought to go in and arouse him, and summon him to matins. He would not wish to miss them."

He opened the door, which was not fastened on the inside, and entered, Hubert following. All was still and silent. A dark-robed figure, with clasped hands, knelt before the cross, as if in prayer. But Hubert knew in that moment that the prayers of Jean Charlier Gerson were ended.

Silent and tearless in his sorrow, he stood beside the dead, while the stunned, bewildered monk went to tell the prior and the rest.

Whether his solitary watch was long or short Hubert never knew. Probably soon enough the little cell was filled with awe-struck, lamenting monks, the prior at their head. Then Hubert silently withdrew. Alone with his sorrow, which was yet a sorrow full of hope and joy, he paced the cloister. One thought filled his heart — "Until the day break, and the shadows flee away."

Soon the prior joined him, and they talked together of the dead, Hubert learning many things of the humility, self-abnegation, and charity which beautified the closing years of the great chancellor. The rest of the day he spent in solitude and prayer.

When evening came he went once more to the Church of St. Paul. They had laid the dead, in all reverence and honour, before the high altar, to await his final rest. The altar candles shed their soft light on the pale features, while the priests who were standing around chanted requiems and prayers for his soul. The raiment he loved best had been put upon him; not the chancellor's robe of state, but the humble pilgrim's garb in which he left Constance. The pilgrim's staff had been placed in his cold hand, and the pilgrim's wallet by his side. In death as in life, "a stranger here," he bore witness that he desired the better country.

Hubert drew near, very near, for the right was his; it seemed to him as if the dead was calling him to his side. He looked once more on that beloved face. Sorrow, pain, perplexity — all were gone forever now. In their stead there was peace. There was more than peace; a look of calm triumph, that look we know upon the faces of our dead,

> *As they did hold*
> *Some secret — glorying.*

If they could but speak *once*, and tell us what it is! But in vain do we sob our hearts out in that cry. There is no voice, nor answer, "until the heavens be no more." Yet, let us be patient. We shall know their secret one day — perhaps we can guess it even now. "Did I not say to you that, if you would believe, you should *see the glory of God*?"

As Hubert stood and gazed, the thought flashed over him that once, and once only, he had seen that look of mysterious ineffable peace upon a *living* face — the face of the man who stood alone amidst his enemies in the Cathedral of Constance. Accepted in one Saviour, cleansed in one fountain, partaking one joy, martyr and persecutor stood together now before the throne of God. Hubert thought that to him who was the longer there, and the nearer to his Lord, the joy had perhaps been given of welcoming and leading in the new-comer. In him, too, he would see the answer — one answer at least — to his earnest prayer for those who slew him in their ignorance.

Jean Charlier Gerson, noblest son of France and of the Church, was laid to rest, according to his own desire, in the Church of St. Paul, where he had provided that bread and wine should be continually distributed in his name to the poor. Around his tomb may still be read the words he loved, and used to repeat often: "Repent, and believe the Gospel;" and also his favourite motto, "*Sursum corda*" — "Lift up your hearts."

Gladly do we respond to this voice from the tomb, *We lift them up to the Lord*. We thank Him for all His *servants, departed this life in His faith and fear*, though stained by many faults, tarnished by many errors, and led by divers, often by devious, pathways, into the light and glory of His presence. It is well with them there forever.

426

XXXI

THE END, WHICH IS ALSO A BEGINNING

And in the tumult and excess
Of act and passion under sun,
We sometimes hear — oh, soft and far,
As silver star did touch with star,
In kiss of Peace and Righteousness,
Through all things that are done.

— E.B. Browning

The little group of men and women whose fortunes we have been following fade away from our vision. The mists of time rise up between us and them, and we see them no more. They pass from us with lives uncompleted, with stories half told. But then no story ever is, or can be, all told upon earth. Out of the complex fulness of real human lives, flitting, fleeting, imperfect glances are all we can hope to catch — still more, all that we can present to others.

One more such glimpse, and we are finished. Nearly fifty years have passed away since the ashes of the martyr of Constance were flung into the Rhine. They have been years of terrible suffering for those who reverenced his name and followed his faith. It is true that three times, with heroic courage, the little kingdom of Bohemia hurled back from her frontiers the invading host of crusaders; and that the soldiers and servants of the Cup extorted a measure of toleration from the Council of Basle. But Rome accomplished by art, of which she has ever been so consummate a mistress, what the arms of her votaries failed to effect. She divided her adversaries, and used the more moderate party, the Calixtines or Utraquists, to crush those who had gone further than themselves in the path of reform. The fierce fanaticism engendered by persecution, the extreme views of a section of the Taborites, and the excesses they perpetrated, contributed

427

not only to their own undoing, but also to that of their more sober brethren. Again the land was the scene of woe and bloodshed, again martyr-piles were kindled, and tortures and cruelties without number inflicted.

Amidst the confusion of those troublous days, those who feared the Lord and thought upon His name "spoke often one to another." The men who had drunk deepest of the teachings of Huss searched the Scriptures diligently, praying earnestly for the Divine guidance, and finding out more and more of the mind and will of God. While doing this, they drew many disciples to themselves, or rather to their Divine Master. In spite of continual persecution, they grew and multiplied. These "Brethren," as they called each other, arose chiefly from among the Taborites, through whom they received the traditional teachings of Huss; but they had little in common with the fierce brethren of the Cup who fought under Zisca and Procopius. They were truly Christ-like, gentle, loving, forgiving, "doing infinitely good to all, and harm to none." Being reviled they blessed, being persecuted they suffered it, being defamed they entreated. Blameless and harmless in the midst of a crooked and perverse generation, even their adversaries were obliged to confess that they were indeed the children of God.

Rorkyzana, the Archbishop of Prague, favoured them secretly; and his nephew, Gregory, a humble and holy man of God, was their most beloved and trusted leader. He obtained from his uncle a place of refuge for them, in the district called Litiz. There they sought to know the will of the Lord with prayer and supplication, and with much study of His Word. At last it became clear to them that the fulness of the time was come for a decisive separation from the corrupt Church of their day. They determined to organize their own communion upon a simple and primitive basis. But they were minded to do nothing rashly; they were anxious to retain all that was good, all that was apostolic, all that was harmless even, in the constitution of the Church they were forced to abandon. So they met upon a certain day to elect elders, one or more of whom was intended to receive episcopal consecration, by the laying on of the hands of those who were competent to bestow it.

Around a table, in a simple, quiet room, sat a little company of men, most of them advanced in years. A few were priests, the rest laymen of various ranks, including peasants unlearned in human lore, but mighty in the Scriptures. We see among them, for the last time, the good knight, Sir Hubert Bohun, his head white with the snows of more than sixty vivid, varied, toilsome years, but his eye still bright with the fire of the olden days, softened now and sanctified by long and close communion with God. Beside him sat a young man whom he had adopted and maintained at the University of Prague, a German, the son of "one named Robert," of Constance, and already a devoted pastor and eloquent preacher. His own two sons, and his beloved brother-in-arms, Baron Václav of Chlum and Pihel, are with him also in Litiz, though they do not share in this first solemn act of the infant Church.

Sir Hubert's grandson, a handsome boy named Prokop, entered the room, and at a signal from the president of the little assembly took his place beside an urn which lay on the table. With an awed and reverent air he drew from it a slip of folded paper, which he presented to the president; then did the same in turn to each of those present. They received it in solemn silence; the lips of most were moving in prayer and no doubt the hearts of all were lifted up to God. Three of these slips bore upon them the one word "*Est;*" the rest were blank. Those who drew the first were to be the elders — if God so willed, the bishops of the Church.

Sir Hubert Bohun had drawn a blank. No matter. It was honour enough for him, though unknown and unnoticed in history, to have been among the *Beginners of the Church of the United Brethren*. When those who turn many to righteousness shine as the stars forever and ever, no part of the Church of Christ will contribute a more glorious galaxy to the grand illumination than the beloved and honoured *Church of the Unity*. It was in its own land pre-eminently the Church of Martyrs. After loving, serving, and suffering there for nearly three hundred eventful years, it sent forth that goodly shoot, that fruitful bough hanging over the wall, which, under its modern designation of the *Church of the United Brethren of Bohemia and Moravia*, has become pre-eminently the Church of Missionaries.

There rests no stain upon the white banner of *The Unity*. Never have the Brethren done violence to any; seldom, if ever, have they even resisted wrong. Those who most detest their principles have had to bear witness once and again that God was in them of a truth.

Nor is their work done yet; either in their own beloved Bohemia, or through the length and breadth of the world, where there is no land, however remote and inhospitable, untrodden by the feet of their missionaries. We shall read the whole story of earth in the illumining light of its completion, before we know all that God has done, is doing, and will yet do through the harvest which has sprung from the ashes of the martyr of Constance.

Well, therefore, may we join the Churches of the Brethren in the words of prayer and praise that conclude their beautiful Easter Morning Litany:

Keep us in everlasting fellowship with our brethren and our sisters who have entered into the joy of their Lord; and with the whole Church triumphant; and let us eternally rest with them in Thy Presence.

Glory be to Him who is the Resurrection and the Life: He was dead, and, behold! He is alive forevermore; and he that believes in Him, though he were dead, yet shall he live.

Glory be to Him in the Church which waits for Him, and in that which is around Him, forever and ever. Amen!

Done and Dared in Old France
by Deborah Alcock

Gaspard, a French Huguenot boy, was taken in by a group of out-laws, smugglars of salt. After several adventures he met the famous Huguenot pastor, Claude Brousson. Then the main story begins. Skillfully theauthor, in her last novel, intertwined the historical facts about Brousson with the fictional account of Gaspard and Tardiff.Shortly after it was written a mother of four boys wrote: "The boys are getting very critical of books for reading aloud on Sunday afternoon, but they all declare this is 'a ripping book.' "

— E. Boyd Baily in *The Author of "The Spanish Brothers"*

Time: 1685-1700	**Age: 11-99**
ISBN 1-894666-03-8	**Can.\$14.95 U.S.\$12.90**

The Romance of Protestantism
by Deborah Alcock

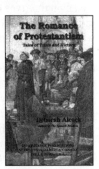

The Romance of Protestantism addresses one of the most damaging and (historically) effective slanders against the Reformed faith, which is that it is cold and doctrinaire. What a delight to find a book which documents the true warmth of the Protestant soul. I recommend this book highly.

— Douglas Wilson, editor of *Credenda/Agenda*

Time: 1390-1800	**Age: 12-99**
ISBN 0-921100-88-4	**Can.\$11.95 U.S.\$9.90**

The Spanish Brothers by Deborah Alcock
A Tale of the Sixteenth Century

Christine Farenhorst in *Christian Renewal*: This historical novel which is set in Spain a number of years after the Reformation, deals with the discovery of Reformed truth in that country. It's not often that we come across a book that touches upon people and places with regard to Biblical truth in Spain. As a matter of fact, we generally think of Spain as one of the most zealous and fiery arms of the Inquisition. Yet Spain itself most certainly also had its own martyrs and heroes of the faith. For this reason alone, the book would be a worthwhile read - to acquaint people with the historical facts of the rise and fall of the early Protestant church in Spain.

Two brothers, one a soldier and the other a student of theology, are the protagonists. Sons of a nobleman who disappeared when they were children, their search for him leads both to a confrontation with the Gospel. How they react, how their friends and relatives react to them, and what their struggles and thoughts are, form the main body of the book.

An excellent read, this book should be in every church and home library.

Time: 1550-1565	**Age: 14-99**
ISBN 1-984666-02-x	**Can.\$14.95 U.S.\$12.90**

The William & Mary Trilogy
by Marjorie Bowen

The life of William III, Prince of Orange, Stadtholder of the United Netherlands, and King of England (with Queen Mary II) is one of the most fascinating in all of history. Both the author and the publisher of this book have been interested in this subject for many years. Although the story as told in this book is partly fictional, all the main events are faithful to history.

F. Pronk wrote in *The Messenger* about Volume 1: The author is well-known for her well-researched fiction based on the lives of famous historical characters. The religious convictions of the main characters are portrayed with authenticity and integrity. This book is sure to enrich one's understanding of Protestant Holland and will hold the reader spell-bound.

D.J. Engelsma wrote in *The Standard Bearer* about Volume 1: This is great reading for all ages, high school and older. *I Will Maintain* is well written historical fiction with a solid, significant, moving historical base . . . No small part of the appeal and worth of the book is the lively account of the important history of one of the

world's greatest nations, the Dutch. This history was bound up with the Reformed faith and had implications for the exercise of Protestantism throughout Europe. Christian high schools could profitably assign the book, indeed, the whole trilogy, for history or literature classes.

C. Farenhorst wrote in *Christian Renewal* about Volume 1: An excellent tool for assimilating historical knowledge without being pained in the process, *I Will Maintain* is a very good read. Take it along on your holidays. Its sequel *Defender of the Faith*, is much looked forward to.

Time: 1670 - 1702	Age: 14-99

Volume 1 - *I Will Maintain*
     ISBN 0-921100-42-6   Can.$17.95 U.S.$15.90
Volume 2 - *Defender of the Faith*
     ISBN 0-921100-43-4   Can.$15.95 U.S.$13.90
Volume 3 - *For God and the King*
     ISBN 0-921100-44-2   Can.$17.95 U.S.$15.90